EMERGENCE

Second Edition

Copyright © by Carol Buhler, 2016

Cover Art by Les Petersen

A Novel of the Lillith Chronicles*

Thank you Tony Lavely for ideas and keeping me on track.

*This novel was originally released in 2014 under the name EMERGENCE. It has been modified from the previous version.

In Memory of Easter Son

1970 to 2006
One in a million

Contents

Chapter 1

~Lillith

Memmyon burst into view from above the council building and aimed his telepathic shout directly at me. "Now's the time." He landed in a flurry before me in the Joe mansion east garden. "Raedon's fuming. He's just dealt with one too many council members telling him what to do." He lowered his mental voice once we stood nose to nose. "He's on his way."

"It's about time!" I whirled and led my co-conspirator into a shadowed area behind the mansion. There, we found my husband Lillyon grazing quietly among the bushes. He looked up and bent a quizzical eye on me. "You're going through with this then?"

"Yes, dear. We have to." I swept past him on my way to a corner next to Joedon's study. "Something has to make Joedon change his mind and this is the best plan we've come up with." I quivered with excitement. "Time's running out!" Memm and Lillyon crowded beside me as I shielded myself from don-mate inside and prepared to eavesdrop on the upcoming conversation.

~Joedon

I was attempting to read a book when the noise my best friend Raedon made striding down the path and slashing at the ancient trees drooping over him brought my head up. His roiling anger hit my mind; normally I couldn't read him so clearly. Metal boot heels rang across the stone courtyard; the front door slammed open; and feet clattered through the tiled entryway. Inside the study, I rose from the armchair, laid the book aside, and uncorked a bottle of Lareina, pouring two glasses of the purple wine. Gulping half of one, I shuttered my sensitivity to maintain calm.

"Good," Lillith said from wherever she was. "Don't get wrapped up in Raedon's fury."

"Joedon!" Raedon stood spread-eagled in the doorway. "I can't take anymore!" Brows snapped down over glaring brown eyes as he stormed into the room. "I've got to get away from here!"

We'd both been frustrated at having to stay in Center; the Speaker's Council had ordered us into town for the wedding preparations, then refused us any input. Only my aunt's insistence had gotten me out of Eyrie in the face of the stupid council command.

I tried to sooth Raedon with the glass of wine but he ignored me and stalked toward the windows shouting. "I'm sick of them. I want to take Sara and run away."

"You have to cope." I struggled to keep my tone level. "It's only four more days." Forcing enthusiasm into my words, I said, "Focus on your honeymoon."

Raedon swung away from the window and glowered, his face flushed a deep red. "If they're this bad now, how much interference do we face later?" He flung himself around the room as if he couldn't control his arms and legs, then crashed a fist down on the desk. "I want them to leave us alone."

"Isn't going to happen." Refraining from "I told you so," I sent soothing waves as I gripped Raedon's arm. He shook me off.

"How's Sara coping?" I tried projecting images of her calm face.

He snarled, "I don't know. They won't let me see her. It's bad luck, they say." He spun away to pace. "You'd think they were a bunch of old femm instead of idiot politicians."

They're both, I thought and heard Lillith's chuckle.

Not as hot-headed as Raedon, I was still just as irritated, but I strove for an air of patience. He continued to hurl himself around the big room, side-stepping clusters of sofas, tables and chairs, ranting about the Council. I didn't even flinch as the gesturing arms came close to toppling valuable treasures. When he failed to respond to any of my efforts, I called for help.

"Let him rave." Lillith allowed the words to float gently into my mind. "It's good for him to get it out." I struggled harder to contain my irritation. Knowing this would happen, I'd warned him.

Finally, he stopped and stared out the picture window as if mesmerized. A minute later, he swung around, his eyes huge, his face excited. "I know," he said. "Let's go to Pith. We could find a street football game. Drink some beer. Party with the humans."

I backed a step, heart thudding madly. I tried reason. "Now's not a good time to chance it. You know how the Council feels about humans."

Lillith injected a quick, "Shut up!"

As Raedon stormed toward the door, saying, "I'll go by myself, then. I've had enough!" Lillith nudged me to follow. Unconvinced of the wisdom of this action, I did.

~Lillith

"Well handled, Memmyon!" I turned to my husband. "Are you coming with us?"

"No. Joedon would wonder why I was following along." Lillyon moved away to resume grazing. "Call if you need me."

Shortly, Joedon and Raedon joined Memm and I outside the mansion. They'd changed into tight fitting riding-suits and tall boots. Flinging themselves astride, they wrapped long legs around our barrels, tangled slender fingers into our flowing manes, and balanced slim torsos slightly behind our heavily muscled shoulders. Once I felt Joedon settle firmly in place, I trotted to the cliff edge, extended my twenty foot wings, and dropped off to glide toward the pass into the far off plains of Pith. Memm followed.

"Lillith." Joedon sounded strained. "Can't Memm help Raedon get through this mess?" His concern translated to fidgeting on my back.

"He's trying…" I concentrated on reassuring him. "But he's not a soother, and he's as frustrated as Raedon with the Council.

7

After all, it's his wedding too. We've agreed that it'll be good for you both to get away for a few hours. That's why I shut you up when Raedon mentioned it. He's already relaxing the further we go. Can't you sense it?"

"Yes. And I have to admit, I'm glad of a respite. This royal wedding is developing into a royal pain." Joedon reached out and stroked my neck; I arched into the caress, feeling slightly guilty about what I'd set up.

We flew steadily for two hours, weaving through clouds and staying out of sight of human civilization. As we approached the city, Memm and I extended the mental illusions that rendered us invisible to don and humans. We glided silently over the huge city and landed south of Pith in one of the willow groves along the river.

Joedon and Raedon swung lightly off and assumed similar illusions of young human males, a foot and a half shorter than they really were, long hair tied tightly back, wearing loose shirts and trousers. Joedon caught Raedon's arm. "If we can find a game, we'll play for a couple of hours and get back before the Council notices, right?"

Raedon scowled and broke away. "You worry too much!" He walked a few steps and then stopped. "Yes, right," he said grudgingly.

"Just making sure you'll go back soon."

"Oh, leave off. I know I have to if I want Sara. It just shouldn't be like this."

"Have fun!" I called and Joedon turned to wave as Memm and I left the grove. We flew only a short distance, then, safely out of sight, we landed on a hill in a stand of pine trees to watch as our mind-mates strode through an open field, headed for the outskirts of the sprawling city.

Later, I grew tired of watching the game they'd joined. "Football is an interesting sport," I commented. "It seems more like war than our rolo matches are." I flicked an ear at Memm, who stood leaning against a nearby tree. "Why does Raedon like it so?"

Memm twitched his ear my way and chuckled. "It gives him a sense of superiority. He and Joedon obviously outplay the humans. They jump higher, run faster, throw farther, tackle harder. Whenever they play, Raedon challenges Joedon to exert less energy but accomplish more than he does." The mobile ear twitched toward the city. "Besides, it's physically satisfying. No one plays rolo in Center anymore." Memm's wistful tone made me realize he would like to be playing, too.

I was glad we didn't. *He's still young.* I sighed and turned my attention back to the game. Joedon stood all alone at one end of the field when a troop of gray-uniformed city guards burst onto the grassy expanse and started detaining players.

~Joedon

"What the…" A guard sprinted toward me shouting; I shifted my image to a doddering old man struggling across the open grass.

As he got close, he seemed to hesitate. "Get out of here, old man," he ordered, sounding hoarse. "You almost got arrested for playing football!"

I shook my head and snorted. "Football! You're crazy!" I hobbled away, sensing him watching my retreat. Then, he glanced back at his troop starting to herd the other players off. As he jogged back to join the rest, I relaxed.

Switching my image to a street urchin, barefoot and barely four feet tall, I shadowed the guards as they escorted Raedon and the other players through the streets. "Why doesn't he do something to escape?" I muttered. He didn't make an effort, seeming to go along with them willingly. "Chut, Raedon. Do something!" Of course, he couldn't hear me.

As they approached a corner where a farmer's market had set up--flimsy stalls holding fruits, vegetables, and breads--I had an idea. Just when the troop reached the intersection, I dashed forward, snatched an apple and tipped over the end stall. It crashed with a racket, the farmed screamed "Stop, Thief!" and I hid behind a broad tree trunk.

Raedon didn't jerk away; not a single guard even glanced at the still shouting farmer. "What?" I couldn't understand.

Dropping the stolen apple, I continued to trail the guards, mumbling imprecations at Raedon. The guards man-handled their captured players into the prison itself and the heavy metal door clanged shut with finality. Not knowing what else to do, I returned to the market to see what I could learn about the guards' strange behavior.

The farmer was struggling to gather his scattered produce; I reached down to help him collect some potatoes. "What was that all about?" I asked, struggling to keep my voice steady.

"That thief?" He straightened, pressed big hands into the small of his back, and grunted. As he shook his head, a wave of disgust crossed his tired face and his words rumbled. "Happens all the time lately. The guards are no help. They're too busy arresting football players and hauling them off to prison for six days."

Six days! I cried inside. I mentally shouted at Lillith. "What should I do?" To my shock, she didn't reply.

Dazed, I helped the farmer resettle his produce and, to my shame, he gave me an apple for my aid.

~Lillith

I forced my mind to return only emptiness to Joedon's cry for help. When I felt the overwhelming sense of loss and despair swirling through him, I sagged to my knees, but held my shield strong, blocking his every plea.

Memm shoved away from his tree and gazed at me with admiration. "How did you get those patrollers to arrest Raedon?"

"I didn't have to," I said, allowing a hint of smugness to seep into my tone. "One of Lord Metz' favorite guards was severely injured in a street football match. Since both Joedon and Raedon love the game, I thought it might be useful to plant the notion that street football was too dangerous to allow. Metz did the rest."

"That's why you wanted me to urge Raedon's in that direction, isn't it?"

"Of course. And it worked just as I hoped." Nodding in satisfaction, I jerked an ear toward the chunky bay. "Keep Raedon muddled. Can't have him escaping by himself."

Dimly, I heard a horn sound and caught my breath as on the narrow cobblestone street, a distracted Joedon dodged away from an oncoming car, then darted down a back alley. Settling my thudding heart, I asked Memm, "How will we keep Joedon from rescuing him?"

"I have an idea." Memm's mind swirled with mischief. "We'll see how well it works when Joedon finds him in the prison."

Chapter 2

~Joedon

Moving from one rowdy pub to another wearing the image of an old wino cadging drinks, I carefully asked questions about the new anti-street-football law and the prison system. Emotions ran high on the law, but no one seemed to know a thing about the prison. *How'm I going to get Raedon out?* Lillith still wasn't responding. *I'm on my own*—a terrifying thought. I'd never been completely on my own.

Around midnight, reeling with frustration, I entered another smoky, noisy place, crowded with what must have been off duty guardsmen from their rumpled uniforms. A couple played guitars and sang melancholy songs, apparently appreciated by the patrons who shushed me as I tried to get them talking.

Well away from the guards, a tattered human seated alone caught my eye. His emotions were clouded with drink but at my quiet question, he burst into vitriolic mutters about being seized and forced to mop prison floors all day for no pay. I probed for more; the drunk's complaints became louder until he was yelling and everyone turned to glare at us. I slunk away and fled out the door, but at least I'd gained some information.

By dawn, I was crouched on a street corner near the prison, determined to get inside and get Raedon out. *If I have to, I'll mop floors.* Shivering in the cool night air, I wished passionately that I'd talked him out of coming, and that I was safe at home in my warm bed.

~ Lillith

Memm had long since given up watching; Lillyon had joined me in my night's vigil. When Joedon finally settled miserably on his corner, I cast an impatient glance at the slumbering bay, stretched out on his side under a broad pine. "If he starts to snore, I think I'll kick him." I swung my head and caught Lillyon's envious eye trained on the young reeth. "I suppose you'd like to be sleeping, too!"

"Not if you need me!" he answered quickly, eyes forced wide and innocent.

I paced over to his side, pressed my forehead against his sturdy shoulder, and stood quietly. Well aware that the uncertainty in my heart would transmit clearly to this one I loved, I whispered, "I have to admit—but only to you. It's harder to stay out of Joedon's mind when he calls so frantically than I expected it to be."

"Of course it is, love." I smiled at his bracing tone. "You've spent his whole life helping him. Now, you love him enough that you know you must force him to resolve problems on his own."

"Or he will never lead!" I nuzzled his jaw. "Thanks for throwing my words back at me."

"Now can we sleep?" His plaintive words made me laugh.

I led him to a grassy stretch under some tall evergreens, folded my knees, and sank to the ground. "Yes, love. Let's rest while we can."

~Joedon

The morning grew brighter as I slouched against a high brick wall facing the south side of the block-wide, six story stone palace. I scanned the building. No windows on this side, only the one door. People scurried past me: men with tool belts, women with baskets of fruits and vegetables, children in uniform on their way to school. I bounced their gaze away; only one person could be allowed to notice me. The metal door across from me banged open with a loud clang and I sent a quick thought to prod the other people into hurrying along. Within seconds, the heavy-set guard's attention locked on my grubby image.

"You there. Come with me!"

I cowered and whined."I ain't done nothin, sir."

"Shut up! You're coming with me." The guard was tall for a human, but still a foot shorter than me. Dressed in an ill-fitting, stained blue uniform, he had an especially ugly face: bulbous nose and overhanging brows over tiny eyes, frown lines etched permanently into his dark skin. However, he moved rapidly for such a heavy human, reaching for me, the apparent vagrant.

I sidled away. *Can't let him touch me and learn how much taller I am than I seem.* "Oh no sir, I cain't go to prison. I got family to support. I gotta work."

"Shut up, I said. You're gonna work in the prison today. Don't give me no crap about family. I imagine your earnings go down yer gullet from the look of ya. Family, my foot!" The guard prodded me with his truncheon, herding me toward the open prison door. "Get a move on. I got work's gotta be done."

I allowed him to push me into a small room; he locked the door behind us. "Here, you!" The gravelly voice stopped me. "What's yer name. Can't just call you drudge all day."

"Name's Jug, sir."

"Jug! Jug Bait you mean. Well, get over here." He pointed to a bucket of water. "Take this bucket 'n mop. Start washing down the floors in this here room. I'll be watching you, be sure o' that." Timidly, I picked up the mop as he glared through narrowed, angry eyes. Once I'd started listlessly swishing the heavy strands, the guard walked to a second door in the small room and opened it. "Knock on this door when yer done. And make it quick." Disappearing into a dark hallway beyond, he slammed the door behind him.

"Yes sir, Mr. Guard, sir." I sneered after him in case he was watching.

~ Lillith

In the pine grove, Memm snorted to catch my attention. "I'm going back to Center," he said. "The girls are getting anxious with me gone. No one will let Saradon see Raedon and she's fretting enough to disturb Sissith. I can't hide my location from her much longer."

"Yes, go!" I waved a wing at him. "We can continue here. The coma will last a while yet, right?"

14

"Until I release him." The bay nodded, then trotted to the south and took off.

Lillyon gazed after him. "You know," he said thoughtfully. "It might not have been a bad idea to include Saradon and Sissith in this plot of yours."

I huffed. "Saradon maybe, but not Sissith. She has way too many gossipy friends. She may be mind-mated to the Royal Fem, but I don't think she's mature enough to hide our activities successfully from the others always around. Once she's married to Memm, she'll settle down, I expect." I turned back to stare toward Pith, feeling Joedon's mind focused on getting deeper into the prison.

Lillyon joined me, letting a wing rest lightly on me back. "What's he doing now?"

"Still mopping, but he's in one of the internal hallways now."

~ Joedon

I squinted through the tiny slot on the thick cell door labeled twenty-three, then started and almost dropped my image. Glancing quickly at the guard, I breathed a sigh of relief—he hadn't noticed. Raedon lay on the cot in the cell curled in a ball. Finally, I understood why I hadn't sensed the other earlier; he'd withdrawn into a self-induced coma. *Why'd he do that?* I fumed. *If he'd remained conscious, we could have projected guard images and walked right out.* From the cell door, Raedon appeared human, but if anyone checked him, a touch might reveal the odd body behind the illusion. *What now?*

I'd just stepped back from Raedon's cell door when a bell clanged overhead. The guard snapped, "Jugbutt. Mop that water up quick. Then, head back up front. Move it, now."

Where is Lillith? I sloshed the water around and fretted.

We returned a few minutes later, followed by guards opening doors and releasing prisoners for something called, "Morning exercise." No one stopped at Raedon's cell to let him out.

15

~ Lillith

With Lillyon projecting an invisibility screen for me, I hovered over the palace building. A wide-open courtyard below looked big enough for me to land to rescue Joedon and Raedon if things got out of hand. But, I worried about the several guards milling around the trees and planters glowing with flowers. Guns in holsters, they simply watched prisoners run in the sunshine.

Joedon had been locked inside the prison while the prisoners exercised; he was no longer mopping. For just a moment, he'd slumped against a wall and dropped his image, giving his mind a break. *He's so tired.* I quickly recited my reasons for making him suffer through this to keep from interfering.

~ Joedon

Left alone at last, I dropped the mop and knelt to examine Raedon's cell door. Flinging a strong mental shout at the still figure brought no response. I considered my options. Bend the window bars? *The opening's too small to be useful.* The door lock? The hinges? I pushed with all my strength against the wooden door. It screeched and sagged but neither lock nor hinges gave. I caught a sound—*the outside door's squeaking open.* Dashing to get my bucket before the guard stuck his head through enough to see, I resumed my image, mop sloshing the floor.

"Get a move on, Jughead. You got ten minutes to finish this hallway."

"Yes, sir, Mr. Guard, sir."

"What else can I try?" I despaired, muttering. "Where the dung is Lillith?"

The outside door slammed open and men filed back into the hall. Barely holding on to my illusion, I preceded the truncheon as the troop re-celled their charges. We all trudged back to the front of the prison. Near the entry room, I stumbled over something and almost fell, feeling my image waver. Struggling,

16

I barely managed to pull it back together before anyone noticed.

~ Lillith

I spun in the air and flew rapidly south.

"Where are you going?" Lillyon's voice was loud in my mind as he followed.

"I have to get away. If I stay here, I'm going to break down and help him and everything will be for naught." I stroked harder.

"How far away?"

"I don't know. Until I can't hear him. Until I can't feel him. Maybe all the way to Mont!"

An hour later, my resolve firmly back under control, I returned with Lillyon to hover over the prison. Joedon was about to his limit; I could feel the weariness in his mind more than his muscles. He'd been awake for almost thirty-six hours, throwing images at humans the entire time. The guard, however, seemed to have mellowed toward him.

"Hey there, Jugbait. You tired?" I heard through Joedon's ears. "You worked good here today, better than the last drudges I got. How 'bout you stick around?"

"Yes sir, Mr. Guard, sir," Joedon mumbled.

"You don't really got a family to support, do you?" The guard sounded concerned. I provided a tiny mental nudge.

"No sir, Mr. Guard, sir. I got nobody but my own self." Even Joedon's physical voice sounded exhausted.

"Well, I kinda like you." The guard greeted another guard, who'd just arrived. "Here's the night man and we're off duty. Let's find you a spot to bed down. Your day's over but you gotta start again at six in the morning. You won't get paid, but you'll always get good food, like today."

Injecting a twinge of pleading into his words, Joedon pretended amazement. "You mean, Mr. Guard, sir, that I can stay here?"

17

"Not here, but close." The guard pushed Joedon out the door and herded him along the outside of the prison, around the corner to a small door halfway down the east side of the building. "These here's the servants' rooms. They ain't great but you can sleep and be safe. Better'n where I found you."

The narrow hall they entered was lined on both sides by small doors. I nudged again; the guard paused, shook his head as if confused, then led the way to the fifth door on the inside wall. The room was small, empty except for a cot across the back wall and a chamber pot.

"Now, Jug, I don't 'xactly trust you to be here in the morning, so's I'm gonna lock you in. I'll be back at five-thirty." He stepped back, then closed and locked the door. "See ya in the morning, Jughead."

Joedon panicked and threw himself against the door to simply bounce off. His mind cried out, more frantic with each word, "I'm locked in a dark, tiny, stone room for the next ten hours. I'm running out of time! Lillith, where are you?"

I leaned on Lillyon for extra strength. Fortunately, Joedon forced himself to develop calm and lie down; bone and mind weary, he cleared his mind so it could recharge and put himself to sleep.

"Clever, my love." Lillyon nuzzled my ear and I let myself relax. "You aimed that guard masterfully!"

"Didn't I though?" Although almost as tired as Joedon, I allowed myself a chuckle from deep in my throat. "The discovery of that room and its secret is what started me on this path in the first place. Juldon did us a good service getting that information."

"What's next?"

I reached out very gently and touched Joedon's mind. "He's sleeping soundly, and recuperating well. In a bit, I'll wake him and send him onto the next phase."

"How long?" Lillyon gazed longingly toward a broad grassy stretch of ground on the other side of the Pith River, tempting in the evening glow.

"Yes, love. Let's go graze." I lifted lightly off the ground and together we drifted over the river to land in the grass on the other side.

~ Joedon

Suddenly, I was awake. Looking quickly around, I remembered where I was and what I was supposed to be doing: rescuing Raedon. The room was pitch black. Feeling carefully along the wall, I found the wooden door and started shoving against it with my shoulder. No give. *Wish I'd paid better attention to the lock picking class. A lark at the time, a needed skill now.*

I poked and prodded at the stones around the door, trying to separate it from the wall. No give there either. I dropped to my knees to explore the floor, stood on the cot to examine the ceiling, ran my hands over both end walls. No stone moved. Stifling my frustration and anxiety, I dragged the cot to the front wall and started on the back.

A loud click startled me. Then, a section of the wall turned to my pressure; I fell through into an even darker beyond, landing on steep stone stairs. Before I could react, the opening screeched closed behind me. "Well, I wanted out of that room." Slowly, feeling carefully along wall and steps, I started up since down seemed a less sensible option.

Chapter 3

~Joedon

It felt like hours since I'd fallen out of the servant's room as I picked my way along my fourth dank, pitch-black, narrow hall. Five flights of stairs and hallways back and forth seemed to be leading me through the innards of the building. The prison, the palace, and the barracks all connected, but where I was now, I hadn't a clue.

I stopped to calm my pounding heart and firmly suppress my imagination. *There has to be an end to this darkness—a way out somewhere.* Forcing my breathing to slow by taking unhurried, deep breaths, I rubbed my aching fingers, scraped along stone walls not wide enough to fully extend my arms. My bare toes ached too; I'd removed my boots early on, expecting my feet to warn me of impossible-to-see openings in the floor. I'd found several small cavities on either side wall, rough cut just big enough for my hand to fit through; my wrists and forearms felt slimy with blood. The entire hallway-stairway system was tightly constructed of gritty stone; I couldn't imagine why it had been built.

After a few moments of rest, I started forward again. When I tripped on something, the wall to my right swung away from my hand and streaming light momentarily blinded me. I stumbled quickly through before the opening closed behind me to find myself in a large room facing two young humans, one dressed in an outlandishly huge ball gown while the other pinned a hem. The one on her knees screamed and sagged in a faint.

As my vision cleared, the lady raised her brows, asking in a haughty voice, "Who are you? How did you get in here?" No fear in her voice or posture. Tall for a human female, she was different from any human women I'd ever seen: flaming red hair, emerald eyes over high cheekbones, a slightly tipped nose and full, luscious lips. Even the odd dress—I recognized a traditional wedding costume—did not diminish her striking appearance. She couldn't have been more than twenty.

Stunned, I took in the double doors, ornate wallpaper, divans and upholstered chairs with wooden feet, small inlaid tables with vases against the walls, and wide, thick carpets on the floor. A fancy salon.

"How did you get in here?" Her demand jerked my attention back to the girl.

Why isn't she angry? "I fell through that opening." I was mesmerized and forgot to project a human image.

"Get it open again, please!" she pleaded, breaking the spell.

"I don't know how I opened it in the first place. In my original room, a doorway opened because I was pushing on one of the stones in the wall."

She threw me a sharp glance, crossed the room, and began pushing on the stones, barely reaching the wall past her hooped skirt. Her determination compelled me to help. Then, the screaming started. The maid had recovered.

The lady whirled around, the swinging skirt almost toppling her over. As she regained her balance, she shouted. "Go bar the door before that damn noise brings in the guards!"

I sprinted across the room and slammed down the bar at the door, just in time from the sounds in the hall: boots slapping on stone, then fists pounding the door. I turned to see the girl slap the maid on the cheek. It didn't stop the screaming so I threw out a command of silence and the maid crumpled.

"What did you do?" demanded the lady. "Cari's not dead, is she?"

I glanced at the crumpled woman, short and plump with black curls tied up in a blue bow that matched her uniform. Jewel-headed pins were scattered all around her. "No, she's not dead."

"Good." The girl turned back to the wall I'd blundered through. "Come help me open the doorway."

"Wait just a minute." I frowned at her. "You can stop ordering me around and tell me what's going on."

"We have no time. If those guards break through the door and find you here, they'll lock me up in my room."

"Don't you mean they'll lock me up?" My frown deepened. *What's wrong with this girl? She doesn't make sense. She isn't afraid of a stranger in her room. In fact, she has the gall to order me around!* She seemed frantic to get away from the guards, yet she wore a very expensive wedding dress. She should be one happy young lady.

"Of course they'll lock you up, but so what? They might put you in prison for a few days. But, they're going to make me marry Lord Roark. That's forever! I was in despair until you fell through that opening." Her wide eyes pleaded with me for understanding.

The dark hallways must have muddled my thinking. Then, in a flash, I began to understand. "You're Soer Jaym, aren't you? Your wedding is tomorrow." I focused on her black vest and skirt to see Lord Metz' blue coat of arms entwined with Lord Roark's red in the embroidery. What was Metz thinking to subject his daughter to such an existence? Before I'd seen the girl, I hadn't thought a thing about what a Soer's life would be like as Roark's wife. Now, I couldn't image a worse fate for her.

"Tell me something I don't already know," she snapped.

The pounding on the door stopped. A tenor voice called, "Soer Jaym, are you alright?"

"Of course I'm alright, Garard," she shouted back.

"My Soer, the guards say they heard screaming. And your door is bolted. How did you lower the bolt? It's very heavy."

"I want to be left alone. Go away." She'd lowered her tone to one of firmness but her angry green eyes bored into mine.

"I'm sorry, My Soer. I must see for myself that you're alright," came the voice.

"Who is Garard?" I whispered.

"My father's majordomo. He won't go away." She looked frantically around before coming to rest on my face again.

"Everyone knows I've refused to marry Lord Roark," she said earnestly. "I've sworn to kill myself if they make me do it. I know it sounds melodramatic, but—I am serious. Garard may be the only person who believes me. He will not leave me alone until after the wedding. Then, if I kill myself, he won't be held responsible."

"My Soer. Please, unbolt this door and we'll talk reasonably," called Garard. I caught the note of panic behind the studied calm of the words. "Listen. I'm sending the guards away. It'll be just me who comes in." The guards tromped noisily away from the door.

"Will he really send all the troops away?" I said quietly, doubting the noise.

"Yes, he will. Garard is an honorable man. He's caught in this horrible situation just as I am. He has to make sure this wedding happens."

I studied the girl intently, then, moved to the door. "Okay, this is what we do. I'll lift this bolt. You open the door, grab him, and pull him into the room. I'll slam down the bolt and hide while you talk to him."

"What am I going to talk to him about?" Soer Jaym placed her hands on her hips and the green glare flashed again. "Everything's been said. I will not marry Lord Roark and he must make sure I do."

"Do you know how to get outside the palace?"

"What? Well…no. I've never been allowed past the second floor drawing rooms." Her eyes clouded with confusion. "We have a garden in the back where we walk to get our exercise and where the children play, but the ground floor is a mystery to me. There's no exit from the gardens to the outside." She cocked her head to one side and considered me, confusion replaced by speculation. "In fact, I'm not sure I could even find my way out of the drawing rooms to get to the bottom floor."

"Then we need Garard. I don't know how to get out and if you don't either, then Garard has to help."

"You're crazy. Garard's not going to help."

"Trust me. He'll help if you get him into this room and keep his attention so I can slip up behind him. He won't have any choice."

The girl glowered, nose in the air. "Why would you help me?"

"I have to." I shrugged; glancing around as if hoping for an answer in the room somewhere, I settled my gaze back on her face. "I have to get out of here, and I have to take you with me. Nothing will go right in my life ever again if I don't." I sighed and said with conviction, "The second that wall opened and I saw you, I felt a compulsion." I held out my hand to stop her from speaking. "Don't ask me to explain because I can't. Maybe later I'll figure out what's going on. For now, I know I have to help you."

Soer Jaym nodded and moved toward the door. "Ready."

I leaned forward grasping the end of the bolt. She called, "Garard, we can talk through the door. Lean forward so you'll hear what I say."

I yanked upward on the bolt and pulled the door open. Sure enough, Garard was leaning forward just outside the door. Soer Jaym grabbed the front of his tunic with both hands and jerked. Although he was a big man, she seemed quite strong for a woman, and Garard was off balance. He stumbled into the room, falling to his knees on the deep carpet. I slammed the door, dropped the bolt, and darted behind a divan before the man gathered his wits and lurched upright.

"What game are you playing, My Soer?" Garard pulled himself into a type of parade-rest. He was a handsome man with a well-groomed head of dark brown hair and a small mustache, dressed in the palace blue uniform made of finer cloth than the that of the prison guards and embroidered with his badge of office on the sleeve. He leaned slightly toward Jaym.

"It's no game, Garard. I'm leaving here today. I will not marry Lord Roark." The girl held her head high, her body pulled up to her full height. She was a glorious creature at that moment, but I had to focus on Garard. Slipping up behind the man, I lightly touched fingers to either side of the man's head, just above his graying temples.

"How will you do that, My Soer?"

"With my help, and yours, Garard," I said softly into the man's ear.

With a cry, Garard tried to wheel around to see who was talking. He was unable to move. "Who is that? What have you done to me?" he shouted. His body still, his face contorted with effort. Then, his eyes widened as I stepped between him and Soer Jaym.

"Who are you?" Garard's voice squeaked; I sensed quickly suppressed dismay.

Soer Jaym stretched a hand toward the stiff majordomo, then stopped. "What have you done to him?"

"Nothing much. He's lost control over the larger muscles of his body. He can breathe, blink, talk if I let him, wiggle his fingers and toes, swallow; that's about it. The rest of his muscles will be controlled by me for a time."

She questioned me with her eyes. Ignoring her, I turned to Garard saying, "We have to get out of the palace. You will help us."

"If you get out, where will you go?" The man had regained his commanding tone.

"I have a place."

"You'll have to move fast. The guards are assembling all over the palace. How will you get out the front door?"

"You will help us. You'll be our shield."

"Don't be stupid. They'll shoot through me to get to you. They won't let you take Soer Jaym out of here."

"They will. I'm leaving and she's coming with me." I glanced at the girl. "Are you ready?"

She nodded defiantly at Garard. "Sooner the better."

"Take his arm, then. Walk to the door." Turning my attention back to the man, I ordered, "Garard, walk to the door." I lifted the bolt, then motioned to Soer Jaym. She cautiously opened the door and peered into the hall.

"Everyone's gone."

"Garard," I ordered again, "take us the quickest, but safest, way to the front door. You may not call for help."

After shooting me a look of anger mixed with fear, Garard went left down the ornately furnished hall, Soer Jaym at his side. I closed the door behind them and followed. At the end of the hall, the man turned right and proceeded down a similar hall. At the end, we found a wide stone staircase covered with a blue patterned runner that appeared to go down through the floors, possibly to the very bottom.

"I've never seen this stairway before," Soer Jaym said, puzzled.

"Of course not, My Soer. You've always stayed in the women's quarters. This is where the men go about their business. You, man!" Garard spoke to me even though his head couldn't move. "Do you even have a weapon?"

"Just myself."

"Down this hall to the right, past the stairway, is a room of weapons on display. I suggest you get something to protect Soer Jaym."

"Good idea. Wait here." I dashed down the hall, swept a gaze over the weapons, and grabbed what I needed. I returned minutes later with a huge shield and a heavy sword, both plain but serviceable.

Garard's mind was throwing daggers. *If he could move, I'd be dead.* "What do you think you can accomplish with those, you fool?" His voice broke with anxiety and I knew he hated himself for that break.

Placed a comforting hand on his shoulder, I backed it with soothing mind-thought. "You will see, old man." As Garard's turmoil subsided, I asked, "Now, will this stairway take us straight to the bottom floor?"

"Right to the front door." His words seemed dragged out of him but he added quickly, "How do you plan to open it?"

"I have no idea. What do you suggest?" I said pleasantly, comrade-like. I couldn't help but feel a fondness for this crusty majordomo and caught the notion that the man hoped Jaym could escape her difficulties.

"The front door has a bolt similar to the one on the door to the Grand Salon, the room we just left. Flip up the bolt and push open the door..." The tone became belligerent. "...if you're strong enough. And if the guards let you get that far."

I whirled as screaming came from the room we'd just left. "Chut! The maid woke up."

"Oh, I'm glad she's alive." Soer Jaym let out the breath she'd been holding. "But I wish she'd stayed quiet longer." Seconds later, we heard an alarm and the girl's emotions flared into turmoil. "She's pushed the panic button!"

"Right. Here we go." I slung her over my shoulder. The skirts of her costume billowed around us so I slashed at them with the sword in my right hand, managing to tame the material somewhat.

"Pick up the shield and use it to cover us from behind," I shouted as doors all down the stairway slammed open and men poured out. I squatted to allow her to grab the shield, and glanced once more at Garard. "The stasis will wear off in about an hour. Then, you'll be fine."

The man stood frozen, glaring as I swung the sword with my right hand and started down the five flights of stairs at a run. Guards charged out of doorways to stop us. At the fourth floor landing, I swung the sword at two, who jumped violently back and tripped each other. Dodging a third, I flipped the sword lightly and cracked the guard on the back of the head with the hilt, sending him tumbling down the stairs.

At the third floor, the guards had drawn their guns. I spun away from two, slapping them hard in the body with the edge of the shield Soer Jaym held, knocking them rolling out of the way. One of the rollers took out a third guard, tumbling him head over heels down the stairway. Leaping over the other roller, I caught the head of a fourth with the flat of the sword.

The second floor guards stopped their forward charge and drew weapons, but held their fire as we flashed past. *Didn't think they'd shoot at their Soer.*

Seconds later, we reached the ground floor. At the door, I paused and cast an illusion that made us seem to shrink behind the shield. Bullets struck the stonework around the doorway but not our shield. I reached for the bolt with my left hand, flipped it upward, and shoved. The door flew outward as if struck by a battering ram and I was running down another set of stairs. Glancing in all directions for a destination, I saw no guards outside. The street was dim and empty and I recognized the early morning light. *I'd been in the passageways all night!*

"Go round a corner so we can't be seen from the door," Soer Jaym shouted from my shoulder. I swung left, never breaking pace from my headlong dash.

"Put me down. I can walk on my own." She sounded breathless, *fear or excitement?* "I have an idea. If you put your arm through mine, we can stroll quietly away as if we were newlyweds." *Ah, exhilaration!* Arm in arm, we walked calmly into the rising sunshine.

~ Lillith

"Lillith!" Lillyon sounded strained.

I opened my eyes to discover myself lying on my side beside a bushy hedge, Lillyon nudging me urgently with his nose.

"What happened?" I felt dizzy.

"You passed out!" *Lillyon is really upset!* I thought.

"Oh!" Memory flooded back: the mad dash down the stairs, bolstering Joedon's deceptive images without his awareness. "Did they get out of the palace?"

"You said they did just before you collapsed."

"Where are they now?"

"I don't know. Can't you find him?"

"Yes, of course." I braced front hooves and heaved upward with bunching hip muscles, only to stumble awkwardly against Lillyon. He supported me with a shoulder under my wing as I struggled to steady myself. Finally solidly on my feet, I sought Joedon's mind, careful to not alert him to my presence. "Good. They're on their way to a car rental. We'll follow."

"Stop!" Lillyon swung himself around to block my path. "Rest first."

I glared but he didn't move. "Whatever you were doing stressed you too much. If they're fine, then you're going to rest here until you feel stronger!" His ears pinned back, he bared his teeth and hunched his shoulders aggressively.

"Okay." I dipped my head. "I'll just keep a light touch. We can stay right here in the shadows of this hedge until he leaves Pith."

"Sensible—for once." Lillyon's shoulders and ears lost their rigidity. "We'll go soon."

I aimed a probe at the girl to follow her thinking.

~ Jaym

Surprised that my rescuer breathed evenly despite the strenuous activity, I glanced sideways at him and stopped abruptly. The young man I strolled with looked nothing like the one who'd just run down the stairs with me. He was short, plump, dark-haired and well-groomed in a wedding suit: white shirt, black embroidered trousers and vest.

He stopped and smiled, a thick, dark eyebrow flicking upward. "What is it, love?" His voice was the same, but it didn't match the face I was looking at. And that face was at least two feet below where it should have been. *He's shorter than me!*

"You know I love you dearly, sweetheart, but if we don't hurry, we'll miss our flight. Stop daydreaming and let us hurry along a bit." The man pulled me gently down the street. "There are people watching us over to the right," he whispered. "Pull yourself together. Remember your role."

I glanced around at the buildings, shuddered a bit, then projected my words. "Yes dear. You're right. I got lost in the beauty of the morning." I nodded absently at a trio of girls standing to the right, then focused on a distant cloud. Forcing my face to hold a smile, which I hoped looked somewhat natural, I demanded in a whisper, "Who are you? How did you do that? You sound the same but look totally different."

He pulled me close and nuzzled an ear. I couldn't help it. I stiffened, then tried to relax into him with limited success. "I'll explain later," he said very softly, as if whispering loving words. "Right now we have to get to a car stand before the word gets out about what happened at the palace." Releasing me with a quick kiss, he tucked my hand into the crook of his arm, and walked on, pitching his voice for me alone. "To the rest of the world, we're both as short as I appear to you. I project into people's minds what I want them to see, rather than letting them see what is real. I can't change what they hear, so be careful what you say." He patted my hand. "We still have to get out of the city." Struggling to put his words together into something I could understand, I kept walking at his side.

Chapter 4

~ Lillith

"What are you doing now?" Lillyon's words broke me away from the mind I'd been following.

"'I' was listening to the girl's thoughts. She's going to be perfect."

"What makes you think so?"

"Let me share this conversation I just overheard." I cocked a hip, flashed my eyes, and said, in the light tone that was Jaym's, "Was that real money you gave him?"

In my own voice, I explained. "That's Soer Jaym. She's referring to the man they rented the car from. I could hug her for being so composed."

Then, I straightened my body, opened my eyes wide as if surprised, and in Joedon's deeper inflection said, "Of course it was real. Do you think I would have counterfeit money?"

Projecting the girl into Lillyon's mind as Joedon saw her, I continued in the girl's tone. "Well, not everything about you is as it seems." Lillyon saw the red-head point a finger at her companion. "Right now, you're dressed in a wedding costume, short, plump, dark-haired, and making off with the daughter of the Lord of the city. And, you appear to be carrying a set of luggage." Her eyebrows shot up and her words dripped with innocence. "Why shouldn't you have counterfeit money as well?"

Joedon laughed aloud. "You have me there."

"He's laughing!" Lillyon's shock rang in his words.

"Yes," I breathed, my heart swelling with happiness. "He's laughing."

Stalking out of the bushes I'd been hiding behind, I took off, flying north. "I want to follow them, follow her mind, learn what I can about her."

Jaym was gazing avidly out the window, trying to match what she saw to what she'd only read about. Unable to see through her eyes, I felt the images through her thoughts. She marveled at the central buildings of Pith which she knew were over a hundred years old. Several stories high and constructed of light-pink limestone shipped in from the Melton Mountains far to the south, they were majestic and imposing to her. Stretched along both sides of the broad Pith River, the city had served as a major trading post for decades, connecting the locals and northern villages to the Bonn Sea one hundred miles south.

"She's bright and inquiring," I commented. "Awed, but not scared. Like I said, perfect."

"What's Joedon thinking?"

"He's not thinking about the girl; he's concentrating on getting out of the city without attracting undue attention. He's driving much more cautiously than normal."

"I thought so, from what I can see." I grinned at the ironic tone in his mind.

The heavy traffic along the river bank made the girl claustrophobic, but I still detected no fear. When the car turned onto a wide tree-lined boulevard and the multi-storied business buildings with broad glass facades changed into lower warehouses and spreading residential developments, she relaxed further.

Quietly absorbing the surroundings until Joedon veered right and headed north on the freeway, the girl finally uttered a question. "Now that we're out of the palace, I see you can find your way around." She continued to watch through the tinted windows: wood and stone buildings of many sizes, wide streets lined with trees, individual homes and apartment complexes, and parks easily seen from the elevated roadway.

"Yes, I've been to Pith many times. I know my way around the city."

She glanced at him and registered amazement. Joedon had dropped the disguise and I approved of her reaction: he'd changed into the glorious man she'd first seen in the Grand

Salon. *Good girl. He is glorious.* I carefully refrained from planting my ideas into the girl's head. *She must make up her own mind.*

The girl's next statement startled me. "I've never seen the city before, except by looking out the window in the top floor play room." And the reason behind the statement was even stranger. "The *Lord's women* are not allowed out of the palace. They're not to be seen by the *common folk* according to my step-mother."

For a moment, Jaym fought off threatening tears. The bitterness she felt at the life she'd had to live vibrated throughout her words. "My step-mother and my oldest half-sister are perfectly happy to live in the palace, never go anywhere, never see the outside, as long as they have their gowns and jewelry and gentlemen at the balls." Then, her mind bloomed happily with pictures of two younger girls with dark curls tumbling down their backs. "My other two half-sisters are still with their tutor."

"I didn't realize she'd been so unhappy all her life," I told Lillyon as we followed the speeding car northward, above and out of sight. "I thought her troubles evolved with this marriage to Lord Roark. And yet, she's valiantly suppressing her tears in front of Joedon. Better and better."

Although driving much faster now that he was on the highway, Joedon continually tried to contact me; I refused to answer. Instead, I followed Jaym's thoughts as the girl silently gazed out the car window at the countryside flashing past. The city gave way to farms that produced the fruits and vegetables Pith shipped to other city-states. Stone farmhouses with large storage sheds appeared once in awhile, surrounded by fields and connected by straight, paved roads. Between fields, she noted the broad irrigation canals; she'd read they carried water from the Pith River, which she assumed was off to her right among the trees snaking across the flat plain. Cottonwoods, she remembered, lined the river throughout Pith state.

To my right, I saw the tall spreading trees. *Cottonwoods? Strange name. They look nothing like cotton.*

Jaym had studied geography and economics with her half-sisters and knew what products each city-state produced. She longed to visit all of Pith, and the other cities. Pith was one of the largest city-states on Garador; wealth coming from agriculture. Located in a broad river valley and protected on the west and south by mountains, Pith had good soil and plentiful rainfall allowing it to be extremely productive. Her father owned large tracts of farmland somewhere and derived his income from produce, but where it was located, she hadn't a clue.

"She seems to be well educated," I said to Lillyon. "Especially in light of the life she's lived, confined to the palace."

"Odd they would bother to teach her anything." Lillyon feigned interest; I knew he was trying to provide his support, as he always did. "What's she supposed to do with an education, I wonder?"

"Now she's guessing at the vegetation she's seeing. Pretty shrewd guesses."

"Why does she care?"

"She's filled with curiosity. A fine trait, I think." I proceeded to relay Jaym's guesses. Maybe the vine things held grapes, the girl thought, and the tall roundish trees seemed to have oranges. The sweetness she remembered of eating an orange made me wonder if I would like one. As the car sped past an immense grove of very tall trees, Jaym compared them to the date palms pictured in one of her books. She was stumped by a field of short, spiky, light green vegetation edging the road; she wanted to ask Joedon what they were but kept silent. I had to stop myself from answering her question even as I shuddered at the thought of onions.

Then, the girl lost interest in the view and her mind shifted to contemplate her abductor. She wondered why she felt no fear of the man. Again, I clamped my thoughts behind a thick mental wall and stopped sharing with Lillyon to insure I wasn't accidentally leaking my own emotions. But she continued to think of Joedon without becoming upset.

The first time she saw him, Jaym thought, she'd worried only of escape. She should be afraid. From what she'd seen, he could hurt her easily. He was at least a foot taller than she and very strong, not to mention all of the little tricks he played. But, even in that mad dash down the stairs, she hadn't feared he might stumble or drop her.

"Good," I said to Lillyon, ignoring his air of resignation. "Joedon has finally stopped calling me and is starting to pay attention to Soer Jaym. He's sensing the shifting emotions roiling through her and starting to react, to talk to her." I followed their conversation a few wing strokes. "Now, he's wondering what he's going to do with her."

"Are you going to nudge him into bringing her to Eyrie?"

"I want him to think of it himself. But if I have to, I will." I began to relate Joedon's thoughts. "He's been so busy planning their escape that he hasn't thought through how it will end and he's swirling with emotion for the first time in years."

Lillyon flicked his ears back, then slowed to a hover. "Trouble," he said.

I banked to see a police car, red lights flashing, speeding down the highway not far behind Joedon's rental car. Beneath us, Joedon had already slowed and I felt his image waver into a long-haired blond woman. Jaym had morphed into a young boy, blond, with facial features similar to his own. Then, he pulled over to the side of the road and stopped. Two men in uniform approached either side of the car, hands on their holstered weapons.

"Do something!" Lillyon hissed.

"No! He's handling it," I hissed back.

"Ma'am," the officer said as Joedon rolled down his window. "You were driving mighty fast. What's the hurry?"

Joedon projected confusion, then embarrassment. "I'm sorry, officer. We were singing and I didn't notice how fast I was going. I'm taking my son to the Sapphire Sea for holiday. We're really not in a hurry and I didn't mean to speed."

35

I caught an urgent communication from one man to the other and the one next to Joedon's door backed away saying, "Just slow down, ma'am, and pay closer attention." The officer backed faster, spun, and jogged to the patrol car. They pulled out, did a u-turn, and headed rapidly back the way they'd come.

"I don't understand what happened," Lillyon whined as he watched the patrol car disappear.

"I'm probing."

As Joedon dropped the images and pulled back onto the road, I explained to Lillyon what I'd learned by reading the policeman's thoughts. "The man on the girl's side received an urgent call from Neff Casino; they were ordered back to the Casino to receive instructions..." I started to chuckle. "... on how to deal with two special fugitives." I grinned at Lillyon, baring all my teeth. "And Joedon's decided to drive within the speed limit until they get to the plateau."

Lillyon grinned back. "Humans!" We increased our speed to catch up with the rental car. "When are you going to let Joedon reach you?"

"Soon. When they reach the plateau, don't you think?"

"In about an hour, then, at this speed."

"If it's that soon, I'd better arrange for us to meet them!"

I noticed a tension I hadn't been aware of fade from my shoulders and neck as I finally answered Joedon's continual calls.

"Lillith! Where have you been? I couldn't hear you!" His relief was immense, but short lived as he heard the sound of sirens. He reassembled his disguises just as two patrol cars shot by and disappeared over the rise in front of them. For the first time, he sensed the girl's fear. Trying to reassure her, he said, "Whatever has them stirred up must not have anything to do with us. Fortunately, we'll leave the highway soon."

The girl did not relax. *She fears going back.* I dropped lower but stayed out of sight. "I'm sorry, Joedon. Since you were gone, Lillyon and I decided to take a break too. We were far away. I heard you for the first time just a few minutes ago."

Lillyon's snort of derision rattled my concentration and I shot him an angry glare. Shielding from Joedon, I snapped, "I'll deal with you later!" He snorted again.

"I need your help!" Joedon wailed. Rapidly, he outlined everything that had happened to him since he'd last seen me. Answering with sounds of sympathy and shock while maintaining a light contact with the girl, I saw her anxiety increasing at his apparent silence. I sent her an easing.

Joedon's rapid words slowed; confusion and embarrassment coloring them. "I've brought a guest, a human."

"I can sense her." I forced a foreign coldness into my voice. "Who is she?"

"I had to bring her! She's Lord Metz' daughter, Soer Jaym, and they're forcing her to marry Lord Roark. I couldn't leave her to face it." He grew more confident. "Besides, I'm going to use her to trade for Raedon!"

Sarcasm seeped in. "Why did you rescue her if you're going to give her back?"

"I haven't worked out the details but I will. You just have to get us safely to Eyrie." He flashed a glance at Jaym who was leaning against her window staring at him with a nervous expression. He smiled as if to reassure her. She tentatively smiled back. "Meet us at the top of Flagstone Canyon." He assumed I was still far away and I didn't indicate differently.

Suddenly, Jaym's anxiety spiked. She'd looked away from Joedon and saw three more patrol cars appear in the distance. Joedon felt her start, then caught a glimpse of them in the mirror. Above them, I supplemented Joedon's quick, inventive projection and the three cars whizzed past the beat up pickup.

"What are they doing?" Jaym's physical and mental voice was shrill as Joedon's hands clenched the steering wheel.

Lillyon echoed the girl. "What are they doing?"

I sped up and rose high enough to look ahead. "They're setting up roadblocks. We have to find somewhere else to meet them."

Joedon continued through the foothills unaware of the danger ahead; rise after rise, each a bit higher than the last, he slowly gained on the mountains while Lillyon and I searched for an alternative. He glanced constantly through his rear-view mirror; Jaym's nervousness increased with each shift of his head.

"Finally!" I landed in a copse of trees close to where the highway crossed the river, just short of the turnoff Joedon expected to take. While in the air, I could see the flashing lights of the roadblock, but once I landed, they were out of sight.

"Stop just before the bridge and scramble down to the river," I said urgently to Joedon. "The police are waiting for you up the road."

He stopped abruptly in the middle of the highway and clambered out, pulling Jaym with him. As the pair slipped and slid down the embankment, a patrol car topped the rise beyond the bridge. It squealed to a halt and officers piled out, shouting, "Stop or we'll shoot."

Ignoring them, Joedon continued to pull Jaym down the bank. They disappeared into the underbrush as shots sang over their heads. "They don't want to kill you," he shouted at her. "Keep moving."

"Where are we going?" Jaym yelled, breathing hard. When they exited the brush, she slid to a stop and gasped.

"Quick. Throw her on Lillyon." I nudged Joedon in the back. "He's wearing a harness; buckle her tight." I looked up at the bridge. "We have to get out of here."

Cursorily, I probed the girl. Her eyes were wide and gleaming, her grin almost split her face, and her body radiated excitement, even though she didn't say a word. Joedon lifted her up, showed her how to straddle the harness, and buckled her in. Then, he threw himself on my back and we took off to the east, keeping trees between us and the bridge.

Once I felt we were completely out of sight, I rose higher and slowed, positioning myself to Lillyon's left, level with the girl. "Welcome, Soer Jaym. You are most Well Come." The girl started, not sure if she heard it aloud or only in her mind; but she smiled, wide and glorious.

I couldn't help but gloat at the thoughts flowing through her head: beautiful creatures, sunlight glimmering on white coats as if they wore thousands of tiny crystals; huge wings spread wide tipping forward then back to catch the currents; warm brown eyes glinting with a variety of colors, like gemstones; manes and tails, like those of a horse, fluttering gossamer fine on the air currents.

I love this girl!

"I am Lillith, mind-mate of Joedon." I dipped my head, then turned to flick an ear toward my rider. Again pointing with an ear, I added, "You are on my handsome husband, Lillyon. Do not fear..." I didn't sense any anxiety at all in the girl, only joy. "... we'll take very good care of you."

Jaym replied aloud, impressing me with her courage. "Lillith, I don't know how to address you properly. I'm very glad to meet you. I've never seen anything as splendid as you and your husband."

"My Soer, you are very gracious. Simply call me Lillith. Lillyon and I will carry you to safety."

"You can understand her!" Joedon sounded stunned. "I never knew a human could understand reeth."

"Any human could understand us if they wanted to," I said dryly. "Most never tried so we stopped talking to them."

Lillyon's deep voice caused Jaym to glance curiously at him. "We must hurry. There's a plane approaching."

We increased our speed, deployed the invisibility illusions, and veered away from the plane. Jaym quickly found her balance and was bold enough to gaze avidly down at the plateau we knew well. A vast expanse of rolling grass sparsely dotted with trees spread out below. Here and there, outcroppings of dark rock jutted upward, breaking the monotonous flow of green.

I told her we would take a long route to safety as she was enjoying the flight so much. We passed over valley after valley separated by high ridges of rocky peaks; streams plunged through blankets of evergreens joining rivers in valleys dotted with yellow, orange, and blue patches of wild flowers. Lillyon flew close to sheer red cliffs, then swung far out above mesas of shrubs and pockets of lacy trees, tall with white bark. At one point, we passed a waterfall cascading down a rocky incline, pooling at the bottom in a dark, mysterious pond. We hovered briefly over a high basin filled to the brim with water, shadowed and lined with a broad-leafed, low-growing dark-green bush. Patches of white peaked through the ground cover. Jaym loved it all, throwing back her head and laughing into the wind.

I snatched the shout of exultation from Jaym's mind and transferred it to Lillyon and Joedon. "I'm free! I could fly like this forever!"

Shielding from Joedon and the girl, I asked, "What do you think of her now, my love?"

"Like you said, she's perfect."

Chapter 5

~ Joedon

After Lillith's surprising tour of the mountains, evidently inspired by Soer Jaym's exhilaration, we flew straight at a sheer face of rock and landed on the narrow ledge leading into our immense cavern home. I had to assume she'd forgiven me for bringing a human when she sent the girl words of approval for her lack of fear. I jumped down to help Soer Jaym dismount; when her legs wobbled, she leaned on Lillyon's shoulder to catch her breath.

"Take your time." Lillyon's voice rumbled. "You aren't used to riding or flying. You'll feel better shortly." Even he sounds like he likes Soer Jaym and he's the most conservative of the pair.

The girl gazed around the cavern, marveling aloud at rooms that flowed from one to the next with no doors, rather walls that curved and provided privacy. Lillith explained that since individuals of both species lived here, it had been especially designed to accommodate everyone. "Lillyon and I occupy this portion. Joedon has his own suite down that hallway." Her friendliness amazed me.

Soer Jaym's first step came close to bringing disaster. "Probably the altitude," Lillith said at the girl's waver. I took her arm and led her into the dining room. She gazed around in awe, finally contemplating the rounded stone ceiling soaring high overhead. A grating sound caught her attention. She stared at Nanadon, our charge-de-house, and her aide, both typically very tall and graceful, arranging heavy wooden chairs around our equally heavy table. A third aide stuffed grass into scattered round tubs: a seemingly amazing sight to her, everyday activities to me. Lillith didn't stop to introduce our guest but all three dipped their heads in a semi-curtsey and smiled.

Soer Jaym clutched at my arm and whispered, "Who are you people?"

I bounced the question to Lillith; she stepped back and left the explanation to me as if to say: you started this, you take it from

41

here. I guided Soer Jaym to a seat at a table and took the chair beside her.

"I am Joedon. My people are the don," I said, then noticed my unconsciously possessive tone. Swallowing my embarrassment, I forged on, "These..." I waved at the three moving quietly about the room, doing domestic tasks. "... are don. The correct term for them is femm—female don, plural." I glanced at Lillith. "How many don live here? I've lost track."

"Fifteen."

The girl's emotional aura glowed with fascination fueling my interest. Indicating Lillith, I explained. "Many don have a mind-mate who is a reeth. What that means is Lillith and I have a mental connection, established when I was born. We communicate telepathically. Although she can understand what I say, she obviously can't form the sounds of our language with her mouth."

Jaym nodded as if she understood.

"Lillith and Lillyon live here with many of their family members. The mind-mates of the don living here reside with their families in this cavern, too, along with various members of Lillith's family. Plus, there are always colts here for training." I grinned at Lillyon. "I never know exactly how many reeth actually occupy this place at any one time." Lillith shrugged. She didn't know either.

"Why have I never heard of your people?" Soer Jaym glanced all around her. "I know I've been kept isolated in Pith Palace, but surely someone, at some time, would have mentioned non-human species living on Garador!"

"No, they wouldn't have." I sighed, then rose to pace around the table, forcing the girl to swivel in her chair to watch me. Lillith backed away, keeping her physical presence out of my thoughts. *Is this her punishment? Making me recount ancient history?*

"A few centuries ago, don, reeth, and humans co-existed on the planet in an uneasy alliance." I had fallen into a lecturer's tone; it seemed to fit the situation and helped me get through the story. Soer Jaym followed me with her eyes, obviously intently soaking in the information. "The don and reeth have been on Garador forever." I stopped and faced her. "Garador, by the way, is the human name for our planet, Gareeth. Humans came by spaceship about four hundred years ago—"

She flung up a hand, her brow crinkled. "Wait a minute. What's a spaceship?"

Surprised, I looked at her with keen interest. "A spaceship is a type of plane that carries humans from one planet to another in the universe."

"What's a universe?" More crinkles.

"You've never studied astronomy?" That was hard to believe except her eyes were free of guile. Placing my hands behind my back, I resumed pacing, dropping again into lecture mode. "In brief, this planet is not the only planet with life on it. Somewhere out among the stars, human life developed. They invented spaceships and spread themselves to other planets, Gareeth being one of them. Then, their supply ships stopped coming and those left here were cut off from their ancestors."

"I don't understand any of what you're saying." She radiated confusion mixed with curiosity and I discovered that I liked her inquiring mind. *Not a typical human female.* Lillith lifted one lip to flash her teeth in a reeth-sized smirk even though I didn't really see it. Neither had Soer Jaym.

"Later, I'll show you my science room and try to explain the universe to you." I stopped walking and gave the girl a confident grin. "For now, take my word for it. The human species did not develop here, on this planet. It came from elsewhere."

Assuming that would satisfy her, I started to pace again. "At first, our ancestors tried to work with the humans to make the planet a pleasant place for all of us. There's plenty of room and we worked well together. But gradually, humans started asking don to do more and more for them, because of our mental abilities and our strength. When my grandfather and his contemporaries refused, some of the humans tried to take them under control by capturing their reeth-mates."

"Why did they refuse the requests?"

"Partially because they didn't approve of what humans asked of them, and also because there were just too many things they wanted." I shook my head, recalling the ancient stories. "Humans never did understand the connection between don and reeth. Once, they accidentally killed a reeth. The don went crazy; some factions called for annihilation." I shot her a glance—she was listening intently. "Don and humans fought until all reeth were rescued. The situation might have developed into death for one or other of the species." Her emotions were so easy to read; catching her sudden worry, I smiled to calm her. "Fortunately, the warmongers were not in charge of our council and saner ones prevailed. My grandfather came up with a plan to slowly end the conflict and disappear.

"We allowed the humans to believe they were winning. Whenever a don came near a human, he planted a suggestion that don and reeth were dying off. The more mentally powerful traveled through human cities in disguise, planting suggestions in the minds of men, women and children not involved in the fighting and they began to question what their troops were doing."

She approved. "So, no one actually told humans that the don and reeth were dying, they just suggested it, and rumors spread?"

"Exactly." *She's quick.* "No human could say why they thought it was true and no one could remember who had told them. Eventually, the deception convinced the humans they had killed us all."

Totally absorbed in my story and rapt audience, I dropped back into the chair, straddling the seat. "Next, my grandfather's friends planted suggestions in human minds that don and reeth had never existed in the first place and that idea spread. They also manipulated targeted humans into destroying written or pictorial proof and replaced their records with legends of our species. After several decades, humans had convinced themselves that we …" I nodded to Lillith. "…were just characters in stories mothers use to scare their children into behaving."

I shifted my image into a cranky old woman scolding with a crooked index finger. "Behave or the wicked don will carry you away." She laughed and I allowed the image to vanish. "It worked beautifully. Since then, for more than three hundred fifty years, the Speaker's Council has kept our existence a secret."

I slumped and looked away to stare at the far wall. "After today, however, things might seriously change."

"Why do you say that?"

That inquiring mind again. "Too many people saw the things I did today and stories will spread. Garard did not appear to be a stupid man and he studied me the whole time." I paused, remembering, then frowned. "And I forgot to project a human image for him to see until we started down the stairs. He's going to put his experiences together in a way the Council won't like."

She straightened and glared at me. "What did you do to him? He must have been terrified, not being able to move except by your command."

"Garard wasn't terrified. That's what bothers me about him. He should've been."

"But how did you do it?" A demanding tone I'd heard before.

I pointed with both index fingers to my head. "There are points just above the temples that I can use to temporarily paralyze a person's muscles. I have to be able to touch both points at the same time when I send a message to their brain. The stasis only lasts for about an hour so if I need it to last longer, I have to do it again."

I'd completely forgotten Lillith's presence. And I probably could have talked for hours if the servers hadn't interrupted us to set the table.

Lillith strode forward. "Why don't you take Jaym into your suite so she can clean up and rest before dinner. In case you haven't noticed, she's drooping in her seat." She cocked an ear toward me. "You don't look too lively either."

Chagrined, I jumped up to offer an arm of assistance. Lillith sent a smile into the girl's mind. "When you come back for the evening meal, I'd love to introduce you to my family."

Nodding, Soer Jaym rose gracefully while admitting to being very tired. I escorted her along a stone hallway to my front door which opened as we approached. The girl stopped and stared at me, eyes wide and slightly suspicious. "How did you do that?"

I had to laugh. "It has an electronic sensor that I snitched from some humans. It opens as I approach." I pulled her gently through the door. "I can do many things that may seem like magic to you but I can't move physical material. I can only influence minds and emotions. I promise to explain everything to you, but first, I must rest."

Releasing her arm, I pointed to a short hallway. "To the left, the first door leads to a room where you may relax, the second into the guest bath. I plan to sleep for a couple of hours. I'll call you when I arise. Help yourself to whatever you need. There may be clothes in the closet that will fit if you want to get out of that costume."

She nodded and turned away. I waited until she entered the room, then started toward my own, totally aware of my exhaustion. Somehow, I hadn't noticed it as I'd been talking with the girl. I collapsed onto the bed, instantly asleep.

~ Lillith

"Good. He's finally resting." I said to Lillyon and switched to monitoring the girl. She was rummaging through the armoire. Surprised that she found a tunic that would fit, she struggled out of the wedding costume—not an easy task. I was on the verge of sending her help when she finally got the last button undone. She examined the heavy skirt, decided it was ruined from the sword work, and tossed it into a pile in a corner.

46

The ruffled white blouse and embroidered vest she carefully hung in the closet. Then, she twirled in the room as if feeling lighter than she ever had, as if some sort of silken bonds had been removed from her heart. Her mind catalogued the lovely furnishings: extra-wide soft bed covered in luxurious silken sheets and a warm, fluffy comforter patterned in greens; two elegant embroidered chairs, also in greens, situated to either side of a carved dressing table with a tall beveled mirror; the armoire, carved to match the table and bed. Thinking she would be too nervous, excited, or afraid to actually sleep, she lay down on the bed, and pulled the covers up to her chin. She intended to mull over what had happened, and what she'd heard. Then, the pillow is heavenly, she thought. She was asleep in seconds.

For the four hours the pair slept, I kept a portion of my mind touching each one as I directed my don helpers to prepare for a party and sent word to my closest relatives to be present for the evening meal. Joedon slept dream free but Jaym flew, soaring through the clouds and gazing down on tiny landscapes. I wasn't sure whether the girl flew on a reeth or by herself. *So glad she's not afraid of heights.*

~ Jaym

I woke to a soft knocking followed by Joedon calling, "Soer Jaym. Are you ready for the rest of the day? I promised to tell you my story."

I sat up quickly, disoriented for a moment, then remembered. Replacing my concern with a happy grin, I called back. "Do I have time for a shower?"

"Of course. Help yourself. I'll be in the living room when you're ready."

I jumped off the bed, feeling more energy than I had in a long time, and rummaged through the closet, my tongue turning over the sound of his name—Joedon. An odd name, somehow endowed with power. A fitting name. I recalled his face, his actions, his lovely tenor voice. Then, I thought again of how relaxed I felt with him, here in his home, even though I was totally powerless, without protection. Never before had I been so alone with a man.

Gazing around the room, I whispered, "I feel more at home here than I've ever felt in the palace."

Cutting off that line of thought, I selected a set of grey trousers and a loose green shirt made of silk-like fabric. Rubbing the sleeve between my fingers, I enjoyed the softness. *So fine.* Never had I worn such loose, comfortable clothing. With nothing overtly feminine about them, I wondered if they'd belonged to a much younger Joedon.

The warm shower water and lavender scented soap felt heavenly. Using a fluffy cream-colored towel to dry my hair, I gazed at myself in the mirror: a lovely young woman, although tall. I scowled, then. My step-mother always denigrated my appearance in favor of her own daughter who was short and beautifully rounded with dark wavy hair and eyes that seemed like deep pools. I'd overheard a notable flattering my half-sister with that very phrase at a palace dinner once.

Shaking my despicable—according to my step-mother—flame-colored hair, I banished the ugly memory of that dinner. *Here I am in a new world.* I decided to enjoy as much of it as I could before I had to return. Reveling in the freedom of leaving my hair loose instead of coifed tightly to my head, I wiggled with abandon in the comfy clothes and relished the dream of freedom I'd held close ever since I first saw Joedon standing in the opening in the Grand Salon wall.

Joedon glanced up from the paper he was reading and smiled as I shyly entered the room. "Quite a change," he said. "You certainly are a beautiful woman, even more so without that heavy wedding costume." He looked me up and down, then nodded approval. "Trousers suit you. Many of our femm wear trousers but they also love their silks and gauzes."

I blushed at his words even as they lifted my spirits. He appeared very fine in a multi-colored shirt over dark trousers, although not nearly as magnificent as he had in the Grand Salon. However, he seemed more friendly and relaxed. I took the seat across the low, oval table from him, quelling nervousness.

"Are you hungry?" he asked.

"Why, yes I am."

"We'll go to the kitchen first, then. I'll make us a salad." He threw a grin back over his shoulder as I followed. "Lillith expects us for dinner so we dare not eat much now."

Although I'd studied food preparation, I'd never actually seen the palace kitchen. "What a beautiful room!" Avidly, I examined the wood accents surrounding the shiny metal machines I'd only read about and watched in awe as Joedon took a bag of salad greens, a handful of mushrooms, and three wrapped cheeses from a refrigerator. Bread came from a cupboard and he plucked various fruits from a bin. He quickly assembled a salad, setting the food on a round wooden table.

I settled into one of the carved chairs. "Everything is greener or brighter than what we get at the palace. How do you have such fresh fruits and vegetables way up in the mountains?"

Joedon's grin made him less formal, almost mischievous, I thought as he said, "We have much faster ways to transport our produce than you humans. Although reeth are not necessarily faster than your airplanes, planes can't take off and land just anywhere. Thus, we have fresh fruit and you don't."

"You use those beautiful creatures to transport cargo?" I said in outrage.

"No, no. Lillith and Lillyon don't usually transport cargo." He sank into a chair and spooned a large helping of the salad onto his plate, then handed a set of tongs to me. Awkwardly, I managed to copy him. I'd never even served myself at table.

"They're royalty, just as you are a soer of the palace," he said, "and I am of the don royalty. You saw some of our helpers earlier; they routinely work in fields and their reeth transport produce and other goods." He poured some thick purple sauce over his salad and passed me the bottle. "Our species never developed any type of mechanical means to travel; we never had to. But we all work together to do whatever needs to be done, which means that sometimes I harvest grass and Lillith carries produce."

The salad was wonderful. "What is this delicious sauce?"

"Lareina wine and apple vinegar. We use Lareina, which means 'the queen' in some long dead language, for dressings and sauces. Would you like to try some of the wine itself?"

At my nod, Joedon opened a chilled bottle, plucked two wine glasses from a cupboard, and poured half a glass for each of us. Because of its color, I expected a heavy wine like those served at the palace formal dinners—this was light and fruity.

"This is delightful. It's better than fresh lemonade."

Joedon snorted. "It's more expensive too. One of our don families produces this wine exclusively and it's not widely available. That's why it's called 'The Queen'—Lareina." He held his glass forward as if making a toast. "The fruit itself is even better. It grows only in the lower areas of Delt and has to be harvested by hand. Both don and reeth use the peel for medicines. I'm sorry I don't have any for you to try."

"Well, the rest of these fruits look delicious." I reached for a pear. "Marvelous!"

We ate in companionable silence, a meal more pleasant that any I'd had since my mother died. When Joedon rose to clear the table, I scrambled to help, following his lead in stacking dishes in what he said was a dishwasher. Then, he stretched out his hand to take mine. "Come. I'd like to show you my home. Then, we'll join Lillith for the rest of the evening.

"You've seen the kitchen." He led me into what he called a formal dining room containing a heavy wooden table and chairs with a matching bureau. "Not that we ever formally dine! And you've seen the living room." Decorated in muted colors, with dim lights, the rooms seemed warm and comfortable even though neither had windows. I felt the home must be circular in nature because after we left the living room, we'd arrived back in the entry hall. "I could live here," I muttered. "I'd never get lost!"

"Lillith's calling for us." Joedon's words interrupted my contemplation of the comfortable home. "I'll show you the rest after dinner."

Chapter 6

~ Lillith

While waiting for Joedon and Jaym to appear, I shared their conversation with Lillyon. "He's brighter, happier than he's been for a long time, extending himself to make her feel safe. She's good for him."

Although he said nothing, I felt his agreement.

Behind me, noise and laughter flowed from one of the larger rooms. I savored Jaym's enchanted gasp when she saw many reeth, in various sizes and colors, mingling with don. The girl looked quickly around, saw everyone dressed in trousers and loose shirts, just as she was, and relaxed.

I moved to greet her. "Welcome, again, Soer Jaym. Allow me to introduce you to my family." I extended a wing and directed Jaym to place her left hand on the crook. Then, I led the girl forward, relishing her every thought, every reaction.

Surprised at the soft feel of the wing, Jaym ran her hand experimentally along it as she walked forward. "Not at all like feathers I've felt before."

"The larger, stiffer feathers are underneath," I explained. "Now, greet each reeth with a light stroke down the neck, start close to the ears, and go with the lay of the hair. Use your right hand. Don shake hands like humans do."

Excited to practice, Jaym turned to the smallish gray mare I invited over. "My oldest daughter, Lillene," I said. Jaym reached out and stroked lightly down the mare's neck with her palm thinking the very short hair was like the finest silk from Bonn. Eyes glowing with pleasure, she noticed a smaller, darker version hiding behind his mother.

"My grandson, Bukkyon." I allowed my pride in the youngster to flow freely and sent out a smile as the girl knelt to put herself on the colt's eye level.

He awkwardly projected his voice. "Welcome, Soer Jaym." His pronunciation was off but the girl didn't mind. She stroked his neck as I had instructed and he puffed up and preened, leaning into the pressure of her hand.

"That's enough, Bukkyon," I reminded him before he knocked the girl over. Jaym started to pat him but I stopped her. "Don't pat. It's annoying. Always stroke."

She learned fast and made an effort to greet others correctly: my beautiful younger sister Lillity, golden with a flowing white mane and tail that waved rather than hung straight; my older brother and his wife, both grey; various don and reeth employees. Jaym confessed to giving up trying to remember names although she obviously felt comfortable thinking her greetings to reeth, rather than speaking aloud. I couldn't have been prouder of the girl than if she'd been my own child.

When several sizes of youngsters pranced forward, I introduced them as my younger twin daughter and son and multiple nieces and nephews. The twins were very much alike with a deep chocolate color, black manes, tails, legs, and wings, and shining, mischievous brown eyes. She studied them, then noticed a slight whirl of white on the colt's forehead, a marking absent on the filly. I muffled my shock over the human's determination to find a way to tell them apart. *She looked close enough to notice something that small!* I flashed the amazing incident to Lillyon. When I refocused on Jaym, I got another shock.

The girl observed the youngsters' ears twitching constantly and decided they were laughing; she began to laugh with them, a clear, joyous sound. Struggling with the idea that Jaym could be so intuitive, I almost missed stopping a disaster in the making. The youngest of the group could barely hold still for the girl's greeting and she started to hug him. Knocking her arms aside, I explained that the colt might strike, that he was still a baby, and hadn't mastered company manners yet.

Chastened, she stroked the colt as my cousin, the colt's mother, and I warned him not to move. Her words gratified both of us. "His coat feels like cushiony cotton balls." Tears welled in her eyes. "He's just precious." Released by his parent, the colt dashed away; the girl's eyes followed. "His legs appear stronger than some of the others." When he flung up his short tail, then kicked out with both hind feet in excitement, she murmured, "That could hurt!"

Throughout the evening, I provided individual characteristics to help the girl associate names with faces. When Jaym asked to see the rest of my home, I called for Nanadon, Charge-de-House, and urged her to explain the intricacies of managing a home of such dissimilar species: the daily sweeping of the rooms and weekly changing of bedding; the preparation of distinct meals for each species; the monthly cleaning of the bathing pools, and the basics of grooming. When we reached my own room, Nana demonstrated how she brushed the pure white hair so that it lay smoothly along my barrel. Then, she handed Jaym the brush and urged her to try; the girl grinned and swept the brush smoothly along my back and over a hip.

I quivered. "Such a light touch is ticklish. Please press more firmly. You can't hurt me."

We ended our tour in the huge room whose floor was covered with deep sand that we used as an exercise arena. "This is where we reeth run to maintain strength in our legs," I said. The youngsters demonstrated races for her; their joyous play enchanted the girl and even though she couldn't follow what they said to each other, she laughed and clapped at their antics.

Returned to the dining hall, we found everyone gathered, hungry and ready for dinner. As usual, reeth spaced themselves randomly around the walls where the huge wooden containers held piles of grasses. Joedon escorted Jaym to one of the tables that dotted the center of the room and pulled out a chair. Noting that Lillyon and I were close, she sank into the chair with an air of expectation.

Nana and her helpers had outdone their usual fare; bowls of fruit salads, nut breads, vegetables doused in delicate sauces, and a number of other dishes began circulating, each person serving themselves. Jaym said she couldn't identify everything and Joedon explained as best he could. To my satisfaction, the girl sampled each dish and showed no sign of missing meat. I could gratefully banish that worry. And Joedon, laughing and telling stories to his table mates, had centered his attention on the girl. *Progressing nicely!*

After dinner, I followed Jaym's gaze toward the colt she'd wanted to hug earlier; he was stretched out on straw in a corner of the dining room, sound asleep. Tears once more sparkled as the girl said, "He's adorable." She looked around the room and smiled. "Thank you so much for allowing me into your home and letting me experience such a wonderful way of living."

My heart as full as hers, I wished the girl well as she turned to follow Joedon from the room. Lillyon came up behind me and put his head gently on my shoulder. "I really liked her. I didn't expect to, but I really did."

"Of course you did." I couldn't help feeling smug. "I picked her didn't I? She'll do."

Chapter 7

~ Jaym

"I have one more room to show you," Joedon said as he escorted me into his suite. "It's very special to me and it's where we'll talk. Please, come with me."

He led me into the living room, then through a door I hadn't noticed before. We entered a huge curved room, obviously his bedroom. One side of the room had a wide bowed window with a view of millions of stars.

I approached the window and gazed out. "It's beautiful at night."

"I often sit by this window simply watching day become night and back to day again. It's soothing." His tone became brisk and he motioned me to a comfortable chair. "But, I promised you a story. Please, sit here near the window. I'll sit across from you."

I sat and composed myself to listen. Continuing to gaze out the window, I felt self-conscious being here alone with him in his bedroom. *Lady Jill would be furious*, i thought, smothering my smile of defiance toward my step-mother.

"The don and reeth are an old species," Joedon began. I watched his reflection in the glass as he sat on the edge of his chair, elbows resting on his knees, hands clasped together. "Our history dates back long before humans came from outer space. Do you remember what I told you earlier?"

I turned to see him intently watching me. "Yes. Don severed their relationship with humans and made humans think don and reeth were legends."

"That's right. Humans refused to understand that reeth and don are irrevocably linked and only saw reeth as animals. They didn't realize that if they killed a mind-mated reeth, its don-mate would die as well. Although they didn't do it, they threatened."

He sighed. "We've lived happily here in the mountains without human contact for a long time." Then, his posture became more intense and his smile slipped. "Ironically, the problem today is that the don species is truly dying, with few don being born." I held my breath; he was so edgy. Finally, he continued softly, "We've only had fourteen babies born in the last twenty-five years, none in the last two."

"There've been more born among the ladies at Pith Palace alone in the last twenty-five years!" I muttered. "That's terrible."

He nodded, his eyes forlorn. "In my generation, there's only one unmarried fem: my cousin, Saradon. And she's supposed to marry my best friend Raedon within the week."

My heart clenched, "Do you love Saradon?"

"Oh, no. You have it wrong." He turned back to face me with a wry smile. "I'm the last of the royal Joe line and everyone thought she should marry me. And I was always cast as her suitor when we were growing up. We spent quite a lot of time together in the past. Our fathers were cousins, you see."

He shook his head, his smile genuine and caring. "Maybe when she was really young, we might have thought about it. But as she grew up—well, we realized we are just too much alike to ever get along as a married couple." His face changed, the look rueful as he shook his head. "It's funny, really. Raedon and I always hated it when we got stuck bringing Sara along for something. Then, we didn't see her much for several years. We were busy—I guess you'd say getting into trouble." His grin flashed. "The older don would certainly characterize our actions that way." He sobered again. "About this time, a year ago, Raedon ran into Sara at a party I didn't attend. The moment he saw her, he was in love."

Joedon got up from his chair and took a turn around the room. "She worked him around her little finger and sunk the hooks in deep. I thought at first she was toying with him, but she apparently loves him as much as he loves her. She wanted to make sure of him before she conceded her heart."

He came back to sit by me again, facing me. "Now, though, we have a major problem."

"What?" Fascinated, I couldn't imagine what it could be.

"Raedon is headstrong. He wasn't brought up to be the leader. He does what he wants, when he wants, without regard for the consequences." His face became mischievous. "I've always admired that quality in him and I'm pretty sure it attracted Sara also. With this marriage, he'll have to take over a leadership role with our people, and he's scared. He loves Sara with all his heart, but he's not in love with the political position of being her hom, her husband."

"I don't understand. I thought you said you were the descendant of royal blood. Why does he have to take over just because he's marrying Sara?"

The smile gone, the face went serious. "He's not actually taking over, but because Sara is the only fem left of any royal line, when she bears a child, Raedon will be the father and guardian of that child: a child who will eventually be leader of the don."

"What about other unmarried femm? Surely there are some, even if younger? Won't you marry one of them when she grows up? Wouldn't your child inherit the position?"

"I'm not going to marry anyone and I don't want the job." From his flat tone, I assumed his mind was made up. "No, their child will become the next leader. I will be left alone, like I want."

I sat quietly, thinking about being alone. Then, I asked. "How old are you?"

His eyebrows went up. "What difference does it make?"

"None. I was just curious."

"I've just turned forty-three."

I studied his face thinking he looked much younger. "How long do don live, then?"

"Our normal life span is around two hundred years."

"Oh." *Two hundred years is a long time to be alone*, I thought. Reaching out, I lightly touched his clasped hands and changed the subject. "Please tell me what the problem is and how I came to be part of it."

Joedon rose and started walking and gesturing again as he explained. "With the Council taking over the wedding plans, as I knew they would, Raedon panicked over what he feared the rest of his life would be like. A couple of days ago, he was ready to explode with frustration. So, we set off for Pith. Then, he was arrested playing street football of all things. I spent a full day trying to find him in the prison. When I finally located him, he was in a coma. If I don't get him out soon, he'll die there."

Turning in my chair, I watched as he recounted his time as a drudge and what he learned from the main guard. "I thought I was going along fabulously, certain I'd be able to get Raedon out last night, until that guard locked me in."

He described, with appropriate gestures, his night up to the time he tripped on something and stumbled through the opening wall to find me and my maid.

"Who promptly screamed and fainted," I added with a slight grin.

"Just as well. I couldn't have gotten you both out. She was better off asleep. Especially since all she wanted to do was scream." We exchanged rueful glances at the memory.

I leaned forward and mimicked his earlier pose, elbows on knees, hands clasped before me. My head tilted to one side as I looked up at him. "So, now you're going to trade me for Raedon."

"That's my plan. I've already blown any secrecy. Garard and anyone he's consulting will come to the conclusion that I am don. I sent a message to your father to meet me at the plateau tomorrow at noon and to bring Raedon for an exchange. They'll assume he's don, too. They know he's important to me. They'll take care of him and bring him safely to the exchange."

"And me?"

He stopped in front of my chair, a serious expression on his face. "I am sorry for it, My Soer. I've no other option. I must rescue Raedon. I'm guaranteed to get him back if I trade you for him. His health and return, in reality, mean the continued existence of my people. Your unhappiness, although I regret it, cannot be considered."

I stared into his face a moment, then turned toward the window, breaking eye contact. "I see." I struggled to keep my voice even, to not let my dismay show. "At least I've had this glorious day. And I have until noon tomorrow. I'll ask Lillyon to fly me over Pith so I can see it from the air."

Joedon returned to his chair. We sat silently for several minutes watching the stars, each deep in our own thoughts.

~ Joedon

I glanced at the girl, feeling surprised at how comfortable I felt having her in my home. She was neither stiff nor shy, but cordial in the way of femm. I'd expected her to be haughty or proud but she had an enthusiasm for life, refreshing after the overwhelming monotony of the last several years. *It's not right that she marry Lord Roark.*

I reached out to touch her shoulder, causing her to start. Her brows raised in inquiry. "I've told you our story. It's time you told me yours. Why is everyone bent on you marrying Lord Roark? There must be hundreds of lovely royal ladies on Gareeth who would be happy to marry him. Why you?"

Jaym sighed and dropped her eyes to her hands in her lap. I thought she wouldn't answer. Then, she began speaking calmly but with a sad overtone that tugged at my heart.

Maybe I should stop her right now. It's already going to be hard to take her back. I thought it. I didn't follow through.

"It's a complicated story," she said. "Although he appears gruff to outsiders, my father is a tender-hearted man. He can't stand to have anyone injured or suffering, no matter what the cause."

"I can believe that."

She was diverted for a moment. "How?"

60

I shrugged. "Remember, I've been in your prison. I saw how the prisoners were treated."

She smiled, wistfully. "I didn't know about the prison. It sounds like him. He suddenly decided to ban street football because some players got seriously hurt and their injuries will affect them for life. My step-mother Lady Jill said the sons of two of father's favorite guardsmen had tendons in their knees torn so badly during a street football game that they'll have to have operations so they can walk again.

"And, just a couple of weeks ago, another boy died during a street game. Father used to love street football, but when that happened to Leld's son, he felt everyone should stop playing before something else bad happened."

Something didn't jibe. "How does his tender-heartedness translate into you marrying Lord Roark? It seems to me he'd be dead set against such a marriage."

Her eyes glinted in anger. "Oh, he is but he's also dead set against Lord Roark attacking Pith and injuring or killing our citizens. He's convinced himself this royal marriage Roark is demanding won't be too bad for me, but having a war with Roark will be disastrous for Pith."

"I've heard nothing of an impending war!"

"Lord Roark made the threat; my father's keeping it quiet. As far as the populace knows, this is a good match and I'm excited by it." The resentment intensified. "Lady Jill is furious with me for not being willing to become Lady Roark. She's even more irritated with Lord Roark for insisting on marrying the eldest daughter. She wants him to marry her daughter. As far as I'm concerned, Kelt can have him. She's a spoiled rotten child. She wouldn't care if he loved her as long as she could be Lady Kelt and have whatever that would bring." Jaym's sneer distorted her face and I didn't like it.

"How old is she?" I asked, thinking again I shouldn't be listening to this. *She's had plenty of unhappiness. And I just want to use her.*

"Eighteen, old enough to be married. I believe her personality would suit him. She'd agree with everything he said, probably join in his plans to conquer the planet. She's as avaricious as he is."

Thinking to distract her, I followed the lead about Roark. "Do you think that's what he wants, to conquer the planet?"

Fortunately, her face relaxed a bit. "I'm sure of it and so is Garard. He's starting with Pith because we're closest. And my father has no son to inherit. All he has is daughters." She shuddered. "That's why Roark demands the eldest—me—so the line will pass to him through an infant son."

"Your human laws are strict on inheritance, aren't they?"

Again, she glinted with anger. "Yes, and they're stupid." She stood and paced, as I had earlier. "Women cannot inherit, leaving Pith open for Roark's scheme. When I marry the man, Father can put off worrying about his city and his people."

I reached out to stop her and look keenly at her face. "Maybe you're being a bit harsh on your father. He's caught in a bad situation. He doesn't see any other way out."

She stiffened, pulled away, and walked to the window. Then, her shoulders slumped. "You're probably right, but I'm the one being sacrificed and I can't help being bitter."

"I can understand that." Hearing the sympathy in my tone, I grimaced. She fell silent, gazing at the stars. I wondered what she was thinking. Her emotions were easy to read but they didn't really tell me much. Suddenly, I wondered when I'd stopped thinking of her as Soer Jaym. The title put distance between us. *I should stick with it.*

Remembering a suggestion I'd made earlier in the day, I smiled. "Enough gloom for one evening. I promised to teach you about astronomy. Here..." I held out my hand. "Come with me." With a quizzical smile, she took it.

Passing through the doorway at the end of my bedroom, I led her into my lab: a room full of telescopes, microscopes, and other instruments. She said she'd never seen such things before. For the next two hours, I explained as much as I could about astronomy to the sponge that was Jaym's mind. She absorbed information with excitement and asked intelligent questions. I enjoyed the lesson immensely, especially since she obviously had too.

At her third yawn, I knew I couldn't prolong the evening any more. The most enjoyable evening I'd spent in a long time still had to come to an end. We passed through the bedroom on the way back to the guest room. Jaym pulled me to a sudden stop and gazed wide-eyed at me. I waited, puzzled. *What can she possibly be thinking to put that gleam in her eye?*

Finally, she said: "This is going to sound strange. I've just thought of something you can do for me that will change everything." She paused a long time, her eyes locked on mine.

I broke the spell. "Well … What is it? If I have it in my power, I'll do it."

"Will you?" She quirked an eyebrow.

Now, she really had me conjecturing, but I could think of nothing I had that she might need. "Just name it," I said confidently.

She blushed a rosy red. "There's something about our inheritance laws that gives me a loophole, if you're willing. Lord Roark will not marry me if I'm no longer a virgin."

I couldn't figure her expression and her emotions bouncing from embarrassed to breathless gave no clue to her meaning. "What are you saying?"

"This is very difficult to say and you're not making it easier." She sounded as testy as she'd been back at the palace talking to Garard. Drawing in a deep breath as if gathering her courage, she blurted "If I'm not a virgin when you trade me for Raedon tomorrow, I can get out of the marriage. My father will disown me and Soer Kelt can marry Lord Roark as my father's oldest daughter."

I said nothing; confusion, and a sudden wonder, tied my tongue into knots.

With exasperation, she snapped. "You can insure I'm not a virgin."

My heart began pounding and I started to sweat. *She's asking me to lay with her.* I'd been incredibly attracted to her from the moment I fell through that door, a feeling I'd suppressed all day as a good don kidnapper should.

I can't take advantage of a woman so thoroughly in my power.

My bad side said, "It never occurred to you she might be a virgin."

I thought human women ended their virginity early in life, as don do. She's telling me she'd never been with a man.

"She's in her twenties for foal's sake. Do it!"

She's asking me to be her first! I can't. I shouldn't.

I couldn't think clearly. I asked, stupidly, "Why are you still a virgin?"

She blushed crimson and turned away, but sarcasm flowed through her words. "Royal *women* must be virgins when they wed. It's one of those restrictions the inheritance laws put on us." Her voice rose, becoming shrill. "Besides, when would I ever have been allowed to be alone with a man when I've been confined and watched over my entire life?" By the time she reached the end of her speech, she was furious, at me, at her life, at everything. For the first time all day, she burst into tears.

I was lost. Taking her into my arms, I intended to comfort her; the comfort quickly became something more. I knew instantly she'd never been kissed. Taking it slow, I taught her how to kiss. *She might be inexperienced, but she learns quickly.* Gradually, gently, I taught her to be loved and to love in return.

In the back of my mind, I thought I might regret this evening but it didn't stop me. *I've done many things I should be sorry for. Not this exquisite pleasure.*

Sometime later, I fell asleep with her wrapped in my arms.

~ Lillith

In our room, I nestled against Lillyon, his large wing covering me, absolutely ecstatic. I had Joedon and Jaym where I wanted them and I hadn't even had to meddle much to get them there. *Good will come of this day.*

Chapter 8

~ Lillith

The morning dawned cheerily with blazing sunshine in a dazzling blue sky devoid of clouds. Standing on the cavern ledge, gazing at the valley below, I took the brightness as a sign of beautiful things to come. As I felt the girl stirring, I extended a tendril to monitor her; Joedon was already in his lab wrestling with his feelings from the night before. I let him stew in his uncertainty.

~ Jaym

I woke and stretched, feeling contented like never before. Then, my emotions plummeted when I remembered that this day I would have to go back to the palace. Determined to be cheerful and enjoy my last morning of freedom, I jumped out of bed and explored Joedon's bedroom for the shower.

It was a big bedroom, bigger than any I'd seen at the palace, but the window was the most eye-catching feature. Looking around, I realized the rest of the furnishings, bed, chairs, a couch, were arranged to draw the eye to the window. On either side of the immense piece of glass stood tall bookshelves in a grayish hue, making a perfect frame, with no curtains to shut out the view. For several minutes, I enjoyed the light that revealed an extraordinary world.

Straight down, the mountain fell in ledges, rocky and sheer, to a narrow valley far below. Off to the right—I had no idea what direction it might be—I saw another range of craggy mountains, covered in dark green conifers, too far away to determine what kind. To the left, I could see what had to be the Sapphire Sea, previously seen only on maps as I'd been forced to study the social/political situations of the city-states around it with my step-mother. It was far, but I could see it clearly, and now understood its name. The color was blinding. Remembering that the sea lay directly north of Pith, I decided the mountain range must be west and south, the Melton Mountains.

Pulling away from the breath-taking view, I found the bathroom through a door at one end of the room; a soft light blue-green robe hung on a hook inside. Once again, I reveled in the warm shower, the spray soft and gentle with the same fragrance as the guest room. After my shower, I wrapped myself in the robe and sat down at the window. "I could enjoy this view for the rest of my life."

~ Lillith

I yanked my perception away from the girl when Tallyon called a warning: the acting Head-Speaker, Taldon, and two others were almost to Eyrie. Focusing on the reeth winging toward me, I realized the second was Coccyon, so distinctively mustard colored. His fair mane, whipping in the wind of their flight, hid his mind-mate, but it must be Samdon. *Drat!* I spied a second rider: Pildon, the biggest trouble maker in Center. *There goes my peaceful day!*

I fired off notice to Lillyon and Joedon; Lillyon joined me on the ledge and Joedon scrambled into presentable clothing to wait impatiently at his door. Stifling my anxiety, I greeted the visitors as cordially as I could manage, then sent the two reeth with Lillyon for refreshments and escorted the three don to Joedon's door. As usual, Pildon ignored me as if I weren't there. I returned the favor.

As soon as the door closed behind them, I heard Pildon's voice raise in complaint. *Is that don never happy?* Choosing not to delve into the turmoil, I turned my attention back to Jaym only to realize the girl had heard the arguing and was listening at the bedroom door.

~ Jaym

"We haven't done anything different than you did in your younger years." Pressing my ear to the door, I easily recognized Joedon, sounding as if he barely controlled his temper.

"Yes, you have. You got caught. We never did," a voice shouted back, shrill and high pitched.

"Because of what you did, the consequences will be disastrous," another voice, much lower, but also angry.

"Why is that?" Joedon again. "What do you think the humans can do to us?"

The lower voice said, "They'll capture us and our reeth; make us do their bidding."

"How do you think they'll do that?" Joedon's words dripped with scorn. "Think, Samdon, even in ancient history, humans never found our homes. Even with planes and helicopters, they have no way to get to us, unless we let them."

"Then we'll be locked in our homes unable to leave," shouted the shrill one.

Joedon laughed mockingly. "Don't be stupid, Pildon. The humans will never find Center on their own. You never leave anyway. I'm surprised to see you here, outside the safety of your house."

"Now, Joedon, Pildon, let's get our tempers under control and decide what to do about fixing this mess."

At least there's one calm don out there. I liked the sound of the mellow, slow words.

The shrill voice I'd heard shouting earlier was calmer but drenched in venom. "We have to leave the humans with no memory of the last day. Give them the girl, get Raedon, wipe their memories."

"I don't want my memory wiped," I wailed softly. "I want to remember forever!"

"Do you have the ability to do that, Pildon?" Joedon, sounding sarcastic.

"You know I don't. But you do."

"I won't."

My heart flew into my throat. *He can do such a thing?* It then plopped back down again. *But he won't.* I didn't know what to think. I felt a reassurance that Joedon would never wipe a memory of the innocent. *Lillith's voice.* I relaxed, not considering why I felt so suddenly confident.

The one called Pildon was shouting again. "You fool. You endanger us all."

"Stop!" ordered the calmer voice. "Samdon, Pildon, sit down over there. Joedon, come sit here with me. Now, Joedon, explain."

Joedon paused and I wondered what he would say. I still had no idea why he'd rescued me. *Maybe he'll say why.* I hunkered down and listened harder.

He spoke hesitantly. "Taldon, I believe we have the power to overcome any attack humans might try, especially with reeth aid. But that's not the point." He sounded steadier. "I think it's time we try again to co-exist with humans."

"This is preposterous." *Antagonism from Pildon.* "You'll doom us all!"

"He sounds like an arrogant ass," I muttered. *I know the type.*

"He is," I clearly heard. *Lillith, for sure.* Jerking my head away from the door, I realized she was listening in on me.

"Don't mind me," she said. "Go on and eavesdrop. I am."

"We can start anew with humans." Joedon's words now rang with conviction. "This time we'll set rules. Our ancestors didn't know to set limits when they dealt with the early humans. Raedon and I have learned much in our forays into their cities. Most go about life with no desire to cause problems for anyone, just like we do. Only a few are constantly starting trouble."

I wondered if Joedon was up pacing, hands clasped behind his back. Lillith said, "He is."

I heard his passion deepen as he developed his theme. "We won't let them know our secrets. We'll reveal our presence but not share our powers. We'll make them deal with us with respect and a certain amount of fear."

He paused and I pictured him gathering arguments. "I did a lot of extraordinary things yesterday; I'm sure I left behind a feeling of awe, and yes, alarm in those who saw me. They have no way of knowing we can't all do such things or that others have different talents. And when we meet today to exchange Raedon for Soer Jaym, I'll make sure they leave with a sense of caution in contacting us further—"

"I won't have it!" Pildon's strident voice interrupted. "Where's the girl. I'll throw her off the cliff! That'll take care of it."

Joedon roared. "Get him out of here before *I* throw *him* over the cliff."

"Settle down, both of you." The don named Taldon tried to insert calm and reason. "We're not destroying anyone today!"

"He's talking about destroying our way of life!" Pildon again.

Joedon fired back, "I am the Supreme Don and I'll do what I think is right. You can't stop me."

Pildon snarled, "I thought you didn't want to be Supreme Don anymore, were going to give it up for Raedon's brat."

"I've changed my mind!" A sudden swell of triumph swept over me—from Lillith. At my confusion, she promised, "I'll explain later."

The sounds of the argument in the living room faded and I fled from the door. A few minutes later, the bedroom door opened. Joedon strode in, splendid in a black body suit with silver trim. He wore shining leather boots, black leather gloves, and belted around his waist was a leather sword belt crusted with jewels and silver, as was the hilt of the sword in its scabbard. A small jeweled crown twinkled in his short white hair. But most striking was the look of thunder on his face. I gasped and fell back.

He froze at my reaction, then took several deep breaths. The red in his face faded, his hunched shoulders relaxed, and he unclenched his fists. Finally, he smiled and pulled the crown from his head. His voice barely quivered as he said, "Sometimes, it helps to put on the trappings. I haven't worn this outfit for years. But, it came in handy just now. And it will come in handy again later."

Rising from my semi-defensive cower, I asked, "What is it?" pleased that my voice didn't quaver.

"The informal dress of the crowned leader of the don. It's usually only worn when don are married or buried. I think it's ridiculous, but it inspires awe in everyone who sees it, at least among don. I hope it'll have a similar effect on your father and his men."

I heartily wished he would take me in his arms and kiss me. He didn't. In fact, he kept his distance.

He turned away, shoulders tight. "You don't have to wear the wedding costume today. Nanadon brought a number of gowns for you to choose from. The femm in Lillith's household love beautiful clothes and she's a good seamstress. If one you like doesn't quite fit, she'll alter it for you." He drew in another deep breath and turned back, his face firmly under control. "Are you hungry?"

"Yes, I am. Let me slip into my trousers and shirt and I'll be right with you."

"I'll bring the gowns in for you to try. We'll leave soon after breakfast so you need to choose one before we eat. I'll be in the kitchen."

He evidently didn't care about the night that had changed my life completely. Clearly, it touched him little. "Well! I can't complain," I muttered as I dashed tears away. "I got what I wanted. I can't be forced into marriage with Lord Roark."

I glanced around the beautiful room and gazed out the window through tear-filled eyes. "I didn't know it would hurt like this."

~ Lillith

In my own bedroom, I suffered the girl's misery but refrained from sending comfort. Whatever happened next had to come from Joedon and although I knew I would meddle and nudge, the final decision had to be his or it would never serve.

Minutes later, I silently applauded Jaym's resolution. She'd slipped a gown over her head, brushed out her long, wavy hair, nodded briskly at the lady in the mirror, pasted a smile on her face, and swept her way to the door. The day had begun.

~ Jaym

An hour later, Joedon escorted me to the cavern entrance where Lillith and Lillyon waited. I felt magnificent in the gown I'd selected. Soft material, brilliant teal, flowed from my shoulders with tiny tucks under the bodice, styled totally differently from anything I'd had ever seen before. The skirt was tucked up into flaring pantaloons, cuffed at the ankles, with a panel dropping from the bodice to hide the division. It fit well, as if fashioned for my body. "Designed for riding," Lillith said.

"For once, I feel lucky I'm so tall," I told her. "Most human women would be dwarfed by this dress, but I feel regal." *And, I intend to be regal all day, no matter how it hurts. I am, after all, Soer Jaym of Pith and proud of it!*

Both reeth bowed to us as we got close.

"Oh, get up," Joedon snapped. "You don't have to make fun of me like this."

"We aren't making fun." Lillith's soft words floated in my head. "You both look very stately this morning. We were paying homage to the sight."

Joedon harrumphed, then said brusquely to me, "Lillyon is happy to grant your wish to fly over Pith and any other location you would like before we go to Flagstone Plateau. We have a few hours so simply tell him where you want to go."

"Thank you both, Lillith, Lillyon." I dipped in a small curtsy. "The only things I know about Garador … excuse me, Gareeth … are what I studied in geography. I'd prefer you take me to see what you think best, and tell me about the places as we see them. I'm in your hands." I grinned. "Or, maybe I should say wings." They flipped up their upper lips and bobbed their heads. *Laughter,* I decided. Joedon's mouth even quirked up slightly.

He stepped forward to help me mount. My arm thrilled at his touch but he backed away immediately.

As I settled comfortably on Lillyon's broad back, I watched Joedon vault onto Lillith. *They are definitely a sight to see.* She, so snowy white; he in black and silver.

"You're a beautiful sight as well," Lillith responded. "You're splendid in that dress and cloak. Especially on my handsome husband." I laughed and felt fantastic. After breakfast, Joedon had given me a long, fluffy, white cloak to wear over the dress.

He'd also given me a silver bracelet, a small replica of a white reeth with a rider dressed in black dangling from it. He said it was to remember them by. *As if I would ever forget.* He'd placed it on my arm with the reeth resting on the inside of my wrist. Now, it swayed and shivers shot up my arm as the small figure brushed me softly.

Lillith distracted me. "First the Sapphire Sea." Both reeth dropped off the ledge and flew directly north. *Wow! Wouldn't want to try that without Lillyon.*

And yet, I thrilled at the rush of fear.

We reached the Sapphire Sea within minutes. The blue-green water sparkled like a huge sapphire, ringed in white sand resembling a silver brooch. To the north, I saw a broad, meandering silver river, seemingly a chain holding the giant's gem. *No wonder everyone describes its beauty. I'm lucky to view it from above.* Glancing down, I could see to the depths just off the shore line, darker shadows shifting in the huge jewel.

As we left the Sea, I asked if we could visit Delt and the growers of the Lareina fruit. Obligingly, the reeth turned east and I became captivated by the passing landscape with its varying shades of green in the growing season. The land was patched with squares and circles, rolling here, flat there, sometimes sections outlined by darker tree lines. Lillith kept me informed of what area we were crossing as well as what was growing beneath us. In Delt, dark rounded Lareina trees marched up the slopes of low hills, lighter rice paddies stretched along the banks of an ocean. "Is that the Blade Ocean?" I thought, trying to aim the question at Lillyon.

"Yes, it is." His rumbling deep voice was pleasant.

"I'm so happy to have seen an ocean. It is so intensely blue!" My thoughts felt as if they were becoming more focused as I concentrated on thinking my questions at the reeth. Joedon was as morose as a gloomy day and I ignored him as he did me.

When I asked to see Lord Roark's capital city, they flew over Kavv. It squatted dismally in its valley, dingy gray stone with no trees or lawns to break up the bleak urban area. I couldn't help but shudder at how close I'd come from being imprisoned there.

To cheer me up, Lillyon said he was headed for my home, Pith. It glowed in the sunshine, its pink and white limestone buildings clean and bright. Trees, bushes, and draping flowers broke up the expanse of buildings and large areas of park grass dotted the city. People in the streets moved briskly about their business and the city radiated joy, sensed even from above. The difference between the two capitals was remarkable.

I heard Joedon asking something but the reeth had separated enough for me to miss the words. Lillith repeated them for me. "Why did you never mention how different the cities appear from the air?" Surprising me, the repeated question formed in my mind in Joedon's voice. *How strange it is to hear Joedon with my mind instead of my ears!*

"We reeth can imitate whatever we hear," Lillith explained. "We decide what we want to sound like when we communicate with don—or humans for that matter—but we can change it anytime we want. Those with a wider range become our recorders, keepers of our history."

Lillith continued talking, changing her vocal tones every other sentence. I laughed as the voices ranged from high squeaky girl to deep male base. I knew she was doing it to help keep my mind off the thought of returning to the palace and losing my freedom again. It was working.

"We need to start for the plateau." Lillyon broke into Lillith's monologue and both veered north. Within a few minutes we were approaching the Plateau. From the west came a large group of reeth, heading straight for us.

"Trouble?" Joedon asked, his concern evident.

"No. They're in full support. They want to provide a show of strength before the humans," Lillith said.

Gradually, I recognized a few reeth I'd met the night before. Even the young ones, minus the precious colt, appeared very strong with their wings at full span. But I counted many more reeth than those of Lillith's household. A single fem rode one of the leaders.

Once more, Lillith explained. "They're members of my family and Lillyon's. I also see Memmyon, Raedon's mind-mate, with his family. The fem is Saradon, riding her mate Sissith. They've come to back Joedon's move to retrieve Raedon and confront your father." My heart swelled in pride at being a part of this wondrous flight.

I listened as Lillith directed the incoming reeth to fan out behind her and Lillyon. Over a hundred formed rank after wider rank, each individual a wing span apart from their neighbor. I craned around to see them and felt Lillyon shifting under my change of balance. "I won't let you fall," he said.

Reeth colors shone in the sunshine and wings sparkled with flecks of light. An enthralling sight that sent my spirit soaring.

"They form their ranks by family affiliation with the older, larger reeth at the fore," Lillith said. "The final rank includes the youngsters, excited to be part of this day although they can't possibly understand its significance. The vee maneuver is something new and fun for them and it tests their flying skills."

Lillyon added, his deep voice lending dignity to the wondrous sight. "They fly because it's a beautiful day."

Chapter 9

~ Lillith

While appreciating Jaym's sense of awe at the sight of the reeth, I chose not to share Joedon's humble feelings of thankfulness for their support. He'd never considered reeth might back him in the insanity he'd devised so quickly. *Little does he know we've been pushing for just such a confrontation.*

As the cloud of reeth approached the cars, I asked the ends of the vee to circle. When the herd landed, they completely surrounded the human group who stood frozen and gaping. I came to rest directly in front of the three men in the lead and studied them as Joedon sat unmoving on my back.

In the center stood Lord Metz, a benevolent ruler I'd heard, beloved by his people due to his hands-off policy. Jaym's father and his city-state prospered through the individual innovation of citizens. He didn't resemble Jaym, being shorter and rounder, with the curly blond hair and beak nose that had marked the rulers of Pith for generations.

The man to his right had to be Garard. I'd heard much of him. He offered solid support, sage advice, and unswerving loyalty to the royal house of Pith, which I knew included Soer Jaym. On Metz' left, I encountered the seething mass of ambition and greed that was Lord Roark of Kavv, who ruled with a heavy hand. His city-state continually floundered even though it was similar in size and resources to Pith. Thus, he cast covetous eyes on his neighbor.

The three men couldn't be more dissimilar, I thought. *Roark, dark and sinister; Metz, sunny and easy-going; Garard solemnly in staunch support.*

When Joedon swung down to stride forward, I caught a whiff from a fourth man, standing toward the rear, his aura radiating excitement and deep personal interest. I raised my head to look past those in front and Joedon stopped in his tracks. *Who is this?* A history professor, derided by his colleagues because of a lifelong belief and search for reeth and don. I sought him out, following the exaltation he radiated. Finally, I saw him, behind the bank of guards: a tall, middle aged man, dressed in tweed jacket and wrinkled dark trousers. *I can use this man.*

As I turned my attention back to the leaders, I urged Joedon to continue forward. Then, I felt a wave of fear and hatred. Jerking my head to the side, I spotted two women helping a third to her feet. The malevolent mind had been blank but as soon as the over-dressed woman spied Soer Jaym, she bristled with loathing. *Has to be Lady Jill, Soer Jaym's stepmother.*

A modestly dressed woman tried to soothe the hateful one but the virago shoved her aside and advanced on Lord Metz, shrieking. Metz sent her away. Garard took her arm and forced her back to the other two who grasped her arms tightly.

Ignoring the incident, Metz stepped forward. Joedon strode to meet him, stopping within an arm's span. I folded my wings back to my body and sent word to the others to do the same. Relief flowed through all the men facing Joedon. *Yes, worry. Recognize we are a strong force!*

"So you are Joedon, the infamous don who kidnapped my daughter?" Metz started belligerently. I decided his tone reflected his worry, overly harsh to bolster his sagging courage.

"Yes, I kidnapped Soer Jaym." Joedon kept his voice reasonable and calm. "I am here to return her safely today in exchange for my friend. I see you've brought him."

Metz' eyebrows quirked up in surprise. "He expected a more violent answer," I told Joedon.

The man relaxed suddenly and indicated the stretcher on wheels with two large, white clad attendants standing by. "We have him here. Whatever his condition is, it's not within our experience to tell."

Again, Joedon maintained his conciliatory manner. "My mind-mate, Lillith, informs me that Raedon will recover once we get him home. I believe his falling into your guards' hands and being put in prison was a misunderstanding on his part and he induced this coma himself to protect his identity."

Metz began to smile, nodding in agreement at Joedon's words; his overly stiff posture softened considerably. I picked up Jaym's start of surprise. "He's afraid!" the girl whispered in amazement.

Joedon pointed at the stretcher. "If you will have your people bring the carry-along, I'll strap Raedon onto his mind-mate, Memmyon. He'll be accompanied by his fiancé, Saradon, and her mind-mate Sissith."

Memm stepped forward. Husky, with bulging muscles, he unconsciously intimidated the humans as he approached; several backed away. Sissith stepped up next to him and Sara swung lightly down. As tall as Joedon, she was dressed in Joe family black and silver. Her body suit gave her fluid mobility and I felt Jaym's sharp stab of envy. I had to contain my glee. *Serious things are happening. I shouldn't be laughing.* I stiffened my body.

Sara's voice, low and velvety, carried clearly. "I thank you, Lord Metz, for taking care of Raedon. He's very dear to me and to these reeth." Human male awareness locked on the fem as she stood between the reeth, one hand resting on her reeth-mate, the other stroking the larger reeth's neck. "We're relieved to find he is well and will be able to be released from his coma soon."

Oh, well played. The right touch of gracious authority.

Metz appeared speechless. He shook his head and finally said, "You are welcome, My Lady." I thought he was going to bow, but he stopped himself.

"If I had but known of his presence earlier, maybe all of these unpleasant circumstances could've been avoided." The man was definitely conciliatory.

"It is ending well that matters." Sara's smile and tilted head were just a bit condescending as she waited expectantly for Metz to motion the stretcher-bearers forward.

He turned to do so when Roark barked, "Wait just a bloody minute. Are you bamboozled, Lord Metz? This creature kidnapped Soer Jaym and you're about to hand over his compatriot without securing her release. If you let them strap this fellow onto that winged beast, there's nothing stopping them from flying off with him. And her!"

Metz swung to look at Roark. I, and the hundred with me, did too. Wings flared and eyes glowed red. Roark paled, but didn't step back as the others did. *No one said he wasn't brave*, I thought as I sent a soothing wave through our supporters.

Joedon snapped, "Who are you?"

Roark drew in a deep breath, straightened his shoulders, and stepped forward. "I am Lord Roark, affianced of Soer Jaym. I demand she be returned to her father before you take control over this being."

"You demand, do you?" A deep scowl crossed Joedon's face. "How do you intend to enforce your demand?" Before Roark could reply, Joedon continued. "Soer Jaym informed me she does not wish to marry you. Choose someone else as your wife." He turned his back on the man to face Metz once more.

Metz blanched, Roark flushed. Lady Jill moaned and slumped, causing everyone to stare at her. Garard caught her and helped her stand. As Jill regained her feet and clung to her companions, Jaym indicated to Lillyon that she wished to dismount. He dropped on one knee and she swung off in a decent imitation of Sara. I caught her mutter, "Thanks be for divided skirts." And again almost laughed.

Jaym walked rapidly forward, one hand outstretched. "Father, do not fear. I have a solution. As you can see, I am not a prisoner of either reeth or don. I'm free to do as I please. They've treated me more graciously than I've ever been treated in your home." She faced Roark, shoulders back, head held high, and spoke boldly. "Lord Roark. You cannot marry me. I am no longer a virgin." *Bravo, Jaym.*

Everyone stood still for a second, then Jill shrieked and collapsed onto the ground before anyone could catch her. A quick probe assured me the woman was fine and I didn't interfere as the man, Garard, revived her. For moments no human moved, shock written on their faces and I caught Jaym stifling a grin at the outrage on Roark's.

The girl stood quietly, totally composed until Jill stood again. Then, she spoke. "Under our laws, I must be disowned. I assure you my actions were of my own choosing. I was not forced or coerced in any way. That leaves my sister, Soer Kelt, as my father's eldest." Her tone dropped as if speaking solely to Roark. "She has loved you in silence, Lord Roark, and will make you a far more acceptable wife than I would have."

"What are you saying, girl!" Metz grabbed Jaym's arm and swung her toward him, shouting into her face.

I sent Joedon a sharp command, "Leave him be!" He clenched his hands but remained still, his face like granite.

Jaym faced her angry father calmly, placing both hands on his upper arms. "If you'll contain your rage a moment and think about this, you'll see it's a much better arrangement than my marriage to Lord Roark would have been. If you disown me, as you must, then Kelt is your eldest daughter. Lord Roark will be marrying your first-born and any offspring will still fulfill his desires. Also, he'll be much happier with Kelt than with a troublemaker like me. My step-mother and Kelt herself will be ecstatic. It's the perfect solution."

"For everyone but you," he said quietly, his eyes telling her he understood her actions. "You'll be banished forever to the ladies' quarters and never have a family of your own." Despite the anguish Jaym felt at his bewilderment, she held firm in her resolve. I applauded silently.

"I know that, Father. It truly is better this way. I'll be fine with my life in those circumstances."

Roark found his voice. "This is preposterous. You can't be switching around brides like this. If this is a hoax to get me to marry the wrong girl, I assure you, it won't work. You won't thwart me this way, Metz. My threat still stands." He strode angrily forward with the obvious intention of snatching Soer Jaym to his side. Memm stepped into his path, blocking him with a broad shoulder. Roark stumbled backward, bouncing off the heavy body.

I thanked Memm for his quick action as Jaym schooled her face into serenity, then responded to Roark's accusation. "This is no hoax. Do you think my father could conjure a host of reeth and don to do his bidding? Everything that has occurred in the last two days has taken place by chance with we players," she waved her arm at Joedon and the rest of us, "including don and reeth, being carried along by happenstance. But the outcome is simple. Kelt will truly be my father's eldest daughter and worthy of the position as your wife. She will serve you well. Please, give yourself a chance to know her before your reject this solution."

Roark started forward once more, trying to sidestep Memm. "Damn, you. Get out of my way!" His raised fist bounced off Memm's bony jaw, causing the man to clutch it in pain. I aimed mental pressure at Roark so hard that he shook his head as if to reject a headache. He stopped moving, stood absolutely still a few seconds, then stepped back and spoke to Metz. "Lord Metz, Lady Jill, let's return to the palace with this woman who is no longer your daughter and I'll meet Soer Kelt. Perhaps, this is the best solution."

I breathed a sigh of relief. Jill moved toward Roark, laying her hand on his arm and Metz motioned the stretcher-bearers to bring Raedon to the waiting Memm. Again, I came close to laughter as the two approached the large bay cautiously with their burden. Their minds said he was awfully big and fearsome to look on. I thought it best not to share their fear with the young bay—he might do more to provoke them.

Joedon and Sara met them at Memm's side. She leapt gracefully onto the reeth's back positioning herself to gather Raedon in and hold him. Joedon hoisted the limp body off the stretcher and handed him up, then helped her with the straps. Sara remained on Memm; Joedon returned to me.

During the maneuver, I watched the faces of the humans. They observed my slender don-mate pick up the unconscious Raedon by himself and hoist him upward, yet it had taken two muscled stretcher-bearers to carry the unconscious don. *Good lesson for them, and he does it totally unconsciously.* My heart swelled with pride.

Jaym walked over to lay a hand on my neck, struggling to contain her tears. "Thank you and Lillyon for all you have done for me. I enjoyed getting to know you."

"And we are glad to have met you," I answered so that all the humans would hear. I ducked my head and Jaym stroked softly down my forehead. Then, the girl reached out to touch Lillyon. Finally, she turned to Joedon. His pale face resembled carved ivory and he held his hands clenched at his side. He did not smile and I felt Jaym's heart crumple.

But, she squared her shoulders and raised her head. "Thank you, for everything."

He nodded stiffly.

As Jaym moved away, walking toward her father, I spoke into her mind. "Take care of yourself. Do not despair. It is not over."

With powerful wing strokes that churned the dust around the silent humans, we reeth rose as one and flew west toward the mountains. Jaym's gaze warmed my behind for a long time.

Once I was sure we were out of sight, I asked Joedon to change to Lillyon's back. "I'm going to follow them to insure Soer Jaym's safety. You go on to Citadel and get started awakening Raedon. I'll join you there." He nodded, lifted himself up onto his fingers and toes, then flipped sideways to land easily on Lillyon's broad back.

I banked to one side, performing a one-hundred-eighty-degree turn, and extended first my perception, then my invisibility illusion. Back at the Plateau, Jaym had started toward Jill who shrank from her, pulling her female friends with her. "Don't touch me, you harlot," the woman shrieked.

Sensing Jaym's self-enforced calm slipping, I hurled another encouragement. "It's not over yet. Keep a good heart!" Then, I flew as fast as I could, arriving silently above the group of humans just as Jaym stepped into a car. The girl began to sob quietly. Her heart had carried her through the confrontation, but now tears streamed down her face although she held her head high so those outside wouldn't realize her misery. I rejoiced in Jaym's sorrow; the girl was crying because she'd had to leave Joedon and us. Nowhere in the girl's mind could I find fear for her own future or shame for her actions.

Chapter 10

~ Joedon

The newlyweds had departed on their honeymoon; Lillith and Lillyon had gone to a family get-together; I sat down to a solitary meal, relieved and exhausted. I always felt like a loose ball rattling around the six-hundred year old Joe mansion in Center. Tonight, it felt even emptier than usual. I'd often talked about razing the numerous guest bedrooms to make Lillith's part of the home larger but she always stopped me saying she enjoyed having only enough room for herself and Lillyon. When they were in residence, she sent the rest of her family to the Lill ancestral home, claiming it was her way to enjoy her husband without the rest of the herd.

Wandering down an echoing hall toward my bedroom suite, a bottle of Lareina in my hand, I thought of the humans and sniggered. If they ever did find Center, they would be shocked. Most of Center's homes had quarters for reeth built right onto them and all rooms and doorways were large enough for mind-mates to wander freely inside. I grinned to myself and swallowed more Lareina. In some ways, reeth resembled the human's horses; we don loved their aroma, but humans only tolerated it, and not ever inside their homes. I tried to picture either Lord Metz or Lord Roark sharing their Palaces with their horses and laughed hysterically.

I didn't know any royal ladies but I doubted they would allow horses inside, either, although Soer Jaym had seemed comfortable with the reeth at Eyrie. But, Soer Jaym, by her own telling, differed from other royals. Stopped in the middle of my bedroom, I swayed from the Lareina and forced my thoughts away from Soer Jaym.

"I'll never be completely alone," I mumbled to the vacant room. "Lillith is always here, within mind's reach." If she were ever killed, I would die too and the reverse was also true. My mind fuzzy, I focused on Raedon. He'd never understood why I refused some of the wilder ideas we'd contemplated in our crazy, younger years. "I would never cause Lillyon the anguish of living without her," I declared to the empty bottle in my hand. Not mind-mated to Lillyon, I loved the big guy anyway.

Thinking about them, how they were always there behind me, Lillith in my mind and Lillyon like a shadow with her, brought me to wonder why I couldn't contact her from the prison. Or later as we escaped Pith.

"Lillith?" I projected.

"Not now, Joedon. We can discuss it later if you insist."

"What do we have to discuss?"

"Later."

"She shut me off!" I shouted into the emptiness. My alarm grew as I tried over and over to reach her.

~ Lillith

Lillyon and I left the family party just after Joedon's contact. To avoid the crowds of relatives, I chose to walk through the river valley rather than fly home. The huge Lill family complex consisted of clearings in the cedar trees and scrub oak that blanketed the northeast corner of the river valley.

Confident all the resting spots that might hold stragglers from the party were empty, Lillyon began to tease. "I told you he'd figure it out. Just as soon as you let him stop jumping from one crisis to the next. Now what are you going to tell him?"

I arched my neck and reeth-grinned at him, my upper lip raised to show my teeth, my eyes sparkling. Stretching my neck, I nuzzled him along the jaw line. "I intend to convince Joedon, with your help, of course, that the melancholy of facing the wedding, so reminiscent of our own, caused us to want to be alone for a second honeymoon. We thought the time he and Raedon were in Pith a perfect time for us to seclude ourselves from everyone to enjoy one another as we did right after our marriage."

He stopped. "You little hussy, you. Why didn't we actually do that, then?" He whiffled back in my face, his nostrils vibrating. "I'd have enjoyed it immensely."

I trotted ahead, arching my neck more and swishing my tail. Without slowing, I glanced back to see him behind me. "You did enjoy it! Just picture that and you'll be fine in supporting my little white lie." I looked forward again and continued to trot slowly away, tempting him to follow. "We couldn't actually do such a thing. I had to be nearby to rescue them if all went horribly wrong."

Lillyon caught up and matched my gait. "So what are you going to do next, my love?" His plaintive tone made me laugh. We trotted side-by-side through the underbrush, moving comfortably in coordination, mind and body, occasionally detouring around a bigger tree.

I shook her head. "It depends on what Lord Metz and Lord Roark do."

"Don are going to panic as humans try to find us." Lillyon snorted at a small rodent scurrying across his path. He kicked out a hind foot as if to emphasize his displeasure at the furry creature. "That newscast we saw today will stir up the humans like a bunch of wasps."

"We'll have to make sure they don't succeed. I'd think the video would've scared most of them. And soon, we'll find out what Lord Metz intends to do with Jaym. Then, I'll make an effort to see her."

Suddenly, Lillyon cantered faster past me, then spun to block my path, a wicked gleam in his eye. "Since we're going to tell Joedon we had a second honeymoon, why don't we have one right now?" His head swung around and he dropped his voice seductively. "This is a beautiful grove of trees. The moon is shining. The breeze is aromatic with grass and pine." An ear twitched forward. "I can even hear water trickling." He bowed and waved a wing in a dramatic gesture. "Come away with me, my love, for a few stolen hours of bliss. Joedon can wait."

I pranced coquettishly toward him. "I thought you'd never ask."

Chapter 11

~ Lillith

Three weeks had flown by and I stood once more on the ledge staring at sheets of rain pounding the mountain that housed Eyrie. I glared at the weather as if doing so could alleviate my frustration. My head and shoulders drenched, my soggy mane hung heavy dripping on the floor. The cold shower didn't make me feel better. With Memm and Sissith still gone on honeymoon with their mind-mates, Joedon had retreated once more into his lab, his mind again locked tighter than a grain barrel.

The only thing I accomplished was to stir up trouble in the council. My emotions matched the miserable weather. *And that cauldron's about to boil over.*

I felt Joedon's hand on my neck before I sensed him; he'd approached so quietly that my roiling thoughts hid his presence. Then, his words brought me rays of brightness.

"She's okay, isn't she? Soer Jaym I mean?"

I stilled my jubilation before answering calmly. "Yes, she's fine. Lord Metz banished her and her maid to a small cottage on one of his palm tree plantations where she's happy gardening and making new friends." I paused to study his now open mind. "As far as I know, Lord Roark is satisfied with Kelt as his bride and shows no interest in what happened to Jaym."

"You've checked on her personally?"

"Yes, I did."

A haze of strain drained away from him. He wrapped both arms about my neck, ignoring the rain that pelted us, and laid his forehead on my withers. "I've been an ass, Lillith, and I'm sorry." He sighed and buried his face in my mane. "I've struggled these last weeks trying to untangle my feelings. I know you thought I'd shut you out, but I needed to figure out what I wanted."

Silently, I snaked my neck around his body to hold him close in the reeth way. After a moment, he choked out more words. "I was so scared. I felt totally lost without you. But I loved every second of my adventure." I waited for him to continue. "I don't want to live alone, quietly, for the next hundred-fifty years."

"Joedon, you were never meant to be a hermit."

"I know that. But what do I do now?"

I stopped myself from telling him exactly what I thought. *Don't break this fragile accord,* I thought. Instead, I said, "Let's go in and talk. I don't know what to do anymore than you. However, together, we should be able to do anything!"

In my bedroom, Joedon grabbed a water blade and sluiced the rain water off my sides, back, and belly. Then, he picked up two oversized towels and massaged my shoulders, mane, tail, and legs until I was relatively dry. He vigorously rubbed down his own hair with one of the towels and shed his soaked shirt and trousers. Finally, he flung an absorbent cover over me, pulled another around his shoulders, and sank into the bed of fresh straw. I folded my legs and dropped next to him.

"It's been a long time since you've groomed me." I kept my voice soft, empty of any tint of criticism.

"I know. I'm sorry I got so wrapped up in being miserable that I neglected you completely."

"It's done now," I said more briskly. "What is it you've decided you want?"

"Well … How old is Mosedon now? Maybe I should go see her."

Not what I expected, or wanted, but it was a beginning. I decided not to tell him about the threat coming from the Council. *Let's see where this takes us.*

The next day, we went to Center. I dropped Joedon in front of the Mos estate and watched him stride toward the front door. I'd promised not to listen in so I flew off to visit my uncle-in-law, the Lill leader and newly-retired reeth leader. On the way, I tried to picture young Mosedon as I'd last seen her over two years ago: thick brown hair tumbling down her back and warm expression snapping with intelligence. Other features I couldn't bring into focus. *Is she as tall as Sara?* I decided not. *Pleasant looking compared to Sara's stunning beauty.*

Ruefully, I remembered the fem's reeth-mate better: a slim liver chestnut with lighter points and a wide blaze. Her coloring and dainty conformation were arresting in any reeth gathering. *Maybe that's why I can't picture her don-mate.*

I shook my head and gave up the struggle, switching my attention to what I would say to Lillolf when I found him. I finally tracked him down high up on the side of the mountain that rose sharply behind the homestead, sampling some new growth. He looked up and greeted me with pointed ears as I landed.

"Lillith. What are you doing way up here?"

"Searching for you, of course." I teased this well-loved member of my husband's family. "Why do you have to always be so far away when I need to consult you?"

"Because I'm trying not to be consulted!" His tone put the lie to his words as he moved out of the sunshine into the shade of a broad, old oak tree. "What brings you here with such a serious mind-set?"

I tilted my head and considered him. Still the virtual leader of all reeth even though he'd supposedly retired in favor of his son, he surely would know what was breeding in the Speaker's Council. I decided to proceed boldly. "They're planning to charge Joedon with treason," I said bluntly. "What support can I count on from you in this mess?"

He ducked his head and turned to stare at the capitol city and the out-of-sight council building. "I've already been approached by Tallyon," he admitted. "He says his mind-mate is losing standing among the Speakers, that radical factions are building, threatening to take power into their own hands. Pildon, of course." When he turned back to meet my eye, I realized he wavered between staunch opposition to the don extremist and an old reeth's desire to stay out of it. "You've asked for my support. Here's a question. Why did Joedon reveal himself to the humans?"

I paused to gather arguments, then sighed. "I set him up and pushed him along. I wanted to propel him out of his isolation into seizing back the leadership."

"Another question. Did you succeed?"

Surprisingly, I sensed no anger. Could it be he actually would lend his support in the upcoming battle for control?

"I think so." I lifted one corner of my upper lip in a grin. "He's right now investigating whether Mosedon would suit him as a consort."

Lillolf snorted a laugh. "I expected they'd have a human consort shoved down their throats."

I allowed my relief to explode. "So you aren't angry about his antics?"

"Not at all. In my opinion, it's high time don ended their foolish isolation and reestablished contact with humans." I could only gape at him, my mouth hanging open. He shrugged. "Tallyon and I have quietly gathered a small group of family leaders. We've worked out a plan with Head Recorder Memmiard to tell the true story of what happened years ago and to train his young recorders to spread the word." When I didn't respond, he continued, obviously enjoying my speechless state. "You know our ancestors scared don deliberately to separate them from humans until they worked out how to deal with the creatures. They evidently did too good a job. We never expected this isolation to last so long."

He strolled over to a gurgling stream and dropped his head for a drink, then flashed me a smile with droplets falling from his muzzle. "I guess you didn't know."

"I've never heard anyone say such a thing before!" sounding petulant at being left in the dark.

Lillolf seemed pensive, staring at nothing, almost like he was peering into the past. "Probably because everyone assumed you already knew when you melded with Joedon. We normally told any new meldee, but you were much older than normal."

"You don't need to remind me," I snapped. "What really happened back then?"

"Go to Memmiard's next presentation and you'll learn. In the meantime, we need to subtly suggest the possibility of using humans in place of don to help non-melded reeth in their homes."

I only thought I'd felt shock before. This statement about knocked me off my feet. "What? Replace don with humans?" I shrieked.

"No, no." Lillolf raised a wing in protest and flicked his ears away from me in negation. "Not replace don. Supplement them." I didn't follow. "I know Sissith shared the concept of asking humans to help research don infertility. What they must not have mentioned, or maybe they don't realize, with the lack of don children, many reeth families have no melds within their entire herd."

I considered what living without Joedon would mean after all these years. I'd been happy pre-meld. I couldn't stand the thought of it now. "That's sad."

"Those of you who are melded often don't understand how those of us who aren't feel about the connection. I would have liked to be melded." I sensed a strong yearning, then realized he'd allowed me to feel it. "It's an experience·I missed out on," he explained. "With humans, it could never be the same, but at least the herds would have more help."

"The Speaker's Council will be appalled."

"We know. That's why we're rather pleased Joedon blew the subject wide open…" His tone carried amusement and a touch of admonition. "… even if we didn't know ahead of time about your scheme."

I ducked my head. "I'm sorry. I didn't even think to inform you."

"It's alright, Lillith. To answer your original question, you and Joedon have my support and the backing of many other herd leaders. Proceed onward, but, please. In the future, keep me informed." Much relieved, I promised.

When I arrived back at Center, Joedon was anxiously waiting for me on the pathway outside Mosedon's home. Surprised, I asked, "How did it go?"

Trying to hide his impatience to be gone, he flung himself on my back. Yet, his tone was forced casual. "She's lovely. She's nice and sweet. Not at all like Sara."

"Then why are you so unsettled?" I took off toward Eyrie; the green Center valley passed quickly below and within minutes we were out of sight of the city.

"She's too young!" The words exploded as if he'd been suppressing them.

Keeping my mental voice extremely level, I said, "She's the same age as Soer Jaym."

"She can't be!"

"Are you aware that Lord Metz himself is only a few years older than you? Or that Lord Roark is ten years younger?"

He rode in silence the whole way to Eyrie. As he dismounted, he said, with confusion, "It must be their metabolism. Humans must age twice as fast as we do."

I answered carefully. "Maybe you're right. I haven't seen Mosedon for several years, but most fem are still immature at her age. Soer Jaym did not seem a flighty young female at all. Quite down to earth, I thought." I stopped short of elaborating further. *Don't push too hard.*

"Sara will be back soon." Joedon led the way into the dining room rather than heading off to his own suite. "I'll talk to her— and Raedon, of course. Have you heard from them?" He selected an apple from a fruit bowl decorating the center of one table.

"I haven't but they must return early next week." He raised a brow in inquiry. "The Speaker's Council meets next Wedday," I reminded him. His mouth full of apple, he scowled instead of voicing his disgust. "You have to prepare to face them..." I said firmly. "...and the Royal Couple can help!"

He laughed derisively at my use of Raedon and Sara's official title. "You're right." He nibbled around the apple core, then handed it to me. "Better get hold of her father too. I'll need his support. Will you please set up a meeting? I can be available anytime the rest of the week, I guess." He sighed, then turned to go back to his own room. "He's not going to like this any more than I do."

At least you're prepared to face them, I thought as he walked away. He was brisk, confident, and appeared thoroughly fit. *Six months ago, I doubt you would have been.*

Chapter 12

~ Joedon

On Lunday, Lillith and I flew slowly over the tree-lined pathways that snaked haphazardly through Center, inspecting the state of our ancient governmental center. As far as we knew, Center had existed for over a thousand years. Even before moving their permanent homes to hide from the human settlers, our ancestors had maintained at least temporary residences on the bluff overlooking the high mountain valley. In those early days, family Speakers had converged on Center for governing duties only on council days, if nothing else demanded their attention. They left behind the large block of apartments along the north side of the square where Raedon kept his suite for council days and a few other mansions beside the sprawling edifice of the Joe family, my childhood home.

"It's hard to image how it was back then," I said, "with the bluff almost empty and only the council building, apartments, and the Joe mansion."

"There were a few other estates. You know that." Lillith, having reached the west edge of the bluff, curved right to head back over the city.

"Yes, but, just think how empty the valley appeared except on council day." I leaned over to inspect my family estate. "It seems smaller from up here."

Ignoring my words, Lillith flew further east checking the buildings Taldon had listed as deteriorating. "I've never particularly noticed the uniformity of architecture," she said. "Gray granite, tile roofs, central home with two wings."

"All the newer ones sprawl on one level." I glanced from right to left. "Of course, the term new is relative. Everything here's a couple hundred years old, like Sara said."

Lillith laughed, although the subject wasn't funny. Center homes were ancient and we saw clearly the disrepair Taldon had talked about.

"Estates are so spread out! Makes it hard to maintain pathways and services." The scene below changed as Lillith completed a lazy circle over the edge of the bluff; the land dropped steeply away and we soared above the valley. "Lillolf says the bowl is filling up." She nodded toward the huge Lill family complex. "Even the Lill are running out of new living areas for young couples."

"We have some really big problems." I mulled over the strange situation our people had fallen into. "Don aren't having babies and reeth are having too many." Shifting my balance, I pressed my left leg into Lillith's side. "I've seen enough. How about you?"

She immediately turned toward home. "Yes, let's go."

**

Two days later, I knelt before an ancient trunk stashed in an unused upstairs bedroom in the mansion. Lillith provided me with running commentary on Sara's reactions to her first Speaker's Council meeting as The Royal Fem; my loving mind-mate was attempting to make the next minutes easier as I focused on the trunk. It hadn't been opened in fifteen years.

My hand shook as I reached for the clasps. I fumbled at the lock and raised the lid slowly. Father's scent battered me, emanating from the black cape trimmed in ermine folded carefully at the top. The last time he'd worn it was a week before he died.

Father had loved wearing the formal uniform—I'd avoided it for years.

"It is necessary," Lillith said to bolster my resolve. "You have to remind the council of the Joe family power and of your rightful place."

Gently, I drew the cape from the trunk, then took out the broad sword and heavy crown, running my fingers over the black diamonds set deep in worked silver. Lillith carried on her murmuring over my whisper. "I never wanted to wear this." Holding the crown out before me, I couldn't stop my hands from trembling.

"You must wear it," Lillith insisted.

I shuddered, then stood and slowly drew on the trousers. Once I was fully outfitted, I walked with what composure I could muster to the great room and placed my hand firmly on Lillith's withers. She carefully touched my cheek with her muzzle, then stepped away, refusing to leave a single white hair on the solid black tunic.

"Sit, try to relax. It will be awhile before they call for you." Proceeding to play the scene in the chamber transmitted to her from Sara via Sissith, she emphasized my cousin's anticipation in an effort to distract me.

I heard Raedon's voice, in the tone I'd heard often. "I warn you, the meetings are never fun. The same don complain about the same things, every time."

I grinned slightly from my seat by the window. "He's bored already."

Lillith sent me a chuckle, then sobered. "Only thirty-seven families represented, like last time. Taldon's calling the meeting to order, calling for old business. Ylsdon, again." I echoed the groan she relayed from Raedon.

The meeting droned on; Lillith stopped projecting. My edginess increasing, I went to get water, then returned to pace the great room. "Foal, will they never call?" She waited with me, helping me maintain as much patience as possible, following the proceedings but not reporting them to me.

Suddenly, her head jerked up and I swung around to stare at her. "Sara's going to speak," she said. Incredulously, we listened to the relay from Memm through Raedon's eyes.

My cousin, the Royal Fem, stepped up to the podium and boldly faced the assembled Speakers. As tall as any in the room but more slender, she presented a startling contrast to most who spoke from the dais. Her long blue skirt and buttoned-down, high-collared tunic mimicked Raedon's typical Speaker suit, with gold piping on the long sleeves and down each side of her skirt. Her black hair wove intricately through a delicate silver crown above her face, then dropped in waves to her waist. Her eyes snapped, her customary laugh lines drowned in the sternness with which she confronted them.

"Well done, Sara," I crowed.

"We should be able to work this out, Ylsdon." Sara's mellow voice didn't wobble. "Surely there's someone here beside Raedon and I who will help with repairs." She focused on someone and Raedon turned to see who. It was Quodon, the sole don electrician. "I assume you know what to do." Her right eyebrow quirked upward. "You just need help to get it done, don't you?"

Quodon twitched, then nodded.

"Good. Now, who's going to help with the electrical project?" She singled out Speakers, one after another, until she had three who agreed to help. "Bring your fymm. We'll make it a family outing." She made her smile into a command. I was laughing silently, wishing I'd been there to see her face down the Speakers.

When Sara turned toward Taldon, her skirt swirled around her, emphasizing her feminine figure and she used his startled pause to say, sweetly, "Thank you for allowing me to speak." As she walked calmly back to her chair, Speakers' heads followed her amid a deep silence.

I laughed out loud and Lillith snorted with delight. Then, she reported Memm's reaction. "The reeth out here are in a turmoil." Mirth echoed through his tone. "They're going on about Saradon doing something crazy. Their don-mates are shocked at how forceful she was. None of them expected something like that. To their thinking, she's supposed to sit there, look beautiful, listen, and nod graciously."

"Guess they're learning just what type of fem their 'royal observer' is going to be," I said, grinning, now totally relaxed.

The call finally came. I swung the ermine-lined cape around my shoulders, placed the heavy crown on my head, and marched out my front door and across the plaza to the Speakers' building. Lillith said she and Lillyon were joining Memm and Sissith—they'd follow the proceedings together from the bowl.

~ Lillith

The four of us formed a tight, intense herd, heads up, ears twitching, wings held taunt against our sides as if we expected a physical attack. Hiding our worry from our don-mates, we linked our minds to share the scene in the council chamber while shielding our thoughts from outsiders.

In the council chamber, Raedon whispered. "Look at Pildon and his cronies. They're just waiting to lambaste him. Smug old fool." Sara had never seen Pildon in council uniform; he appeared elegant in dark blue with white piping, colors that complemented his dark features. His face however, seemed cold and treacherous to her.

Joedon swept into the meeting hall in full formal royal uniform, strode down the aisle, and stopped just in front of the seated Taldon. Sara caught her breath at his magnificence.

In the silence that fell, he spoke clearly. "I understand I have been called before the council. I am here at your pleasure." Instead of taking the seat of the Joe family Speaker, he remained standing in the middle of the room, relaxed but alert. The cape dropped from his squared shoulders to the floor, the sword jutted aggressively at his side, and the sight of the crown seemed to hold the older don frozen in place. I'd known it would have a profound effect on them, as if they'd forgotten just who Joedon was.

Taldon said nothing but through Sara's eyes we could see he was not surprised. Then, he evidently remembered the prepared charges; he stood, moved to the podium, and began to read tonelessly, eyes aimed resolutely at the paper in his hands.

"The don council has asked you here to examine the events of four weeks ago when you brought a human into your home against law and custom. We will also examine your extraordinary demonstration of don and reeth existence to the humans at Flagstone Plateau that same day. Finally, we will investigate the reoccurring appearances of human flights over, and human explorers in, the mountains that have always been

98

the home of the don and the reeth and which have been hidden from humans for centuries."

He paused and raised his eyes. Joedon's commanding stance and the overwhelming quiet did not seem to bother him. I sent the don a compliment on his poise. He shrugged slightly in reaction, dropped his head, and continued reading. "Members of the council have laid charges that you have irrevocably breached our security and caused imminent danger to the don and reeth who accompanied you that day to the Plateau, as well as to the homes, lifestyles, and lives of all don and all reeth. These charges, if substantiated, will result in the council's order for your death."

The bland tone rolled out the words. No one moved. Then, Sara gasped and jumped to her feet. Raedon pulled her back into her seat and whispered, "Wait, love. Let Joedon handle it." She trembled with fury, then followed his gaze. Joedon still stood like a statue. I sent them both waves of support, saying, "We are prepared."

After a sharp glance at Sara for her outburst, Taldon continued his speech. "Evidence of the charges will be presented at this time. Joedon, please take your seat. The chair recognizes the Special Prosecutor." As per our plan, Joedon did not comply with the direction and remained standing defiantly in place.

The prosecutor, an old widower dressed in maroon with blue— rather an ugly combination Sara thought—stood at the podium and began reading the charges in a monotone. "The investigative committee has sufficient evidence to find Joedon guilty on both charges. Every don has seen the human broadcasts of the exchange of the human for Raedon. Don and reeth were exposed to not only a few humans on Gareeth, but to all humans on the planet. Due to Joedon's actions, don will no longer be able to maintain the secrecy of our existence."

He paused, then nodded in Pildon's direction. His voice rose, taking on some inflection, as he continued to read. "Additionally, it is clear that the humans will not leave us alone. The number of human flights over Center has tripled since that day of exchange. They are seeking us with every means at their disposal, not only by air but by ground." He directed a glare at Joedon and his voice shook with disgust. "My reeth-mate and I saw a group of four climbers as we flew from Sanctuary to Center today!"

"Senile old fussbudget," I commented quietly to my audience.

Drawing in a breath, the Special Prosecutor acidly announced his recommendation. "We should find Joedon guilty as charged."

Joedon remained stone faced and immobile. The prosecutor frowned, folded up his paper, and took his seat.

Taldon intoned the traditional phrase. "Joedon, do you speak for yourself or do you request counsel?"

"I speak for myself." He mounted the platform and took up a position of ease just behind the podium, forcing Taldon to move away to his family desk. Joedon swept the cape around his torso, causing the silver ermine lining to flash against the black of his uniform, a visual aid to remind the Speakers of his hereditary right. "First, I remind the council it has no jurisdiction over the Supreme Don. Only other members of the royal family may sit in judgment on one of their own." His words fell like bombs.

Pildon jumped up, shouting. "That is preposterous. That's an ancient and totally outdated law and cannot be considered in today's times. Why, there's only three full members of the royal family alive."

Joedon focused on Pildon and the ermine flashed again. "Precisely my point. That law is no more outdated than the laws I am accused of breaking. Both other members of the royal family are present." He turned toward Sara and his iron-like face relaxed into a smile. "Ask if she will stand in judgment."

"Outrageous," shouted Pildon. "She's only a fem. What does she know about security and safety of the species?"

Sara rose slowly to her full height in the sudden silence, her face stone-cold in fury. "I would say, Pildon, that I know a great deal about the safety of the species since I'm the one expected to save us through my children." She shifted toward Taldon and smiled a tight, half smile. "I will not stand judgment against Joedon on this matter. In fact, I'm so in support of Joedon that I willingly accompanied him that day to retrieve my betrothed from the humans." She swept the assembly with a sneer. "You might as well charge me, too!"

She nodded to her father, seated at the Sar family desk. He stood and said, clearly. "Neither will I."

Sara knew full well no one would charge her with anything. She was the expected savior of the species. "A ridiculous concept, but I'm not going to tell them that. They're only homm," she added to Sissith as she returned to her seat.

Pildon spluttered and shouted; Taldon banged his gavel and ordered silence. As Pildon's friends convinced him to shut up and sit down, Taldon nodded to Joedon. "Continue your defense."

Joedon's pale face settled into a serious, hard-as-granite expression. "As far as the charge that I brought a human to my home, I am guilty. As far as the charge that I demonstrated the existence of don and reeth with my actions both in Pith and at Flagstone Plateau, I am guilty."

Pildon jumped to his feet, again. "Aha, he admits it!"

Taldon banged his gavel. "Order."

Joedon stood quietly until the room settled back down and then continued. "I maintain that the laws passed centuries ago, that we have been upholding without thinking about, are..." He threw a hand toward the furious don. "... as Pildon said, outdated and should not be considered in today's times."

Pildon started to protest, Taldon pointed his gavel at him and out-shouted him. "Not another word or I will throw you out of the council chamber!" Pildon sat, glowering.

Unperturbed, Joedon continued. "The laws passed by our forefathers over three hundred years ago were necessary at that time to isolate don and reeth from the humans. They are no longer necessary. We have learned much about humans since then. Everyone in this room has been among the humans at some point in their lives." Again, he pointed at the outraged don. "Yes, even you, Pildon."

Then, he swept the hand to include all those present. "You have not been detected. By going out among them, we've learned much that our forefathers didn't know. Now, we can guard against them."

Joedon bowed briefly to Taldon, then spread his hands out wide. "I admit, I have irrevocably breached don secrecy. However, I do not admit, nor do I believe, that I caused imminent danger to any don or reeth. The day we went to the Plateau, we went in a position of power." He paused. "As the prosecutor said, you've seen broadcasts from the human networks. Humans believe we are strong and powerful. Saradon and I were the only don at the exchange..." He raised his voice. "... but there were over a hundred reeth." Again, he swept his gaze slowly around the room, making eye contact with several. "You are don. You know I did not command reeth to either be there or to act as they did. Humans are now aware of us. They are also in awe of us. We will keep it that way."

Through Sara's eyes, we saw council members nodding their heads in agreement. Every don knew they could not command reeth; even Pildon knew that. Neither partner in a mind-meld controlled the other; I urged all reeth listening to remind their Speaker mind-mates of that fact.

"I deny that I have caused any danger to any home, lifestyle, or life. Yes, the flights over the mountains have increased recently. But, we are not, and have not been, mounting extra security because of those flights. It's been four weeks and they've found nothing. As to explorers on the ground, I've not heard of anyone mounting extra security around their homes, and again, it's been four weeks. Has anyone here encountered a human even close to their home?"

He waited, one white eyebrow raised. Don shifted in their seats, glanced at each other. No one responded.

"We're well hidden," Joedon continued, "and our defenses have been in place for hundreds of years. Soon, humans will tire of searching and give up. I have not caused any danger with my actions."

I spoke to him, passed on the reeth ultimatum. Although I couldn't see him, I sensed his eyes glaze as he listened. I nodded briskly, satisfied. Every melded Speaker would recognize that expression. Then, his eyes cleared and he locked gazes with one after another. When he spoke, his words carried the weight of us two thousand reeth behind them. "Consult your mind-mates before you decide to condemn me. Your decision affects more than me."

He focused on Taldon and said, "I conclude my defense." Bowing, he took his seat at the Joe family desk, his face a calm mask of indifference. I was so proud of his handling of the defense I could hardly contain myself.

The Speakers sat stunned as they considered Joedon's final words. I received their thoughts from their listening reeth-mates. How could they find Joedon guilty and subsequently vote to put him to death without having to deal with the huge Lill family? Did the committee think of that when they put their charges together? The charge just leveled at Joedon was disastrous. Even holding such a vote could cause our civilization to collapse. If don executed Joedon, then Lillith would die too. Reeth might pull away, refuse to live with don any longer. They might even leave!

Sara began to tremble at the thought of losing Sissith. Raedon grasped her hand and then, put his arm around her as he shared her vision of loss. I did not send comfort and forbid Memm and Sissith to do so. Fear dawned on other faces and reeth refused to respond to their anxiety. Speakers sat stunned when they realized how close they were to causing their own catastrophe. Through Sara's eyes via Sissith, I saw that even Pildon went unnaturally pale although I knew he couldn't actually feel the fury emanating from the reeth surrounding the meeting chamber.

Taldon stood slowly and rapped his gavel out of habit. He seemed dazed when he called on the prosecutor to present his closing. I'd worried that Tallyon would warn him of our impending action.

The elderly prosecutor peered at the council members as if bewildered before he approached the podium. His voice, low and reedy with tension, carried easily in the silence. "The evidence is available to convict Joedon of breaking the laws of which he stands accused." He hesitated, looked anxiously around as if seeking support, and stopped to stare at Sara. He shook himself, stood straighter, spoke more firmly. "However, I recognize that the laws are ancient." Focused on Sara, as if speaking directly to her alone, he seemed to gain confidence as he continued. "I recommend the council take the case under advisement and reconvene in the morning for discussion and vote. Tonight, the investigative committee will meet to discuss the ramifications of the charges." He nodded sharply. "And I, for one, will consult with my reeth-mate."

Taldon accepted the recommendation, adjourning for the day.

Chapter 13

~ Lillith

The meeting ended and I followed Joedon's mind as he, Raedon, and Saradon retired to Raedon's suite where they sat in glum silence, each so lost in imagining life without reeth that they didn't notice our temporary absence of from their minds. Turning toward my companions, I passed out assignments.

"Memmyon, poll your family, especially Memmiard, and any others you feel comfortable talking to. See what reactions they're hearing. Sissith, same for you. Lillyon, would you talk to Lillolf and then work with Tallyon contacting the political mind-mates? We need to have a good sense of others' reactions before we get together to plan the next step." They stepped away from me to begin their tasks and I focused on the three in Raedon's home.

~ Joedon

Raedon shifted uncomfortably in his chair and finally broke the quiet between us. "You know… I thought it a big lark, you against that fool Pildon. I never had any doubt about how it would end and I was enjoying your defense until you said that last part." His dark brows met. "It wasn't so much the words—it was the way you said them, the way you looked—like doom was upon us. It unnerved me."

"It did me, too." I stared blankly at my feet, still enclosed in father's boots, my thoughts churning with uncertainty. Somehow, I'd myself, lost my sense of right.

"It was horrid." Sara's shrill tone brought my head up; her body was stiff with tension and I wanted to comfort her. *Not my place. I can't even comfort myself.*

But, I hated the dazed way she mumbled, "If don have gone so far as to even think about trying to execute you, then life with the reeth might be over." Raedon moved closer, put his arm around her. They slumped into each other, a picture of mutual misery.

I glanced away. *At least she has Raedon.* I sighed, then spoke softly, slowly. "I think it was Lillith … using me to pass on a warning." He shook his head. "I don't mean just Lillith, but all of them through her, telling us we need to pay attention to someone besides ourselves." Gradually, I firmed my words with resolution. "We've been caught up in petty problems when we should be concentrating on survival, or at least helping reeth to survive without us."

"I'm depressed." Sara sat up suddenly, glancing wildly around. "I don't feel Sissith. Where is she?" For a moment, I shared her panic, my heart beating erratically.

Lillith's words calmed. "It's okay. We're here. We were conferring."

Sara stood abruptly and headed for the door. "I'm going to find Sissith. I need her."

"I'll go with you." Raedon caught her hand, pulled her to him for a quick hug, and then accompanied her to the door. "Joedon, what about you?" he asked over his shoulder.

"I'm going to sit here and think. I'll find you later."

After staring fiercely at the wall, running explanations for everything I'd experienced recently around fruitlessly, I finally reached out. "Lillith, did you put those words in my head?"

"Joedon, come outside and walk with me." She sent sympathy, soothing my turmoil. "I'd prefer your physical presence for my explanation."

My tension faded. "Where are you?"

"Near the fountain in the south quarter. We're munching sunflowers. So good this time of year. A big field—you can't see it from the fountain but if you walk south, you'll spot us."

I had to smile at the mundane nature of sunflowers. Lillith loved them so. "I'll be there in a few minutes." The sunflowers were not tall; both Lillith and Lillyon stood above them by a foot. Although not alone, their gleaming white bodies were easy to spot. I moved easily through other reeth, stroking greetings when I recognized one.

"Lillith," I said aloud as I caressed her supple neck. She leaned into me, her touch bringing us both comfort. I slapped Lillyon on the shoulder and he head butted me gently in the chest.

Lillith nuzzled my arm, then moved slowly toward the east. "Come this way." She continued munching sunflowers as I strolled beside her, hand on her withers, just above her wings. Lillyon fell behind.

"Lillith, did you put those words in my head?" I asked again, hesitantly.

"Yes, Joedon, I did." She snatched up another sunflower with her teeth and I felt the muscles ripple through her neck as she chewed. "When we learned of the charges and punishment those idiots proposed, it scared many of us. We finally acknowledged something we've felt for some time—don are taking their comfortable lives for granted. In their complacency, even those with mind-mates didn't consider the ramifications to reeth. We decided their selfishness is no longer tolerable." Her jaws working vigorously, she swung her head to focus her left eye on me as if to emphasize her concern. Her tone mismatched her appearance—extremely solemn—effective even with the sunflower dangling out of her mouth to the right. I felt no urge to laugh as she continued her mental diatribe. "We felt attacked, especially the Lill. For the first time in centuries, we decided to intervene outright, to convince the council beyond a shadow of a doubt that they couldn't, ever, complete the action they proposed."

She finished the sunflower and reached for another, letting me out from under her glare. But her anger simmered. "All don, including you, have to understand the path you've been following will no longer work. Our suggestions, nudges, and subtle counseling have not changed the council's direction." She stomped on the base of a plant almost as if she were stomping on a Speaker, ripped it apart, and shook it. I gulped as her voice thundered in my head. "We threatened. They will listen. Things will change."

"I see." I eyed the numerous reeth grazing around us. I was alone among them. They seemed peaceful, contentedly eating.

But I knew they weren't. They were aware of what had happened in the council meeting and what Lillith lectured me about. For the first time in my life, I felt a frisson of fear of reeth. They wouldn't attack me; rather, they would leave. I whispered, "Living without you is unthinkable."

My head throbbed as I walked unseeing toward the edge of the plateau. Lillith joined me and I placed my hand once more on her withers. "The declining birth rate isn't a crisis for me," I said as I pulled realization out of the chaos of my thoughts. "Whether or not there are more children, I will still live my life."

We reached the cliff's edge and I stared out over the huge valley: varicolored patches of cultivation intermingled with expanses of luxuriant grass; a coat of deep green evergreens climbed up the far mountain; the river snaked through the middle ending in a mirrored lake that reflected the sheer cliffs to the north. *Center valley had always provided a beautiful home for reeth. It would be overwhelmingly lonely without them.*

"The implications of your threat are clear." I turned my back on the valley and gazed again over the reeth in the field with us. Lillith had stopped eating and was quietly watching me. "You think the humans are the answer, don't you?"

She nodded, her eyes gleamed blue-green with satisfaction. "Yes, we do. Reconnection with humans will benefit our community in many ways. Obviously, Pildon's followers will resist, and maybe some of the older, more traditional Speakers. There may be reeth who oppose the move, too. We, you and I, have to change their minds."

I made her a formal vow, both mentally and aloud. "Whatever it takes, I will do."

She rubbed her nose up my arm to nuzzle at my ear. The anger left her mind as she focused on the future. "I suggest we plan for tomorrow. Whatever the committee recommends, and whatever the vote gives us, we must be ready."

On the second day of the council meeting, I sat at the Joe family desk on the bottom tier, facing Sara and Raedon on the royal dais. Surrounding me, and all other Speakers' desks, extra chairs and family members packed the aisles. The scene, although even more brightly colored than the previous day, seemed bizarre. Never could I remember the chamber being so crowded.

I watched Sara catch sight of an elder fem, dressed in deep purple with orange trim, staring at her. Sara pulled her shoulders up to sit proudly in the Royal chair, pasted a smile on her face, and inclined her head in what I interpreted as her regal nod. The old fem smiled and nodded back. Concealing my sudden mirth behind a solid mask of indifference, I said mentally to Lillith. "She's a perfect Royal Fem."

Taldon started the meeting and called for a report from the special prosecutor. I maintained my unconcerned posture, burying my anxiety deep inside. Silence reigned as the old don made his way slowly to the podium from the top tier, stepping carefully around the closely seated Speakers and their families.

He stood painfully straight and spoke loudly. "The committee met last night. We recommend the council find Joedon guilty as charged for exposing don and reeth to humans. We recommend the charge that he irrevocably breached don security and caused imminent danger to don and reeth be dropped. As punishment, the committee recommends confinement to Center for one year and assignment to regular rotation on the camouflage team for the same term." He looked defiantly around, avoiding Pildon, then made his way back to his desk. Lillith breathed a sigh of relief. *Despite her stated certainty, she'd been worried, too.*

Taldon rapped his gavel. "You have heard the committee's recommendation. Is there discussion?"

Forcing myself to remain calm, I watched Pildon stride angrily to the podium. As usual, he was loud and condescending. "Fellow council members, I demand Joedon receive a more stringent punishment in the face of this crime. The committee did not present all the facts. Perhaps they don't know them." He flung out his arm and pointed at me. Emphasizing the name with a sneer, he said, "Joedon willfully disregarded our chairman's counsel when he chose to publicly return the human female in exchange for Raedon. He could have made the exchange without exposing don and reeth to any human. Instead, he chose to make a flamboyant statement that destroyed over three hundred years of effort on the part of this council."

He left the podium to advance across the floor toward me. I'd dressed today in an ordinary Speaker suit. "Less provocative," Lillith had said. Rising to meet him, I stood at ease.

Pildon almost spat in my face. "I was there! I heard Taldon tell you not to go. And I heard you state that, as Supreme Don, you would do what you wanted."

Pildon's rage intensified at my lack of reaction and for a moment, I braced for a blow. Then, he swung around to sweep the audience with his glare, continuing to point at me with an accusing right hand. "Now, he blithely assures us humans will not find us … humans will not disturb us … humans will give up searching." He smacked his chest. "I don't believe him and neither should you!"

He stomped back to the podium, sneering once again. "Due solely to his wanton actions, humans will seek us for years, until they find us and force us into their service. They did it once. They'll do it again. We have to do more than slap his hand."

When Pildon took his seat, still scowling, another mounted the podium. I identified him to Lillith: Holden, non-melded.

"My friends," he said. "You know I don't live at Center. My community, Sanctuary, and the others: Warren, Enclave, Labyrinth—none have the excellent protection of Center. Humans may find us. I believe as Pildon does about one thing: I don't trust humans to leave off searching. Joedon must pay for his crime by helping the rest of us defend our homes from discovery. And if we're found, he must suffer consequences."

Another unmelded don joined him. "I do live at Center," Dogdon said, "but I don't feel the proposed punishment is sufficient. And I'm not sure I agree we should fear reeth retaliation for our chosen penalty. I don't advocate the death penalty, but we shouldn't fear to penalize him sufficiently." He paused; the assembly rustled in their seats.

Dogdon placed a hand on Holdon's shoulder and singled out others with his gaze. I noted the ones he focused on. "All non-melded," Lillith confirmed seconds later.

Dogdon's words surprised both of us. "I've lived for one hundred thirty-six years without a reeth-mate. There's no reeth mated to anyone in my family, yet my son, my grandson, and I help gather for them." He pulled Holdon forward. "There's no reeth mated to anyone in my good friend Holdon's family either, but they help with the gather every year too."

He stepped forward to stand in front of the lectern, bringing Holdon with him, and his voice rose. "Yesterday, Joedon called on Speakers to consult their reeth-mates before they voted. Well, we have none to consult and some of the rest of you don't either." Again he swept the audience, then settled serious eyes on me. "I cannot know what reeth intended when they accompanied you to the exchange, but I *am* afraid of the results. I believe you should be more severely punished." In that moment, I agreed with him. Lillith kept me from saying so. "We will protect them—the non-melded," she promised me.

Another Speaker approached the podium, one of Lillith's employees. "I can't believe what I'm hearing." His deep voice boomed with exasperation. "No one in my family is mind-mated either, but we still feel reeth are of supreme importance to us. If not for them, we would be fighting amongst ourselves, not verbally but physically, and possibly killing each other." He bristled at Pildon's sneer, and his words thundered through the room. "The joy reeth provide is worth everything to me and my family. This is foolishness."

He took a deep breath as if gathering his patience, then held his hands wide in supplication. This time, he persuaded. "Let's give it a chance and see if humans stop hunting us before we make a decision based on what we think they'll do." He looked again at Pildon. "I've never known Joedon, or Lillith, to be stupid or self-serving and you can't convince me they are now. The committee's proposed punishment is sufficient and so I will vote."

"I agree." This Speaker, Weedon, did not bother with the podium but rose to speak from his desk. "You all know my family is the largest ..." He waved a hand to indicate the seventeen grey and green suits surrounding him. "... and we only have one reeth-mate, my grandfather's. He provides joy for our entire family and none of us would want to live without it. But that's not the point of the upcoming vote." He glowered at Pildon. "The Wee have lived among humans all our lives and we unanimously support Joedon's statement. They will lose interest. As soon as something comes up on Gareeth to attract their newscasters' attention, we'll fade from their minds and they'll stop searching."

My emotions rose and fell as other Speakers continued the debate and I strained to maintain my granite face. Lillith shared encouraging words gleaned from incoming reeth reports. "Don't' fret. The majority is not against you. Most of the non-melded yes, but they're outnumbered. Let the sour ones have their say."

Finally, Taldon stood at the podium and waited through several quiet moments. No one else approached or stood to speak. "Do I have a motion?"

As planned, my pseudo-uncle, Sara's father Sardon, stood at his desk and called out, "I move to accept the sub-committee's recommendation as stated."

Someone called, "Second that motion." I didn't recognize the voice; it came from behind me.

Holdon also stood at his desk. "I wish to amend the motion to state that Joedon must help the other communities in their defense, not just Center." Another from Sanctuary called a second.

"Do you agree to the amendment to your motion?" Taldon asked Sardon, who nodded acceptance.

Rustling in the room increased as Taldon declared, "I hereby call for a vote of the council to accept the sub-committee's recommendation as amended."

Pildon leaped up. "Is that all we're going to do?" He threw his arms out and shouted. "He should be at least locked up for a year, not allowed to wander wherever."

"Where would we lock him up?" Taldon scowled at Pildon. "Are you saying if we impose this punishment, we couldn't trust his word to comply?"

"We couldn't trust him before!" Pildon looked around for support.

Eyes turned away from him as Taldon retorted, loud in his anger. "We never before specifically forbade him from going among humans."

"But the laws!"

Taldon pounded his gavel. "The committee made its recommendation. You spoke your piece." He pointed the gavel. "Now sit down and be quiet." The Chairman took a deep breath, then said calmly, "Speakers will vote by family. Bailiff, call the roll."

"I've never seen a roll call vote," I said to Lillith. "Nothing's ever been that important." The bailiff stood, roll call book in hand. "Taldon planned ahead — the bailiff's already prepared."

The bailiff walked stiffly to the lectern and opened the book reverently. He first read the motion, his voice crisp and clear, then reminded the Speakers of how to cast their vote. "When I call your family name, please respond with one vote in consensus of your family by saying clearly 'for' or 'against'. Speak loudly so that the council may hear and record." A shiver sweep down my back at the ancient ritual.

The bailiff read the family name Abo and paused. Then, he said, "No family Speaker alive." My stomach clenched at the terrible words. Faint gasps whispered through the air as others realized the same feeling of doom—an entire family gone forever.

The bailiff moved on. "Ara family, Speaker Aradon."

The grey haired don dressed in yellow and green rose and said clearly, "For". The bailiff made a mark in the book and continued alphabetically down the roll.

At the Pil family, Speaker Pildon, I wasn't surprised. "Against."

But, every time I heard, "No family Speaker alive," I shuddered inside. Knowing families had died out and hearing their names called to vote with no response evoked totally different emotions. "My people really are in trouble," I silently acknowledged to Lillith.

Finally, the bailiff called the last name, Zoe family, and Pildon's best friend voted "Against".

The bailiff closed his roll book, took off his glasses, and raised his head. "Twenty against, forty-one for. The vote has passed."

I let out a slow breath. "I told you not to worry," Lillith told me. The bailiff's announcement made it official.

"Joedon, please approach the podium." Taldon waited for me to walk onto the platform. I moved calmly although my heart raced with relief. "The motion has passed. Do you understand the punishment as the council voted?"

"Yes, and I will comply."

Chapter 14

~ Lillith

When Taldon adjourned the meeting, don clambered noisily out of the chambers. Raedon, Saradon, her parents, and Joedon waited for us reeth-mates in the shade of an overhanging limb just outside the council building. As we hurried toward them over the crowd, Joedon turned toward Sara's father intending to thank him for his support. I saw something whiz by his ear. Spinning, he caught the blow of an oncoming paving tile on his right temple and dropped like a brick.

I screamed, physically and mentally. Landing in the square, I rushed forward, knocking don aside as they reeled from my psychic assault. Raedon knelt over the limp body; I probed frantically. His mind blank, his eyes open but cloudy, Joedon lay on his side, blood streaming down the side of his face dripping steadily onto the flagstone walk. Sara pressed a folded kerchief against the wound while I sent a call to the doctors. Within seconds, both Nandon and Eledon flung themselves off their reeth-mates and converged upon us clustered around my unconscious mind-mate.

"What happened!" snapped Nandon.

"Someone threw a stone." Raedon moved back, giving the doctor room. Then, he spun on me, mind boiling with conjecture. "Did you catch any sense of who?" He waved toward his father-in-law, who held the stone in his hand.

I shook my head and glanced at the other reeth, quizzing each for their observations. No one had any impression of the attacker.

"Pildon?" Raedon's voice was sharp.

"No way of knowing." Forcing aside my own anxiety, I cautioned him to be patient as we watched Nandon daub at the blood. Eledon held Joedon's wrist in his hand—he was counting, emanating despair. I flashed a fear-filled plea at Memmyon: "Help."

He shook his head. "Not like Raedon's," he said gently.

"What should I do," I wailed.

"Reach for him, Lillith." The bay came near and placed his head on my back. "We'll help."

I felt Sissith rest her forehead against my hip. Vaguely, I felt Tallyon arrive and lightly touch my shoulder with his wing; Lillyon was at my other shoulder. Reeth after reeth joined us, each in physical contact with one touching me, if only with an ear.

The power of the Lill herd surged through my heart, then the Memm, then the Siss, followed in rapid succession by other herds. I didn't consider how they did it. I simply focused my appeal on Joedon's mind, sending a thread of myself deep into the darkness that enveloped him.

There! A spark. I begged, "Joedon, come back." More minds clicked in. I sent more power toward the spark. And it flared!

I pulled and felt the supporting power strengthen. The flame drifted slowly toward me until, finally, fire exploded in my mind. I dropped to my knees, lay my head down, and let the surge subside. "He is back," I whispered, then knew no more.

Sometime later, I woke. Lillyon was hovering over me as I lay on the square outside the council chamber where I'd collapsed. "Joedon?" My voice crackled with fear.

Lillyon stroked my face with the tip of his wing. "He'll be fine," he said. "Nandon says. But he's very groggy." He continued stroking my sweat-crusted neck, smoothing my ruffled hair as well as my frazzled nerves. "They took him to the mansion. Both Nandon and Eledon are staying with him …" His thoughts held a touch of sarcasm. "… along with just about every other don who can squeeze into the building." He stroked my back. "I felt it best to leave you here. You were recuperating and needed to be alone."

"How long?"

"About three hours."

"What did Raedon do?"

"Taldon restrained him from attempting to kill Pildon. When they did go to question him, he and ten of his cronies were commiserating over the vote. No way it could have been him, or even one of his usual supporters. He claimed to have no knowledge of a plan to attack Joedon and Taldon had to believe him. Unless you can read his mind, they can't charge him."

"Who then?"

Lillyon shrugged. "They're trying to find out but I have no idea how they'll proceed. You can quiz Tallyon when you feel better."

I grunted and gathered my hindquarters for the heave to my feet. Surprisingly, I felt steady. "I want to see him."

The walk was short. Someone had seen us coming and the door swung wide. I made my way to Joedon's bedside, shoving worried don out of my way. His head wrapped in bandages, he seemed unnaturally still. A quick probe assured me he was simply sleeping, not lost again in the awful blackness of earlier. I touched his cheek with my nose, locked my knees, and prepared to stand vigil until he woke.

While I waited, I followed the investigation through Tallyon. The square had been full of don families leaving the meeting, but no one reported anything useful. Tallyon contacted all melded reeth; none registered suspicious behavior from their mates. And no one could probe non-melded don to check the veracity of their stories. A frustrated Taldon finally appeared at my side with apologies. He promised to continue investigating, but offered little hope of finding a perpetrator.

"I can't understand it," he said, worry clouding his thoughts. "We've been non-violent for centuries. What would prompt someone to do such a thing?"

"Anger," I replied. "Or hatred."

By the time Joedon woke, Taldon and Raedon had cleared the house of well-wishers who only got in the way. He tried to sit up and pain ripped through his brain with blistering waves; groaning, he fell back as I sagged against Lillyon in reaction.

"Hold still." I kept my words as gentle as possible, for both our sakes. Gradually, the pounding subsided. He sat up slowly. His vision blurred and the room spun with bright colors. Despite my attempts to stop him, he swung his legs gently sideways and perched on the edge of the bed, leaning forward to brace hands on knees. His hands swam in and out of focus. His stomach rebelled from the spinning input and he spewed vomit across the rug. Fortunately, reeth can't puke or I'd have mirrored him, making an even bigger mess. Still, I felt totally unsettled.

I stroked his back with my muzzle as others rushed to clean up. "Nandon said you were to stay still." As the wrenching spasm subsided, I nudged. "Now lay back down, at least for my sake if not your own. He'll be here in a few minutes."

"What happened?" Joedon sounded terribly weak; his head drooped and his arms dangled limply. Another pain lanced across my mind, echoing his. He arched back, falling sideways across the bed. Gulping to control his roiling stomach, he closed his eyes against the swirling room and relieved me of the experience. I nuzzled with sympathy as I explained the attack.

"Nandon said you would be woozy. Head injuries are funny, he said. You have to be careful how you move until the dizziness subsides. So stay down!" Behind me, the door opened and Nandon entered. None too steady myself, I carefully stepped back as he made his way through the dim room.

"You have a huge bruise on the side of your head." Nandon's voice was quiet but brisk. "From the description Lillith gave, I'm pretty sure you have a major concussion. Which means you have to be extremely cautious with any movement."

"How long." Joedon struggled through the pain to squint. Nandon blurred in and out of my focus through Joedon's eyes.

"No way to know." The doctor took an arm and carefully pulled Joedon more fully onto the bed, straightening his legs. "We have to take it one day at a time," he said sternly. "I'm warning you, Joedon. You have to stay still!"

"I feel pretty miserable!"

"I'm sure you do." He helped Joedon sit slowly up, high enough to swallow. "Drink this. Then, go back to sleep. Making you rest is all we can do for you right now." Turning to me, he continued, "You need rest too, Lillith. Open your mouth and I'll put this Lareina mash on your tongue. It'll help stifle the symptoms you're catching from him."

~ Joedon

I woke into total darkness. I started to sit up, then felt Lillith's head pushing at my chest. "Where am I?" I muttered.

"In your room at the mansion. Now, stay still!" She hovered a moment and saw that I obeyed. I couldn't do much else since my muscles felt like jelly and my head ached abominably.

"Do you remember what happened?" Soft as her voice was, it still rasped against my pain.

"No."

"What is the last thing you recall doing?"

"Putting on my father's clothes to face the council." I wavered with confusion. "Did we go to the meeting?"

Lillith's anxiety spiked and she quickly hid it from me, saying only, "Yes, we went. Nandon says not to tell you what happened. He's hoping the memory will come back on its own." She moved toward the door and pushed against a light switch with her nose; dim lights came on. "He says you're not to struggle to remember right now, so don't."

"My head hurts."

"I know. I've sent for Eledon. He's staying here tonight. He'll give you something. How's your vision?"

"You're fuzzy." I rolled my head—a mistake. At the flash of pain across Lillith's face, I shut my eyes and tried to will the agony away.

Eledon entered and I moaned, "Don't be so loud."

Through tiny slits, I saw Lillith's distressed glance at the doctor; evidently he'd entered quietly. Focusing on him, I gained some reassurance from his confident air. Lillith's closed mind alarmed me. *How badly am I hurt?*

Eledon moved forward, picked up my wrist, and commenced silently counting. A moment later, he asked me to open my eyes and studied them. "Your heart rate is fine, but your breathing is erratic and your eyes are dilated." He moved toward a table at the side of the bed and poured a glass of Lareina he said was mixed with a sleeping draught. "Drink this."

"I don't want to sleep anymore." My words grated crankily. "I want to know what happened."

"You have to heal first." Eledon picked me up by my shoulders and held the glass to my lips. "Drink!"

I tried to resist. Dismayed by my weakness, I had to swallow and Eledon lowered me gently. "You'll feel stronger tomorrow." I didn't believe his words. Neither did he.

Lillith asked him to wait for her outside, then lingered until I couldn't keep my eyes open any longer. I didn't want to sleep. I wanted to understand. "It can wait until tomorrow," she said.

~ Lillith

"What are you afraid of?" I demanded of Eledon outside the door to Joedon's room.

"I forgot you can read me as easily as Fennyon does." He walked away down the hall and I followed. "We don't know much about concussion. Nandon and I are worried that such a blow to the head could seriously change Joedon's behavior, his personality. He could have future problems with mental and-or physical coordination." He stopped walking and turned to stare at her, trouble shading his mind. "We just don't know!"

He doesn't deserve my antagonism, I reminded myself as I forced stillness I didn't feel. "What would help?"

120

He paused, then sighed. "I know you can tell I'm not trying to push you into my own agenda, but we need to consult a human specialist, or at least the human medical library in Hilt."

"One of you go tomorrow to Hilt," I said. "I'll see what I can do about the other." I felt his shocked gaze as I re-entered the bedroom.

Chapter 15

~ Lillith

The next morning, I conferred with Nandon, asking him to keep Joedon sedated for the day if he felt it necessary. Then, joining Lillyon on the patio, I explained my mission and we left for Pith. Two hours later, we landed once again in the back garden of Pith Palace and took refuge behind the large, spreading pine tree. Lillyon maintained our invisibility while I probed the palace. Before long, I encountered the mind I'd been searching for. I felt him freeze in the middle of a sentence, then continue as if he hadn't heard a strange voice in his head. Shortly, he isolated himself within a storeroom and sent a probing question my way.

"Is this really Lillith? Joedon's reeth-mate?" A picture of me bloomed in his mind as he recalled seeing me at the exchange. *I'm not that big!* I thought to myself.

"Yes, Garard. I've been following your actions since the exchange and feel I can count on you for help."

"This feels very strange, talking to a being I can't see, or actually hear." He experimented with thinking rather than speaking and I responded amiably. "Well." He stood quietly a moment and mulled over the ramifications of conversing with a previously mythical creature, then steadied his breathing. "What can I do for you?"

"I need a human doctor, a specialist in concussion." At his query, I refused to explain further. "The doctor must be capable of keeping a very important secret, must disappear for a few days without raising questions, and must be very good."

"How soon?" I liked his brevity and determination.

"Yesterday!"

"Give me two hours." He started moving out of his hiding place, growing confident that he could communicate with me using his mind and not his voice. From others around him, I learned that although he might appear preoccupied, such a countenance was normal for him. In another part of the palace, he met with the man I'd noticed at the exchange, the history professor. Curious, I extended my range to listen in on both sides of the conversation.

"Talmadge," Garard said. "Who is the best person at the University to consult about concussion?"

The man who must be named Talmadge had been furiously writing notes when interrupted. To my surprise, the notes concerned don and reeth and his mind was filled with conjectures about us. "I'll have to consult the directory," the professor answered. "I don't know anyone in particular."

"Maybe we should talk to Dr. Grey at the Hospital, then. The one who examined the prisoner for us. What did you think of him?"

From the professor, I felt nothing but admiration of the named doctor. "Curious about the don, wanted to study more," he said. Talmadge himself shared that desire. "Professional, handled the media smoothly. Who has a concussion?"

Garard avoided a direct answer. "Someone I know wants to talk to a specialist. Surely, Dr. Grey would know the best in Pith."

"Do you want me to go see him?"

"You, no. Every reporter in Pith would follow you. Me, neither." Garard sounded perplexed. "How to get a hold of him?"

"Can't you just ask him to come here? Maybe your friend could meet him here in the palace somewhere. There's plenty of room and sufficient security to keep the media out."

Garard evidently paced, unsettled, while Talmadge remained seated. Of course, the professor had no idea the friend who needed the specialist was a reeth, therefore, he was calmer about the conversation. I considered talking directly to Talmadge, then decided not to. Instead, I prompted him for a solution.

"Have Soer Marn call him," Talmadge said. "The media won't think a thing about her making contact." Affection swirled in the man's mind as he pictured the woman—the brown haired sister of Lady Jill that I remembered seeing at the exchange. I also recalled picking up feelings of comfort from Soer Jaym when the girl thought about a woman named Marn. I sent Garard a nudge.

"Good idea. I'll talk to her right now."

"I'll go with you." Talmadge rose and walked with Garard toward the ladies' quarters. I had to grin at the professor's eagerness, sensing a budding romance. The two men managed to spirit Soer Marn away from her overbearing sister's side, saying Lord Metz wanted to see her. Evidently, Lady Jill never resisted Metz' orders. I shuddered at the animosity in the woman's mind as she watched her mild-mannered sister leave with Garard. *What a spiteful woman.* I transferred her attention to the younger one.

Soer Marn agreed readily to phone Dr. Grey and soon arranged a meeting for later in the day. Garard left the professor and the unappreciated younger sister chatting happily and walked out into a garden.

"Were you able to hear?" He struggled to aim his thoughts outward.

"Yes, thank you." I felt him relax at my response. "I'll return at three to see what you learn from the doctor." I paused, then said, "Are you aware of the attachment between those two?"

Garard seemed surprised. "Talmadge and Soer Marn?" He glanced toward the room where he'd left them. "They've only known each other a few weeks!"

"Nevertheless, they're quite fond of each other." Then, I felt contrite. "I hope I haven't ruined anything for them?"

"No, no." Garard remained relaxed. "They're wonderful people and deserve each other." He attempted a mental smile and I appreciated his effort. "Metz would approve. He's impressed with the professor and he's always liked Soer Marn. She should be rescued from her sister." Then, he paused uneasily and I waited for the question. "I would like to see you." His remembered vision didn't match my self-image; for now, I decided, I'd leave him believing me large and formidable.

124

"Perhaps later." I withdrew my voice but continued to follow his thoughts. Once free of my influence, he puzzled over why he'd taken to communicating with me so easily. *Because you are quite intelligent,* I thought to myself. *And adept at dealing with difficult situations.*

**

Just before three, Lillyon and I landed in what we'd begun to consider our garden outside the palace. I briefly contacted Garard to make him aware of my presence, then lightly touched each of the others in the room with him. "Shall I include the professor and Soer Marn in my communications?" I asked my husband.

"Stick to Garard for now," Lillyon counseled. "I know you feel an affinity for the professor, and female sympathy for the woman, but don't get carried away with your trust."

I stroked his neck with my head. "Yes, of course. Thank you, love, for keeping me centered."

The doctor arrived on time, ushered into the ground floor parlor with awe tempered by unease filling his mind. He relaxed immediately at Garard's friendly greeting and shook hands with Talmadge and Soer Marn. Garard directed them each into seats that I sensed formed a closely confined circle.

"What can I do for you, Soer Marn?" The doctor, confused by the presence of both Garard and the professor, contained his curiosity. I probed a bit deeper and learned that human doctors never met female patients with males present, certainly non-husband males. *How odd.*

"It's not me." I liked the calm, confident tone of Soer Marn's words. *She doesn't seem a tormented woman. Handles her sister's animosity well.* My liking of the human rose considerably at Marn's explanation. "We needed you to meet with Garard and Professor Talmadge, neither of whom could have contacted you directly without media intervention. So, I'm the messenger." A self-conscious smile filled her mind. "I don't even know what this is about."

Garard took over. "I have a close friend who needs the services of a brain specialist for several days, someone extensively conversant with concussions." The doctor's mind sharpened with interest. "Also, someone who can disappear for a short time without sparking undue notice." His words caused intense curiosity in his companions while he held his expression blandly in check. "We thought you would know such a person."

All three stared at him, rampant surmises running through two of the minds. "Not Jaym!" Marn whispered.

"No, no. Jaym is fine."

Talmadge discarded his first notion, then felt totally at sea. "Who then?" He knew nothing about Garard's background or family.

Neither do I! Feeling dizzy following all four minds, I decided to focus on Garard and Dr. Grey, although I savored the other two humans. I'd never expected to feel that way about any human.

"I can't tell anyone without permission," Garard was saying. "I have to interview the physician first, and judge for myself how trustworthy he or she will be."

Dr. Grey had settled into mild attention, suspicious of the apparently melodramatic trio before him. Hesitantly, he offered, "I specialized in brain trauma before I became Chief Surgeon at the Hospital." Digging deeply into his memories, I found that indeed, he had extensive experience in his past medical practice, even before he'd become affiliated with the hospital.

I prompted Garard. "Ask if he can be gone for several days."

At Garard's question, the doctor stalled. "Where, and what for?"

Garard went still, his face contorting slightly in his effort to communicate with me. The doctor pounced. "What are you doing?" His mistrust intensified. "Why are you asking this? What's going on?"

I sighed. "Bring them out to the back garden," I said to Garard.

The doctor cynical, the professor inquisitive, the woman content to be included in what appeared to be important, the three followed a grave Garard through the palace. I remained hidden behind Lillyon's illusion until they entered the garden and peered anxiously around.

"Are you sure you want to do this?" Lillyon eyed the humans warily.

"I can read their personalities. They're good people, the kind of humans we need to start with if we're going get don to open up to them." I rubbed against him as I walked out of the covering illusion, radiating confidence.

"Hello. I am Lillith," I broadcast. Garard grinned with relief and strode forward; Talmadge snatched at an astonished Marn's arm and pulled her excitedly after him; the doctor froze in place, his jaw dropped.

"I am the one who needs a specialist." Shock appeared on human faces making me laugh. "Not for me!" Bobbing my head in Dr. Grey's direction, I continued. "One of our people has suffered what our physicians say is a major concussion. They feel it is serious and would greatly appreciate your consultation on how to handle the patient."

Dr. Grey shut his mouth. The lines around his eyes crinkled and his mouth slowly curved into a broad grin. "A reeth!" He approached to stand next to Garard; all four ogled me.

"I understand, Dr. Grey, that you examined Raedon when he was in the coma, and that you are anxious to learn more."

Before the doctor could respond, Talmadge surged forward. "I want to learn too!"

I sent him a soothing. "Your chance will come, Professor Talmadge, soon I hope. And yours too, Soer Marn."

"Please, call me Stephon." Talmadge was bouncing on his toes. "How soon?"

"That I can't say. Right now, I urgently need the doctor." Turning my head toward Dr. Grey, I asked, "Can you come immediately?"

"I can be gone for two days only." Dr. Grey raised a hand to his chin and rubbed. He was relatively short for a human, and on the slim side. His grey streaked dark hair lent him an air of seriousness that I sensed was not part of his true character. Presently, he radiated the excitement of a young boy with a new toy, although not as animated as the professor who was glaring at him with envy. "I have to return to the hospital to pick up some different supplies. How will I get wherever you need me?"

"You can ride on my back." I heard Stephon growl in frustration and caught a quickly suppressed stab of jealousy from Garard. "You'll all have the experience soon, I promise." To Dr. Grey, I said, "I can meet you in Willow Park at the south end of Main Street, near the bridge. How soon can you be there?"

"One hour."

Dr. Grey hurried away and I said to Garard, "Thank you for such a quick response to my request. I will keep in touch with you. And Stephon, and Marn as well. But you must keep this story to yourselves."

**

Proving to be an excellent rider, Dr. Grey showed no nervousness whatsoever and maintained a constant flow of conversation. With Lillyon providing invisibility coverage, I landed at the Joe mansion front door feeling confident I'd done the right thing in bringing him. As he slid agilely off my side, I explained that, for security, I would erase from his memory anything he had seen during our flight. After a moment's alarm, he calmed himself and said he understood. "I like this man!" I said aside to Lillyon.

Nandon and Eledon were both in attendance on Joedon, who was, to my relief, sitting up, looking more alert. A quick scan revealed the massive headache had subsided, but he still felt nauseous and dizzy. Nor had his memory of the attack returned.

The don physicians eyeballed Dr. Grey as he bustled forward, hand outstretched. "Lillith's explained the problem. Which of you is Eledon?"

Eledon took Dr. Grey's hand and the man exclaimed, "Okay, black hair—Eledon, brown—Nandon. I'll remember." He shook the other don's hand, then swung toward Joedon, pulling an instrument out of his chest pocket. "And you are Joedon?" He stood still for a moment, examining Joedon carefully without touching him, then said, "Tell me what you've done so far."

The don unbent rapidly; the three doctors converged on Joedon and medical phrases flew between them. I met Joedon's eyes for a moment, sending him my confidence condensed in a summary of the human doctor's qualifications and experience. As he grimaced his thanks, I backed out of the room, leaving the doctors to their work.

Chapter 16

~ Lillith

Much relieved by my consultation with the doctors, I retired to my own chamber to rest and unwind. Lillyon brought Nana over from Eyrie to massage me into total relaxation. Knowing the fem would be happy to stay to visit her brother and his family, I allowed myself to fade into a deep sleep, confident Nana would be there when I woke.

I woke instantly to Lillyon's distressed call. "My cousin's youngest colt has disappeared in the far west mountains!"

"Disappeared?" I scrambled up and trotted toward the outside door. "How? Can't they sense him?"

"His mother says not. They've always had trouble keeping track of him; he's so inquisitive. She was listening to him ramble about an adventure. Then, he was gone." Lillyon was already far away, on his way to the canyon home of his favorite cousin.

"Where exactly are you?" I asked as I took to the air.

"Over Warren canyon."

"Stay there. I'll meet you." Ten minutes later, I saw him standing at the mouth of the gorge; he launched up to meet me. Together, we sped west while Lillyon passed on what little information he had.

We'd just passed the third mountain range west of Center when I detected outrage from Jaym. I flared my nostrils to catch Lillyon's attention. "Something is upsetting Jaym. I have to go." Flicking my ears forward, then clamping them back, I concentrated on the scene far away. Then, I swung sharply left, lashing my tail in fury. "Keep me posted," I shouted.

"Do you need my help?" Lillyon's voice wavered with indecision.

"No. Go help your cousin."

"Be careful, my love."

I hid myself in a palm grove just behind the cottage Jaym now lived in. A young grove, the trees stood only ten feet high with broad spreading leaves, and the thick underbrush, as yet unmown, concealed me well. Thankful I didn't have to expend energy on an invisibility shield, I blocked my mind from everyone but those in the cottage, trusting my ears to warn me of someone's approach.

Inside, the air whirled with conflicting emotions. Jaym was talking with Soer Marn and another woman. Although introduced by Marn as a friend, I read only massive ambition in the unknown's mind. Marn struggled to appear calm and relaxed while, in reality, she churned with doubt. And Cari, Jaym's former maid, was quietly agitated. Jaym's emotions flitted between accepting the unknown woman's false smile and seeming harmlessness, and something that made her hackles rise.

I focused on Jaym to sort out what was happening.

~ Jaym

The woman's eager eyes don't match her careful words. I'd listened politely and tried my best to treat her as Aunt Marn's friend, but… she's trying too hard to make me like her. When Marn and Cari both excused themselves to prepare tea and snacks, I steeled myself for something unpleasant. Then, with a flash of inspiration, I asked, "Do you happen to be a psychiatrist, Dr. Bothwell?"

The woman quickly suppressed her surprise. "Why do you ask?" I shivered at the sweet tone.

"Because that's what you seem like. Why are you here?" Despite my efforts to remain calm, I heard my voice rise as it always did when I was mad.

"Just to get to know you better, my dear," the doctor said with bland innocence.

I didn't believe her. "Why do you want to know me at all?"

The woman smiled again with her fake warmth and leaned toward me. "My dear Jaym, I am here to help you." I sank back, revolted as she tried to touch me. Undeterred, she continued in what she evidently supposed to be a soothing tone. "Your friends say you're quiet and withdrawn when others aren't around. And you refuse to talk about your ordeal. It must have been simply horrifying to be kidnapped and I understand why you're reluctant to discuss it. But, it's best to remember the misadventure, speak about it to someone with professional training, so you can get past it and move on."

What is she talking about?

I tried to clarify. "Dr. Bothwell, there's nothing terrible to talk about. I remember every moment of my kidnapping clearly." Delight filled me. "The experience fills me with joy every time I think about it."

The skeptical expression showed that Dr. Bothwell didn't believe me; I tried again. "Really. I'm not sad or depressed. I don't understand who could have told you such a thing." I paused, remembered the backward glance Marn had sent me, then got up and started toward the kitchen. "I'm sure it wasn't Marn. She's only been here once before today."

Dr. Bothwell jumped up, intending to head me off, to keep me in the living room. Maintaining the semblance of being a hostess, I stepped around the shorter woman instead of snarling at her and knocking her out of the way. Sweeping into the kitchen, I found the two I sought sitting at the table, tense and unhappy.

"What's going on?" I demanded. Shame flooded Cari's face and she started to cry. "Cari, what have you told this woman?" Marn flinched and I swung to confront her, scowling. "Or, is it what have you told Soer Marn?"

Marn pulled herself together and answered. "Cari said she was very worried about you. You didn't seem at all like the la ... girl she used to know in Pith and she's afraid you're unhappy, even though you always have a smile on your face."

Astonished, I allowed Marn to escort me to a chair at the table. Cari had curled up in her own chair and continued a muffled weeping. Dr. Bothwell took the fourth seat. "Now, Joys, tell

Jaym your theory, just as you told it to me," Marn said to the doctor.

Evidently, Dr. Bothwell decided to drop the pretense and spoke in crisp measured tones. "We know for a fact, Soer Jaym, that the don who kidnapped you was capable of manipulating minds. I believe he manipulated yours so you would think you enjoyed your kidnapping when you actually were raped, isolated, and treated with a degree of mental violence ..."

I killed my first impulse to leap across the table and knock the doctor out of her chair. Shaking with rage, I rose slowly and ordered the woman out of my house.

"Just listen, Soer Jaym. You don't know for sure what's in your—"

"Get out!" I screamed. I strode around the table at her, my eyes flashing and my breath coming hard. "Get out before I throw you out with my bare hands!"

She scrambled out of her chair, then stopped with hands raised to fend me off. "Really, Soer Jaym—"

As I reached for her shoulder, intending to spin her around and march her toward the door, she must have read my purpose in the wrath in my face. She dashed out the back door and, seconds later, I heard a car start, then peel away from the cottage; pebbles pinged against the front windows through the heavy vines crawling up the walls.

Incensed, I turned on Aunt Marn, and then on the one I'd considered my best friend, only to discover I was so outraged, I couldn't say a thing. I whirled and dashed into my room, slamming the door behind me. Throwing myself on my bed, I wailed.

An hour later, I woke feeling rather sick to my stomach. My head hurt from the crying; my body felt as if someone had beaten me. I concluded that someone had—emotionally. *How could a trained professional come up with such tripe?*

Thinking rationally was difficult. Maybe confronting Marn and Cari would help me understand what had prompted Dr.

Bothwell's ludicrous diagnosis. What if others thought I'd gone crazy, just because I was filled with joy here in the country? Then, my shoulders slumped and I dropped my head into my hands. *I'm not filled with joy; I'm lonely, even with Cari and all the locals who fill my days.*

"The doctor is right in a certain way," I muttered. "I have emotional baggage I haven't dealt with. Somehow, I have to live without them—Lillith, Lillyon, Joedon, the precious colt. They won't leave my dreams, but they aren't here in reality, either."

Running my fingers through my tangled mess of hair, I massaged my scalp to easy the headache. "It *would* help to talk about it, but with whom? Not Cari." I shook my head, a mistake as the throb intensified. "Not now. If she still harbors such fear, she won't listen to my longings with anything helpful to say." Marn? Maybe. "But will she understand my extreme feeling of loss?"

It came to me in a rush. Talmadge. His broadcasts about the Exchange had been truthful and revealing. And I'd eagerly absorbed whatever news the reporters dug up as they interviewed anyone with a tale to tell of don or reeth. While Professor Talmadge had shot to stardom, asked to rule on the believability of every don-reeth story uncovered, he'd remained humble and passionate about the two species.

I nodded my head in decision, opened the door prepared to confront Marn and Cari, and ran into a crowd in the sitting room. They'd been joined by Father and Garard. My personal guards, Turl and Seth, in uniform, stood propping up the wall next to the door, stiff as statues. My heart sank.

"I must look a fright," I blurted before anyone could utter a word. "Give me a minute to wash up." I dashed across the sitting room to the bathroom and shut the door. Nausea from my roller-coaster emotions threatened to choke me.

After I'd washed my face and pressed a cold, wet cloth to my eyes, I gazed in the mirror. No way to erase the red, the swelling. My mind roiled with the scene I'd just run through: Marn strained and tense; Garard and Father confused; Turl and Seth, frighteningly stern. Their crisp guard uniforms, in place of the civilian clothes I was used to, disconcerted me. They're armed!

I blinked as the realization hit me and sagged with a rush of relief. Leaning heavily on the small counter surrounding the sink, I grimaced at the strained face in the mirror. Of course. They're the only bodyguards permitted here. "They aren't here to arrest you, stupid," I said to that face. "They're here to guard Father." I'd never seen Father without a contingent of guards standing stiffly around. I laughed weakly, silently.

A moment later, I shook myself, ripped a brush through my unruly hair, arranged my face into serenity, red eyes and all, and left the bathroom to confront my father.

Cari curled into Marn on the couch and hid her face. The others contemplated me with worried eyes and the guards avoided my eyes. I took the seat they'd left me at what seemed the top of the group, my back to the guards, and smiled wanly.

"So. Why are you here?" I locked gazes with Father.

Glancing at Garard, as he often did for support, he cleared his throat, and said, "We're concerned. We thought Dr. Bothwell might have a clue as to why you're so unhappy."

Fury blazed for a second, but I clamped down on it. Controlling my voice so it wouldn't rise or squeak, I answered him directly. "Father, in no way am I unhappy here. Dr. Bothwell is an idiot—reading something into my situation that's ludicrous in the extreme. Is she perhaps anxious for an award or publicity?"

Father shrugged, his face creased in worry lines. "Not that we know of."

"Well, she's made up her own scenario that's far from the truth. Everything she believes has come from her imagination."

Garard leaned toward me, intense. "Are you sure?"

I shot him a contemptuous glare, which he really didn't deserve, but remained focused on Father—the one I truly had to convince. "Of course I am. Don't you remember what I said right after the Exchange? That I was crying because I had to leave them?"

Father hated controversy—it always made him uncomfortable. Now, he frowned unhappily. "Dr. Bothwell said Joedon controlled you even then. Made you say those things."

I sat back and stared from one to the other of my worried audience. "I have no idea exactly what I can do to convince you. Dr. Bothwell is completely making this up." Baffled, I asked Marn, "Tell me what Cari said that started this nonsense. Maybe then, I would know what to say to convince you."

Behind me, Turl choked. Then, he said, "Sir. May I speak?" I spun in my chair in surprise. Father must have nodded because Turl started talking. "Cari's been worried for weeks about you sitting outside alone on the patio, late at night, staring at the stars. She says you fall into long periods of silence, even during the daytime." His face stiff with torment, he turned his head toward the still weeping Cari, muffled against Marn's shoulder. "In the palace, you never went outside at night, she says. It's not natural for you to do it now." He paused, pulled himself up as tall as he could and rushed through the last. "Cari thinks Joedon is controlling you by planting notions in your head every night through your bracelet because she knows the stasis he used on Garard could only last a short time and that's why you sit outside at night by yourself." He stopped and shot a final, anguished glance at Cari. Then, "I told Soer Marn."

I felt those I loved had gone mad, and in my distress, I reached for the bracelet that never left my wrist. How could Cari have come up with such a notion? I saw it in their faces. Father, Garard, Aunt Marn, all thought it might be true. Sighing deeply, I look down at my hands, struggling to not curl them into fists and start pounding sense into my family. When I'd succeeded in forcing my face into a controlled calm, I raised my head and gazed deeply into Father's eyes.

"The doctor is a little, tiny bit right. I do think it would help if I could talk to someone about my experience." I jerked up a quick hand to stop him from speaking. "Not her!" I said firmly. "I want to talk to Professor Talmadge. I think he'll understand, and can help me convince you how wrong Dr. Bothwell is." Pausing, I forced myself to plead. "Please, father. Give me that opportunity before you consign me to the loony bin."

"Of course, Jaym." The relief in his voice was clear, but his smile didn't appear. "Garard, get him down here immediately."

"Yes, my Lord." He too seemed relieved; he relaxed back into his chair.

"Do you think Soer Marn could stay here for a day or two with Cari and I?"

Cari sat up quickly, tears still streaming. "You don't hate me?" Cari asked. "You aren't going to throw me out like you did the doctor?"

I think my tired smile convinced the woman even more than my words. "Of course not, Cari. You are my best friend. You may have a too active imagination, but I don't want to lose you over it." I stood and walked to Cari, holding out my hand. Cari took it and I pulled her up into her arms, giving her a tight, sincere hug. Holding her away again, my hands on my friend's shoulders, I continued. "I *am* going to convince you—along with everyone else." I swept my gaze over the others in the room—even Turl and the carved in stone Seth, still leaning against the outer wall as if part of it.

"I should have dealt with this earlier." I walked over to hug Father in his chair. "Don't worry any more, Father. Professor Talmadge will help me clear this up."

~ Lillith

I left the cottage confident Jaym had things under control for the moment and that Talmadge would serve her well. Since it was only early evening, I flew rapidly to the west to join the search for the missing baby. Pondering the thoughts Jaym had revealed, I searched for a way to help her. It surprised me that Jaym dreamed about us and missed us so profoundly. Should I soothe her dreams, make her night times strengthen her for the

Chapter 17
~ ?????

He woke, feeling sun beating down on his belly. His belly? His legs felt cramped, pains shot through his hips into his hocks. He twitched. Something rasped down his sides. His head and neck hurt. His under-developed wings felt as if something attempted to yank them off.

He kicked. His hind legs worked, with an increase in the now throbbing pain. His forelegs tingled. Trying to move them caused unbearable cramps in his shoulders. He held still.

Where was he? Gradually, he opened his eyes and attempted to look around. His head wouldn't move side to side. He curled his neck forward, then dropped back in despair. Wedged tightly, he lay upside down in a crevice so narrow the sides pressed into his shoulders, pinning his wings extended upward toward the sky.

He screamed aloud, and with his mind. Nothing answered. He screamed until exhaustion stopped him. Then, he whimpered.

**

Caleb sat on the rock ledge and ate lunch: egg, bread, water. He split the egg with the dog and added a bite of bread. His constant companion, the dog wagged his tail in thanks. Lunch finished, he glared at their charges, a ragged flock of sheep grazing scattered on the narrow steppe just below.

He was thoroughly sick of sheep. They were ugly, and timid. If it weren't for him and the dog, they'd never last a moment here on the mountainside. He stood up to stretch and the flock rushed away from him. A sharp whistle sent the dog to bring them back. After days and days watching this flock, he still couldn't move without startling them!

He hated sheep.

He turned and gazed at the peak behind. If he didn't have to tend sheep, he and the dog could wander freely. He wanted to see everything the mountains had to offer; there had to be green valleys, craggy peaks, and maybe caves to explore. These dry benches bored him. He wanted to climb higher, touch the snow, see what was on the other side of that peak.

The dog came back, bringing the sheep like always. Caleb smiled and reached down to pat, wishing he had another piece of bread to share. Six hours, by the sun, before he could take the sheep home and eat supper.

He glanced down in surprise as the dog nudged him urgently on the thigh. He looked up quickly and counted: all there. What did the dog want? When he dropped his hand, the dog took it into its mouth and pulled. He yielded and followed, climbing up and to the right, ever higher. Then, he heard it: a whimper. The dog led him to a crevice and what he saw made him scramble, seeking a branch to use as a lever. He found a dead tree and wrenched off a thick branch. Rushing back to the crevice, he dropped in at the head of the animal. His slim body fit with room to spare; not so the animal's.

Bending to listen, he felt breath on his face. Large, dark eyes sprang open and peered directly into his; pain and fear slammed into his head. He reached out and stroked the long white face in reassurance, then shoved the broad end of his branch under the creature's shoulders, using a square rock as his fulcrum.

He leaned on the other end of the branch and the front part of the body slowly rose. He felt its pain; rough sides of the crevice scraped long gashes into the velvety black hide. Blood seeped and he stopped, wondering if he should continue.

"Yes," he heard in his mind. Shock almost made him jump away but then he would drop the animal, possibly wedging it harder into the gap. An image accompanied the word prompting him to continue. His muscles strained. Bracing his feet on the side of the fracture behind him, he leaned his body weight onto the branch. The creature slowly rolled into a ball, then stopped. Caleb bounced on his lever and the body rolled a bit further. Its shoulders no longer crushed between rock walls, it struggled, kicking down with hind legs as if trying to rock its forelegs forward.

Caleb jammed his branch further under and suffered the pain as a knot dug into the animal's back. Again, he received an image begging him to continue; he labored harder.

All at once, the animal rolled the rest of the way over, its legs hanging down, its back to the sky. It struck out with forelegs and gained purchase on the edge of the crevice. Caleb leaped backward, away from the scrambling hind legs as the animal heaved itself up and out.

Wearily pulling himself out of the crevice, he expected to find the animal gone, but it lay on its side, lungs heaving, blood spurting from multiple wounds. He ripped off his shirt and ran to the nearby stream. He bathed the cuts and abrasions.

As he washed away blood, he worried; the animal's breathing didn't slow. Then, he noticed muscle spasms racing up the animal's shoulders, forcing the small wings to flutter erratically. He remembered when he'd pulled a muscle in his calf stepping crookedly on a rock, his mother had kneaded the leg until it relaxed. Not knowing if he was helping or aggravating, he began to rub the animal's shoulder with circular motions working down the leg. A thick knot of muscles flexed and rolled beneath his palms as an awareness of soothing caressed his mind. He glanced at the animal's head, saw the upward eye focused on him. He nodded and massaged harder. The eye closed; again he sensed relief.

A new image appeared in his head. The animal wanted to roll over. He gripped the bottom front hoof in one hand and the bottom back hoof in the other; the animal tucked its visible wing tight to its torso; and Caleb heaved upward. To his surprise, the critter rolled smoothly over, presenting its other side for bathing and massage.

Gradually, the heavy breathing calmed, the muscle spasms diminished, and the critter lay quiet, eyes closed. Caleb sat back, dropped his head onto bent knees and breathed deeply.

Later, Caleb squatted to survey his find: twice as tall as his biggest sheep, longer in body and leg, thin neck with a head seemingly too big to be supported easily. Its hide was covered with fine, soft black hair, more like the dog than a sheep.

Reaching out to stroke the tail, he found extremely long, course black hairs—longer than his arm. Similar long black hairs draped down from the crest of its neck. The four legs, black to the knee, then snowy white except where the blood still seeped, were three times as long as a sheep's but spindly looking. They ended in pointed solid hooves, half the size of his hand, with light and dark vertical streaks.

He tugged gently on a black wing, way too small to be of any use, feathers as soft as the goose down in his mattress. With torso thicker than a deer but more slender than his father's oxen, he wondered what it was and where it had come from to tumble so disastrously into the ravine.

Finally, he stretched out on his stomach, face almost touching the animal's head. Two small ears, black with white tips, twitched above a face as long as his forearm, white down the center, black outside the eyes, one on each side of the face. It couldn't see directly in front of itself, like a sheep. Soft nostrils flared as the critter breathed, more like the oxen. With those heavy round jawbones, skin tucked tightly along them, he wondered what the creature ate. Probably hay, grass, grain like the ox. He reached out to lift a flexible upper lip and the animal shifted, opened a warm brown eye with a tinge of blue in the center. Just as he thought: squared off teeth to cut grass.

He met the animal's gaze; warm, loving, grateful emotions suffused his brain. "Lilliod". Caleb didn't understand. An image of the animal he was facing formed in his mind, followed by the word "Lilliod". He repeated, using his mind, "Lilliod".

He placed his palm flat on the animal's broad forehead and thought again. "Lilliod." And sensed confirmation. The animal was a lilliod. Denial struck and he heard "reeth." Oh! The animal was a reeth whose name was Lilliod. Now he understood. He placed his palm flat to his own forehead and thought "Caleb".

The animal repeated, "Caleb" and nudged at him with its muzzle. He reached down to stroke the jaw and grinned. Lilliod could talk, in a way that Caleb could hear, clearer than he ever heard his family.

Caleb loved the dog. He loved all of the animals on the farm, even the sheep if he had to admit it. But Lilliod! He could hear Lilliod. He could talk to Lilliod. Using his mind instead of a voice he'd never had. His heart swelled.

For the first time in his life, he could have a friend, someone he could communicate easily with. He reached his hand out again and stroked the nicked, blood spattered neck, happier than he'd ever been.

**

Caleb and Lilliod soaked up the sunshine, nose to forehead, developing a language as the one Lilliod used, Caleb didn't understand. They spoke with emotions, images, sensations, and understood one another.

"Where are you from?"   "I don't know."

"Are there others like you?"   "I don't know."

"How did you fall in the ravine?"   "I don't know."

Caleb stopped asking as Lilliod's agitation increased with each question. He stood, stretched, then knelt at the reeth's back to massage hip muscles. He worked slowly down each leg, then rolled the reeth over as he'd done before, repeating his treatment for the other side. Lilliod enveloped him with waves of pleasure.

He examined the cuts; they'd stopped bleeding.

The dog appeared, touching Caleb's face with his nose. Then, to Caleb's surprise, he swiped a quick tongue down Lilliod's jaw. The dog sat down, barked once, and raced away.

"Time to go." Caleb formed the picture in his mind. Lilliod pushed himself up with his forelegs, flapping his wings to help with balance. He pulled his hind legs under, but couldn't force them to lift. Caleb nodded understanding and scooted over to place his shoulders, back to the reeth, against the hip, bracing his feet solidly against the small rise at the lip of the ravine. Together they took a deep breath: Lilliod strained, Caleb shoved, and the reeth stood, legs wobbling, but upright.

Following Lilliod's pictorial instructions, Caleb pulled on his tail, heard a slight pop. Then, he took the left hind hoof and pulled that leg forward, stretching it; supporting the hoof, he bent the leg up towards Lilliod's hip; then stretched it out to the back. Changing sides, he repeated the exercise with the right hind. Next, he picked up the right front hoof and stretched Lilliod's foreleg out, then back; repeated it with the other foreleg.

Lilliod stretched his head as far as he could, forward, then down, and instructed Caleb to place both hands on his crest, just behind his ears to pull with one, push with the other, massaging thick, ropey muscles down the neck to where it attached to his body. Finally, he asked the human to stretch each wing, forward, to the side, and then back.

As Caleb worked, he felt muscles tighten, then loosen, and gradually Lilliod was able to move each appendage on his own, the ache he felt echoing through his own body. Slowly, they started down the mountain to gather Caleb's sheep and head for home.

The sheep scattered at the sight of his companion. With a shrill whistle, he sent the dog to gather them and pushed them down to their night resting place, just above the farm, where they would be safe without his supervision overnight. Caleb's stomach rumbled, but he knew he couldn't take Lilliod home. His father, his brothers would do something to his wonderful friend. He trilled three times and the dog gathered the sheep in a tight little herd, holding them in a slight hollow while Caleb directed Lilliod to a copse of trees, one hillock over from the farmhouse—a place Lilliod could hide and Caleb could check on easily. With a trickle of water available, Lilliod declared the spot perfect and started to graze.

Stroking his hand down the soft black neck, Caleb promised to be back after nightfall, as soon as he could escape undetected. He hurried off to collect the sheep and finish the journey to their night pen: a high sided circular structure of slender poles tied together upright and staked periodically to the ground. Small predators that roamed this side of the mountains couldn't breach the pen and he felt confident that Lilliod, with his sharp hoofs and teeth, would be able to defend himself as well. He'd been moving fluidly by the time they'd reached the trees, sore but mending quickly.

At the farm, it was early to bed, early to rise. Caleb was back by Lilliod's side by ten, belly full, with a big old quilt for cover. He stretched his body along Lilliod's back, arranged the quilt over both of them, and they slept, human head cushioned against reeth neck, the dog curled up at the base of Caleb's spine.

Chapter 18

~ Lillith

Four days we searched to find no sign of the colt. I left the distraught family with a heavy heart. "I have to return to Center," I told Lillyon. "Dr. Grey has stayed two extra days, patiently, but he insists his hospital will begin searching for him if he doesn't show up today."

"I'll stay as long as they need me."

"Keep me posted."

When I arrived at the Joe mansion, I saw Joedon up and walking with Nandon on one side steadying him. The three of us made our way slowly to the bedroom where we found Dr. Grey and Eledon in deep conversation. Both stopped speaking at my entrance making me wonder what they were up to. Dr. Grey assured me that Joedon was on the mend, that he would get stronger, more sure of himself every day, and that his memory would gradually come back.

"How much longer?" I watched Joedon return to his bed and lay back, sighing with exhaustion.

"A couple of weeks at the most. He's an extremely healthy young m... whatever." Dr. Grey indicated the other don in the room with a waved arm: both doctors and their wives, Sara, Raedon, and Nana. "You all are. Wish I could study you to find your secrets. Humans need to be healthier."

Without responding to his hint, I spoke pointedly to the assembled don. "I would like some time alone with Joedon, please."

"Of course." Raedon ushered the rest out of the room. "We'll be in the parlor."

When I walked to the bed, Joedon opened his eyes and raised a hand to stroke my face. He lay receptive to my scrutiny; I probed for mental and physical states to reassure myself. "How have you been?"

"I'm much better. No more dizziness or nausea. Just so blasted weak!"

"What do you think of Dr. Grey?"

"I like him. He's a fine example of what's good about humans. He didn't say much more than either Eledon or Nandon, but he certainly helped their confidence." A quizzical gleam appeared in his expression. "They've been discussing the birth rate problem, you know."

"I thought they might. Confine three medical personnel in a house for four days, they're going to talk shop." I flicked an ear toward the front of the house. "What have they concluded, do you know?"

Joedon grinned for the first time and I cherished his returning sense of humor. "Dr. Grey is going to talk with a pair of researchers on staff at his hospital." He pointedly looked away from my face and dropped his voice. "If someone were to smuggle them to Eyrie, he believes they could set up a sufficient lab in my science room and teach our doctors and their wives how to search for an answer."

I eyed him lovingly. "And what does our Supreme Don think of such clandestine activities?"

"Our Supreme Don is being punished for a year, confined to Center, under close surveillance. Our Supreme Don won't know what's happening in his own home!"

We laughed together. "I take it your memory has come back?"

"Not completely. Nothing after I agreed to their absurd penalty. Dr. Grey says I may never recall the attack itself." He paused. "Quote. The closer the action is to the time concussion occurs, the less likely a subject is to remember. Unquote. The good Dr. Grey includes thoughts, emotions, and reactions in his definition of action."

I gave thanks for his good-humored words.

Then, his face changed expression, his mind dropped into seriousness. "Not a sign of the missing colt?"

147

"Not even a hair." Troubled, I looked away. "One would think if a predator got him, we'd have found some trace."

"I didn't think we had predators that could take on something his size. How old was he?" He winced at the past tense.

"Three, but excessively small for his age. Lillyon determined he was about the size of a typical yearling." I paused and evaluated him once more. "Everyone will be invited to the funeral. If you feel up to it, I think you should go."

"Of course. Why everyone? We don't usually attend a non-melded funeral."

"It's what Lillyon's cousin wants. I'm not sure why."

His grin was lopsided. "And you didn't ask?"

I threw my head up in a mock-huff. "Since you are getting so sassy, I'm leaving. Have to get Dr. Grey back to Pith before they send out search parties!"

On my way down the hall, I sent a query to Tallyon. "Any news?"

"Nothing," he replied. "We've no new leads."

"What are the thoughts of the council leaders?"

"Most are appalled." *They should be,* I thought as he continued. "Pildon and his supporters are silent on the subject."

"Well something may turn up in time. Have we successfully kept Dr. Grey's presence hidden?"

"Of course."

"Excellent. I'm taking him back to Pith shortly. Has Taldon talked with him?"

"Several times. His plan for Eyrie has our support."

The doctor came walking down the hall and I bid Tallyon farewell. Then, I asked Dr. Grey to place his hand on my withers and extended my invisibility illusion. Together we left the Joe mansion, he easily mounted, and I dropped off the cliff. During the two hour flight, our conversation ranged from views of the terrain to medical problems humans suffered. During his visit to Center, the doctor had become adept at telepathy. *An adaptable man*, I thought.

As he dismounted in the willow grove, he shot me a quizzical look. "Did you know Joedon allowed me to take blood and urine samples to study? As did the others I met."

"He didn't mention it." I rose to his challenge. "What do you plan to use them for?"

"Comparison. For my own curiosity." He tilted his head at me, his eyes gleaming with mischief and daring. "I don't think don are much different from us humans. The birthrate problem might easily be solved!"

My heart leapt into my throat as I considered his implication. "Please, let me know what you find."

His grin was triumphant. "Contact me in three days. And thank you very much for introducing me to your world."

I nodded. "The pleasure was mine."

Leaving him among the willows, I flew to Palmyra to check on Jaym, his insinuation heavy in my mind. Then, I put it aside to focus on the current problem. *It's been five days. Has Talmadge come yet?*

A battered, oversized vehicle parked in front of the cottage led me to probe the interior: Metz, Garard, Talmadge, the obnoxious doctor, even the two guards were inside. From the gist of their conversation, they'd only just arrived.

I heard Jaym welcome the professor and sensed her offering a hand. The professor covered his shock and shook her hand enthusiastically; he'd been prepared to bow to a princess. "It's very much my pleasure to meet you at last, Soer Jaym. Marn has told me so much about you I feel I know you already. Please, call me Stephon."

"My pleasure. I'm so happy to have you here. I've watched everything broadcast about you. It's been fascinating to learn all you've shared about don and reeth."

"Thank you for the kind words, Soer Jaym." The professor's elation was palatable. I settled in the palm grove to listen thinking, *I like this man more every time I'm around him.*

"Please, just call me Jaym. How did you come to know Marn?"

Marn answered. "We became acquainted as Stephon came to the palace to talk to Lord Metz. Your father kindly included me in the discussions."

Jaym easily noticed the affection between Stephon and Marn and speculated; "When did this happen?" I picked out of her thoughts. She didn't ask however, too intent on talking about don and reeth.

I pictured her leaning forward from the passion in her tone. "I've been dying to talk to someone about what I learned from Joedon and Lillith, but Cari refuses to listen. She insists on being afraid."

"Please," Stephon said. He was probably leaning forward too; his mind bubbled with excitement. "Tell me about your experiences and I'll ask questions as we go along."

Jaym explained everything Joedon had said and done while they escaped, none of it new to the professor except the mental blow to Cari. Off to one side, Dr. Bothwell sat smugly, as if Jaym's words confirmed her theories. The others listened with tangled emotions which I soon blocked out in order to concentrate better.

"He told me he didn't know how he did it," Jaym was saying. "He needed her quiet so he kind of hurled that thought at her and she fell down in a swoon."

Cari entered the conversation with a smoldering frustration. "And you don't want me to be afraid of him! He knocks me out without even touching me and I shouldn't be terrified?"

"He didn't mean to knock you out, Cari." Jaym's voice was taut with annoyance. "He just needed you to be quiet. And it didn't do any permanent harm, now did it?"

Cari subsided but didn't verbally agree. *She still has fear of us.*

150

While Jaym recounted what she could remember of Joedon's history between don, reeth, and humans, I focused on Stephon: open, interested, and completely unaware of other tensions in the room. *No one told him about Bothwell's theories. Just as well. His reactions will be more believable since he hasn't been prepared.*

Jaym became lost in the joy of her story. Having someone listen raptly as she recalled every moment, she unconsciously projected her feelings with her voice, her face, her whole body. Metz, Garard, and Marn were sucked into her delight; the doctor remained firmly closed-minded; Cari kept dredging up her fear to resist the effect of Jaym's cheerful narrative.

When Jaym described the message of hope she'd received as the reeth left, Dr. Bothwell surged with triumph and shouted, "I told you they were controlling her mind!"

My flash of fury broadcast for a second before I muffled it. Everyone inside gaped at the elated doctor as they suffered instant headaches and I feared humans for miles around might have been affected, too. I completely blocked my mind, projected my invisibility shield, and leapt out of my nook, flying hard and fast to the west, struggling to dissipate my rage at the doctor's arrogance.

After a half-hour of exhausting physical effort, I'd regained a calm and controlled mental state and returned to my position in the copse behind the cottage. The scene inside had changed. The two guards held the irate doctor. She didn't struggle, but her twisted, sinfully ambitious mind had been released from its earlier binding, open to my reading. *This woman is dangerous—and not only to Jaym.*

Stephon generated a whirlwind of turmoil; he must be striding around in the tiny room, unable to release his agitation among the bodies and furniture he had to avoid. I sensed his words, more than heard them. "Who the hell do you think you are ..." He exploded with wrath as he confronted the woman."... to come up with such an outrageous explanation from the bits of information these people gave you?" His words battered against an ego so filled with self-righteousness they simply bounced away.

I'm going to have to deal with it. She's too steeped in her opinion to listen. The thoughts of past treatments I read in the woman's mind almost made me ill. I pondered options for several minutes while the verbal and mental storm ranged inside. Then, I struck.

Reaching for, and receiving, an open feed from other reeth, I hurled enough focused mental energy at the cottage to force the occupants into unconsciousness. It only took a second. Then, I picked through each one's memories and erased all awareness of interactions with Dr. Bothwell, starting from when Marn first met with the megalomaniacal woman.

Recognizing that Cari had talked herself into her terror, I softened the fear and strengthened the woman's self-image and courage so she could work a solution out for herself. The others would settle down easily without Cari's panic to spur them on.

Then, I went to work on the doctor, made a small change here, and another tweak there. While I was implanting compassion and caring into Dr. Bothwell's mind, I heard the sound of my sister's arrival close by, bringing my favorite don employee. I sent him into the cottage and a few moments later, he returned with the insensate doctor slung over his shoulder.

I nodded my head in satisfaction. When the rest awoke, they would think they were in the middle of a pleasant visit. I directed Juldon to tie the doctor safely onto my back and mount behind to hold her still. Then, Lillity and I flew to Pith, invisibility screens projected.

Landing in a pleasant park, near the doctor's office, I had Juldon carefully arrange the limp woman on a bench so that when she woke, she wouldn't fall. As we left, I sent another mental shaft into the doctor's mind and felt her awakening slowly. Satisfied, I flew wearily toward Eyrie, listening passively to Lillity's description of the continued search for the missing colt.

Chapter 19

~ Lillith

I slept through the evening and on into the night. The next morning I found Lillity waiting for me in the Joe mansion parlor, more solemn than usual. I quirked an ear at my sister in inquiry.

"Lillith. Are you totally comfortable with what you did to that doctor?" My sister's mind tone expressed unease and I looked sharply at her.

"What are you worried about?" I loved and respected this golden younger sister. The mare was level-headed, although soft-spoken and usually stayed out of any sort of controversy. Her concern surprised me, but I had enough sisterly love not to pry directly.

Lillity dipped her head as if to soften the severity of her words. "The manipulation you did of the doctor's mind was beyond what reeth should do to other beings." Her head came up and she locked gazes with me. "I know you're more powerful than the rest of us, and you've been tasked with guiding the don onto a different path, but I'm not convinced you should make decisions on massive changes in any being's mind without consulting anyone."

I suppressed my first spurt of offense. Instead, I cocked my head and considered. She doesn't mean to censor me—she's asking for an explanation of my motives. Shielding my mind, I assessed. *Have I acted too hastily, too drastically, because it was Jaym involved?* No, I decided. The woman's ideas were dangerous on many levels: she'd displayed no compassion for her subject and saw Jaym simply as a means to a glorified future for herself. If not Jaym, then it would have been someone else. And in reviewing what I'd found in that twisted mind, Jaym hadn't been the first to catch her attention.

I played scenes from the doctor's memory into my sister's mind. The woman had tortured a man until he succumbed to her manipulation and acted the part she needed to advance herself among her peers at a conference. Then, she abandoned him to wander lost until he committed suicide. She'd planned the same type of treatment for Jaym. Before I was done, Lillity was shuddering, just as I was.

"The woman was insane to some degree," I said. "Rearranging her thoughts and attitudes was better than outright killing her."

Breaking eye contact, I started to walk in a circle in front of my sister. "If I'd had time, I might have done things differently, but she was forcing herself on Jaym. Her theories were starting to seem logical to the others since don haven't appeared since the Exchange. By claiming Joedon was continuing to manipulate Jaym, she concealed the web she was weaving. I never realized a human could be so devious." I stopped and glanced at Lillity, ears pointed rigidly forward, eyes wide, and tail slashing. "I'll watch individual humans more closely in the future."

I settled myself and forced my tail and ears to relax. "You're the only one who knows what I did." I regarded her solemnly, projecting warm thoughts and love. "Are you okay with keeping this between ourselves for now? I believe the doctor will prosper since I instilled compassion. We can check on her periodically; if things don't work out like I expect, we'll deal with it then."

Lillity considered and I didn't pry into her thoughts. "Yes, I can accept that," she said finally. "But you have to be more careful not to overstep."

~ Joedon

A funeral without a body is a terrible thing, I thought as I watched the swarm of reeth along the cliff ledge just below me form themselves into a tight herd, facing the sheer drop. I squeezed Sara's hand, standing on my left with Raedon. Others, spaced an arm's length apart to my right, hand in hand, lined the upper level. Reeth mourners ranked themselves by family, Lill at the fore of the solid block of bodies. I could see Lillith clearly in the front row, Lillyon at her side.

The silent herd dropped their heads in unison, noses touching the ground. I'd never seen the pose reeth took in grief: hips

154

rolled under with tails dragging, spines arched up, and necks dropped down. Each formed a perfect curve, so close together they resembled huge, furry balls stuffed into a tight framework. Lillith's terse instruction swept over us watchers: "bow your heads." Sara gripped my hand tighter and I heard her in-swept gasp. Thankful to be above the herd, I watched the incredible ceremony raptly.

An ominous moan swept up from the reeth mourners and rolled over the rise behind. *How did they make that sound?* It pulsed from over a hundred throats and battered against my hearing. The front line of heads came up and screamed, followed in a wave by row after row. Screams echoed back and forth along the canyon walls and I understood why they'd chosen this spot. I felt buffeted as if by a harsh wind. The screams rose and fell for ten full minutes.

Finally, the bunched reeth dropped their heads again, assuming the arched position, and the moan once more swept over us, followed by utter silence. I heard Lillith before the herd started breaking apart. "It's over. You can relax now." My muscles too tense for relaxation, I felt strung tight. Tears streamed down Sara's face; my own eyes welled and I blinked rapidly to stop them from spilling over. Exhaustion buckled my knees and I sat abruptly. A long time passed before I recovered from the emotional onslaught of the reeth dirge.

~ Lillith

"Lillith, I'm sorry to bother you, but, if you can get away, I think you should hear this."

"Maffair!" I hadn't heard his voice for years. A close friend of my grandfather's, his mind-mate led the older don faction in the Speaker's Council. "What's going on? Can you relay to me?"

"Do my best," he responded. "I'm outside Dogdon's home in Center. He called a meeting of friends and relatives, invited them to discuss the threat reeth made at the Speaker's Council meeting. I think he's gotten more than he bargained for. There's over sixty don inside, very few of them melded."

Not a flexible reeth, he seemed unable to imitate the tones he must be hearing through his mind-mate, making the conversations he reported hard to follow. He recited them verbatim with no inflection whatsoever.

"Twenty percent of don families have not one melded member and forty-six percent of individuals are un-melded. That's a lot." ... "Has it always been that way?" ... "Not according to the record book. Most don used to be melded." ... "Are some families not good enough for reeth?"

I gnashed my teeth. "I can't believe this. Like it's our fault!" I snapped. "Can you tell who's saying what?"

"Not really. I'm just sending what I hear." I felt his chagrin and sent a soothing, asking him to continue. *I'll get what I can out if it.*

His monotone started again. "How can reeth help us if we're not melded?" ... "What about the joy? Why don't they help me feel joy?" ... "If they're supposed to help us with happiness, they aren't doing their job." ... "That's the problem. They don't have a job. It's us that do the work—gathering all the feed for them." ... "No one makes you gather for the reeth. If you don't want to help, don't."

Maffair added his own comment, with pride, "That was my mind-mate. He's standing up to them!"

Again, the monotone. "Why *do* we help with fodder gathers?" ... "I think we need to confront them, tell them we won't have their interference in our decisions."

"Enough, Maffair." I struggled to contain my anger. "Can you ask Oredon to give you list of those present?"

"He's leaving now. Said he couldn't stand to listen anymore. I'll ask him and get back to you."

My sides heaving in fury, my eyes flashing red, I fumed for several minutes. A filly walking toward me veered sharply away, reminding me I stood among the funeral attendees. Breathing deeply and concentrating on getting my heart rate under control, I sought Joedon. He sat on the higher ridge, struggling with his own reaction to the ceremony. Slowly, I worked my way toward him.

"What has you so upset?" Joedon didn't get up as I joined him so I dropped my muzzle lightly onto the top of his head and explained the information I'd just received. "Not a reaction I'd anticipated."

Joedon glanced at the reeth clustered below. "What about non-melded reeth?"

"Lillolf said they want to contact humans. Families need help they aren't getting from don. And not just non-melded reeth families. Older don widows with reeth families to support have the same concerns."

"The Council's not going to like that."

"The Council may not have anything to say about it!" I lifted my head and gazed toward Center. "Tallyon, I just received disturbing news from Maffair—of a group of non-melded don. Can you get with him, see what you think?"

Chapter 20
~ Joedon

The funeral was over, no new information developed on the attack, and nothing but talk came from the non-meld meeting. I was sick of being house-bound.

"They won't even let me read," I fumed to Lillith. "I can't go out, I can't go back to Eyrie to my lab. I can't just sit here!"

"Maybe you could do a couple of hours a day at the illusion base." I felt like a young child begging for a treat as I flung her a hopeful glance. She asked Eledon's reeth-mate to send the physician over when he was available. That afternoon, after lunch, he appeared.

"I don't know." Eledon studied me carefully. "I guess, as long as you promise to quit as soon as you feel a headache coming on, or if you start feeling dizzy. You could supplement their efforts for a few hours. I don't want you carrying a full load yourself."

"Thank you, Eledon." I almost felt like hugging him. "I'm going stir-crazy in this house!"

He gazed slowly around at the elegant room and huge dining table covered with delicacies for me to enjoy and burst into laughter. "I should be so stir-crazy," he said. He held up a hand as I advanced on him. "No, no. I know what you mean. Just do as I say and you should be fine."

Over the next week, I spent two hours a day at the illusion center while Lillith monitored my energy level. The next week, with Eledon's approval, we traveled from one small village to another arranging for security around the three outlying communities: Sanctuary, Warren, and Enclave. The two oldsters at Labyrinth waved us and our offers of security help away. "We have reeth, old but experienced. We'll do just fine," they said.

"But Sara promised to bring Quodon here to fix my electricity," Ylsdon added. "And you need to examine Opudon's walls." He waved an arm toward the rock house across the small valley. "Something needs to be done before they cave in."

I studied the structure. From a distance, it didn't seem too bad, certainly not like others in the vicinity. The small settlement of Labyrinth, even older than Center, withered in stark decay. Only these two old ones held on.

Then, I looked over the valley. *Charming. Rushing stream, narrow meadow sloping gently to the creek bed, evergreen trees lining the far side.* There on Ylsdon's front deck, I saw the steep slope into the eastern gorge where the stream tumbled into the valley below. I couldn't see the old mine entrances, abandoned now, hidden amongst the trees along the cliffs.

Drawing in a deep breath of the crisp, pine scented air, I felt a profound sense of peace settle around me. *No wonder they don't want to leave.* "We'll be back in a couple of days," I promised.

**

Three days later, Sara, Raedon and I collected the don electrician and visited Labyrinth. Ylsdon solemnly showed us his electrical problems while our reeth followed his reeth-mate to a high mountain meadow to graze. Then, leaving Quodon behind to map out the system needed, our host took us to view Opudon's disintegrating house.

"You remember Regdon died several years ago, don't you?" I was examining a massive crack running up the south facing wall. "Without him, we don't have any good masons." I placed my hand on the widest part of the crack, a full palm width. "Even if we could come up with laborers, we don't know what to do to make these walls safe again. I don't know how to fix this. Do you?"

Opudon, looking miserable, shook his head.

Sara placed her hand on the old don's arm. "You and Ylsdon both have apartments in Center where you and your families could be more comfortable than here at Labyrinth." She smiled at Opudon's fym standing a few paces away, her thin face pinched with hope. "You could move back to Center while

Quodon investigates the electricity problem and we work out something for these walls."

"I would much prefer to return to Center." Lillith shared Opudon's reeth-mate's comment in a voice much deeper than her own. "Labyrinth is no longer comfortable for me; it's too cold at night."

Ylsdon's reeth-mate added, again via Lillith, "In Center, we have heated mats under our straw. It's much nicer sleeping there."

The old don sighed deeply and glanced at his fym. "I guess we could move to Center for a while."

She sent Sara a relieved expression, then hurried off to start packing before he changed his mind. "I'm just tired of living in this crumbling old place," I overheard her confide to Sara as they walked into the house, leaving us homm investigating more problems. "I'm so glad he spoke up. He always gets Opudon to do what he wants." She expressed no jealousy that the reeth had more influence with her hom than she.

After making me promise repairs would be investigated at last, Ylsdon decided to also move back to Center, temporarily. Lillith and I shared a triumphant moment. Mission accomplished!

**

A couple of days later, Lillith sent word that Quodon and the Royal Couple waited outside the camouflage center for me to finish my shift. "What are they doing here?" I asked.

"Quodon has a proposal, Sara says. They want to wait until you're here to tell us about it." She was moving away from the building. "I'll join the others in the park. Sara'll bring you when you get off."

When I walked out of the building, Sara was seated on the lowest step in front. "I've never liked this ugly, blocky building," she said as she took my arm. "It's all angles and squares, with nothing graceful about it at all. Well, I guess it was designed for working, not pleasure." She was right. Inside, four illusionists per shift kept Center hidden from human airplanes at all times, projecting an image of craggy peaks over the valley.

"I'm glad I'm one of the weakest projectionists," Sara murmured. "I couldn't stand spending day after day in that hideous building. What's worse, the image they project has to always be the same or humans would notice. I would go insane."

The work didn't bother me, but I agreed with her anyway as we wandered toward the park. Reeth heads popped up from munching grass; Raedon and Quodon stepped forward. "Tell him, Quodon," Sara said, face gleaming with mischief.

"Joedon, Lillith." Quodon seemed hesitant, standing with his feet spread and his hands clasped behind his back." *Looks like one of Metz' guards*, Lillith said to me.

The sandy-haired don in workman's coveralls took a deep breath and plunged in. "Since Sara wasn't able to get any don to show up for work on Ylsdon's wiring, I suggest I hire a couple of workers I know from Bonn. I could hire a helicopter to fly them to Labyrinth, and you could erase their memories afterward."

My eyebrows soared in surprise. "Humans?"

"Well, of course they're humans. But they're as trained as I am, have lots of experience, and we could be done in two days." Quodon's voice rang with confidence. "Nobody but us needs to know how we got it done."

I had to laugh. "You! To suggest something so outrageous!" Quodon blushed but didn't back down. I turned my attention to Sara. "What happened to the ones that said they would help?"

Her eyes flashed. "They won't come," she spat. She bobbed her head from side to side and whined. "They're all" - to the left - "too busy" - to the right - "to help" - back to the left. Her voice returned to normal. "Unidon's too busy making glass and Jonadon is having a luncheon she's preparing for; Zoedon and Veladon are helping Pildon plan a party; and Gepdon's spending the week in Warren with his in-laws. They're the ones who said they'd help." She glared indignantly at the rest of us.

161

"What have we come to, that going to luncheons and parties is more important than helping our elderly?" Then, she smiled and nodded at Quodon. "I think you have the solution."

The electrician relaxed. "Labyrinth is not obviously don. It's just like any small human community in the Melton Mountains. If my helpers can't see how they got there, and they don't meet any don or reeth while they're there, they'll never know whose house they worked on."

"You know these two you want to hire?" Lillith asked with no indication of disapproval.

He nodded. "I was in school with them and talked with them when I went back for refresher training." He radiated confidence. "Working with them, I'll have that wiring fixed in no time."

She chuckled. "Do it then." Swinging her head to look at me, she lifted her upper lip in a grin. "Someday, we might tell the council about it!" She followed the comment with a full reeth laugh, snorting so hard her wings wobbled along her sides.

Chapter 21

~ Lillith

I woke suddenly and pushed myself up on my forelegs. Shaking my head, I wondered what had woken me—a dream? A nightmare? No, a call. *Jaym needs me!*

"Lillyon!" I nudged him hard with my head. "Keep Joedon occupied today. I have to go see Jaym."

~ Jaym

I awoke feeling sick for the second morning in a row. I barely made it to the bathroom before I threw up.

"That's it. I'm calling Soer Marn for help. She'll know what to do." Cari left me in the bathroom, returning in a few minutes. "Marn promised to be here as quickly as she can. I'll make more tea."

I felt awful; I sat on the floor and moaned. My head ached. But yesterday afternoon, I'd felt fine. *What could possibly be wrong?* I vomited again. Then, it passed, again. I made my way to the kitchen, sank weakly into a chair, and drank the cup of tea Cari handed me.

We both heard the tapping on the back door and exchanged started glances. No one we knew came to the back door. Cari went to see who was there, leaving me staring into my tea.

~ Lillith

I read Cari's mind and stopped the girl from fainting when she opened the door. Surprisingly, the girl then stepped outside and closed the door behind her, facing me defiantly.

"Good morning, Cari. I am Lillith. May I see Jaym, please?" I kept my words soft and gentle.

"I can hear you," the girl exclaimed.

"Of course you can." My tone remained warm and soothing. "You love Jaym as much as I do so you'll always be able to hear me. May I come in?"

Cari scrunched her eyes to slits and leaned forward aggressively "You love Jaym?" Her disbelief rang clearly.

"Very much. And I want to help her, and you, of course." I bobbed my head gently, peaceably, and then stood perfectly still and waited.

"Why don't you call her yourself?" Cari pulled herself up tall and planted her fists on her hips belligerently. "I thought she could hear you too."

"She can, Cari, but right now her head is hurting so much she isn't listening. If you will take me to her, I'll make the headache and morning sickness go away."

Cari's jaw dropped. "Morning sickness?" She paused to consider. "Do you mean she could be pregnant?"

"Yes. I'm sure she is. The child called me."

"Wow! I'll get her. Wait here." She held out a hand, palm forward, as if to stop me from moving, then whirled toward the door.

"Of course, dear."

When Jaym appeared at the back door and saw me, she burst into tears and threw her arms around my shoulders. "Dear Jaym." I made sure Cari heard as I carefully encircled Jaym with my neck. "You've had a bad time, but I assure you, this will go away. He's already deciding he's comfortable where he is and will leave you alone now."

Jaym's muffled words came from a mouth pressed into a furry neck. "Who's he?"

"Joedon's child, growing in your womb. This is what I hoped for."

Jaym pulled back, bemused. "I'm carrying Joedon's child?"

"Yes. I can sense his emotions and he's happy, now. How do you feel?"

Jaym looked at her stomach and placed one hand on it. She reached up to touch her forehead with the other. Astonishment swept across her face. "Actually, I feel great."

164

"I knew you would as soon as he settled down. He just became self-aware. Now, everything will be easier."

"How can you hear him?" Jaym asked. At her side, Cari gradually relaxed from her initial fear. I shifted slightly toward her and the girl reached tentatively out to touch.

"You know I can communicate with all don," I said. "I'll be able to converse with your child when he's coherent. You'll be able to hear him, too."

Jaym dropped her other hand to cradle her stomach with a protective gesture. "But this child cannot be don. I'm not don."

"He is." My voice was firm.

Dazed, Jaym gazed vaguely around; Cari took her arm and conducted her to her favorite chair on the porch. Following them, I snagged Cari's panicked thought: *What am I going to do?*

Sending reassurances directly into the girl's mind, I answered. "Cari, everything will be just fine. Don babies are easy to carry and to birth. Soon, Jaym will begin to hear him and after that, everything will go smoothly."

Jaym broke Cari's bemusement. "But I'm not don."

I stroked Jaym's face with the tip of my right wing. "No, but it doesn't matter. I have it on the best of authorities that don are not much different from humans. They have developed atypically because of their long association with reeth. But as a species, don and human are identical."

I felt Jaym and Cari struggling with the concept; I continued stroking and talking. "Yes, they're taller, stronger, and have acquired some unique talents, but nothing humans couldn't develop if they would listen. In fact, although our stories don't support the theory, I think don are humans who arrived earlier in time and mutated through contact with reeth." I stopped stroking and stepped back. *I've given them enough to think about.*

I changed my tone along with the subject. "You'll be able to carry this baby and deliver him easily. He'll be the salvation of the don." My satisfaction with the results of my plan escaped with my words.

"I can't have a don baby!" Jaym's anxiety suddenly soared out of the calmness I had coaxed into her. "If word of this gets out, we'll be swamped by reporters. They'll want to lock me up, to test me and the baby. I'll never be free again!" The baby took umbrage at her turmoil; Jaym threw up all over the patio and herself.

"Calm yourself, Jaym," I said. "We won't let such a thing happen. Reeth will allow no one to bother you while you carry this child."

The gentle words eased Jaym's agitation and she sank back into the chair. "Yes, the feeling's stopped." With a beseeching look, she sent Cari running to collect water and towels. She strove to stay calm, carefully enunciating her words. "But Lillith, I said at Exchange I was no longer a virgin. Everyone heard me. When they learn I'm pregnant, they'll know the baby is Joedon's."

Again, I stroked Jaym's cheek as Cari poured water on the floor of the porch and began to clean. "I know that's what you said, dear. However, none of those people remember. Your stepmother thinks you were exiled and disowned because of your refusal to marry Lord Roark. Even your father believes he gave in to your pleading and allowed you to retire to the country." Cari stopped swabbing the floor and peered at me with awe. "Only four people know the truth. I've watched them closely and they've been silent on the matter of your virginity. Therefore, I haven't manipulated their memories."

I swung my head toward Cari. "Yes, you are one, of course, and Garard, Talmadge, Marn." After a glimpse of the hope on Jaym's face, she gentled her words. "No, I won't tell Joedon yet. Don are struggling with embracing the future instead of living the past. They *are* making progress. Announcing this pregnancy would upset the dynamics of change. Until the baby is born, and we know what his powers will be, we'll not inform any don of his existence."

I stroked Jaym's arm with my muzzle. "I know you want him to come to you, but he's quelled his feelings for you. He's deliberately focusing on problems to keep himself from thinking about what you meant to him that night. Now is not the time to let him know about the baby. He must not be forced into making a decision without recognizing how he feels."

Jaym paled and Cari grasped her shoulder, intending to object. I spread a raised wing, stopping Cari, as I continued. "It's hard, I know, but you have the strength to be patient. Believe me, Jaym. I know Joedon very well. I'm certain he'll recognize his love, eventually." Stepping away from them, I flicked my ears forward to listen. "Marn's almost here. They brought the helicopter. You must have scared her, Cari."

"I didn't mean to." Cari twisted damp towels in her hands. "But I insisted she come. I don't like to deal with sick people."

I felt her embarrassment when her words came out whiney. "No harm done. The helicopter has landed. I'm going to project my invisibility screen until everyone is gone except Marn. I'll be listening in."

~ Jaym

Lillith disappeared as a loud knock sounded at the front door. Cari glanced at me frantically and then I heard her run through the house. "Oh, Soer Marn!" she said loudly. "You're here so fast. I didn't mean for the rest of you to come."

Who is it? I wondered, jumping out of my chair and peeking through the back door. Garard, Turl, Seth! *What are they doing here?*

"Come in, Soer Marn," Cari said, her voice wobbling from horror to relief. "I'm sorry for my panicky call. Jaym's doing much better."

"Where is she?" Marn asked gently.

"She's on the patio getting some fresh air. She's still in her night gown so I must ask you gentlemen to stay outside until she's properly dressed." Cari hustled the three men back out the front door, took Marn's arm, and led her to me on the patio.

167

"Here's Soer Marn," she babbled. "Turl, Seth and even Garard are here. You must come in to get cleaned up. What should I do with them?"

I hugged Aunt Marn and said to Cari, "Let them into the living room and feed them cherry tarts or something. Marn and I will talk here for a bit and then come join you."

"But I told them you were still in your nightgown and needed to dress."

"Well, okay. Aunt Marn and I will go into my bedroom and I'll change. Then you can let them into the living room and feed them tarts." I pushed Cari gently before me and we reentered the house.

"Be calm, Cari," I heard Lillith say. I glanced at Marn—she hadn't heard. We disappeared into the bedroom as Cari drew in a deep breath to gather her composure. The door squeaked open and she invited the men in.

"What's gotten into Cari?" Marn asked. "She seems a nervous wreck. And you're blooming with health. What's going on?" Her worried frown deepened at my mischievous smile.

"We've had an interesting discovery this morning." I slipped out of my soiled gown and selected another. Pulling it over my head, I turned her back for Marn to zip it. "Indeed, I was very sick yesterday morning but felt fine the rest of the afternoon and evening. I woke up this morning, sick again." My eyes were twinkling as I grinned at Marn. "Does that mean anything to you?"

"Could you be pregnant?"

"I am. Lillith said you, Stephon, and Garard are the only ones she hasn't caused to forget how I got out of the marriage to Roark." I placed my hand on Marn's shoulder. "So, you should immediately realize I'm pregnant with Joedon's child. We found out after Cari called you so frantically this morning."

"Lillith said?" Marn studied my face with confusion. "I thought you had no contact with don or reeth since Exchange."

I settled on the bed and patted the spot next to me. "She arrived this morning. Evidently, she's been keeping an eye on me and she knew immediately when the baby became what she called self-aware." Marn sat, or rather collapsed onto the bed. I couldn't stop the elation vibrating through my words. "Lillith said *he* would give me trouble at first, then settle down as he realized he was comfortable. I'm still trying to come to terms with the idea. I suspect Cari's in shock."

Marn shook her head. "I'm lost. Lillith was here this morning?"

"She's still here. I think she wants to talk with you. I don't think she wants to talk to the men." I looked at the ceiling. "Is that right, Lillith?"

"Yes, Jaym." Marn gasped. "I would very much like to speak with Marn. This is not the time to involve the gentlemen."

Marn twitched, then followed my gaze. "Is she on the roof?" she whispered.

"No," Jaym whispered back. "I don't know where she is but she can speak to us from just about anywhere, I think."

They heard a chuckle. Then, "Do you think you can get the men to go back to Pith and leave Marn here for a few days?"

"We can try."

The men stood when Marn and I entered the living room; Cari had indeed served cherry tarts. I greeted them and told Garard I felt much better. "I think something at dinner disagreed with me and Cari panicked." Garard stared closely at me, but with Lillith's backing, I convinced him I was truly well now.

"I would feel better if Soer Marn stayed for a few days," Garard suggested. I'd felt the surge of suggestion Lillith had sent him and hid my grin. "I didn't realize Cari felt so uncomfortable dealing with sickness. Would either of you mind if she stayed?" He glanced from one to the other.

"I'd love to have her stay," I said quickly.

"I'd love to stay," said Marn, at the same time and we grinned at each other.

"All right." Garard gave in to the subtle pressure. "I'll have one of the men bring you back some extra clothes. I'm glad this was a false alarm." He started abruptly toward the door. "Turl, Seth. Let's get back to the palace." The guards each grabbed an extra handful of tarts and followed him out the door.

"That was easy," said Marn as she gazed after them.

"I believe many things are easy when Lillith is around." I led Marn toward the back door. "She seems to get what she wants. Isn't that right, Lillith?"

~ Lillith

"Most of the time." I projected to all three women. "Marn, it's important that you not talk to anyone about what you hear today, not even Stephon."

"Why not?" Marn bristled. "He can be trusted."

"I know, dear, but it's important that he hear the details from me so he understands the importance of this baby. I promise to tell him when next we meet." Marn relaxed and Jaym showed her to a chair, then sat herself. Cari, still uneasy with me, rocked from one foot to another for a moment, then finally sat down.

I launched into the subject of most interest. "Don babies begin to communicate around three months with their mothers. Unfortunately, it's a skill usually lost shortly after they're born, but it helps during birthing to keep baby and mother confident." I nodded to Jaym. "You'll not hear words but feel emotions from him throughout your pregnancy, ten months, not nine like humans." I turned to focus on Marn. "I'd like for you to stay with Jaym for that time."

"We'd have to find somewhere else to live." Jaym begged Marn for compliance with her eyes. "Cari and I don't really want to move, but we'd both feel better if you could stay and help."

"I have an idea," I slipped in, grateful for Jaym's mention of moving. "I know I'm an interfering being but I want the best for everyone. I really do" I cocked head and flicked an ear at Cari.

"I suggest Cari and Turl go ahead and get married. You could live in that nice farmhouse down the road."

Cari spluttered, "What?"

"You know that's what you both want. You're so worried about what you feel is your duty that you talk around it, and never get to the point. If you and Turl married, Marn and Jaym could continue to live here, you could come in to cook for them, and Turl could guard you all from outside interference."

Jaym laughed. "You really do like to control everyone, don't you Lillith?"

"Yes, I do," I said, joining her laughter. "However, I have the best intentions. I promise, if you three let me direct you for the next several months, your lives will be happier in the long run. Once this baby is born, then I might leave you alone to muddle about." I bent a knee and bowed at the three women staring at me. "This is what reeth do: we insure the happiness of those around us. It's our power and our joy."

Cari remained strangely silent. Then, to everyone's alarm, she burst into tears, sobs breaking from her as she curled herself into a ball on her chair.

"She's worried everyone thinks Turl is her cousin." I approached the sobbing woman and touched her softly with her muzzle. "Cari, dear, I can handle that. I can change everyone's perception of Turl, if it bothers you so."

Cari stared with tear-filled eyes. "What do you mean?"

"I've removed memories of how Jaym got out of the marriage with Roark. I can do the same with the locals' memories of Turl."

"Oh! You'd do that for me?"

"Yes, Cari. You're important to us all." I stepped back and stretched out a wingtip, placing it on Cari's shoulder. "You need to continue to take good care of Jaym, and eventually, her son."

I felt Marn's ire rising and swung to face her. "If Cari can marry Turl, why can't I marry Stephon?" the woman demanded.

I nodded, acknowledging Marn's distress. "Because Stephon is famous, not likely to be left alone down here. Someone would stumble onto Jaym's pregnancy if he lived in this area as he plans. And right now, Jaym needs you as much as Cari." I paused, read Marn's stubbornness, and curled my upper lip, baring my teeth in my version of an evil grin. "I could wipe out Stephon's fame, but I don't think he'd be happy, do you? He can wait."

Marn paled at the thought of Stephon losing the recognition he richly deserved and reveled in. "No, I don't want that."

Cari's face went red; the tears had stopped but her eyes grew wide. "Turl hasn't proposed!"

The rest of us laughed; Cari glared at the others, then swung toward me, all signs of her earlier fear gone. "And Lillith, you can't make him propose." She shook a finger in my face. "I'd never believe in him if you did that!" Her eyes, still wet, flashed sparks. "Don't you dare make him do it!"

I stepped back and suppressed my mirth. "No, no, Cari. I promise I won't. We'll just see what happens in the next little while."

Chapter 22
~ Lillith

After leaving the cottage, I decided to swing by Pith hospital to consult with Dr. Grey. Saradon had been bothering me about the research he'd talked about and now, I had news to share. Invisibly hovering over the hospital, I probed for his mental flavor. To my relief, he was doggedly reviewing reports instead of intensely involved in a medical emergency. He tossed his papers aside, hurried down to the front door, and caught a taxi. Ten minutes later, he met me in the willow grove.

"Lillith! I wondered when you would call." Dressed in a white lab coat, his tie askew, he reeked of medical chemicals.

Ignoring the odor, I extended my head to touch his out-stretched hand. "Dr. Grey. I have great news. You were right!"

He looked puzzled. "About what?"

I grinned, my upper lip raised to show my teeth. "Don can reproduce with humans!" His eyebrows shot up as I continued. "Lord Metz' eldest daughter is pregnant with Joedon's son. I'm sure you've heard the story of the kidnapping and exchange."

"Of course. I had no idea that might be a consequence. How's Joedon taking it?"

I shook my head. "He doesn't know yet, and you can't let any of the others know either until I'm in a position to spread the word safely." I felt his agreement and appreciated his quick understanding of the problems this pregnancy could cause. *He spent his time in Center wisely, learning much of our world,* I thought. "I'm going to need a human obstetrician, and a pediatrician, I guess."

"It just so happens that my twin sister is head of Obstetrics. And we have a number of excellent pediatricians."

"Good. I'll leave that worry in your capable hands." I felt his pleasure at my words, then changed the subject. "Now, I need to know about your researchers."

"I've spoken to them about the project and they're in. One is absolutely brilliant, but absent minded. I'm not sure he listened thoroughly. His partner, although not quite as astute, keeps him on track and focused. I think it would be best for Nandon and Eledon to meet them in the hospital before we make arrangements to send them and their teams to Eyrie."

"Two days time sufficient?"

"Yes. Ten o'clock, my office?"

"I'll have them there."

**

Next stop, Memmiard. I found the master story teller and official reeth historian standing in a small meadow above the home he shared with his mare, meditating and enjoying the sunshine. The ancient bay was graying along his topline and hips. His formerly chunky body had begun shrinking, leaving loose pouches of skin behind his shoulders and below his hips. I wondered exactly how old he was.

His voice, as he shared the history, showed no sign of age and listening to him, I pictured a much younger reeth. "Don stories portray us as suffering at the hands of humans," he said bluntly. "What really happened is our ancestors were badly frightened. They'd never before encountered a species that tried to capture them. It was the nets, specifically, that terrified them." His tone rose with anger, as if he couldn't help adding the emotions he constantly used in his presentations. "Humans tied ropes around feet and necks and locked individuals into tiny stalls." He nodded and dropped his voice back to normal. "But if injuries happened, humans treated their prisoners just as they would valuable horses. My grandfather said his friends purposefully planted horror stories in don minds because they were so afraid at the time."

"I thought humans killed some reeth," I said. "Pildon's using the play Conquest of Bonn to scare his guests."

Memmiard snorted and stamped a foot. "And who wrote that play? Not a reeth. Not even a melded don."

He wasn't large, but he projected a large presence as he moved grandly with each shift of his body. I decided his mannerisms were a result of his century and a half of storytelling. "A human hunting party accidentally killed one reeth," he said. "But the oldsters knew that reeth simply appeared in the wrong place at the wrong time. According to my grandfather, no humans injured a reeth on purpose." He developed an overtone of anger. "They tried to use reeth captives to control don and they threatened our relationships with their ignorance. When those captured were freed, our ancestors withdrew, believing it simpler than trying to get humans to understand."

I twitched my ears in puzzlement. "So you're saying that at the time, our ancestors felt anger and fear. But I don't feel that way now!"

"Of course not. Recorders stopped telling those stories long ago. Think about it. Have you ever heard one of our story tellers talking about humans? It's don who keep such stories alive. We know our powers and our strengths. We know what to avoid in dealing with them."

"So..." I projected mental persuasion. "Will you and the other recorders help us spread a favorable view of humans? Will you incorporate good stories into your presentations?"

He shrugged, an exaggerated movement causing his wings to rise and fall. "I don't know any good stories about humans."

"Oh. That's a problem." My head sank. "Could you at least start telling what really happened back then to counteract Pildon's scare tactics? You reach so many with your stories, and in such a different way than I do."

"I already have, at Lillolf's request. Join us at the Memm family reunion and you'll hear. And see."

**

Two days later, Lillyon and I, and others of their friends and supporters, stood on the top level of a valley with a natural amphitheater, exactly the venue Memmiard loved best for his performances. Unlike many recorders, the Master used not only changing tones of his mental voice during his tellings, but also his head, wings, hooves, and sometimes even his whole body. I had always heard that to thoroughly enjoy one of his presentations, you had to both see and hear him.

Memm family members spaced themselves up the hillside, shifting so everyone could see well. Raedon and Joedon had helped prepare the area, placing a twelve-foot square, low wooden platform on the ground at Memmiard's request. They were not allowed to stay for the presentation, however, as the Master only presented for reeth.

To my shock, Memmiard opened the scene by projecting an image of two humans moving through underbrush, a huge net hanging from one man's hand. He murmured in two tones, not clear enough to be heard. I realized he portrayed humans conversing as they slunk forward.

The words stopped and I saw the net fly through the air. Memmiard fell, wings pinned tightly to his sides. He threw his head, screaming in fear, and thrashed around on the ground. With a mighty bulge of muscles, he lunged upright, keeping his wings pinned, and stomped his feet, moving around the meadow in tight circles, fighting an imaginary net.

I shuddered. The story-teller's contortions were so real, I thought I felt the net cutting into my wings. Then, Memmiard stopped fighting and hung his head, his body sagging in exhaustion. I stepped closer to Lillyon as I heard the hoarse, desperate words. "What do you want with me?" His voice trembled with despair.

Again, a human spoke. "What was that? Did you hear that?" A third voice said, "Hear what? I didn't hear anything."

The first human's words rang clear. "I just heard someone talking to me."

"You're imagining things. Let's get this beast home. He'll make a good hostage."

Such a harsh word, calling a reeth a beast. I recoiled as one human fling a rope and Memmiard jerked, as if the rope choked. My throat constricted in sympathy.

Memmiard stalked forward, his head and neck stretched as far ahead as possible. He resisted the invisible pull with every step, his wings still pinned to his sides. Stopping in front of the audience, he shook his head as the imaginary rope was removed, and weakly fluttered his wings with the removal of the net. He stood still, then ate and drank. He portrayed a conversation between the two humans as they spoke of feed and water. He flinched; his audience saw humans smear a stinging salve on his rope burns. He pulled his wing away, feathers bent at an odd angle, as humans examined torn feathers. I succumbed to his growing fear; he stood locked in a small high sided wooden box.

It was a story. I knew that. But I'd never seen Memmiard perform and was unprepared for how real it would feel.

In his visuals and actions, humans cared for their captive, examining his hooves for damage, grooming him, feeding him treats, all the while ignoring his attempts to communicate. I lived it in my imagination, couldn't force myself to look away.

Then, the Master changed the scene; he reared and struck at imaginary walls. He pounded hooves on the wooden platform; wood splintering echoed around the valley. He rushed through a visualized door and flew away, free, ecstatic. I swear I felt the air moving by me and heard humans shouting as they were left far behind.

Landing once more in front of his audience, Memmiard drooped with exhaustion; his wings drug the ground; his legs quivered. He told his imaginary don-mate of his capture and escape, two distinct voices, Memmiard's deep bass, the other a mild baritone. Fear and anger swept through me at the forced separation. I understood the panic planted in don minds.

Memmiard ended by walking away, his imaginary don at his side. The story had been told, as promised. I sagged against Lillyon; he gave unsteadily. Gradually, I became aware of him moving beside me, propping me up, encouraging me to stand on my own. Turning my head, I saw that, although he wasn't as drained as me, he too had been greatly moved. "I had no idea it would be like that," I whispered, surprised at my weakness.

Chapter 23

~ Joedon

Lillith went to Eyrie to check on the human research team that had moved into our home there leaving me sprawled in a brocade chair in the front parlor brooding about my situation. She sent pictures of computers and research stations set up in my lab with word that the equipment I'd left behind having been stored in one of her back rooms. "Hope they didn't damage anything when they moved," I said nastily.

"They're quite professional looking," Lillith sent back in a tone meant to chide. "They seem to have what they need for now." Her swinging head showed Nandon and Eledon absorbed in learning to use the new machines that completely filled the space. She felt encouraged about the medical aspect of our future; I had to agree.

Although I'd finally decided to take my place in the Speaker's Council, I couldn't help but wonder if the Speakers would follow me after my absence of fifteen years. Especially if word leaked about the research going on at Eyrie with my approval. "I think I'd better start building support, calling in favors, if I have any." Jubilation flared from her and I sighed. "I know. You've been after me for years to do something. Well, now I'm ready."

"Make a list of who you know will support you," Lillith suggested, her mind whirling with names. "Then, we'll plan a campaign to gather in the rest."

"Raedon, of course. And Sara although she can't vote. Her father."

"I'll call them to meet us this afternoon. We'll go from there."

**

We decided to start with the younger generation and jointly hosted a party several weeks later. The draw of the mansion itself—many had never seen the inside—along with plenty of food and drink, brought well-dressed young don and their reeth-mates crowding into the Joe public rooms. Conversations flowed freely. Lillith and I drifted through the guests with the express plan of introducing fun topics of human-don interaction. We found our job simple as almost everyone had a story to share.

Eledon and Nandon told of a fall festival in Real. "That's when the Realians celebrate the harvest," said Nandon, an unusual twinkle in his eye. "They have tests of skill and crazy mechanical rides."

"We danced and danced," added Eledon, grinning at those surrounding him. "They have this dance called the polka. It's wild and fast, not at all like our dances. Lots of stomping of feet. Everyone in the crowd claps. Lots of noise. Lots of fun. Even the old humans get rowdy." He put his glass down on the table, grabbed his fym around the waist, and swung her in a fast step.

"Especially when everyone's drunk," Nandon added as he snatched his fym's hand and joined the other couple in a fast spin around the room. Both couples stopped, breathless and laughing with those watching their antics.

"Remember that fat old woman with the striped dress? She had to be as broad as Memmyon." Eledon flung his arms out wide; his reeth-mate supplied pictures as he described the scene. "She wore this purple and white striped dress with a huge, hooped skirt. When she swung around, she about knocked the bystanders over. We laughed until we were sick. She finally fell in a heap and lay there chuckling at us."

I gaped at the pair, mesmerized. "What?" Eledon flipped me a saucy look. "We weren't always sober physicians!"

Another young don, non-melded, waved his glass for attention. "We went to ride the roller coaster at Neff Casino, once. You know, we can get the same experience flying with reeth. Humans are crazy to trust themselves to a mechanical contraption that can't even catch you if you fall."

"Or stop if you get sick," put in his brother.

"Or might break," added Raedon. "Joedon and I did that once, too. Don't want to do it again." Neither did I.

One of the young bachelors said, into the pause of agreement, "I was in Gild once in the winter when they were celebrating some religious holiday. The entire month centered on using as much electricity as possible to light up the city buildings, the homes, even decorations out in the yards." Enthusiasm bubbled out of his round face. "Humans evidently have a firm grasp of electricity. I bet they could fix Ylsdon's electrical problems in no time."

Quodon, standing to one side of the group, froze. I stepped in quickly to cover the don's reaction. "Great idea! We could learn more about electricity from humans I'm sure." I wrapped my arm around Quodon's shoulders. "You know Quodon studied in Hilt, don't you?" Murmurs of agreement passed around.

"Speaking of Neff Casino," Raedon said loudly. "That's a mighty beautiful building." He paused to glance at me before continuing. "Humans are good at buildings. I'll bet they could easily repair Opudon's tumbling walls." Some shocked stares met his statement, so he changed the subject to playing football.

"Good one," I mumbled to Raedon later. "You planted the seed! Let's hope it grows."

Throughout the evening, homm shared stories of their adventures among humans. Lillith saw that many a fym learned, for the first time, what her hom had done in his earlier years. Raedon and I, with reeth-mate aid, worked at keeping the stories funny and lighthearted, involving all our guests, some of whom were non-melded. And although Lillith could not influence any non-melded don, she could follow their emotions to keep us informed of those we should draw into the fun.

Sara drifted around, helping as best she could, but I sensed her feeling out of sorts. "There must be something more I can do to help," she muttered when I brought her a glass of Lareina.

Toward midnight, I called for everyone's attention. Perching one hip on the corner of the buffet table, I waited as don and reeth gathered round and grew quiet. "I wanted you to know that at the next council meeting, I'm going to take over as the

Supreme Don." Several of our guests drew in sharp breaths. "I know there will be opposition."

Raedon snorted. Eyes turned toward him and he shrugged. "Everyone knows how I feel about Pildon."

"Precisely." I smiled tightly. "I'm asking for your support although many of you aren't Speakers for your families. We're hoping you'll put in a good word with your Speaker for me." I paused and gazed at the earnest faces, femm and homm both. "When I am again in power, I intend to push for contact with humans to help us solve many of our problems. We heard stories of electricity and buildings, fun and frolic. We didn't hear tales of problems with them, because there are none."

Raedon pushed away from the wall he leaned against. "We ask you to think our plan over and let either me, Joedon, or Sara know your thoughts sometime over the next month."

"And if you have questions, I'll be glad to provide what answers I can." I rose to stand shoulder to shoulder with Raedon and Sara.

"How does Taldon stand on this?" asked one.

"He supports me. He's tired of fighting with strong minded don all wanting their own way."

"And you want to face that?" The voice crackled with laughter.

I grinned. "I know. I guess I'm as crazy as my father was!"

**

The next morning, Lillith heard via reeth chatter that Pildon had entertained a number of older, more politically active couples with a game of charades. The guests, naturally theatrical in nature, participated avidly in the competition, acting out the names of books and plays that Pildon supplied: titles like Murder in the Glade, Ropes and Chains, Withdrawal, First Encounters, Defending Reeth, and Victims. No one at the party commented on the theme of the secret phrases.

"He specifically excluded reeth-mates," she told me. "Big Mistake. Memmiard's stories should counteract his scheme."

Lillith kept close contact with Memmyon and Sissith as we planned our next move and a few days later, the bay mare replayed a scene for us in which Sara and her mother sat in the garden room sipping tea and eating the tiny cakes Suridon's famous cook had served. As Sara reached for her third pastry, she stopped in the middle of her sentence and stared at it. "I've just had the most marvelous idea," she said, beaming at her mother. Suri's puzzled frown prompted an explanation. "Do you remember grandmother's monthly formal teas? We need to reinstitute that tradition."

"Why, dear? It would be a lot of work, you know."

"Yes, but I want to do something to help change don opinions toward supporting Joedon and working with humans. Tea parties would give us an excellent opening."

Suri set down her tea cup, placed both hands on the table, and stared at them. Her fingers were trembling.

"What's wrong, Mother?"

Tears welled in the older fem's eyes. "I'm afraid. What if they do try to enslave us?"

It had never occurred to Lillith or me that Suridon might be afraid of humans. Her husband, Saradon's father, was in full support of our plan.

It obviously hadn't occurred to Sara either. She scooted around to hug her mother. "That won't happen. Raedon and Joedon have been among humans a lot. Please believe me, Mother. They know what they're doing."

"Why are you so sure?" My heart ached at the anxiety in my pseudo-aunt's tone.

Sara struggled to say something that would ease her mother's concern. Taking both of Suri's hands, she squeezed gently. "I guess I'm not sure. But we have to do something. You saw how few are left." She paused. "When the council talked about me rescuing the don through my children, I laughed. I thought it was a supremely stupid thing to say. There's no way a single

183

fem can restart the species. And I might not even get pregnant!"

She peered seriously into her mother's strained face. "The doctors and their fymm are convinced humans can help with the birthrate problem. With many fymm having children, we can save our world. We have no choice but to try."

Suri's tentative smile appeared. "My lovely daughter—full of courage. You will help change our world. With you as my support, I'll do what I can to help."

After sending a congratulatory message to Sara, Lillith thanked Sissith for reporting the scene to us. When I next saw Saradon, she regaled me with her tea-party plan. I thought mobilizing the femm to influence their Speaker husbands and fathers was a brilliant notion. Not to mention her efforts would go a long way toward allaying fears in the feminine part of our culture.

~ Lillith

A week later, Raedon and Joedon went off visiting influential Speakers while their fymm enjoyed tea and cake in the Sar mansion for the first time in over thirty years. Sissith and I monitored the scene through Sara. She leaned against a wall watching, teacup in hand, as young Wynnadon, Weedon's daughter from Delt, fascinated the femm gathered in her mother's parlor. There had not been a young female child at Center for many years and Wynn commanded their attention.

"Papa takes all of us kids with him into the human world, not all at once of course, but one at a time. He says we need to move comfortably among humans without attracting attention. He's been teaching me to disguise myself since I was a baby," said the precocious four year old.

"I thought only some could project images to humans," one fem said. "I can't. Do you mean your father taught you how?"

A merry laugh trilled. "Oh, no. We disguise ourselves physically. Papa says if we move and act like humans, and dress like humans, we blend in quite well." The scamp peered around at the femm seated on all sides. "You all wear body suits and draperies. Well, I wear a skirt and blouse, or trousers, when I go with papa. I wear boots and Mama rolls my hair into a bun. I have to practice not being graceful. Humans are *not* graceful, you know."

She pantomimed her version of human women, walking in heels. Her scrunched, intent face broke into a grin when the femm laughed.

"I often play with two human girls, Sissy and Claire. They're eight and nine years old and don't know I'm only four. I'm just as tall and I'm much smarter, too. We play lots of human games. My favorite uses ten little metal pieces shaped like stars that we throw on the cement. Then, we bounce a ball and try to pick them up and catch the ball. It's called jacks. I'd show you if I could, but I didn't think to bring any." Still, she went through the motions, pretending the jacks were on the floor and she held a small ball.

From her crouch, her eyes gleamed mischief. "I have to be careful to lose sometimes. That's what Papa says is learning to blend in. He says by the time I'm an adult, they won't notice I'm quicker than they are."

"What a concept. Blend in with humans." One of the femm wrinkled her forehead. "I would never have thought to do that."

"I'd not want to do that," the older fem with her shuddered. Neither Sissith nor I knew the femm sitting around the parlor although Sara surely did. She didn't fill us in with names as we watched—not that it mattered. We'd dissect the conversation when it was all over.

Wynn's mother—whom I did recognize—responded to the shudder. "It's a skill that can be learned and it helps us work with them. Weedon, his brother, the boys and cousins all work with humans during the harvest and in the wine presses. No human even notices they're different. It helps us get things done."

"Get things done," someone murmured into the silence.

Wynn bounced on her toes and re-claimed the attention. "Of course, I'm much prettier than Claire and Sissy. There are beautiful human women Papa says so it doesn't matter if I'm beautiful." She posed, her head tilted back, hand on her hair, a wide smile on her face. "Claire and Sissy will get used to it."

She dropped the pose and waved her hand around. "Papa says you all are too radiant, that's a word he really likes, to go among humans but you don't have to be. Humans have stuff—they call it makeup—that you could put on your face to dull the skin." She simpered, batting her eyelashes with exaggeration. "They think it makes them more beautiful." Her expression changed to a sneer. "I think it makes them look sick. If you wanted to use some of their makeup, you could make yourself appear very human. Claire's mother thinks she's gorgeous and she wears lots of makeup. It stops on her chin though and her neck is still old and ugly."

It was almost as if someone had primed the girl to present comical, and utterly safe, images of humans to her audience. I hadn't thought to do it. Sissith denied that she had. Evidently, the child really liked her human playmates and never felt a moment's fear around even their parents. She was very effectively doing our work for us.

Wynn grinned mischievously, slanted a smirk toward her mother, eyes twinkling with glee. "One time, Claire took some of her mother's make up and we put it on each other, me and Claire and Sissy. We looked dead when we looked in the mirror!" Her grin widened as the femm laughed again.

"She's a perfect ambassador," Sara passed on to us eavesdroppers. Leaving her guests in the capable clutches of the entertaining Wynn, she made her way to the guest bathroom where she discovered her good friend Cheradon sobbing on a green velvet settee. She hurried forward. "What's the matter? Have you hurt yourself?"

As Sara wrapped her friend in her arms, the blonde gasped and hiccuped in a struggle to pull her raging emotions into control. "It's so unfair! My brother has his son and that imp Wynn is so precious. I want a baby so badly. Twenty years we've tried. It's just not fair, and now I'm too old," Chera wailed.

I'd heard this story before, from Sara. The two sisters-in-law who didn't speak for lack of a child on one side.

Sara sent a call to Sissith for help. She left my side and called a powerful reeth soother to join her in the house. Before long, the soother had helped Chera contain her whirling despair. "You're not too old," Sara soothed. "The doctors will find a solution." She asked me for permission, which I gave, swore her friend to secrecy, and explained what the physicians were working on in Eyrie.

"You think they'll find something?" the blonde asked. The hope in her mind made me more determined than ever to insure the researchers had everything they needed to succeed for our femm.

Sara actually winced at the yearning in her friend's face and unconsciously echoed my vow. "We're going to work on it as hard as we can," she promised. "If you want to help, I'll ask Lillith if I can take you there. Then, you have to help me get these femm to support Joedon and his efforts. We have to steer the Council in his favor!"

**

Over the summer, Sara and Chera shared hosting other young femm in their homes for discussion groups about things they read about humans in the newspapers Raedon collected weekly from Pith or things they saw on the human broadcasts. Sara's mother Suri always joined them and, gradually, the younger femm brought their mothers, mothers-in-law, grandmothers, and reeth-mates. Sissith reported that femm and mar enjoyed making fun of, but also learning from, humans.

I kept a close eye on Pildon's parties as he and his supporters worked anti-human conversations and entertainment into their social events. One night, Pildon presented a human made war film in his home on his television. After the showing, he and his guests talked about how warlike humans were, how they loved violent conflict, and how they appeared to anger easily. Once the guests had departed, he and his chief associates sat down in Pildon's living room to take stock. I eavesdropped shamelessly.

"I don't think you're getting anywhere." The hom of the couple, mind-melded but meek, sat by the window finishing the wine. "The only ones here tonight are the ones always here. You aren't reaching anyone new. And your numbers are dwindling."

His fym wrung her hands, miserable failure swirling in her mind. "I can't get any more femm to come and bring their homm. Saradon has been too successful with her tea-parties."

"You've gone a couple of times, haven't you?" Pildon asked. He worked hard to maintain a pleasant demeanor with the fem while he discounted the hom's words with disdain. "What's the attraction?"

For an instant, she bloomed with joy. "They're really fun. Everyone laughs a lot. They're learning about humans." Then, her mind fell into worry. "Are you sure they will attack us? They seem pretty harmless from what I've seen at Sara's."

Pildon's rage flared. *He hides it well,* I thought. I gathered, from the fym's reaction, that Pildon smiled, leaned forward, and took her hands in his. "Don't you realize Saradon is very careful what she shows? Of course they seem harmless. But you saw the movie tonight. Were they harmless then?"

The fem vibrated with indecision. *She wants to believe him.* She tried to explain her feeling. "But it was just a movie!"

"And they love that kind of violence. Doesn't that tell you what they're like at heart? And remember the play, <u>Conquest of Bonn?</u> Humans annihilated the families in Bonn three hundred and eighty years ago—humans, don, and reeth."

She sighed. "I guess you're right."

Pildon surged with satisfaction.

I reflected on the conversation. *He's not succeeding. And still ignoring reeth in his plans. No worries yet.*

Chapter 24
~ Lillith

I walked into the great room at Eyrie and found the don physicians and their fymm sipping hot Lareina wine with the female leader of the human research team, Dr. Maun Alls. I moved quietly up behind the group and listened in; Nandon was speaking. "We track our individuals through families. Our Speaker's Council makes all decisions and each family has one vote, proffered by the designated Speaker of the family. Therefore, our council maintains a list of all don. The list is updated every year on a specific date so our bailiff always knows how many don there are, how many died, how many born. That's his job."

"I think we have a definition problem here," said Dr. Maun. Her brow wrinkled in confusion below the squared brown bangs and she tapped a pencil as she made her point. "In human terms, a family consists of a mother, father, and their children."

"A don family includes all descendants from one original don leader and fymm that have married in." He cocked his head as if thinking. "That does imply others we didn't keep track of, doesn't it? Our written records start when don and reeth first melded, over two thousand years ago." Acknowledging my presence, he asked, "Do you know anything different?"

"There must have been others but I don't know what happened to them. You should ask Memmiard." I nodded greetings. "Good day, Dr. Maun. How are things going?"

"As well as can be expected." The woman's smile was warm. I thought of her as the brilliant mouse; her hair, curling softly around her head, was what reeth called gruella, or mousy brown, and her face and mannerisms reminded me of the quietly efficient rodent. She was, I acknowledged, just as intelligent and driven as her partner, but much easier to deal with. "Lots of samples, lots of studies, little news." Dr. Maun grimaced. "Typical." She paused, then said, "Nandon, please continue."

"My sister and I are the last descendants of the Nan family. I was fifteen when my father died and I took over his name and position as Speaker." His voice dropped with an element of despair. "The Nan family has only three living members: me, my fym, and my mother. My sister has two sons but they're part of the Jul family, their father's family, which has five members: Juldon, my sister, the two boys, and Juldon's mother.

"My fym is an only child and we've been married over twenty years." He stopped a moment to draw in a deep breath. I felt him reaching for the comfort of his mind-mate. "When I die, the Nan family will be gone if we don't have a son."

Turning to me, he forced his words into brightness. "We're trying to explain why everyone's been so willing to participate. It seems such cooperation is unusual for a study like this. Dr. Maun also wondered how we keep track of everyone without the aid of the marvelous computers they're using."

"I see." I nodded. "Please, don't let me interrupt."

Nandon slumped with sadness as he continued. "The Len family, my fym's birth family, only has one generation until it will be gone, too. Although there are three couples, there's only one child, my fym. Our story is repeated among other families." He sighed. "Stressful."

Strong empathy radiated from Dr. Maun. The woman couldn't read the emotion that had both doctors tied in tense knots, but she sensed their dismay. Her intuition intrigued me.

"I know this isn't precisely on the subject," the woman said, curiosity coming to the fore of her mind. "But, why do all of your names end in don?"

The don looked at each other as if stumped, having been diverted from their emotional turmoil. I delved more closely into the human's mind. *Did she deflect the direction of their thoughts on purpose? She did!*

"Well..." Eledon wrinkled his brow and essayed an answer. "We have no surnames, so I guess 'don' functions as one. Generally, the first part of our name indicates our family:

Nandon of the Nan family, Eledon of the Ele family, although Benetadon's name doesn't fit that pattern."

His fym, the blonde at his side, grinned. "I was second born. My older sister got the Bel name. Mine came from my great-aunt."

"Our names are handed down from generation to generation, especially for Speakers." Eledon glanced at Nandon. "When a Speaker dies, the eldest son takes his name and Speaker position. If there's no son, then the next oldest brother takes over the name and the family." He gulped. "If there's no brother, the family name dies." The three don sat again in glum silence.

The human tried again. "I just have to ask. Is that a don trait, to never move your hands while talking?"

Both glanced down at their hands resting flat on the table, then laughed self-consciously, the somber mood broken. "I guess it is." Nandon whisked his hands off the table. "Everyone keeps hands on the table while negotiating."

"Probably goes back to the era when don warred among themselves," Eledon added. "You know—no hidden weapons." He dropped his hands into his lap.

Smiling, Dr. Maun rose, saying it was time to go back to work just as noisy bustling erupted near the door. Sara and Cheradon entered with arms linked, followed by their reeth-mates.

"Hello," Sara said. "I've brought Chera to see the lab. She wants to help!"

Dr. Maun moved forward in her gentle manner and took the blonde fem's hand. "Nice to meet you, Cheradon. They call me Dr. Maun. Let me show you around."

The gathering broke up as everyone went back to their projects; I headed off to check with my staff. Nana and I were reviewing supplies in a storage room when a blast of pain lanced through my mind. I galloped through my part of the home, hearing Nana panting behind, and stormed into

191

Joedon's living room. Sara stood pale and shaking surrounded by humans and don. Dr. Maun knelt beside Chera, unconscious on the floor, bathing her face with a damp cloth.

"What happened?" I snapped. Everyone started to explain. I blocked reception and probed Sara. The fem swirled with conflict: overwhelming joy mixed heavily with guilt. *Guilt?* Waving wings for silence, I pieced the scene together: one of the lab assistants had shouted out that Sara's test came back positive, she was pregnant. Chera shrieked and fainted. I remembered the meeting in the ladies' bathroom during the tea party and Chera's intense desire for a child.

I urged everyone to go back to work while Dr. Maun helped Chera recover. Noticing the lab student who'd shouted standing with head down, emanating chagrin, I sent a soothing and nudged the girl on her way. Then, I caught a warning from Lillyon: Samdon, Coccyon, and Pildon were approaching the entrance to Eyrie.

Flicking my ears at Sara, I directed her to help Nana move Chera into the lab, shoved Dr. Maun after them, and ordered everyone to stay hidden. Then, I galloped toward the entrance, sending a note back to Nana to lock Joedon's door behind her.

I reached the ledge just as Coccyon landed with his passengers. Before I could form a welcome, Pildon shouted, "I want to know what's going on here!" The angry don leaped to the ground and advanced belligerently toward me, hands curled in fists, head hunched forward, scowl on his face.

I drew myself up, arched my neck, and bared my teeth. "I don't know what you want, Pildon, but I don't respond to that tone." I swiveled my head toward the reeth who'd brought him, ears pinned. "Take him away!"

Coccyon bowed his head in obedience, then tipped an ear toward his mind-mate who'd followed Pildon to the ground and was now gripping the enraged don by the shoulder. Samdon's voice was soothing, but I didn't relax my aggressive posture.

"Pildon, you can't talk to Lillith that way. Calm down, ask reasonably." Samdon flashed me an appeal which I ignored.

Pildon yanked away and advanced once more. "You've got humans here! I've heard the rumors!" Stopping inches away, he snarled. "You and Joedon won't get away with this."

"Joedon's not even here, you idiot. And it's none of your business what I do in my own home!"

His eyes blazed and he whirled on Samdon. "She doesn't even deny it! I told you the rumors were true."

My words laced with ice, I said to them both. "I don't answer to rumors. Now, get out of here." I advanced a step. Although Pildon towered over me, I knew my strength. All I had to do was force him backwards to the edge. I took another step and shoved his chest with my head. He fell back. "I told you to leave. You can do it with a reeth, or without. Your choice." Another step.

Samdon grabbed Pildon's arm and pulled him toward Coccyon, standing poised for them to mount. Snarling, Pildon flung himself behind his friend and the reeth dropped off the ledge. As they disappeared into the valley below, I saw Lillyon winging rapidly toward me from the north where he'd gone to graze while I visited the humans.

"I saw them just as they topped the ridge," he said as he landed. "Couldn't get here sooner." He stared east. "I guess you routed them."

"Yes, for now." I sighed and leaned against him. "Thanks for the warning, though." Leading the way to Joedon's suite, I explained the situation to those inside.

Nana came to unlock the door, a jubilant Sara just behind her. "I have to go tell Raedon," she bubbled. "I forbid Sissith to send word. I want to see his face!" She rushed past, speaking over her shoulder. "Chera's fine. Dr. Maun has her learning how to input data into the computers to give her something to concentrate on. Talk to you later." And she was gone.

We'd barely stepped into the living room when Dr. Maun cornered us with excitement, her face more animated than I'd ever seen it. "I've had an idea! Something Sara mentioned about her honeymoon. How often do femm leave the mountains, before or after they're married?"

"I'm not sure I'm the best to answer." I considered. "I don't believe many femm leave before, and after marriage, homm settle down so they don't leave then either. Since humans have spread everywhere, few take a chance on encountering them." I cocked an ear at the woman and lifted my lip in a grin. "Sara's an exception. Are you thinking something in the mountains causes their infertility?"

"It's just a notion at the moment, but I'm going to start my assistants following it. I'll keep you posted." The woman whirled away, headed for the lab.

**

By the time Lillyon and I returned to Center, word of Sara's pregnancy had spread. I found Joedon in his study, staring somberly out a window. He swung around as I entered but avoided my gaze. "Guess your worst nightmares are over. Sara's pregnant."

I didn't like his tone. "I heard." I waited for him to indicate what he thought since he had himself tightly closed off. He walked slowly along his desk, fingers trailing over the papers and books he'd been working on. I contained my impatience, striving to wait without interference.

Finally, he said, "I guess I still want to be Supreme Don. Not abdicate to a babe. But ..." He looked away and his voice dropped to a whisper. "I'd like to have a fym, a child."

I buried my exultation, then went forward to console Joedon's loneliness.

Later in the evening, I stood irresolute outside Pildon's door. I sensed intense emotions from inside, mainly fear of reeth. What could have caused his dread? *Maybe I'd better research him more thoroughly. Something is driving his rage.*

194

Chapter 25
~ Lillith

Hovering over Pith, I sent a call into Professor Stephon Talmadge's mind interrupting his frustration with the lecture he was preparing. "Stephon, it's your turn."

He sat up and dropped his pen. "Lillith," he said out loud. "What can I do for you?"

"I would like you to meet Joedon and me in the willow grove at the park just south of Pith. Can you come?"

"Of course. I'll be there in twenty minutes."

Joedon lounged on a park bench. I stood behind him with my head dropped onto his shoulder and watched Stephon arrive, glance around quickly, then stride toward us. He stopped abruptly, eyes wide with astonishment, as Joedon rose and towered over him.

"Joedon," I said. "This is Professor Stephon Talmadge who did all the interviews and documentaries on don and reeth since the Exchange."

He extended a hand. Stephon gulped and took it. "I don't remember you being so tall." He paused. "I always thought I was tall."

Joedon's ice blue eyes twinkled. "You are, for a human."

"Hello Lillith." Stephon stroked a hand down my neck.

"Thank you for coming," I said. "We've come to ask your help. I've told Joedon you're planning on getting married and building a house."

"I am," Stephon nodded, his mind filled with conjecture.

"Congratulations," Joedon said. "I'd like to meet the woman who will tie you down. I've watched all your broadcasts. You're a wily man with a sentence."

Stephon puffed up with Joedon's praise. "I'd love to introduce you to her one day." He followed Joedon to the bench and sat down, steepling his hands in his lap. "What can I do to help?"

"We have an older don who needs repairs on his home." Joedon leaned forward and rested his elbows on his knees. "Lillith came up with the idea of having you contact and hire humans to work on his home to show how useful they could be to us."

I nodded. "We thought if you hired them," I said, "we could fly them in, have them do the work, then return them to their homes and wipe their memories of the location. They won't be hurt and will be richer for their efforts."

"We'll pay them well for their work," Joedon clarified.

Stephon glanced from one to the other. I'd love to help, he thought, then blushed as he remembered I would hear his thoughts. "What kind of work are you talking about?"

Joedon stood and held out a hand, palm up in invitation. "We could fly you there to see for yourself."

Stephon grinned, but shook his head. "I'd love to fly but that won't do any good. I know nothing about construction."

"Well, his walls are unstable and we don't know how to repair them." Joedon regained his seat. "I'm not positive they can be fixed. He might even need a completely new house."

"That would be harder to accomplish. It means meeting with a design firm to plan, finding an architect to create blue prints, and hiring contractors to build. That's what I've been working on for the last month around my teaching schedule." His face lit. "Marn and I don't want to build a house just like everyone else's. We want to create it exactly like we want."

He considered, tilting his head slightly. "We've just hired a design firm I'd highly recommend."

Joedon and I exchanged thoughts, then he shook his head. "I don't think Opudon should contact a human firm himself. The Council would be furious."

Stephon smiled slowly, as if developing an idea. "What if I meet with your friend to find out what he wants. I could present the project to the firm as my vacation home and at least get the design phase finished."

"That sounds possible." Joedon pondered. "We could bring him here."

"I'd be more convincing to the designers if I saw the location."

"Can you go now?" I asked.

Stephon frowned. "No. Next Ursday at the earliest. I'm overloaded right now."

"Okay. We'll talk with Opudon. Then, I'll check back with you." I bathed him in approval. "And thank you for being willing to help."

**

"Where's Joedon?" Stephon asked when he joined me at the same willow grove a week later.

"He got tied up with politics," I said, exasperated. "I'll fly you to your meeting with Opudon and his fym. His reeth-mate will join us so it's essential I be there to translate. Although the old reeth supports our plan, he claims he's too ancient to make the effort of talking directly to you."

"Well, I'm looking forward to meeting more don and reeth. How should I mount? Is it easy to fly?" He dithered around, his nervousness evident from the rapidity of his speech. "I've never even ridden a horse. I don't mean to insult you by comparing you to such a creature, but I don't want to cause you problems with my ineptitude."

I sent him confidence. "It's very simple. Go stand on that table, I'll walk beside you, and you can slide right onto my back." He calmed as I moved away. "I've worn a harness that you fasten around you. You'll be quite safe and not bother me at all."

It happened just as I'd said. He slipped onto my back and found the harness easy to attach. His words and thoughts amused me. "Am I not too big for you to carry?" He felt as if he were too heavy and since his feet didn't touch the ground, he struggled with balance.

"No. I'm very strong. Stop worrying and relax. Simply enjoy the flight." My muscles bunched as I launched into the air; Stephon clutched at my mane and clamped his legs to my sides, hitting my mind with a bolt of fear.

I began to talk, calmly. "Joedon was detained by one of the don who complains about everything we do. He's our most outspoken foe—always harping against anything to do with humans. Joedon and some others created a film about humans doing the sort of things that would help solve don problems. Two of our young don interviewed human contractors on the film and this morning, Pildon appeared, with his cronies, to complain to Joedon about allowing them to expose themselves to such dangerous situations." I felt like I was babbling but Stephon gradually eased out of his anxiety.

As I talked, I continued to let exasperation color my tone. "If he knew what I was doing today, he'd be furious. But the film prompted Opudon to approach Joedon about getting his house rebuilt by humans—so it's already accomplished one of its purposes."

"Your problem don sounds like one of the professors in my department, complains about everything but never has a suggested remedy." He pulled his legs up slightly at the knee, finding it a more comfortable position.

"Pildon wants things to stay the same. But that won't work anymore."

"How long will it take us to get to Opudon's house?"

"About two and a half hours. Are you comfortable?"

Stephon laughed. "I'm starting to feel the rhythm. This feels very different than I expected."

"If you can relax your legs, you won't get so tired. You really don't have to grip with them. I promise not to drop you."

He laughed more. "I trust you, Lillith. Here, I am relaxing, aren't I? Does it tire you to talk while you fly?" He loosened his death grip on my mane and I sensed his effort at reducing the tension in his legs.

"Not at all. It's as easy to talk and fly as it is for you to talk and walk."

"I guess that makes sense. It would seem more difficult to fly." He paused and rolled his head and shoulders. "Well, could you explain a little about the don-reeth relationship? If you're working toward a type of partnership between our three species, I'd like to know more about the other two. Although I can't claim to comprehend the human race."

As I explained, I didn't change the cadence of my wing strokes and his legs relaxed more. "The only way reeth communicate is through telepathy," I said. "Our communication is instantaneous, our discussion open to all. In general, reeth families determine their position and only the family representative joins in discussion and decision making."

When I paused, he shifted his weight, slumping more with his back. I didn't vary my movement, waited for him to be still, then continued. "The major political difference between reeth and don, or human, is that we can't hide an agenda from one another during direct communication. We do shield thoughts and emotions from casual eavesdropping or we'd go mad hearing everything. However, reeth cannot communicate one thing when they actually mean something else. Do you understand the significance of that?"

"Yes, of course. Politics, as we humans know it, don't exist among reeth." He gulped; we were steadily rising, following the lay of the land. He worked hard at ignoring my wing muscles bunching and relaxing beneath his thighs.

"Exactly," I said. "In a way, reeth are separate individuals with one group mind. We don't have major controversies where individuals have different opinions. We come to a consensus almost immediately." I tilted my head as a human would when thinking, then realized I'd copied Dr. Maun. "Sometimes, we're slow to act, but we always act as a unit when we do. In all our history, we've never had a major disagreement on anything."

"I think I saw that at Exchange, when reeth reacted to Roark."

"Exchange is a good example." I nodded and he reacted to the ripple through my backbone. At his mutter, "how does she keep me level when she's moving?" I responded, "Experience."

Then, I continued the lecture. "Although some of the older reeth were not happy about endorsing Joedon's actions, we agreed instantly for that group to arrive in support. No controversy."

"Humans thrive on controversy."

"I know. And in that, don are much like humans. They each have their own opinion and they tend to argue. Everyone has their own agenda. Eventually, don come to an agreement, but often it's only after reeth become involved through their mind-melds. There are non-melded don and they're not easily influenced."

"So not all don are melded?" Stephon, totally engrossed, failed to notice the mountain pass we flew through until we were already on the other side. He blocked his mind from the thought of the cliffs and closed his eyes for a moment.

"No," I said loudly, bringing his attention back. "Not all reeth are melded either. Melded don are more emotionally stable and happier than those not mind-melded. The meld itself, although extremely significant for the two individuals involved, is not particularly important to either species as a whole. All reeth help all don. All don help all reeth. Don argue among themselves but they don't argue with us."

Stephon, for some reason, looked down. His heart jumped into his throat as far below he saw a valley with a waterfall on one side and a stream masked by spreading fern-like trees. I blocked his panic and he relaxed. "Interestingly, prior to my meld with Joedon, I couldn't hear all don mentally as I can now. Also, I couldn't speak to multiple don at the same time. Our meld is slightly different than the others but I don't know why it happens to be unique."

Recognizing that my talking helped him not focus on how high we were above the ground, he asked another question. "How does the meld happen?" I grinned to myself and encouraged him.

"When a don child is born, he or she sometimes makes an immediate mental connection to a reeth. No one understands how it happens. Usually a male child melds with a male reeth and a female child melds with a female reeth. Sometimes the meld doesn't happen until the child is older, maybe four or five."

When my tone became suffused with love, I felt his envy, his longing. "Take Joedon and me. I'm many years older than he and was married with young ones of my own when he was born. Yes, he was of the royal don family and I was of the royal reeth family, but I never expected to meld. It came as a complete surprise." I stopped talking and savored the memory. "It felt as if he reached out and roped me, like the humans catch a horse." His laugh was infectious and I joined him, although not hard enough to shift his balance.

Suddenly, he noticed the mountain we were rapidly approaching and shut his eyes. I shook my head and his eyes snapped back open, but he swayed with the movement, totally unaware of his growing balance. I sent him a grin. "I'm going to relieve you of your worries. We're here and I'll be landing shortly. You've done very well on your first flight."

Chapter 26

~ Lillith

"Garard," I said. I sensed him standing alone in the Grand Salon, polishing something. He immediately laid down his cloth and walked over to a bay window.

"Where are you Lillith?"

"In the back garden. Could you please send Turl to Palm Cottage for some reason? I need him to do something for me."

"I could come!"

"I'm sorry. I appreciate your offer, but for this, I need Turl."

"Consider it done."

Later, I followed Turl's car to Palmyra, then prompted him to stop at the market there. He got out and wandered into the store, unsure of his purpose until he halted in front of a broad display of fresh cut flowers. As he mulled over the selection, he overheard two men talking through an open window.

"That's the car that belongs to that guard who's always down here to see Cari, ain't it?" said one. Turl's head came up.

"Yeah! Nice car. He must make good money. The rest of us ain't got a chance with him coming round. Big city guy like that. I think it's a damn shame how he treats her, that's what I think. If I had Cari lookin' at me, I'd sure as heck not mess around with her. I'd ask her to marry me right now, if she'd notice me."

"You got that right. She's a damn good cook and a looker, too. Sweet as can be. He's probably got some girl on the line back in Pith and just strings poor Cari along."

"Maybe he's even married and just keeping Cari on the side. We oughta teach that guy a lesson, teach him he ought'n mess with a fine gal like her."

"Yeah, you and who else? I ain't tangling with him."

Turl stood frozen, staring unseeing at the flowers as he heard the two men walk away. "Is that how people see me?" he muttered. "Someone playing with Cari's affections?" He'd

202

smash them both if he knew who they were. He glanced around to see if anyone else had heard to discover every eye in the store on him. The worried faces told him how they felt.

Suddenly, he grinned, picked up two bunches of brilliant red roses and strode up to the counter. He looked the counter man in the eye and asked, "You think she'll say yes?"

"Damn straight she will." The man smiled as he handed Turl the change. "Just don't take her away, that's all I ask."

"I won't," Turl responded. He left the shop whistling, feeling better than he had in months.

I nodded in satisfaction, leaving him to complete his task.

**

Three days later, I heaved to my feet and touched Lillyon lightly with my front hoof. He came instantly awake from the anger in my mind. "That idiot Roark has attacked Pith," I snarled. "We can't have a war among humans right now—Pildon will have a hay day with the news coverage. We're going to stop it!"

We galloped through the house sending orders right and left. Joedon met us in the back garden, competently dressed, if rather fussed. Juldon came rushing out of the back, pulling on a jacket. He stopped a second to catch his breath, then leapt onto Lillyon's back. As soon as Joedon was safely aboard, we dropped off the cliff, catching air currents.

Flying furiously eastward, we met Memm and Raedon, accompanied by both doctors, their fymm, and their reeth-mates. Then, the contingent from Eyrie joined us. "As soon as we get near Pith, I'll connect with Garard to see what I can learn. Lillyon, take half the staff and go east. Report what you see. Memm, go north with the doctors. The rest of you scatter to the south. Make sure you're not visible!"

I banked suddenly. "Aren't we going to the palace?" Joedon asked.

"Memm says they're attacking from the north-east. Garard, Talmadge, and Metz are on that roof top." We caught sight of three figures huddled behind a head-high wall atop a ten story apartment building. Roark's army had arrived within a mile of what appeared to be a hastily dug trench just outside the city. I followed the trench with my eye; it ran for miles, lined on the city side by earth-moving equipment parked nose to tail. Armed men and women stood waiting behind the equipment, evenly spaced along a wooden wall erected between the equipment and the first set of buildings. More shooters lined the tops of buildings facing the oncoming army.

"They seem prepared," I said, showing Joedon what I'd seen. The three men had binoculars trained on the vast wave marching across the relatively flat plain towards them. Metz' mind roiled with anxiety as he studied the formidable surge.

"Have faith, my Lord." I heard Garard's sensible voice. "Roml and his forces have frantically trained the civilians. They have plenty of guns and ammunition."

~ Joedon

The three men whirled around at the whoosh of wings as Lillith landed and I slid off. "We're here to help!" I shouted although we immediately realized they were unarmed.

Metz stared, jaw dropped; Garard surged forward. "How?"

I strode to the man, took his arm, and turned him back to face the army. "What's your plan?"

"We've kidnapped women from Kavv, including Kelt. We're going to try to get the troops to give up and desert." He swung sideways and pointed to a jumbotron mounted on a nearby skyscraper.

Peering along the edge of town as far as I could see, I spotted others, dangling from cranes or tall trees. Whirling toward Lillith, I exchanged rapid thoughts with her, then demanded, "Do you have explosives? Bombs?"

Metz had gotten over his shock and answered, "Captain Roml has grenades, over there. Why?" He pointed to a park far to the right where people in uniform milled among the trees.

"You'll see." I threw myself onto Lillith and we headed for the park. Captain Roml seemed a capable commander; he barely blinked when Lillith landed among his troop. Soldiers backed rapidly away from the massive wings, but the captain held his ground.

"Metz says you have grenades," I shouted. "Any other explosives?"

Roml hesitated only a moment. "Not much but what we have, you can use." He waved several of his men forward and ordered them to hand their packs to me. Trembling, the men complied as other reeth landed. I distributed the packs to incoming riders while Lillith repeated instructions for grenade use from Roml's demonstration.

"Where's the rest?"

"Take me with you and we'll collect them."

Definitely a bold commander, Lillith thought as I mounted and pulled Roml up behind me. We spent only half an hour collecting more grenades and other explosives. Lillith sent heavily laden reeth and their riders to surround the approaching army before dropping Roml back with his command.

"When you're ready for us ..." I saluted the captain. "...shout out and Lillith will hear!"

Lillith and I hovered to the right of the army, invisible, watching Metz on the roof top. The men in the lead of Roark's forces came to an abrupt halt and started laughing and pointing at the ditch and the barricade of work equipment. Metz raised his right hand, jumbotrons flashed on noisily. On screen, screaming women and children were being loaded into cargo trucks with the name Pith Moving Company blazoned on the sides. The front line stopped laughing as one after another of Roark's commanding officers evidently recognized their wives, children, or girlfriends. Men now pointed at the jumbotrons and shouted to their fellows. The perfect lines of troops wavered.

The next scene displayed Roark's wife Lady Kelt being carried out of Kavv Palace front door, kicking and screaming. Then, Lord Metz's face appeared, huge and stern. "Your families will be gently cared for in my palace as long as you do not attack."

Loud speakers installed along the front of the trench boomed his words at the Kavv troops. "If you attack, your families will be moved to the front lines."

On the screen, Metz pointed a large finger at Kavv. "Turn around and go home." Next came scenes of the same families in Pith Palace, laughing and enjoying a meal.

"Roark's screaming at them, thrusting his fist," I said quietly to Lillith. "The forces are regrouping, approaching the trench. Their ploy isn't going to work."

"Give me your mind," Lillith said, then reached for energy from the rest of our group. The trench changed into a thirty foot moat full of water and creatures looking strangely like alligators, mouths open, teeth gleaming in the sun. It stretched as far as the eye could see around the city, backed by a tall rock wall. The heavy earth moving equipment had become truck-mounted long range guns preparing to fire.

"We can't hold this illusion for long," I muttered.

Gunfire clattered off the barricade, shattering windows in the front facing buildings. Lillith blanked her mind for a moment, then, catching Roml's shout, steadied her resolve. The Pithians returned fire. Airplanes screamed overhead, Pith, not Kavv. Men dropped sticks of dynamite out the doors. Explosions rocked the crowded troops. Soldiers fell, screaming in pain. Sharpshooters fired out of the illusionary rock wall, picking off commanders. More grunts fell.

Forcing herself to ignore the screams of the wounded and the stench of the smoke, Lillith directed her fellow reeth to swoop on the Kavvan tanks, their riders dropping grenades on the gunners. One tank after another halted in its tracks and soldiers melted away from the uncanny attack of an invisible force that even slightly unnerved me.

With all our explosives gone, Lillith dropped me just behind Roark's jeep. Commanders screamed at their leader for instructions but he stood frozen as I whispered in his ear. "The stasis will fade within an hour. You'll be allowed to return to Kavv but you won't be allowed to do anything else. Remember what happened today. Be content with your own city and lands. Leave the others alone or you'll encounter us again." Lillith allowed Roark to see her land at the vehicle's side and his supposed corporal leap on her back.

The battle ended minutes after it began. The mighty Kavv army ran, having damaged a lot of windows and killed a jumbotron, but not one Pithian.

We gathered our troops well away from the city. Trembling, she marshaled her thoughts, steadied her nerves, then spoke through the noise for everyone to hear. "Thank you for your support today. I know we agree our actions were necessary, but still, we operated against our core mandate to provide joy to others." She specifically targeted the younger reeth. "We avoided as much as possible causing injury to individuals, and I assure you Lord Metz implemented medical care for Kavv wounded immediately." She paused to assess their mental states. "If you have flashbacks, please contact Lillyon or me. We'll do our best to resolve your concerns." She dropped to one knee; she and I bowed our heads to the group. "Thank you again."

Chapter 27

~ Caleb and Lilliod

Spring flew by and the day came to shear the sheep so his mother could prepare the wool for market. Caleb hated being away from Lilliod for the two days it took, but at least he maintained mental contact throughout the day. He knew Lilliod had gone to graze, keeping careful watch for any predators, or any of Caleb's brothers that might be wandering away for a break from the heavy labor.

For the first time ever he had pleasant memories to occupy his mind as he caught sheep after sheep and flipped them on their sides for his oldest brother to work the shears. Noise faded as he thought of the mountains and his traipses through them with Lilliod, the dog, and the sheep.

His father was pleased with him for once. In their wanderings, the trio had found new grazing areas and the sheep were fat and healthy. The lambs screaming for their mothers being sheared were bigger than ever and promised to fetch high prices at the fall market. He hadn't really heard that, but the back slapping and smiles coming his way were different than in previous years.

It seemed strange to Caleb that only he could hear Lilliod, but his friend could hear all of Caleb's family's thoughts. Having Lilliod nearby had made his life easier—Lilliod explained things Caleb couldn't hear. He grinned to himself as he thought about his friend, the most beautiful creature he'd ever seen. They'd spent all spring wandering farther afield than Caleb had ever dared go before. He'd seen valleys, waterfalls, babbling streams, high red cliffs, and snow! Also deer, and something similar but bigger.

Once, they'd encountered a wild pig, big enough to injure Caleb. It charged at the sheep, scattering them, and knocked one over. The dog had barked furiously, attacking the pig from the rear, snapping at its hind legs. Caleb had beat on its head with a thick branch, darting in, then away from the snapping jaws. But Lilliod defeated it. Wheeling, he'd struck hard with hind hoofs, knocking the pig onto its side. Then, he spun and beat the pig's head with sharp front hoofs and wings until its skull caved in. Caleb had butchered the thing immediately, stashed what he couldn't carry in a cave, and packed home fresh meat for his mother. He'd been a hero that night even though he couldn't explain how he'd conquered the pig except through gestures and grunts.

He snapped his head up as his brother boxed his ear. His brother gestured wildly for him to pay attention. Glancing down, he saw the sheep bleeding from a slash in its side; he'd let it wiggle too much and the shears had cut too deep. He hung his head and vowed silently to quit daydreaming.

**

Caleb wished his parents would stop yelling and go to sleep so he could slip out and join Lilliod. Pulling the pillow over his head, he reached for comfort from his friend. "They're arguing about you," Lilliod said from his hideout. "Your mother wants to take you with them to market tomorrow since your birthday's coming. She thinks you deserve a reward for doing so well this year."

Caleb sat up on his sleeping mat. "It's because of you that I've done well."

"She doesn't know that. She thinks you're growing up, becoming mature enough to shoulder more responsibility."

"What does Pa think?" He moved to the small window under the eave to gaze out. It didn't make any difference where he was—he could always hear Lilliod clearly, but he felt better if he could see the tops of the trees where his friend sheltered. His tiny sleeping area above his parent's room was his hideout. His six brothers each had a room of their own on the floor below, tiny but separate, making it easy for him to slip out unnoticed once everyone was snoring.

"Your father wants you to stay home and care for the animals as always. Your mother thinks one of the others should stay this year so you can go."

"Pa never wants me to go 'cause I embarrass him." When Lilliod didn't reply, Caleb knew he'd guessed what Pa was thinking. He was skinny and tall, not stocky and heavy muscled like the others. He also had dirty blond hair over delicate features instead of the dark brown hair and heavy brows he should have. He took after his mother. Pa always avoided having outsiders know about him.

Caleb knew his father didn't like him. The man had never struck him, but he never took him fishing or hunting either, nor taught him how to do any of the chores he expected done. Everything Caleb knew, he'd learned from one of the brothers, who taught him willingly to do whatever that particular brother didn't want to do. Only his mother tried to teach him things. Pa usually stopped her efforts just as he got the hang of something—such as stitching up a wound, or making a fishing fly, or baking a pie.

Some of the brothers, not the oldest, attended school in the village five miles away but he'd never been. Once the family realized he couldn't hear anything but loud noises, they'd decided not to send him. A few times, before he'd grown taller than his oldest brother, they'd taken him to market with them, but he hadn't been in years.

"Can you tell from either of them how old I am?" Caleb asked

"Your mother thinks you'll be fifteen in two weeks," came the answer.

He crunched his brows together. "How many is that?" Lilliod pictured fifteen sheep so Caleb could visualize the number. He returned to his sleeping mat and sat down, cross-legged. "I'd like to go to the market if I didn't have to leave you. I don't remember much about it."

"I think you should go." Pictures began to appear in Caleb's head as Lilliod pulled scenes of being at market from his sleeping brothers. "You deserve to have fun like they've had."

"But I wouldn't know how to go on—I don't think I could do those things." Caleb wondered at what he saw: a big round contraption swinging high in the air with two of his brother's in a box, dangling; people dancing around a bonfire; a long table with platters of food and his brothers cramming pieces of meat in their mouths, juices dribbling down their chins; girls with long blond hair holding ribbons in their hands; his father arguing with another man; money changing hands.

"I can go with you, in your mind, and help you like I do around the farm." Lilliod paused and Caleb could sense him thinking. "I don't know how far is too far apart for us to hear each other. It would be interesting to try it."

Caleb noticed that the noise had stopped below. "Your mother's coming up the stairs to your attic," Lilliod warned. He flopped on his mat and pretended deep sleep. His mother walked over to touch his shoulder. She gave him the warm, loving smile she reserved just for him when they were totally alone. Gesturing for him to get up, she helped him stuff a spare shirt and other clothes into a knapsack, then led him down stairs.

Outside, the brothers and Pa were waiting with the wagon, the two oxen yoked to the front and the sheep gathered, ready to start off to market. He hadn't heard any of the preparations and was surprised to see them all ready. He caught the scowling glare of a younger brother standing in the doorway. His mother motioned for him to fall in behind the sheep, and the family departed for market long before sunrise.

When the sun came up, they stopped for breakfast; Caleb's mother handed around her meat rolls and everyone shared the jug of milk. Afterward, Caleb followed along behind the sheep, the dustiest position, but it left him alone to concentrate on his conversation with Lilliod. He looked avidly around so Lilliod could see everything he saw, and the reeth explained things Caleb didn't understand.

"How do you know what that is?" asked Caleb when they passed through the village and he noticed a fountain spewing water into the air.

"I don't know," Lilliod answered, with a feeling of confusion. "I just do. Just like I knew what the animals were that we saw in the mountains. I can remember lots of things, only nothing about me personally."

"Someday, we'll find out who you are," promised Caleb for the hundredth time.

**

Caleb and Lilliod conversed easily even after the family reached the market in Terra, a name Lilliod didn't recognize. The tall buildings and hundreds of people fascinated the boy although he clung to his mother. His friend couldn't help him with anything he saw; Lilliod had never seen a city.

The family camped by their wagon outside town for three days. Each day Pa took one brother and a few lambs away, returning before dark with money. Caleb's mother took him along when she sold her wool. He watched carefully, and Lilliod explained as best he could, as she bargained with merchant after merchant. Gradually, Caleb began to understand the process. On the last day, his mother took him into another part of the city so he could buy something as his reward for working so hard, and for his birthday. Caleb understood immediately what she was about, because of Lilliod, but, he watched patiently as she pantomimed her intentions.

"She's decided to buy you some picture books since you can't go to school and learn with the others," Lilliod explained.

"What's a picture book?"

"I don't know. From her mental picture, it's similar to the books the brothers bring home. You'll have to wait and see."

They entered a market set up inside a building, not in one of the tent covered stalls. He eagerly scanned shelf after shelf of books while his mother picked up some to examine. An image jumped out at him from one of the shelves and he snatched up the book. On the cover, he saw an animal similar to Lilliod, golden rather than black. Another animal, tall and thin, sort of like a man, stood at the golden one's side. Lilliod's excitement filled his head, matching his own.

212

Caleb whirled and raced to his mother, holding out the book. She glanced at it and said something Lilliod translated as "fairy tale". Caleb begged with his eyes, clutching the book to his chest. Lilliod added mental pleading. With a funny expression on her face, she added it to the stack on the desk. Once the precious book was paid for, Caleb hid it under his shirt, then sat until dark examining the pictures inside, mentally sharing them with Lilliod.

On the way back to the farm, the brothers rode in the back of the wagon where the wool had been. A girl joined them, long blonde hair, pretty face; no one explained who she was, but Lilliod said she was his oldest brother's new wife. The couple rode up front with his mother and Pa. The younger brothers pawed through Caleb's books; he wouldn't let anyone touch the one with the animal on the cover, sitting on it to keep them from snatching it out of his hands. He wasn't as chunky as they were, but was every bit as strong.

The brothers laughed and made fun of him; his mother and oldest brother kept them at bay; Pa ignored them all. Lilliod told him they called him baby because of his fascination with a fairy tale. Caleb disregarded them, sitting quietly in a corner of the wagon anxious to get home and share his treasure with his friend.

**

The weeks following flew by. Caleb learned much from his books, from the pictures; he craved more. One night, he tried to get his mother to read the fairy tale to him, but she couldn't understand what he wanted. He held out the book and pointed to one word, then the next. Lilliod prodded her until she looked at Caleb worriedly. They were alone in the house as the brothers had gone with Pa to a nearby property to work on a house for his oldest brother and his bride.

Finally, Caleb got his mother to sit down. He plopped onto the floor at her side, and she read the story to him, totally unaware he understood every word. When she finished reading, she studied Caleb. Lilliod reported her absorption in his elated face.

"She realizes you understood what she read," Lilliod said. "She's worried about how you heard her words, but she knows you did, somehow."

Caleb grinned, pulled his mother out of the chair, and hugged her. Her head reached his chin. He dropped a kiss onto her hair and rushed up to his tiny space in the attic, leaving her perplexed behind him. After that night, whenever Pa and the brothers left to work on the new house, Caleb and his mother sat in the kitchen and she read to him. She never understood how he knew what she read, but she knew he did. He learned at a tremendous rate, soaking up everything he could. Soon, she was reading the brothers' school books and, within a month, he'd bypassed his youngest brother's grade level in understanding. As she asked him questions, he nodded or shook his head to answer, proving he heard. Neither one told Pa or the brothers.

**

By the time winter arrived, Caleb had stolen enough wood and nails from the new home project to build Lilliod a small shelter among the trees where he hid. Their days of taking the sheep to the mountains came to an end and they huddled with the dog in the tiny enclosure, wondering what they'd do all day during the bad weather.

Caleb's mother knew he could now read and constantly read everything he got his hands on, but the others didn't. He hadn't dared trying to write—he knew one of his brothers would catch him and then, what could he say? One day, when it was raining too hard to go outside, Caleb squirmed on a stood, watching his mother bake bread. Suddenly, she threw her hands in the air, shot him an exasperated look, and said, "That's it. I can't stand your fidgeting any more. Stay here."

"She's got another present for you," said Lilliod. "She was trying to wait until sometime called Thankful Day, but she's lost patience."

She returned in a moment with a large rectangular box, handing it to him. Inside he found heavy sheets of white paper

214

and a box of pencils. Also, a book about drawing. "I want you to try to draw. Take these and sit at the table. Learn to reproduce what you see there." She still didn't understand how he heard her, but she'd long ago forgotten her wonder. She never, ever slipped in front of Pa or the brothers though, just as he didn't.

Caleb took to drawing instantly and soon the house was papered with sketches of animals and landscapes. Mixed in were drawings of a black reeth with white legs and a wide white blaze down his face in all sorts of positions: flying, cantering, sitting on his haunches, upside down with legs tucked up to his belly, sleeping in a snowy meadow. Even Pa started to notice the excellence of the images of sheep, a wild hog, the dog, streams, and the mythical reeth. So did his oldest brother and his wife, and finally the brothers.

After Thankful Day, Caleb's oldest brother joined his mother in the kitchen where Caleb sat drawing yet another picture of the sheep herd with lambs cavorting around.

"Ma," the brother said. "The school's having an art contest. I think you should enter Caleb's work. It's far better than anything people around here have ever seen." Caleb froze in his chair as his spirits soared. He couldn't let on that he'd heard. He felt his mother's eyes on his back.

"You think?"

"Yeah, Ma. Even Pa said so. You could sell some and buy that sewing machine you've always wanted."

"Sell Caleb's drawings? I don't know ..."

"She's worried you wouldn't want her to," Lilliod said. Caleb stiffened in his chair, then turned carefully around as if he'd just noticed his brother standing there. He stood to shake hands. His brother no longer lived in their house so Caleb didn't see him often. His brother regarded him with genuine pleasure. Maybe living with a girl makes him happier, Caleb thought.

"He's proud of you and your talent."

Chapter 28

~ Joedon

On the day of our annual gather, Taldon gazed at those of us assembled and frowned. "Does anyone know what's going on? A quarter of us are missing!"

"Weeks ago, I went to a meeting where they talked about resenting the gather," volunteered someone. "You don't suppose they've decided not to help?"

"And I told them they didn't have to help if they felt that way about it," Wolfdon said. "I was angry at their attitude. I never thought they'd not show up."

"I'll ask Lillith to check it out." Picking up my scythe, I moved toward the field. "In the meantime, let's get started."

At the end of the day, the storage areas were filled, and exhausted, angry workers clustered around me to hear what Lillith had discovered. "It's that group of non-melded don." Lillith's harsh tone betrayed her annoyance. "They've decided to no longer help. They say they want us to quit interfering in don politics." She looked pointedly at Raedon. "Pildon's not the leader, but he's with them."

Quilyle, head of a large non-melded reeth family, stomped a large feathered front hoof. "We don't interfere. How dare they do this?" Only reeth heard him, but we don understood his message; he stood menacingly, massive shoulders hunched, head and neck stretched down in challenge, ears pinned, and eyes glowing red. Those standing nearby backed away.

Lillolf moved to confront the enraged black. "Let us talk of this among ourselves," he said. "Thank the don for their efforts today and take them home." Reeth nodded their obedience and left the clearing, returning their mind-mates to their homes. Then, they shut us out of their minds.

**

"I can't believe those idiots," Raedon fumed as he and Sara followed me into the Joe mansion, accompanied by a large

217

number of those who'd helped with the gather. "Are they trying to destroy our lives?"

"Making reeth angry is worse than exposing us to humans." Sara, thoroughly enraged, stomped around, her voice shrill. "We should knock some sense into them."

"In a way, I can't blame them," Wolfdon said. She snapped her head to glare at the older don. He stepped back and held his hands out as others turned on him. "I know how it feels to be non-melded. Yes, I'm surrounded by my family's reeth." He spoke seriously to those of us glaring at him. "But, I feel lost at times." His eyes, his tone, his stance, entreated us to empathize. I banked my fury and attempted to listen. "Think what it's like to have no one in the family meld." He focused on me. "They're scared. You're pushing new ideas at them and they don't have the leveling effect of a reeth mind to help them cope."

I snapped my eyebrows down in outrage. "You're asking us to forgive them, help them?" I looked around at the others, as shocked as I was at Wolfdon's words. "How do we do that?"

Wolfdon dropped into a nearby chair, his body drooping in dejection. "I don't know," he said so softly I barely caught the words.

A knock on the door brought his head around. When Gemdon entered, I straightened in shock at his ashen face, then strode forward. "You look terrible! What happened?"

Gemdon gripped my shoulders as if he couldn't stand by himself. "I can't reach Carnair!"

I grasped the don's hands and drew him into the room. "They shut themselves off from us for a meeting. Many are furious about the gather. Where were you?"

"What have I done?" Gemdon screeched. He sank into a chair and dropped his head into his hands, mumbling. "They talked me into not going. My sons, my grandsons. My daughter's in-laws refused to go and they pressured me, too. I should've stood up to them."

"None of them are melded?" Sara watched him, appalled.

His tortured face veered toward her. "Only me and one granddaughter-in-law. I didn't believe the reeth would be angry. They're never angry!" He sobbed, deep sounds wrenching from his heart, making everyone uncomfortable.

I squeezed his shoulder, offering comfort. "Maybe Lillith can smooth things over." Then, I sank to a squatting position and peered into the old don's face. "Can you tell us why they decided to do this? Help us understand?"

Gemdon drew in deep breaths and got his breathing under control. "I don't really understand why. I just know ..." He trembled. "I just know how hard it is. Baby after baby. Generation after generation and no mind-melds. And now, there'll be no more babies!" He rolled beseeching eyes on me, then glanced around, his face pleading for understanding. "I have a son and two grandsons with no children. And a great-grandson with no one to marry. I know in my mind the meld comes from the don, but ... well, in my heart it seems as if reeth have abandoned my family."

He slumped again, shaking his head. "I don't know what I've done wrong. I don't know if I've not been a good mind-mate. But I can't stand it if Carnair abandons us too." He started sobbing again.

"Carnair's not going to abandon you," Sara said firmly. She knelt beside Gemdon and wrapped her arms around his hunched shoulders. "It'll be alright soon. We'll hear from them and they'll have made a reasonable decision. That's what reeth do. They make reasonable decisions. It's us don that make stupid ones."

Gemdon struggled again to control himself. "We haven't talked about it. We talk about humans and the worry of what will happen. About reeth wanting us to contact them. But I'm positive the others feel the pain of no melds too." He moaned. "Why are our families left out? What's wrong with us?"

No one answered him.

Then, he cried out, "Oh, thank you. Carnair!"

At the same time, everyone heard from their reeth-mates, with the same message I got. "We've worked it out," Lillith said. "We're going to assign reeth soothers to each non-melded don family to help them with stress. We've been negligent. Gemdon, thank you for your honesty." I shifted to squeeze Gemdon's knee to emphasize her words and Sara hugged him tighter as Lillith continued. "I projected what you said to the others and we felt your pain. You convinced them to work with me toward a solution."

Relief sweep through the living room as every don relaxed and basked in the returned minds of their mates. Gemdon cried again on Sara's shoulder as Raedon hugged them both. Relieved, don wandered out until only Raedon, Sara and I remained, soon joined by our reeth-mates.

"We have to come up with a solution." Lillith shoulders rippled with such tension that her wings bobbled erratically. "The situation among the non-melded reeth was nerve-racking."

"Foal, tempers were strained," Memm added. "Nothing like this ever happened before. I checked with Memmiard for his recollections. Why now?"

"It's because of our threat, I assume," Lillith answered. She interrupted her thought to pass Memm's comment on to Sara and I, complete with pitch and inflection. Then, she continued in her own voice. "We sensed hostility building in don families, but we thought it revolved solely around the lack of children, not the lack of mind-melds." She stopped and considered. "Well, both stresses are there but this one took us all by surprise." Stomping around the room, she wrung her tail in agitation. "I've been lax. I should've realized how serious their defiance was getting."

I stopped her in her tracks. "Lillith, you can't take the sole responsibility for this. None of us saw it coming, and we all were warned."

"We've concentrated too much on Pildon," Raedon said. "I keep thinking he's a fool, but he isn't. Just because he rubs me the wrong way doesn't mean I shouldn't take him seriously. I always thought he was alone in his idiocies. We found out he isn't." He put his arm around Sara. "I had a hard time watching Gemdon's grief."

"Me too." She wrapped both arms around him and snuggled close. "We've never considered how it must feel to be non-melded, to watch child after child not meld. And think it's because of something you've done wrong." She lifted her face to meet his troubled eyes. "What torture he's felt. We have to be more sympathetic, more aware of others' feelings."

**

Eventually, the royal pair left, Lillith returned to the Lill family homestead to continue soothing reeth tempers, and I wandered into the kitchen to prepare a solitary supper. I started to pour a glass of Lareina, then picked up the bottle along with my salad, and walked slowly through the hallway to the study. "Funny," I said aloud to the empty house. "I used to spend weeks alone at Eyrie, experimenting or working, never missing company." Entering the study, I shuddered at the big, silent room. "It's too quiet." Sinking onto a sofa by the window, I stared sightless at the tree branches waving in the evening breeze, my mind on Raedon and Sara, arms wrapped around each other, seeking comfort from the day's turmoil. I must have fallen asleep curled on the sofa, empty bottle dropped on the floor, salad forgotten.

Chapter 29

~ Jaym

I awoke suddenly, heart pounding with fear, trying to remember what I'd been dreaming. Something to do with Roark. Then, I recognized what I was hearing—not a dream, but screaming emotion from my son.

"Get out, get out, get out!"

I snatched a robe as I dashed into the other room, shaking Marn awake. "We have to get out of the house. Now!" I shouted. Marn jumped to her feet and we ran through the back door onto the patio.

"Away, Away." Clutching Marn's hand, I ran toward the closest line of palm trees, toward the river. Not understanding the emotion I heard, I just reacted. Rocks and twigs cut my bare feet as we continued to run.

"Hide." Next to the river, the willows bent low, creating a hollow along the bank that I'd discovered on one of my rambles. Crouching, we squirmed under the branches, then hugged each other in the shadow of the tree limbs, panting.

"What is it?" Marn whispered.

"I don't know. The baby was screaming at me to get out. I think I'm going to be sick." As quietly as I could, I retched off the dark bank into the river. "There, he's settling down. We must be safe enough for now. Help me wrap this dark robe around us to hide these light gowns. Keep your face down."

We heard rustling nearby and held our breath, trying not to make a sound. Bushes crackled, branches broke as several somethings ran through the brush along the river, then something splashed into the water. From further away came a gunshot, then, a piercing scream rent the air, someone in agony. It went on and on but I heard from inside, "Okay, Safe."

More rustling approached as the scream continued, rising and falling.

"Jaym?" A reeth, not Lillith. "Jaym?" again. Dark colored feathered hooves approached. "Jaym? It's okay. We caught them. You can come out now." The baby echoed, "Out now."

I grasped Marn's hand, then scrambled out from under the willow branches. Before me stood a large reeth, very dark, barely visible in the dim light. No moon.

"I am Lofferth, Lillyon's cousin. I'm assigned to your security but these humans did something we were totally unprepared for. Are you alright?"

"Yes, Lofferth. Scratched up is all. What happened?" I raised a hand to hold off his answer as I explained his presence to Marn.

"I don't know exactly," he said, his tone low and gravelly. "We were monitoring some humans driving down the road toward your cottage when they shot something toward the window. Then, you came charging out the back door. How did you know?"

"My son woke me and sent me outside." I shivered.

"You must go to Cari's to stay. We can't check the cottage. We don't know what to search for and I don't want you going back in there." I thought he made excellent sense.

"What is that screaming?" asked Marn.

Lofferth answered, "My brother has an intruder by the arm."

"How is he holding him?"

The reeth's grin gleamed in the dim light. "With his teeth."

"Oh."

"If you can mount Tallalb here," Lofferth continued, "he'll take you to Cari's house. Then, please send Turl back to help us secure these fellows."

"How many are there?" I asked. Squinting, I tried to see another reeth in the darkness.

"Four."

"What happened to the others?"

"They'll have headaches." I sensed humor in Lofferth's words, then started as something brushed softly against me. Reaching out, I encountered a reeth neck. *If this is Tallalb, he must be totally black.*

With Marn's help, I climbed heavily onto Tallalb's back. He walked forward to the table and Marn slipped up behind me. Fortunately, he wasn't as tall as Lofferth.

"Don't fly," I heard Lofferth say. "They're not seated very well."

Tallalb walked quickly but smoothly and soon we reached Cari's home, woke Turl, and sent him back to help. As Cari helped me relax on the couch, Marn placed a call to the palace.

"You have to wake Garard. This is an emergency, but I will speak only with Garard ... Quit wasting my time and get him on the phone! I promise you, he'll be furious if you don't wake him."

A few minutes later, she said, "Garard. Our reeth guards say someone shot something into the cottage from a passing car ... We're fine. I'll explain later how we got out ... The reeth leader wouldn't let us back in ... We're at Cari's house ... She's fine, just tired." Marn looked at me for confirmation. "The reeth say they captured four ... "

~ Lillith

Knowing Jaym was safe with Cari, Lillyon and I veered south to meet Lofferth and his team halfway between Center and Palm Cottage. The trussed men had regained consciousness and I searched their minds.

"They're Roark's men, of course," I relayed. "They were first told to locate Jaym after that stupid war." Frustration tinged my words. "When they reported her pregnancy, he instructed them to bring her to Kavv."

"I'm sorry we let them slip past us." Lofferth hung his head. "We had no idea what their intentions were." His bemusement was clear as a heavy scent. "We watch people drive by the cottage day and night. This group didn't seem at all different."

"It's not your fault, Lofferth." I used a wingtip to lift his head. "You couldn't have expected something like this. And you took effective action. Jaym and Marn are fine."

"Yes. Jaym said her son warned her. She and Marn came rushing out the back door just as the shot was fired."

"He must be incredibly powerful." I gazed in the direction of Palm Cottage, considering. "I heard him too and he isn't even born!" Walking around the stationary patrol, I shared my thoughts. "It's my fault for not providing you with a reeth who could sense emotions. I'll remedy that oversight immediately."

I studied the bound men still strapped to the backs of Lofferth's patrol, all groaning but still. I blocked the pain of the one with the lacerated arm, then wiped four minds of the incident and Roark. "Drop them off somewhere far away, maybe Yole or Narr. Their intentions were not to hurt Jaym and Marn, so if they survive, fine. We won't deal with them more harshly unless they show up again in Pith."

Staring once more toward Palmyra and Jaym, I said, "Round up more of your family and meet Lillyon and me in the palm groves when you're done. Then, we'll confront Roark."

**

I approached Cari's house an hour later, calling Jaym to come out. Garard stormed toward me first. "Those men have to be dealt with," he demanded.

"They will be." Garard recoiled at my fierce tone. "They attacked one of ours. They'll receive our punishment. And so will Roark." I trailed around him, stomping my hoofs so hard my wings bobbled from the blows. I snaked my head toward him as he swiveled to keep up with me. "*You* can't mount more guards without drawing too much attention. I'll increment the reeth guard and they'll keep even closer track of comings and goings in this area." I stopped to face him, teeth showing in a parody of a grin. "I'll make sure Roark doesn't try something like this again, I promise you." Garard gulped and stepped back.

225

Jaym came from the side and placed her hand on my taut neck. "To be fair," she said quietly, "he wasn't trying to harm me."

"That's why he'll live," I snarled. Caressing her cheek quickly with my nostrils, I left.

**

Hovering over a park in Kavv, I spotted our quarry, walking alone with his Lady while his security team surrounded the perimeter. "Roark!" My shout whirled the man around; he tucked Kelt in close to his side. An instant later, large, angry reeth surrounded the pair. Kelt screamed and clutched at Roark while he tensed, grabbing at his hip for the gun that wasn't there.

"Don't try to call for help, Roark. We'll kill them, if we have to." I stalked forward, flaring my wings and flashing red-hot fury from my eyes. Roark didn't move as Kelt shrunk tighter against him.

"I'll give you that, Roark. You are brave." I looked him up and down. "But you will not make another move against Jaym, do you understand?"

Roark glanced quickly around. I read his thoughts. I wasn't large, but I was backed by a number of much larger, extremely angry reeth staring at him.

"You have an interest in the trollop, I guess?" he said.

I swung a wing and slapped him across the face with the tip. It appeared soft as a feather, but it sliced his cheek open and blood welled.

"If you don't care to preserve yourself, you might think about your wife and unborn son," I snapped. Kelt whimpered.

"It must be a great interest in my half-sister-in-law." Roark spoke bravely but his hand trembled as he wiped the blood from his face. "Are you taking an interest in Pith as well?"

"My interest in Jaym is not your business. Know that any further attack on her will result in your painful death." I slapped him again, cutting the other cheek as I planted the vision in his

226

mind of being drawn and quartered. Roark wobbled, then stood firm once more.

"You have my word. Nothing will happen to her at my hands."

"Keep it." And we were gone.

**

Several miles away, I landed in a field, shaking violently. When Lillyon landed next to me, I pressed myself against him. He tossed his head high and sent the others away.

"I can't do this," I cried. "It's so wrong. Why do these stupid humans have to be so stupid?"

"Lillith, love, it's okay. You did what you had to do. Roark wouldn't have listened otherwise. He may not still." He caressed me with his neck and head, soothing my agitation. "I know, dear. It's hard for you to be violent, but it was totally necessary."

"I deliberately sliced him!" I wailed. My mind roiled in turmoil and I knew Lillyon had difficulty understanding my words. Trying for more control, I went on. "I was furious; I could have easily killed him." I buried my head under his wing. "I should've asked Lofferth to handle him."

"You could have, but you'd have hated yourself for it. And you might not have liked what he did. He's feeling terrible that he let you down. This way, you controlled the situation. You did exactly enough." He continued to caress me with his head, nibbling softly with his lips up and down the crest of my neck, biting gently just above her withers. Gradually, my shaking subsided as his caresses helped release my tension.

"Oh, Lillyon. We're supposed to provide joy, happiness, stability—not threats and injury. What have I become?"

"You've not become anything different, love. You're still the most beautiful, the most glorious reeth there ever was. Come, let's walk. You need to move, give your mind a chance to settle." He started off across the field, guiding me with his wing. "We'll go somewhere, give you a chance to grieve for your

227

actions. Then, we'll forget the violence and go back to doing what you do best."

Chapter 30
~ Joedon

On Council day, Speakers and their families packed the chamber. Taldon first called Pildon to defend the actions of the non-melded don at Gather. Surprisingly, Pildon deferred to Kewdon, an older don who had never before spoken before council. I watched him with suspicion, extending my emotion sensor talent. His heavy forehead and bushy brow made him seem brutish. His hands, worn and big knuckled, matched the bulging chest and arms developed from physical labor. Dressed formally in black and green, he swaggered forward throwing arrogance in a wide arc.

I throttled my own temper as Kewdon spoke, contempt underlying his tone. "We have to think of ourselves, *our* families. We don't have reeth-mates to help us with whatever it is they supposedly do." He clenched big hands and upped his belligerence. "But, *we* have to help *them*." As he glared around the chamber, he delivered his final words with a roar. "We're tired of their drain on our families!"

Taldon drew in a deep breath, then glowered. "You know don obligations. They've been in place for centuries. Why are you saying this now?"

Kewdon sneered and his conceit oozed over the podium. "Don't you see what they're doing? Forcing you to contact humans?" He paused. "Think for yourself, for once, Taldon."

Taldon sprang from his chair and drew himself upright, squaring his shoulders. "You shall not talk to me that way. I think for myself. I love Tallyon. I would do anything for him."

"Exactly. He has you bowing and scraping and you're too stupid to see it!"

Before I could move, Ylsdon surged forward and slammed a fist into Kewdon's shoulder, knocking him backward. "That's enough!" he bellowed. "You will not insult Taldon."

The decorum of the council chamber disintegrated. Those standing in Kewdon's support were shoved back into their chairs as others tried to get to the podium to take up Taldon's defense. Then, Sara screamed above the noise, "Something's happened!" She caught Raedon's hand and raced out of the chamber, stopping the commotion. In the sudden quiet, Gemdon also screamed, "No!" and collapsed at his desk.

Outside the chamber, the royal couple leapt on their reeth and were instantly airborne, to be followed shortly by other melded don and reeth. I stared after them, impatiently waiting at the door for Lillith to fetch me. Behind me, I heard Gemdon sobbing. "My daughter-in-law," the old one wailed. "She's not alone. Carnair says there's others, surrounded by blood."

I followed Raedon's movements via Lillith's mind. With Memm's massive wing span and powerful muscles working as hard as possible, Raedon arrived first on the scene to see several young reeth surrounding three still forms on the ground, blood flowing freely from their right legs, pooling. He slid to the ground and ran toward them. "What should I do?" he wailed.

Memm answered. "I'm visualizing the scene to the doctors' reeth-mates. They're coming. Nandon says to tie something tight around their upper legs to stop the blood flow."

Sissith heard the same instructions and passed them to Sara as they landed. Already tearing strips from her council dress, Sara slid to the ground. Two more don landed and the three bound strips tightly above the wounds.

"What now? I think they've lost too much blood," she said via Sissith.

Before Nandon could answer, Lillith spoke to everyone. "Take them to Pith, to the hospital. Joedon and I will meet you there. We're on our way now. Nandon, Eledon, follow us. Sara, organize the others to bring the non-melded from the council chamber to see what happened there."

Raedon and two other don with fast reeth loaded the limp femm and took off for Pith. Raedon passed on Lillith's instructions on. "Maintain your invisibility screen as soon as we reach the edge of the populated area. We're going to land on the roof of the hospital." Lillith and I met them there to assist Dr. Grey's emergency response team.

~ Lillith

From the council chamber, Tallyon supplied me with a running commentary of the chaos there. Kewdon refused to respond to Sara's summons even though his family and friends gratefully accepted rides from melded don and reeth—even Pildon.

"You will come with us," Ylsdon ordered. He flung himself on his reeth-mate, trotted up to Kewdon, and lifted him aboard. The reeth immediately launched himself into the air; Kewdon stopped struggling and rode in stiff silence.

"I don't know what happened," Sara said once everyone had dismounted. "They each had long, deep cuts down the side of their right leg and were bleeding to death. Nandon told us what to do even though he wasn't here yet." She glared at Kewdon. "He sent us vital instructions via his reeth-mate." When he didn't respond, she whipped angrily away. "Lillith told us to take them to Pith to the hospital."

She waved her arm at five young reeth standing to the side. "These reeth found them and called for help. All reeth heard their distress call. Sissith notified me; Memmyon told Raedon, Lillith told Joedon. Without reeth instant communication, they'd have died before we even knew they were missing."

Pildon strode forward, outraged. "You took them to a hospital in Pith? To the humans?"

"Yes, Lillith says they'll save their lives."

"Lillith says. How does she know?" Kewdon demanded. He advanced as if he would strike. Ylsdon yanked him back.

"Kewdon, she knows." Sara rebuked him with contempt. "Shut up and listen to what I'm saying." Ylsdon and Taldon moved to stand behind her. "These sons and daughters of the Quil family, non-melded reeth," she emphasized, "were able to get us here, hopefully in time to save our femm's lives, because of the instant communication between reeth!"

231

She sought her reeth-mate and asked, "Sissith, please display for the other reeth what you saw. The rest of you please display to the non-melded."

Gasps broke out among the newcomers as they recognized the three on the ground, surrounded by blood and guarded by the Quil youngsters.

"Twyladon," Kewdon moaned. "My daughter-in-law." He drew his son into his arms.

"Does anyone know the third?" Sara asked.

"It's my fym, Hera." The hom's voice broke. "She and Twyla are good friends."

"What does Lillith think will happen?" Gemdon asked between sobs.

"I don't know." Sara eyed the circle of don, pinning each individual with reproof. "Nandon will explain the medical part to you through these reeth. Pay attention to how important reeth instant communication is to all of us, not just the melded. I'm going to Pith!"

"Well done, Sara," I said into her mind.

**

Later, at Center, don gathered in the council chamber again, awaiting news. Tallyon described the scene to me from his mind-mate's eyes as Joedon and I returned from Pith. Kewdon stood ramrod stiff in the midst of his family, all of them holding hands, many crying. Other groups huddled around the two other young homm, giving whatever comfort they could. Pildon sat at his desk, alone, unnaturally pale, his head bowed.

"Hopefully, they've learned a lesson, at a huge cost," I muttered.

~ Joedon

Lillith landed outside the chamber. I slid off and flung the door open to rush in, Raedon one step behind me. "They're going to live," I yelled. "Thanks to the humans' quick action!"

As emotion subsided, one father asked, "Do they say what happened?"

"Lillith says the three made a pact to commit suicide." I made my face and voice cold. "They were already unhappy at the lack of children. And then, they didn't want to live with a rift between don and reeth." Kewdon started to speak; I interrupted, speaking louder. "Twyla didn't believe don would survive without reeth. The more you refused to help, the more you argued among yourselves, the more afraid she became." At Kewdon's outraged splutter, I spoke even louder. "Lillith picked it out of her mind. When Twyla learned the other two were just as frightened, they decided to end their misery."

"It's my fault," Kewdon's oldest son said, dropping his head onto his brother's shoulder. His words came out mumbled but I understood. "She tried to talk to me about her fear and I wouldn't listen. I was too wrapped up in my anger." The boy raised his head and pleaded. "I have to go to her, tell her how much I love her, child or not. Will you help me get there?"

"We need to go, too." Two other young don stepped forward, their bodies tense, faces reflecting the same fear.

I frowned, consulted Lillith, then nodded. "We'll arrange it." Again I raised my voice for all to hear and emphasized the name. "The Quil family will take you." I glanced at the other don crammed into the chamber, traded nods with Taldon, and took my seat at the Joe family desk.

Taldon counted, announced that enough voting members were present, and banged his gavel. Several minutes passed before everyone settled so he could recall the meeting to order. "What say you, Kewdon, Pildon, now?" he asked, not quite calmly.

Neither volunteered a word. Silence drug until Dogdon rose and walked to the podium. "My fellow don." He gripped his hands in an unsuccessful effort to stop them from shaking. "I'm sorry for the controversy I inadvertently started." Shorter than most, he was also a bit plump. He untangled his hands and clutched the podium. "I only wanted to know how others felt about being non-melded, and somehow, the business got out of hand. I choose to present my apology, and to pledge my support once again to the council." He bowed toward me. "And to our Supreme Don."

Taldon walked to his side and extended a hand. "Thank you, Dogdon. I appreciate the stress you've felt and welcome your renewed support." He paused, then announced, "New business."

I rose and collected Raedon and Sara's father Sardon before I approached the podium.

"You have new business to bring before this council?" Taldon showed no surprise since we'd discussed this days earlier.

I faced the assembly, the other two arranged in support behind me. "We do, Taldon. It is necessary and proper that the council hear this business and vote a decision at this session." Then, I noticed lines had been drawn; those supporting Pildon wore a dark blue band on their left arm. "Most are non-melded Speakers," I said mentally to Lillith. "The rest are older Speakers from the outlying areas—not Center dwellers. Dogdon just slipped his off."

"Pildon doesn't have a majority. I'll insure he doesn't get one." She broke away from me to contact those reeth-mates of the ones wearing arm bands to see if they were solidly behind Pildon's bid for the chair, or wavering in their thinking.

"What is your business?" Taldon's words jogged me back to awareness of the Council.

"Sardon, Raedon, Saradon and I, along with our mind-mates, Sellyon, Memmyon, Sissith and Lillith, propose the following three items for the council's consideration." I paused to let the presenter's names sink in, knowing my inclusion of reeth names fell totally outside of customary practice; I'd caught their attention.

Then, I reminded them. "Saradon is still with our injured femm or she would be before you, with us now." Pausing, I waited for an outcry from someone. None came.

"First, we propose the council form a committee to study the effects of the reeth demonstration of force at Exchange on humans, both those who were present and others around Gareeth who viewed the broadcasts."

I ignored the rustling as council members took in what I'd said. "We recommend four don be appointed to gather the information and report back to the council: Beedon, Girdon, Mosedon, and Fendon. Their training would be coordinated by the royal couple."

Pildon jumped to his feet. "That's crazy. We can't take the chance on losing these young ones—especially not Mosedon, an unwed fem!" Others shouted agreement.

Taldon pounded his gavel. "Quiet in the house. These are proposals. They're not open for discussion at this time. Sit down and be quiet!"

I proceeded as if nothing had happened. "Second, we propose the council form a committee to work in concert with reeth to investigate and develop defensive and offensive capabilities of both species. We've become lax. Humans came from off planet; another species could arrive any day and we must be ready."

Murmurs of agreement swirled through the chamber.

"Third, we propose the council assign our physicians to study human research records at the Medical University in Hilt and work with human research specialists to seek a solution to our birth-rate crisis."

Again, agreement rippled through the room as members eyed the six Wee children seated to Weedon's right. Then, evidently, the second part of my proposal sank in.

"I object!" Pildon leaped up, his face white. "Learning about humans can't be of help. They're too different."

As Taldon pounded for order, Raedon stepped forward. "According to Eledon, they aren't," he said loudly. "Humans just saved the lives of three of our own. They have large medical facilities and research labs. When Eledon gets back, he'll explain what he told me."

"Absolutely not!" Pildon ranted, pacing before the podium, flinging his arms in supplication. "We can't possibly learn anything from humans. And we can't risk letting them know we have a problem."

"We don't know what we could learn from humans. We've never tried." Raedon held his temper as he appealed to the femm, as he knew Sara would have. "Do you want children or not?"

"Exactly." Shy, quiet Cheradon stood, arms forward, palms up, and shouted. "I speak for the femm in this room. This problem must be solved. It's more critical than anything else." I followed her gaze as she swept the room. Femm whispered in Speaker ears, nudging their homm, their sons, their fathers. Old to young, they responded to her appeal.

Chera's hom stood abruptly at her side, defiant and demanding. "Our fear of humans is ridiculous." His deep tone carried clearly. "If we don't solve this, our most urgent need, we're going to destroy our species!"

My heart thudding in amazement, I watched as couple after young couple gathered around them in support. Many a Speaker censured son or daughter, but no one faltered, making it obvious where they stood on the matter. Quietly, Lillith and I rejoiced.

Taldon pounded his gavel and gradually, the noise settled. Chera and her supporters regained their seats, Raedon stepped back, and I proceeded. "As of today, Taldon is stepping down and I am taking my rightful place as your Supreme Don. We, the royals, present our proposals for your review, for vote during tomorrow's session."

I bowed gravely. Taldon walked to the podium and handed me the gavel, then took his position at the Tal family desk next to his son. I struck the gavel on the podium. "This meeting is adjourned. We'll reconvene tomorrow morning at nine."

Chapter 31
~ Joedon

"Joedon!" The strain in Lillith's voice had me on my feet in seconds. "Raedon needs you." I pulled on a loose shirt, shimmied into trousers, crammed feet into boots, and raced out the door to fling myself on her back. We flew north as she fed me the story she received from Memm. "Kewdon's kidnapped Sara." Her words fell heavily. "He drugged them and left Sissith asleep at his house. No one else is there; she just regained consciousness and called for help." Her words left me cold as ice. "She's frantic. She can't hear Sara anywhere, and neither can I!"

She landed in a cloud of dust outside a modest house on the north edge of Center and we pushed our way through the open front door. In a cramped living room, Memm, Sissith, and Raedon huddled in agony. I strode forward and wrapped my arms around my friend's shoulders while Lillith curled her neck around the bay mare. "We'll find her," she promised as she bathed the room in reassurance.

Reeth landed and feet came running outside; Taldon burst into the room, followed by two young don I didn't recognize.

"Kewdon's sons," Taldon called. "They don't have any idea where he might be but want to help. More are coming."

I held up my hands to quiet the crowd that flowed into the small room. "We at least know she's alive! We'll spread out and search Center, house by house if we have to." I caught Lillith's suggestion and grabbed Raedon by the arm. "Go in pairs. We don't know how dangerous he might be."

All morning reeth flew sweep over Center and don searched abandoned homes from the ground. By midday, no one had found a clue as to Kewdon's whereabouts. "We've completely covered Center," Lillith reported. "I have over fifty reeth seeking any type of emotion out of the ordinary. I can't imagine how he's hiding from us so effectively."

I stroked her neck. "When we find him, we have to figure that out so it can't happen again." The touch helped calm us both.

"What else to try?" She tensed. "Marnith's found him. He's screaming mentally, running south." I vaulted on and we were off. She sent a command to Memm to keep Raedon away until we had Kewdon under control. Reeth from all directions converged on the pathway following the cliff edge; they tracked the running don as he dodged in and out of abandoned homes.

"He's wearing some type of helmet," Lillith reported. "We're only getting fleeting emotions. Something is suppressing his mental signature."

Reeth dove but the don dodged them each time, into a building or a doorway. "See if they can drive him into the path behind Sardon's house," I said. "It ends at the wall next to the cliff. Drop me just outside the back door and I'll try to get behind him."

Lillith swooped down and I dropped off, flexing my knees to take the impact. Running to the end of the path, I closed and locked the high gate to the trail down the cliff. Then, I darted into the doorway leading into Sardon's gardens and settled down to wait.

Following the chase through Lillith, I saw reeth continually dive at Kewdon, forcing him ever south. They dropped riders close to him, forcing him out of hiding time after time. "He's moving slower each time he's routed," Lillith said.

"Just keep driving him this way." I waited, completely still. "Can you read anything from him yet?"

"Not a thing."

I counted, holding intensely still. Then, I heard the rush of wings and the shout of a rider. Another reeth dived at a running don at the end of Sardon's lane causing him to duck into the path. Someone ran past. I sprang out, knocking Kewdon flat. Placing my hands just above Kewdon's ears, I slipped my fingers up under the helmet, found the touch I needed, and sent the command for stasis. Kewdon went limp.

238

Pulling lacerated fingers from under the helmet, I knelt to roll Kewdon over. His eyes spun frantically; he screamed and screamed. Alarmed, I leapt back as spittle leaked from his mouth. Seconds later, Lillith landed next to me and someone dropped off her side: Juldon. He shoved past and yanked the helmet off Kewdon's head, leaving deep cuts in brow and cheeks.

"I can get nothing out of him. His mind's in absolute turmoil." Lillith backed away. "He truly has gone crazy."

More reeth and don arrived. We stood in a group, staring at Kewdon, then looked away from his madness.

"What happened to him?" Juldon's deep voice quavered with revulsion. He turned the helmet around in his hands. "What is this stuff?"

"I don't know." I forced myself to approach, knowing Kewdon couldn't control his muscles to strike under stasis. "Kewdon, stand up," I ordered. Nothing happened. I gripped Kewdon's shoulder. "Kewdon, stand up," I ordered again. No response, other than the screams stopped. Shaken, I said, "He should respond to my commands!"

"I don't think Kewdon can respond to anything right now." Lillith stepped closer. "His mind is churning. He thinks he's striking out in all directions. What I get is a picture of him punching and kicking for all he's worth." She assessed the assembled don, each of them staring horror-struck at the one on the ground, then bolstered their nerve. "I think we'd better get him restrained, before the stasis has a chance to wear off. I'm not sure we should count on it lasting an hour."

Juldon dropped the helmet and knelt at Kewdon's side. Stripping off his heavy jacket, he grabbed a flaccid arm and shoved it into a sleeve so the back covered Kewdon's chest. Then, he flipped the body over, crammed the other arm into the second sleeve, and pulled the sleeves together behind the immobile don's back. "Get some rope," he said. A few minutes later, someone handed him a length of rope and Juldon tied Kewdon's legs together and then his arms. He rose. "Now what?"

"We're not going to find Sara with Kewdon's help." I felt defeated.

Lillith must have sensed my guilty feelings and spoke quickly. "His mind was gone before you put him in stasis. This is not your fault!" She sent instructions to the crowd. "Search all abandoned buildings first. He couldn't have carried Sara far, not without a reeth to help."

I picked up the helmet and examined its rough construction. "Watch for something made of this metal. It must have been blocking Kewdon's emotions from you." I held it up to Lillith, then passed it around to the other don. "Something made of this could be hiding Sara from us."

As the don studied the helmet, Lillith nudged me. "Go get your hands treated. I'll join Memm and Raedon, then pick you up to continue the search. Juldon and his sons will guard Kewdon until we find Sara."

I nodded and walked to Sardon's back door, pounding on it. Shortly, someone let me in. Suridon washed my bleeding hands, doused them with Lareina, then wrapped them as I explained the search so far, Kewdon's capture, and the odd metal helmet. Both parents, although white with worry, seemed to be holding up as well as could be expected. When Lillith arrived with Memm, Raedon went straight to Suri and hugged her, then extended an arm to pull Sardon close. The three stood trembling with their foreheads together for a moment, sharing their anguish.

Their emotion flowed violently over me and I sagged against Lillith, none to steady herself. I briefly thought of Jaym and how I might have had with her what Raedon had with Sara. Lillith broke in. "We'll find her," she said sharply. "Now, quit dawdling and get out there to search."

**

The elder of Kewdon's sons found the metal box in the back of a store room in the deserted Pam mansion, covered with moldy blankets. His shout brought the nearest melded-don who sent the call out via his reeth. The young don searched frantically for something to pry the top off the box and snatched up a crowbar. She was curled inside a space too small for her to stretch out; legs pulled up to her chest, arms wrapped around her belly, her forehead rested on her knees. She did not move. He backed away, shaking as others poured into the storeroom. Raedon dropped on his knees before the box, Sissith dropped her head onto her mind-mate's tangled black hair, Memm braced himself next to his mare's shoulder.

"She breathes," Sissith said as Lillith and I forced our way inside. "She's holding herself deep, like Raedon did." The mare cried, "We have to save her!"

"Memmyon, direct her," Lillith snapped. "All you don clear out and let the reeth in. We'll be ready in just a moment."

I pulled Raedon up and we each wrapped our arms around our mind-mates. Reeth touched reeth, power flowed through them. Sissith called, Sara responded and opened her eyes. Stiffly, she raised her head.

Raedon touched her bruised cheek gently. "Saradon. I love you."

A smile wavered. "I love you too."

Carefully, Raedon and I helped her rise, unfolding joints that creaked and muscles that screamed from pain. Sissith and Lillith combined to block the worst and, gradually, Sara unbent to stand trembling in the opened box. Reeth jostled each other to get out of her way. Through the open door came her parents, faces grey, seemingly twenty years older. Raedon and I lifted her out of the box and she fell limply into her mother's arms.

"Everyone out," Lillith ordered. "Give them room." She spoke directly to Raedon. "When she feels stronger, take her home. We'll come this evening to talk."

"Wait, Lillith." Sara's voice shook. "My baby. Can you hear her?"

Lillith stood still and blocked out the don around her, all projecting high levels of stress, fear, or anger. I held my breath as she probed. There. She sent us the faint flutter, a heartbeat. "Yes," she murmured. "She's alive."

**

That night, we gathered in Sardon's front room to hear Sara's story. "When I returned from Pith hospital, no one was home. I assumed you were all at the Council meeting, so I cleaned up and dressed to join you. Kewdon knocked, nodded politely, and I let him in." She gripped Raedon's hand. "He said he'd come to apologize and to thank me for my care of his daughter-in-law. He sounded absolutely sincere, didn't he, Sissith?"

The bay mare nodded from her place just behind Sara. She rested her head on the back of the chair with the air of never letting Sara out of her sight again.

"We talked for a bit about the young femm and their fears, then he asked if we would give him a lift home. I never thought a thing unusual about it. He had no reeth-mate and we could easily deliver him before coming to the meeting."

She shuddered. "As soon as we landed in front of his house, he invited me in to see something he'd made for Twyla and we, stupidly I guess, followed him. In his living room, he picked something up, turned around, and placed it on his head. The next thing I knew, I was crammed in that box and I couldn't reach Sissith, no matter what I tried." Terror of being locked in rose in her mind; Sissith and Lillith again combined to help her steady herself.

"It will take a long time before Sara will go into small places, I think," Lillith said quietly to Sissith. "You must help her get over this extreme fear." Aloud, to the others, she explained. "We think he had some type of sleep drug in that helmet of his and he sprayed it on you. Then, he must have carried you to the Pam mansion, leaving Sissith behind."

She nodded to me and I produced the helmet. "According to Goldon, this helmet and the metal box are made of pure lead. None of us, including our best metal workers, knew lead would block telepathy. And we don't know how Kewdon knew. We tested it after Goldon told us his theory and indeed, Joedon cannot communicate if he wears the helmet or climbs into the box and closes the lid."

Sara's face filled with fear. "You willingly got in there?"

I smiled ruefully. "Lillith and Goldon were right there. I knew I could get back out. I can't image how you didn't go insane locked in that thing for hours."

Trembling, she hid her face in her hands for a long moment. Then, she steadied herself and looked up. "Kewdon knew of the humans at Eyrie and he hated you for it. He had no way to attack them, or you, so he came after me. He raved his revulsion at me and, unfortunately, I could hear him clearly from inside." She ducked her head. "He hated me for getting pregnant when neither of his daughters-in-law could." Again, she shuddered. "He meant for me to die in that box." Raedon folded her into his arms while the rest of us filed out of the room.

**

As we left the Sar mansion, Lillith shoved me violently to one side and whipped around to face a dark corner where she'd felt something move. Her tension did not abate as Pildon stepped into the light, his hands forward, palms up. Studying him, she decided he was distraught, not aggressive.

"What do you want?" she asked, cold as ice. I went to her side and placed my hand on her shoulder, my mind tightly aligned with hers.

"I ..." Pildon drew in a deep breath; he was trembling. "I wanted to know how Sara is." When neither of us answered, he blurted, "I can't believe what Kewdon did! Honestly, he never said anything about it to me."

"I believe he's sincere," she said aside to me. Aloud, "She'll be alright. No physical harm to her or the baby. Mentally—I don't know."

"Good." Pildon's eyes went wide. "I meant good she's okay."

"I knew what you meant. It's over. Go home!" Lillith let her exhaustion be heard but Pildon didn't leave.

"Please. What will happen to Kewdon?"

"We don't know. When the healer gets through with him, we'll make a decision."

Pildon bowed. "Thank you." He started away and, for the first time ever, left his mind unguarded. Lillith probed.

"I understand now," she told me as we returned to our own home. "His father was cold, fanatical. When Pildon didn't meld by the age of ten, his father shunned him, made him feel unworthy. He thinks he's afraid of reeth. What he really is … is envious. He still wants to please his dead father. Humans are only one small part of his overall anger."

Chapter 32
~ Jaym

My water broke in the middle of the night. I knew it instantly when Joeledon woke me saying in my head, "Mama, out." I pressed the button on the side of my bed and pandemonium burst into the still night. I heard Marn squeak and jump up from the foldout-couch in the living room; Turl and Cari came rushing out of Marn's room, and they bounced off each other with mild curses, grunts, and a whispered "sorry" in their scramble to their positions.

"Calm. Stay calm," said Lillith from outside. She'd been staying at the cottage for a week to help us through the birth.

Turl placed the fetal monitor. Cari, shaking worse than me, took my hands to coach my breathing. Marn, deemed the sensible one, found it difficult to dial the phone in her excitement but finally managed to connect with the hospital where the doctors had been on call for several days. Twenty minutes later a helicopter landed outside the cottage, probably disgorging the birthing team, Garard, Stephon, and who knew what others had forced themselves along. *Hopefully, not Father,* I thought between pushes.

I glanced up in surprise, caught between labor spasms, as people rushed into the room. The medical personnel, two doctors and two nurses, stopped to gape at the finely equipped delivery room they found inside our quaint rural home. But they wasted no time discussing it as they scrubbed.

"Dr. Lyra. I'm Turl. The epidural is ready." He handed her the shot and she administered it. I didn't even feel it.

Cari squeezed my hands. "Look at me." She forced me to focus on her. "Breath in, now out. Stay with me."

Between pushes, I saw the medical team sort themselves out, the observers take to the corners out of the way, and suddenly, Joeledon arrived, as if he'd only been waiting for them to get ready. He wailed, jerked his arms around, kicked his feet at the nurse as she took him from the doctor, and radiated love and happiness throughout the room. Everyone stopped what they were doing to gaze at him with wonder. For the doctors and nurses, it had to be the first time they'd felt the force of a telepathic emotion. The rest of us grinned in delight.

Outside the cottage, Lillith whinnied mightily and then shut herself off. "I can't let the world know about this child just yet," she said to me. "You did wonderfully."

Grinning with an overabundance of joy, the medical team proceeded through their tasks. "A healthy baby boy weighing ten pounds, twelve ounces," said the newborn nurse. "He's twenty-four inches long and has masses of red curly hair, just like his mother."

His hair, however, was the only way he resembled me. Although I'd been told about their doubt of this "don" birth, the doctors easily saw that my son was not a human baby. He was too long, too alert, and had the long and narrow facial features they'd seen on the television screen for weeks after the Exchange.

"He really is don," whispered Dr. Lyra.

The nurses, confused, carried on. "I hope someone explains this someday," one said to the other. She finally laid the baby on my chest and we heard him gurgling mentally with happiness and praising me, his wonderful mother. He broadcast feelings of delight and a sense of my face floated through human minds, followed by a humming purr of contentment. They, and I, experienced the warmth of my skin next to his cheek and belly; my kiss on his forehead; the comfort of my hand on his back; the vision of my face through his eyes once again; and finally "Mama."

Dr. Lyra shook herself out of her inertia and, to my relief, bent to attend to the afterbirth. My son fired a blast of welcome and a second's warning, startling me into a reflexive push and another, much smaller baby slid into her hands. A nurse jumped forward to take the wailing child from the doctor, dried her off, and placed her on my chest alongside her brother. Doctors, nurses, friends marveled at the babies, so much alike except for their size, while Joeledon bathed his little sister in comfort, washing it over us. He soothed with images of me as their mother who loved them and would protect them. Overjoyed, I hummed love out loud and with my mind; the tiny girl stopped crying.

"Her name is Joanadon," I announced.

Outside, Lillith could hardly contain her excitement. "Not only a beautiful baby boy but a girl as well. What a triumph!" she said. I couldn't actually see her but I knew clearly what she was doing as she danced crazily around on all four feet, flapping her wings in the air. She longed to tell the world about this wonder but placed a strong clamp on her mind so nothing would leak. She didn't stop herself from shouting with her body, however, knocking over almost everything on the patio in her gyrations.

Again, Dr. Lyra went back to her task of taking care of me, prompting the rest of the helpers to get back to work. "Five pounds, four ounces, eighteen inches long," announced the nurse of the squirming baby girl.

Dr. Gema, the pediatrician, picked up Joeledon to check him over; he was pleased to oblige and smiled into her mind as she held him. "How strange it feels to have an infant babble in my head," she said. When she reached for the girl, however, Joanadon started to wail again. "I can hear him soothing her with pictures of you. She's relaxing!" The doctor regarded the baby in awe. "What's going on here?"

Before anyone could respond, we heard a commotion from outside the cottage. Then, we heard Joeledon's young mental voice, "Lillity, Lillity," and a pleasant answering voice, "Welcome, Joeledon. I'm so pleased to meet you."

"Good Lord," exclaimed Stephon loudly. "We've just heard a mind-meld! Joeledon has mind-melded with Lillity, whoever she is. I'm going to let her in."

A golden reeth entered the room. I stared in amazement, along with everyone else, but she had eyes only for my son. Moving gracefully forward, she ignored the humans stepping out of her way. She touched her nose gently to his plump belly, breathing in his scent. Joy and satisfaction radiated from her. I heard, "I've long been lonely. Never again."

Wordlessly, I reached up and stroked the golden jaw. Joeledon locked his brown eyes on the blue swirling eyes of his mind-mate and didn't move. My voice wobbled as I gazed in wonder at the large muzzle touching my son. "I understand now. He's yours as well as mine and you're his, aren't you?"

The soft, pleasing voice brought thoughts of chimes with it. "That is so. He'll never be alone."

~ Lillith

Standing just outside the bedroom door with Garard and Stephon by my side, my heart swelled to bursting as I monitored and shared with the two men the emotions swirling in the small room. The pediatrician abruptly sat on the closest chair, tears streaming down her face. Turl and Cari wrapped their arms around each other, immobilized by the affectionate outburst. Dr. Lyra, still sitting at Jaym's feet, felt she had never experienced anything so tender. Although no one explained what had happened, the humans understood the serious bond made between these two beings: the newborn boy and the golden horse-like creature. Every single one of them wanted a reeth of their own, wanted never to be alone.

This is my sister! I thought, speechless with pride. *My baby sister!*

Lillity shifted her gaze to the other baby. "This is *my* baby sister," we heard from Joeledon, as if he'd heard my thought. "We must protect her." She stretched her golden neck and lightly touched Joanadon as if to acknowledge the task placed upon her by her mind-mate.

Marn galvanized herself into action. "Come out into the other room, all of you." She took the pediatrician by the arm and lifted her from the seat. "Let Jaym and the babies rest. As you can see, they're doing well. They need to be alone." She herded them into the living room where they ran into Garard, Stephon, and me.

The medical team stopped in their tracks to gawk at me, smaller but even more dazzling than the golden one, more than one thought. As they struggled with accepting what they saw and felt, Stephon came to their rescue. "Here, Turl," he said. "Help me put up this sofa bed. Now, Doctors. Please be seated. You nurses can sit over here in these chairs. Garard, bring more chairs from the kitchen. Cari, Turl, fix hot tea and whatever you might have to eat. I'm afraid we've thoroughly shocked them. It's now our responsibility to help them absorb what they've experienced."

Marn showed everyone where to wash up and soon they were seated comfortably. Cari served hot tea with plenty of honey; Turl passed around plates of fresh strawberry tarts and triangular meat sandwiches. The food helped to restore their equilibrium as the team devoured everything. Finally, they seemed relaxed.

"Okay. Good," Stephon said. "I'm happy to see you recovering. It's time to tell you our story. Garard, you start at the beginning, I'll pick up where you end. Turl, Cari, and Marn can tell their part. Finally, we'll turn the floor over to Lillith. Fair enough?"

For the next two hours, the medical team asked questions and I controlled the answers about the extraordinary birth they'd assisted. I assured them the day would come when they would be allowed to tell the world about what they'd witnessed, but until then, I could, and would, enforce their silence.

"It's funny," I admitted. "With all our preparations, all our plans, it never occurred to me there might be twins. Don don't have twins. It's obvious now that Joele shielded his sister from us, even in the womb. I never, ever, sensed her."

"Our ultrasounds never worked," Dr. Lyra sat composed on the couch, both hands wrapped around a cup of coffee. "Could he have blocked them?"

I eyed her speculatively. "I wouldn't be surprised. I've never encountered a stronger mentality in a newborn than what's in that boy."

The doctor set down her cup. "I think he also blocked her heart beat. One time, I thought I heard an echo, then never heard it again. With humans, we almost always hear both heartbeats."

"He started out very young to protect his little sister," Stephon said.

"It also never occurred to me that he would mind-meld." Distracted, I allowed my amazement to escape, filling the room with something almost tangible. "I believe I thought he would be mine to watch over." Shaking my head, I laughed, baring my teeth. No one reacted to what could have been considered a threatening move. I guess they were filled with my rueful amusement. "I absolutely ignored the fact that he would meld with whomever was right for him. Lillity is my younger sister. In retrospect, I can see she's the perfect partner." Throwing my head up, I laughed harder. "But of course she is. That's how melds work."

When the doctors checked their patients, all were sound asleep. Lillity stood quietly in the corner, also asleep, but to Dr. Lyra's eyes, she appeared steadfastly on guard. The doctor closed the door quietly.

Chapter 33
~ Caleb and Lilliod

Caleb, Lilliod, and the dog followed the sheep slowly home after a glorious day on the benches. The boy reveled in the late year sunshine as he watched the flock moving downhill. No one wanted to hurry away from the grass—even the ewes sensed the coming of winter. Lilliod reported the dog's sadness although Caleb could see it in the way the dog moved. "I must give him a name," he thought to Lilliod. "He's more to me than just a dog, now."

Since Lilliod had begun sensing the emotions of the other animals, even the stupid sheep, Caleb had changed his opinion of them all. "I'll call him Doc. Close enough to dog but better." He concentrated hard and thought the name toward the dog. Doc looked up, ran toward him, and licked his hand.

"Wow." Caleb's joy radiated to the others. Even the lead ewe looked back as if she understood.

"I don't think so," said Lilliod. "It's just a coincidence that she looked just now. But Doc is happy to have a name."

They continued down the mountain with Caleb storing pictures in his mind for drawings: the deep green of the evergreens with orange, red, and yellow splotches of changing leaves peeping through; the dark blue of the mountain peak, streaked with bands of grey from rock slides and as yet snow free; multiple shades of gray, pale green and brown moss mottling a boulder. His mother had brought home colored pencils from her last trip to town and he couldn't wait to draw.

Lilliod leaped over such a boulder, flared his wings, and trotted quickly toward a rushing stream. He plunged in, water swirling around his knees, and buried his muzzle in the cold water. For the first time, Caleb noticed how much Lilliod had grown. His back now reached Caleb's shoulder, and his wings—they spread very wide.

He heard Lilliod's warning as he approached. "It's awfully cold. I don't think you should step in."

Caleb laughed and stuck out his hand. "Too cold for me!" He backed away, as Doc ran up and lapped.

"Lilliod, your wings are so much bigger now. I wonder if you could fly."

The black reeth cocked his head to regard Caleb with one big, brown, loving eye. "You think?"

Caleb pointed to a long rock layer jutting over a short drop. "Why don't you try? You could jump off that rock ledge and flap. If you don't fly, it won't be far to fall."

He felt the reeth's grin as he watched Lilliod trot toward the ledge, Doc barking madly behind him. Lilliod reached the ledge, flapped his wings vigorously in preparation, and leaped for the sky. He flew! Not far but still. Caleb dashed forward to where he landed, winded, and wrapped long arms around the muscled neck.

"What did it feel like?" His mind swirled with the exhilaration emanating from his friend.

"It was glorious. Got to try it again."

Doc barked at them and dashed toward the flock of sheep. "We've got to get them home." Caleb shared Lilliod's disappointment but they turned toward the sheep anyway.

The boy smiled and placed his hand on the reeth's back. Kneading, he discovered new muscle there. He thought of home and his smile broadened. This last summer had brought many changes to his life. Pa actually liked him now—the drawings brought money into the house for luxuries they'd never had before. Mother had her sewing machine. She'd made new shirts and pants for everyone from material Pa brought home. Caleb had always had new pants, being taller than the brothers, but this fall, everyone got new ones, not just hand-me-downs. And his new shirts fit instead of hanging loose on his bony shoulders as his brother's discards always had.

And mother had new dresses. "I'm going to draw her," Caleb said. "With a big smile on her face in that yellow flowered dress she made last week."

"Your mother will like that." Lilliod ran his muzzle up Caleb's arm to emphasize the warmth he felt for Caleb's mother—who loved without inquiring into the changes that came about in the boy.

"Wonder what's for supper?" Caleb's stomach rumbled as Lilliod pictured his favorite: roast beef with potatoes and biscuits. Caleb's mother made the best biscuits and he always hid some to share with Lilliod. The pair increased their pace toward home at the thought, but the sheep refused to be hurried.

They'd just rounded the last rock outcropping, and the lead ewe was headed strongly toward the sheep pen where she knew grain awaited, when Lilliod flung out a wing and stopped Caleb in his tracks. Doc ran quickly up and planted his hind end in front of Caleb, staring up with urgent eyes.

"What?"

"Your brother and his wife have returned from their visit." Lilliod's tone made Caleb feel sick. "I don't understand, exactly ...," Lilliod continued. "They saw some sort of program ... about reeth, and don, like in your book. Your brothers found my stable."

Lilliod's head swung back and forth as if he cast about for words. "They're waiting for us. For you. They're going to make you explain the drawings." The expression in Lilliod's eye, joy dampened, a slight sheen of red, decided Caleb instantly. His friend was afraid.

He whistled a series, sending Doc to pen the sheep, quickly. He ran down and closed the gate behind the last lamb, then hurried back to where Lilliod still stood. "We're leaving. Now."

~ Lillith

At Center, I sent Joedon a wakeup warning. "Raedon's coming. He has something important to show you." He'd fallen asleep in a chair, again.

"What time is it?" He sounded groggy. "I didn't drink that much Lareina, did I?'

"It's six am. And I think you did." I kept my voice soft, not blaring into his hangover.

"What's he want at this hour?"

"I can't tell. Memm's hiding something." I prodded him into staggering to the bathroom and turning the shower on cold. "I don't understand how he's doing it!"

"I thought he took Sara to the Sapphire Sea for her birthday." Shivering, Joedon stepped out of the shower and toweled himself dry.

"They're flying as fast as they can back here, their thoughts in turmoil. That sneak Memm is somehow blocking me from picking up the subject."

"I never knew he could do that."

"I didn't either!" I stormed into his quarters as he entered the kitchen to make breakfast. Shaking off his offer of carrots and pared apples, I paced around the table, unable to do anything until Raedon and the others arrived. Joedon sat down to eat, the warm grain cereal cheering him after his cold shower. Lillyon arrived with an air of disgust and Joedon reached over to pluck a long straw from his mane.

We waited impatiently for half an hour before Raedon came through the door. "Look at this!" He thrust a book into Joedon's hands. I peered over his shoulder. The cover displayed a black reeth, rearing among a field of wild flowers, broad white blaze running down his face, four white stockings from knee to hoof. I snorted in disbelief and waved Lillyon over.

"Lilliod," Joedon breathed.

"That's what I thought. I'm sorry," Raedon said. "I asked Memm to try to block our thoughts so we could see your reaction without the prejudice of our guesses."

"How did you do that?" I asked at the same time Joedon asked, "Where did you get this?"

Memm answered me. "Sissith and I filled our minds with nonsense as we flew here. It was hard."

Raedon answered Joedon. "A kid had it at a campsite near where we were. Sissith saw it first. I projected a human image and convinced the family to sell it to me for 'my little boy back home'. They said they could easily get another."

My anger subsided into astonishment as I thought about the young reeth pair's tactics. Then, I focused on the picture. "Did you learn where it came from?"

Sara took the book from Joedon's hand and flipped it over. "Some relative sent it to them from Farr. However, they said it was selling everywhere." She pointed at the bottom of the back cover. "Look at the date—just two weeks ago."

She started to leaf through the book, holding it out so Joedon and I could see. Lillyon crowded in. "It seems to tell a story of a boy finding a reeth stuck in a crevice and rescuing it." Sara paused. "The drawings are very good."

"We felt we had to show it to you in person, without any hints." Raedon put his hands on Sara's shoulders, standing close behind her, watching Joedon's reactions. "We didn't want to spread false hopes if we were wrong."

Joedon took the book from Sara's hand. He studied the cover, and then the pictures inside. I rested my head on one shoulder, Lillyon on the other, as he read the story aloud. No drawings of the boy, only pictures portraying a young, plump, happy reeth. "It has to be Lilliod," he said at last. "But, if he's alive, why couldn't anyone hear him?"

"We need to find out about this boy, this story, before we contact my cousin." Lillyon's voice was firm. "We need to go to Farr and track this down." My normally unflappable husband quivered with anxiety, his wing-tips shaking and his tail snapping.

Joedon jumped up from his chair. "Let's go."

"You're still restricted," Raedon pointed out.

"Hasn't stopped me before. We need to see what's going on in Farr." He pointed at the food on the table. "Help yourselves to breakfast. I'll change into riding clothes. I'll just be a moment."

While Raedon and Sara posed as a couple wanting to have portraits done by the talented artist, I probed the publisher's mind. He insisted he didn't know the artist. I only learned of a man in the eastern reaches of Farr, not a name. The publisher had recognized a gold mine, bought the pictures at a farmer's market, put them together in a logical order, and made up the story. The book sold like candy.

We flew east, cloaked in invisibility. The land we crossed gradually rose in altitude and soon I recognized landscapes included in the book. The area seemed sparsely populated, small farms surrounded by grazing animals. *Not as prosperous as Pith,* I thought. A town appeared in the distance; I swerved sharply right. We landed just outside a row of houses, hiding ourselves within a grove of unfamiliar, denuded trees. The don split up, heading into the city projecting human images; Raedon and Sara angled east; Joedon aimed west.

"I've picked up word of the market," I reported. "It's on the south side of town." The don changed their directions and converged on a point at the south of the city, following my mental map. Joedon saw the small, awning covered stand first. He approached carefully, not wanting to overwhelm the proprietor with too much attention. The man fit the description I'd uncovered in the publisher's mind.

Joedon walked toward the pictures, many of the black reeth, but also drawings of sheep, a long-haired black and white dog, mountain meadows, and a farm-stead nestled among broad-leafed trees.

"The prices are reasonable." A big man, not tall but broad, with black hair and heavy brows, came forward. "Do you see something you like?"

Joedon pointed at a drawing of sheep quietly grazing while lambs jumped and played around them. "These are very good," he said. "So life-like I almost feel they are right there next to your booth." He looked the man in the eye. "Do you know the artist?"

"My younger brother." Joedon sensed fondness for the boy. "He's deaf and can't talk. Just last summer ma gave him a book, some paper, and pencils. He's been drawing ever since. Everything he sees ..." The man smiled crookedly at a large drawing of the reeth. "And stuff he imagines." Apprehension hid behind the man's affection.

"He heard reeth are not imaginary," I said. "And the boy disappeared just after. He's worried."

"Do you think I could meet him?" Joedon moved toward a picture of the dog. "Get him to do a portrait of an animal for me?"

"The dog's gone, too," Lillith said. "He evidently left with the boy. His brothers found a shelter hidden among some trees. The family thinks the reeth wasn't so imaginary after all. They're afraid to let the authorities know the boy is gone."

Joedon projected wellbeing along with sincere admiration. After hesitation and careful study, the vendor decided to trust. "I'd have to ask Ma. She protects him pretty much—cause he can't hear you understand." He picked up the drawing of the dog. "How about you buy this one. I'll make you a good deal. Then, come back tomorrow and I'll tell you if Ma'll let you meet Caleb."

Joedon smiled and paid for the picture, knowing as soon as he stepped out of sight, the man would pack up his wares and disappear. "Too many strangers have been asking about the artist and the family is scared," I said.

We consulted in the woods outside town. As usual, I strode around in a circle to dissipate my tension. Lillyon was watching with anxiety building; he'd always been better at hiding it. "A simple family, they had a real fear about the authorities taking the deaf boy from them before, and now that he's gone, accusing them of doing away with him." I swiveled my ears, wrung my tail. "I can't tell if that threat is real. This man believes it." I stopped and stared east. "He's leaving."

Within a half hour, we hovered outside the farm house from the drawings. "The man is reporting to his mother. Several others inside." Jittery from my effort, I spoke quietly. "I've centered on the mother. She suspected for a long time that Lilliod was real because of the tremendous changes that came about in the boy... He's been gone five days."

I rubbed my head down Lillyon's shoulder. Hoping for good to come of our search for the son of his favorite cousin, he was more stressed than I'd ever seen him. I offered what comfort I could. "They tracked him north, then lost sign of him." I went stiff, focused sharply. "They found hoof prints beside the boy's boot marks."

"Okay." Joedon stepped forward and placed his hand on my withers, preparing to remount. "We'll spread out and fly north, calling and listening. Watch for possible hiding places." He swung himself up. "We'll stop every so often to search the ground, and talk to anyone we happen to see. We know what the boy looks like—and the dog."

"He evidently took nothing with him and he didn't have a coat when he left with the sheep the last morning his mother saw him." I left the sheltering trees. "They're frantic with worry."

Chapter 34
~ Lillith

"There's a storm coming," Memm warned. We flew slowly, calling mentally to the young reeth. *Surely the colt will hear us, I thought, as close as we are to each other.* We saw no sign of humans.

The storm rolled toward us from the east, black clouds massing over the mountains, causing the sky to gradually darken even though nightfall was hours away. "Before long, it's going to be hard to see anything," Memm predicted. None of our riders were dressed appropriately for a severe storm.

"Keep watch for an inn or something," I said.

Sissith voiced Sara's protest. "We can't take cover. You said the boy had no coat. We can't leave them out in a snowstorm. The boy could die."

"She's right." I slowed to a hover. "Memm, you and Raedon see if you can locate a place to buy warm clothes and blankets for when we find them." I swooped toward the bay. "Do you have money?"

"No." I followed Memm to a landing and Joedon handed over human money from his pack. The pair veered off to the west; the rest of us continued north.

The ground we flew over was empty of habitation. Foothills rose and fell covered in wildly colored scrub brush with pockets of golden trees we discovered marked streams running down from the higher mountains. Fall had painted the area with splashes of red, orange, yellow, and green. Periodically, we saw larger animals moving through the scrub, deer and even an elk, but no black reeth, no boy, no dog.

"I wouldn't think he could've come this far over this rough land." Lillyon's apprehensive voice swept through mind. "We should head back, shifting further uphill. He's got to be somewhere!" Stress had shrilled his normal deep, calm tone. I sent assurances I didn't really feel.

Keeping our relative positions, we turned south and moved higher up the mountains. The storm caught us within minutes, at first in large, heavy wet snow flakes, soaking us instantly. The wind picked up, snowflakes got smaller and thicker. Soon our visibility was down to only a few feet. Swirling snow flew directly into our faces.

"We've got to take shelter." I assessed the fem: Sara's teeth chattered and her fingers and toes were numb. Her wet black hair clung to her face and neck as the wind swept it madly around her. And Sissith's normally bay body was plastered with white.

"Land!" I squinted and aimed for a heavy thicket, the others following my mental trail. We landed in a clump of trees; broad tree trunks blocked some of the wind. Falling snow clung to branches, causing them to droop. Huddled together, hindquarters to the wind, heads dropped low, we three reeth cradled the two don between our bodies, sharing what heat we could.

"Memm's coming." Sissith raised her head, ears pointed. "He's got blankets, coats."

Just as Memm landed, I heard something and threw my head in the air to listen harder. I started walking deeper into the grove.

~ Joedon

Raedon, bundled from head to toe, quickly handed out long, heavy coats, wool hats, and gloves. We draped thick wool blankets over the shivering reeth, and followed Lillith.

Sara called Lillith to stop and get blanketed, but she refused, saying she was afraid she'd loose the thin thread she followed. Unable to see through the heavy snowfall, I clasped hands with Sara, who reached for Raedon. I followed my mind-mate by the feel of her mind, moving through a silent world where snow fell steadily, dampening sound, and coating the ground with heavy wet. I placed my feet carefully to avoid a fall; unseen roots lumped and gave beneath my boots.

"I can hear it now too," Sissith whispered. "Moaning. Eerie."

"It sounds like the funeral dirge to me," Memm said from the rear.

"I hope we're not too late," Sara murmured.

I stopped abruptly; Sara, then Raedon, ran into me. Lillith was projecting: covered in snow, three figures curled tightly together, the black reeth's back tucked against a log, long human curled between his legs, dog held against the boy's chest.

"Are they alive?"

"Yes!" Lillith's shout was triumphant. I yanked Sara forward. We fell to our knees and swept the snow away from the three on the ground. Raedon took a blanket and started to rub the reeth while I picked up the boy and wrapped him in another blanket, holding him close to my body to share my warmth. Sara dithered around until she bumped into Memm's shoulder, realizing he'd placed it in her way. She felt along his side to the pack and pulled out yet another heavy blanket and more towels. Then, she followed Lillith's mental voice to her side.

She was shivering violently when Sara reached her. Dropping to her knees, she lowered her hind end to the ground in a semi-seated position. Sara rubbed vigorously with the towels, then draped the blanket over her, stripping off her gloves to buckle the thing around Lillith's neck; it was a true horse blanket.

She'd just finished when I grabbed her elbow, turning her toward me. "Help me with this boy." I thrust a slender booted foot into her hand; she struggled with the laces, and growled in frustration. "Here." I handed her a knife; she sliced the laces and pulled off one boot. Together, we wrestled a wool sock and a huge, fleece lined boot over the icy foot, then worked on the other one.

Standing the boy back up, I wrapped him in one of the body-length coats; Sara pulled huge mittens over his hands and I pulled the strings tight to hold the hood over the boy's face. She lead me to the semi-circle of hunkered down reeth Sissith pictured for her surrounding the colt. Lillyon's head rested on

Lillith's flank, Sissith next in line, followed by Memm, each draped in horse-blanket with snow accumulating on top. I snuggled the boy up tight to the colt's belly so he wouldn't be frightened if he woke in the night.

I could barely see Sara as she felt her way to Sissith and collapsed against her flank, dropping her head back in exhaustion. She jerked awake and I saw a wet nose touch a bare spot on her wrist. The little dog whimpered and shivered before her. She took the towel she still held and rubbed him, then gathered him up to tuck him inside her coat, zipping it up so only the tiny black nose stuck out by her neck.

Raedon and I struggled with the tent and then, miraculously, we'd blocked the gusting wind. Light appeared as Raedon stepped back from one of the human-made battery-powered heaters with a spotlight attached.

"Did you buy the entire store?" Sara asked in the relative quiet. He placed a cup of hot coffee in her hand. "You must have!"

He smiled tenderly. "The store manager said I'd need these if we got caught in the snow. The cups automatically heat themselves! Never seen anything like it." He dropped down beside her and they huddled close to weather the storm.

With two heaters running we were soon warm enough to sleep. The snow and wind stopped sometime in the night. By morning, the sun blazed down through the trees, blinding against the white coating everything. *Typical early fall storm*, I thought as I stood and stretched, feeling renewed. *It will all be gone by this afternoon.* Hearing a whine, I watched the dog wiggle inside Sara's coat. The fem unzipped to let him free and he dashed over to curl up next to the boy. Wrapped in his oversized blanket with the boy carefully placed between his legs, the small black reeth appeared simply peacefully asleep.

Lillith studied them. "It's time to reach for them, bring them back to consciousness," she said. "Rouse the others, please."

We shuffled around and took up a position close to the reeth-boy-dog clump. Lillith gathered in the other reeth minds and asked for energy from us three don. Then, she reached out and demanded support from all reeth on the planet. She focused the energy shaft at small Lilliod's mind. Within a second, the power was gone and the black reeth was pushing himself onto his forelegs, his head wobbling weakly.

"What...Who are you?" We started. We'd all heard the young voice.

"Lilliod. I am your cousin Lillyon. We've come to take you home." Our heads swiveled toward the older reeth. We heard him, too!

"No!" The juvenile voice screamed as he tried to force himself upright, tangling his legs in the boy's muffled body. Lillith marveled at his power.

"It's okay," Lillyon soothed. "Caleb will come too—and Doc." A picture of Caleb's mother flashed. "Caleb's family also if you want, and they want."

Lillyon continued to sooth the colt, introducing the others of our party while Lillith floundered in disbelief. She studied each of us. Yes, we were hearing every bit of the conversation between Lillyon and the colt. Sara was crying, Raedon stood with mouth dropped, I stared with startled eyes. "He's incredibly powerful," she said to my unspoken inquiry. "We have to handle this with utmost care."

**

By afternoon, the wet snow had melted, the camp was packed away in carriers strapped on Memm's back, and we walked slowly back toward Caleb's farmhouse, answering rapid questions from both reeth and boy. We'd gotten over our surprise at hearing Lilliod as clearly as we heard Lillith and were absorbed in the story of his rescue and subsequent melding with Caleb.

"It has to have been from the trauma." Lillith's voice was thoughtful. "Do you know if you hit your head when you tumbled into the ravine?"

"No," Lilliod answered. "Do you think so?" He aimed his question at Caleb who now radiated absolute comfort.

263

The boy shook his head. "Not that I could tell." Lilliod automatically repeated every thought Caleb projected, in a voice different from his own. He'd evidently assigned Caleb a voice he thought appropriate, rich and warm with loving overtones lacing every word.

It's hard to realize the boy isn't actually talking if I don't look right at him.

Dark had fallen by the time we reached the farm. "Joedon, take the boy to the house. Depending on their reception, we'll decide what to do next." Lillith explained the plan to the others and I heard Lilliod reassuring Caleb that everything would be fine. Caleb ducked his head at me in bashful awe, especially after I developed a human image, and we walked together toward the front door, dog cavorting around us silently.

I knocked; the man I'd met at the market opened the door and started to speak. When he saw Caleb, a broad smile appeared, and he wrapped his brother in a bear hug. Then, he hollered, "Ma! Caleb's here! He's safe."

I stepped out of the way as the family, six boys I counted, piled out of the house, tears running down their faces, alternately hugging and scolding the boy. Caleb passed from embrace to embrace, resting finally in his mother's arms although he towered over her by a foot.

"I don't think we need to worry they'll harm him," I said to Lillith wryly. Joyful, the family invited me into the house and introduced the entire bunch, including the oldest son's wife. When they finally let me speak, I asked them to be seated to listen to my tale because it was a strange one. They sat nervously around a big table, Caleb's mother still clinging to him as if she could hold him in her lap. He sank cross-legged at her feet and rested his head in her lap instead.

I stood at the head of the table, dropped my human disguise, and talked.

**

The next morning, Lilliod's immediate family arrived, under strict instructions to tell no one else of our find or their destination. Caleb's family stood arm in arm in the farmyard and happily watched the exuberant family of grey reeth land and wrap long necks around their lost baby.

Lillith and I surmised that the ordeal of being trapped in the crevice had stolen Lilliod's early memories and the subsequent ordeal of almost freezing to death had released it. He recognized all of his family members: his parents, two siblings, aunt and uncle and two close cousins.

Caleb's oldest brother and his wife volunteered to stay on the farm and tend the animals while the rest of the family visited the reeth home high in a mountain valley to the east. A widely grinning Caleb sat astride Lilliod's father, Doc cuddled in his arms, Lilliod by his side. The reeth family flew toward the hills, each carrying one of Caleb's brothers, his parents riding together on Lillyon.

"We have to get back," I insisted when invited to join them for the celebration ceremony.

"Remember to keep your minds shielded." Lillith added her warning. "We can't let word get back to Center before we decide how to handle their meld."

Chapter 35

~ Lillith

Three days later, I went looking for Joedon to find him wallowing in self-pity in his study. I listened to his morose ramblings for several minutes before I decided the time had come. "Joedon, you must come with me right now!"

He tried to avoid me by pretending he was busy with paperwork. "Not now. I have to get this training schedule mapped out."

"What I need you for is much more important. Let Sara and Raedon handle it. It's their job, anyway."

He tried to block his mind. "Can't you just tell me? I really don't want to go anywhere right now."

"No. You must come."

He sighed and his thought made me chuckle silently; *sometimes being mind-melded is exasperating.* He walked out of the mansion and vaulted onto my back.

I flew south, then east. Joedon pestered me for the entire flight but I refused to explain why I needed him so urgently. Landing a short way into a palm grove, I asked him to dismount and walk with me. As we stepped out of the woods, his eyes focused on a beautiful trio resting sleepily in the sunshine.

Jaym sat on the patio, rocking both babies, each dressed in blue, the same shade as her gown, their curly red hair gleaming. Joeledon, for once, slept in the warmth, Joanadon beside him on their mother's chest.

~ Joedon

I stopped short. "Jaym," I breathed softly. She looked up in surprise when she heard my voice and I got lost in her eyes. I couldn't move.

She said simply, "Joedon." I heard a world of love and longing in her voice as she spoke my name. The word resonated powerfully in my heart. Finally, I understood the melancholy I'd felt for the past eleven months.

I strode forward to regard her and her bundles, dropping to my knees at her side, reaching to caress her face. "Jaym," I breathed again. "I've missed you so much. You're even more beautiful than I remember and so very dear to me."

~ Jaym

His words, his tone, his intense gaze instantly healed the ache in my heart. I'd been so lonely ... I was happy with my babies but so afraid I'd never mean anything to this don I'd fought hard not to love. I placed a kiss on the palm of his hand as happy tears streamed down my cheeks.

He tried to gather me into his arms, distressed by my tears, but his movement woke up Joele. "Whoa! Who is that?" Joedon exclaimed before he recognized his and my essence in the powerful mind stabbing at him, warning him away from his mother. Father and son locked eyes as Joedon answered the threat. "I loved her first," he told his son, "but I can share."

Lillith and I laughed when we heard the boy's clear answer. "I might share her because she thinks she loves you, but you have to prove yourself worthy."

Joedon threw his head back and laughed harder. Then, he said: "You've been busy, I see."

I flashed him a brilliant smile that shifted into a grin. "Yes, I have. There've been a lot of changes in my life, all because of you. All for the better, because of you." With a look of love that he couldn't ignore, I hugged the babies, then patted the smaller one. "This is Joanadon and *that* ..." I tipped my head at the boy. "... was Joeledon."

~ Joedon

I reached down and swooped my son into my arms. "He's very powerful." I couldn't remove my eyes for the small image of myself.

"Indeed he is. Even from the womb he's kept me informed of his wishes," said Lillith walking closer. "Everyone feels his presence. He mind-melded with Lillity within minutes of his birth."

I glanced up and for the first time noticed the golden one standing nearby. Lillith continued, "It's a powerful mind-meld. She felt his call all the way from Eyrie. They communicate easily, even though it's mostly feelings so far."

"And," added Jaym proudly, "he completely hid his sister's presence from all of the human diagnostic machines and from Lillith herself. We didn't know I was carrying twins until Joanadon arrived. Even then, he tried to protect her from everyone. He's finally trusting Cari, Marn and I to take care with her. As you can see, she's much smaller."

"But very, very precious," said Lillith.

"And just as beautiful as her mother. Jaym, I don't know what to say. What a wonderful gift you've given me. They're glorious. You're glorious. I don't know what else to say." My words became tangled with my emotions. "I never, ever realized that this is what I've been missing. This is what I've wanted, what I've needed. Jaym, you've given me love, a family. I'll do anything to have you with me forever."

She began to cry as she struggled to rise from the chair without dropping Joana. I reached out to help and once she was on her feet, I wrapped my free arm around her, enveloping her and our children.

"You're mine," I commanded. I rethought. Then, "Will you be mine?" I pleaded.

"Of course, Joedon." She blinked away her tears and hugged me back with her one free arm. "I've always been yours. I just didn't know it before I saw you that day in the Grand Salon."

Suddenly, we were laughing at the awkwardness of our embrace. Jaym stepped away and laid our daughter on the settee. I followed suit with our son and we were back in each other's arms, demonstrating the love and longing we felt until Joele let out a loud squawk and Joana started crying. I winced from the mental stab of aggravation from our son and I let his mother go, laughing again.

268

Jaym picked up Joana to comfort her while I scooped up Joele. "It's time for us to have a don to don talk, my son." I held the baby close to my face and began to croon, something I remembered my father doing when I was very young. The boy let out another squawk, then settled into a cooing sound, echoing my elation.

Jaym smiled at us—or maybe it was a smirk. "It's about time you two got acquainted. I've been coping with him for four weeks. It's your turn!"

Joele didn't stay quiet for long. Soon, he squirmed in my arms and loudly demanded to be fed. A middle-aged woman came out of the house at the boy's first scream of hunger. She smiled as she took him out of my arms.

"Joedon, it seems as if I've always known you. I'm Marn, Jaym's aunt. Cari's prepared some delicious treats for you. She'll bring them out in a minute. If you'll hold Joana, we'll take this little monster in and get him fed." She nodded at the baby girl. "She's much quieter and a lot happier than her brother."

I felt as if I'd met a whirlwind, but took my daughter, who'd awakened again at her brother's latest scream. She looked peacefully at me even as Joele warned me to be careful with his sister. Since Jaym also heard the warning, she grinned sympathetically and followed them.

Carefully cradling the small bundle, I turned to Lillith. "Why didn't you tell me?"

"It wasn't the right time. I wanted you to acknowledge to yourself how you felt about Jaym before I told you." She shrugged. "I got tired of waiting."

"I couldn't believe it was possible. All these months, I've been fighting against it, telling myself not to miss her." I dragged in a deep breath. "I believe I fell in love with her the first second I saw her, standing there in that ridiculous wedding outfit demanding to know where I'd come from."

"I'm aware of that. But I wanted to wait until you became aware of it." She twitched an ear. "Sit down and enjoy your daughter."

"I can see why you couldn't just tell me what you wanted to show me this morning." I sank into Jaym's place on the settee. "I wouldn't have believed you." I stared into the vibrant blue eyes of my daughter. "She's so tiny."

"Yes, she's small but she's strong. She's peaceful where he's a fire breather." Lillith dropped her head over my shoulder, eyeing the baby. "She'll be mentally powerful one day, I know it. I can hear her now although no one else seems to. She isn't in the flaming hurry he is."

Another, younger, woman came out of the house carrying a tray with tall glasses of lemonade and some type of cake. She set the tray on the table, scooted a glass toward Lillith, another to Lillity and placed several of the cakes in front of each. Then, she smiled at me.

"I'm Cari, the one who screamed and fainted when I first saw you. I'm not afraid of you now. Jaym and Lillith have taught me how to control my fear and face up to things. I heard what Jaym said about how different her life is, because of you. Mine is different too, wonderful, because of you. Thank you."

She hurried back into the house before I could respond. "Well, that was a surprise. When Marn said Cari had prepared treats, I didn't even think about Jaym's maid. I'd forgotten her name." I stopped and stared at Lillith as she gently placed her lips around the tall stick poking out of the glass Cari had placed in front of her. "What are you doing?"

"Sipping lemonade," she answered. "Marn invented this thing she calls a straw so Lillity and I can enjoy lemonade. And Cari makes delicious date tarts. Have one."

She and Lillity each lipped up a tart from the table. In a moment, I picked up one and popped it in my mouth.

"This is delicious," I said. "Made from dates?"

"Baked in a pastry. We've become addicted to them," Lillith answered. "This is a date farm owned by Lord Metz. Jaym loves dates and we've become quite fond of them, too. Cari makes me pastries to take back to Eyrie whenever I'm here. Lillity is staying here permanently."

"And this has been going on behind my back?" A tiny smile hovered. "How did you manage it?"

"You've been tied up with parties, film making, and politicking. You haven't noticed when I was gone. And Lillyon covered for me."

"So Lillyon knows, too. Anyone else?"

"Only the three of us. Lillity didn't know until Joele called her. She really couldn't help herself."

"That I know." I paused, puzzled. "Don't you think it's a marvelous coincidence this has happened just now? The birth I mean."

"Actually, no I don't. I sort of planned it that way." She sounded smug.

My mouth dropped open. "What ..." I struggled for self-control. "Exactly what do you mean, you planned it that way?" Jaym came out of the house carrying a baby boy projecting his contentment with his full belly, interrupting my thoughts. I stood to welcome them, wrapping an arm around Jaym's shoulders and drawing her as near as possible. The babies between us again, Jaym returned my hug quickly before she stepped away.

"Sit back down. I'll sit here and burp this little glutton while I share your treats."

Cari arrived with a tall glass of lemonade for Jaym and more tarts.

"Cari, stay and sit with us," I said, still on his feet. "Won't Marn come out as well? I'd like to get to know you better."

"Thank you. I'll fetch her and more lemonade."

Seated around the table, the three ladies and Lillith filled me in on everything that had happened to the over the last eleven months. Joele enjoyed a loud burp and consented to be held by his father again. He squirmed and kicked but didn't purposely interrupt our conversation. Jaym took a break to feed Joana while the talk flowed on without her. When she returned, Marn and Cari were describing the shock of the doctors and

271

nurses when Joele loudly announced his arrival and I laughed. Lunch time came and Turl arrived.

"Oh! I forgot to make lunch. We've been talking all morning." Cari rushed into the kitchen.

During lunch, I marveled at how comfortable I felt with these humans, how well they accommodated Lillith and Lillity in their midst. Cari served grain patties with fruit to the reeth and placed a huge salad before me. The humans ate meat and vegetable pies. Although the meal appeared effortless, it obviously required forethought and planning to accomplish.

"This evening, Stephon will be here," Marn said. "He'll be happy to see you again."

"Stephon?"

"Yes, my fiancée, Stephon Talmadge."

I gazed at her in surprise. "So you're the Marn he talked about so much. He knew about these babies too? And never said anything?"

"I wouldn't let him," Lillith said. "Time had to be right, so don't be upset."

"I won't, but still."

We adults took turns strolling around with Joele, keeping his mind occupied while others ate. I told stories while I carried the boy around, stomping my feet so the baby jiggled on my shoulder. Joele loved it and bathed everyone with his giggles. And I had trouble convincing myself this whole scene was real.

Chapter 36
~ Jaym

Lillith allowed Joedon and me two nights together before she said, "The Council's getting ready to meet again today. Now's the time to introduce Jaym and the babies."

"What! Why?" I'd been lounging on the settee on the porch snuggled against Joedon, babies asleep in separate seats nearby. Cari and Marn's voices wafted from the open kitchen window and Lillity dozed in the sunshine.

"Because, now's the time, my love ..." Joedon answered enthusiastically into my ear ... "to really stir them up!"

"I don't understand," I looked at Lillith, not shifting my position as Joedon squirmed behind me.

"Do you remember I told you about the declining birth rate among the don?" he asked.

"Well, yes. You were hoping Saradon would bear a child to help rebuild the race." I kept my eyes trained on Lillith.

"Yes, but you, my love, have borne not one don child but two." He wrapped both arms around me and hugged, dropping a kiss onto the top of my head. "Both are easily recognizable as don. The Council can't ignore them. To save the don, we must re-establish relations with the humans. It's the only way."

"I don't follow." I sat up and turned puzzled brows toward him.

Voice dripping with patience, he explained. "Even though Sara will have a girl, the baby has to grow before she can bear children. Don women don't usually become fertile until they're thirty or older. Even if Sara bore six girls in the next twelve years, they'd have to grow. Sara, by herself, cannot re-establish the don." His tone and rhythm accelerated as he presented his crowning argument. "But there must be more human women than you who could bear a don child. Maybe not all humans could, but, as unique as you are, I doubt you're the only one."

"Oh, I see." Outraged, I elbowed him in the ribs and stood up. "You want us to be broodmares!" Arms akimbo, I glared.

Lillith came between us and interrupted my anger. "You're making a mess of it, Joedon. Shut up before she kicks you out. Or I do. Forget your politics. Think about relationships, support, caring. There's much reeth and don can offer humans, just as there's much humans can offer us."

She herded me to another chair, away from the spluttering Joedon. "Jaym, dear. Let me play some scenes so you'll understand better what's at stake." Lillith paced as she played, in my mind, scenes handed down reeth mind to reeth mind from the earliest days of contact. In Lillith's scenes, don were once fearsome warriors, fighting among themselves. Then, reeth extended their friendship and don accepted. Reeth helped regulate don tempers by projecting happiness and contentment through cooperation and don absorbed the lifestyle change eagerly. Gradually, don became quieter, developing mental powers, and living longer. Both species prospered as they became co-dependent.

Lillith emphasized emotions into the stories she portrayed. "When the humans arrived, reeth and don extended their friendship but humans would have none of it. We withdrew. Unfortunately, that began what appears to be the decline of the don, very slow at first, now more noticeable."

She paused, studied our reactions. Then I realized Joedon was seeing and hearing the same lecture. I listened intently. "When the reeth prompted the withdrawal, they hadn't understood that don require stimulation to thrive. Over their centuries of isolation, both species declined in their activities and their accomplishments. Apprentices failed to learn from masters. Skills vanished. Physical games of agility and endurance ended. Many young don failed to meld. Distress developed on all sides."

Lillith then displayed the last eleven months, with both species more active than any time in the last century, because of Joedon's encounter with me. Lillith showed politicking, parties, controversies, and defiance. Her voice dropped. "Even argument is better than no emotion at all!

"We believe a working relationship between our three species will strengthen all, but many don have been holding tightly on to their fear." Her exasperation flowed over me. "They need to be jolted out of their comfort level and forced to recognize the opportunity before them. Now's the time to apply that jolt."

I sat as if stunned, not saying a word. Joedon, looking just as dumbfounded as I felt, asked, "Why have you never told me all this?"

Lillith stroked his cheek with a wingtip. "You wouldn't have believed me if you hadn't seen it for yourself."

"Yes, I would have."

"No, Joedon, you wouldn't have. You'd have thought you believed, but you wouldn't have acted as you have when you were forced."

Joedon's eyebrows snapped down and he regarded her with an unusual sternness. "What do you mean, forced?"

"When you found yourself stuck in Pith, with no way to rescue Raedon, you had to act for yourself. And you did. Since then, circumstances have continued to push you to seek solutions: with the birth rate, with the reeth threat, with the non-melded. All of this shoved you out of your isolation."

"Have you had a hand in this, Lillith?" I asked with suspicion.

She stood quietly for some time, evidently deciding whether to lie or admit the role I was sure she'd played. She had, once, admitted to being an interfering being. Finally, she answered, focusing on me. "Yes, I have, in a way. We were desperate. We didn't know how to snap the don out of their lethargy and we were falling victim to that same indolence." She shrugged her shoulders. "I thought of a means to save us all—using my mind-meld to spur the most powerful don into forcing a change. And he did."

I gazed at Joedon, pride in my eyes and flowing out of my thoughts as Lillith continued. "Today, it's important that you and

Joedon present the results of our, the reeth's, experiment. Today, we need to present the ultimate joy that will come of combined relationships: the Joe family, we reeth, and your human friends."

She looked at me but I sensed her words were aimed at Joedon. "My dear Jaym, Joedon is not always perceptive where relationships are concerned. He's had little practice. But he's been in love with you since he first saw you. He's tried hard to ignore it but he's been miserable these last months without you."

"Lillith …" Joedon started to protest.

"Hush, Joedon. You know how forlorn you were when not busy."

After a brief pause, he admitted it. "Yes, I was."

She allowed traces of pleading to slip out from mind and voice. "I know, Jaym, that you haven't had much experience either. Your growing years in the palace could not be considered a healthy relationship environment. But you're very much in love with Joedon. If you hadn't been, we wouldn't be here with this happy outcome."

A deep reeth sigh whistled out her nostrils. Dropping to her knees, she spread out her wings in a flourish. "So, Jaym, we need you and your friends to help us start a new chapter on our world."

"Please, Jaym," added Joedon. "I do love you so." He stepped back and stood tall. "But, as important as this is, it doesn't matter because I can't bear to be without you any longer. And if you won't come, I'll happily live here with you."

I smiled and placed a hand softly against his cheek. "You lie, you know. You wouldn't be the Joedon I love if you didn't care about what happens today so much." I drew in a breath and swung toward Lillith. "How are we going to do this?"

Lillith lunged up from her knees, mind brisk. "You get ready with warm cloaks. Take extra clothes and diapers for the babies. I'll carry Joedon and Joana, Lillity will carry you and

Joele. Lillyon is bringing others for Marn and Stephon, Turl and Cari. And thank you, Jaym."

"Lillith, how could I refuse you?" I asked with a grin. "Let's get going. We have to change the world!"

Chapter 37

~ Lillith

I kept our passengers informed of the council proceedings as we flew toward Center. With Joedon absent, Taldon was chairing the meeting, worrying about what had happened to his Supreme Don. Raedon and Sara likewise fretted over his absence. Sending calm thoughts ahead, I explained to the three via their reeth-mates that we'd been delayed and would arrive shortly.

The proposal to allow young don to investigate human attitudes passed relatively smoothly. The one directing reeth and don to investigate defensive and offensive abilities passed with overwhelming support with Ylsdon appointed as committee chair. A decision barely passed to allow Nandon and Eledon to investigate the human medical library, but the council became deadlocked on whether or not to allow them to work with actual human researchers. Since Raedon, as Royal Consort, was so heavily in support of one side, Pildon and his party refused to recognize his vote to break the tie.

"Taldon doesn't know how to proceed. Everyone knows how you will vote, so he's stalling as best he can." I chuckled as I shared the scene. Raedon had mounted a filibuster from his dais and was reading from an old play, despite Pildon's frequent objections. "We'd best hurry."

~ Joedon

The controversy stilled to total silence when I strode into the Council Chambers holding my son, hand in hand with Jaym carrying our daughter. Just behind us walked both human couples, heads held high, smiles pasted over their nervousness, just as we'd discussed. Lillith and Lillity crowded into the chamber after them.

The council members first voiced their indignation at the reeth's bold entrance, then noticed the humans and aimed their ire at the woman holding my hand. Their mental outrage buffeted me as it swirled around Jaym. My son stiffened in my arms,

278

evidently catching the indignant glares aimed at his mother. He screamed and then mentally slapped everyone in the room.

Speakers reeled; some jumped up to stagger against their desks. Other slumped limply in their chairs. Everyone knew the blow hadn't come from me. Jaym and the reeth soothed Joele who gradually settled down and don back settled into their places, headaches abated. Every eye in the chamber drilled into my back as I took my place at the Joe family desk, seating Jaym in the Speaker's chair with Lillith and Lillity aligned behind her. I pulled up chairs next to her for Marn and Cari; Stephon and Turl perched on the edge of the desk, all of them with relaxed faces and muscles. Once I had them settled, I stood firm behind Jaym and stared belligerently outward, waiting for quiet.

"I'm here to speak for the Joe family," I said, projecting to reach the entire chamber. Joele squirmed in my arms and I patted his back. "I apologize for being late. It took longer to bring my family here than I expected. Speakers, I present my wife, Soer Jaym of Pith." I pinned Pildon with a glare, daring him to say something. Seemingly shell-shocked, he didn't.

"This is my son, Joeledon." I held the boy up, now totally still as if he knew the importance of this presentation, so all could see him. Then, I handed him to Marn and picked up my daughter, holding her out in the same way. "And my daughter, Joanadon. Twins born four weeks ago."

Handing her back to Jaym, I faced the assembly, legs spread, head held high, and continued. "You all know my mind-mate Lillith, and this is Lillity, my son's mind-mate, melded at his birth." I paused to let the words sink in, then, turned to the four humans. "These are my close friends, Professor Stephon Talmadge and Soer Marn of Pith, Cari and Turl of Palmyra."

To my surprise, no one had yet interrupted. My face set hard and cold, I said, "I apologize for my son's behavior. He has not yet learned to control his temper and when he felt your outrage aimed at his mother, he struck." Leaving the implication of the boy's immense power float in their minds, I continued, "He's now quiet. We can proceed."

They goggled at me as they massaged their foreheads and temples. Still no one spoke, so I kept going. "Lillith has kept me informed of the council's progress. I hereby cast the Joe family vote in favor of any don being allowed to open any negotiation with humans for any purpose desired, subject to committee approval." Not exactly the proposal at hand, but Lillith approved my words.

For one more moment, the room stayed silent. Then, Pildon yelled, jumping to his feet. "What are these humans doing here? Are you trying to kill us all?"

"Pildon, they are no threat." I tried to stare him down. "They're here to prove a point to this council, a point about human/don/reeth relationships and how strong we can be when we work together."

"I won't listen to this." He stormed toward the door and tried to exit the chamber. Lillyon blocked the doorway and with his head, shoved Pildon back toward his seat. Speaker voices raised in protest.

"You damned reeth, get out of my way." Pildon raised his fist to strike, then stopped as we heard a child cry and a whisper swept our minds.

"Please be quiet. You are upsetting my brother. Please be calm."

I gaped at the tiny girl in my wife's arms. The room became still as don froze, confusion on their faces. As before, Joele's rage swept the room, followed by comforting waves of calm from Joana. The unbelievable strength of both emotions overwhelmed me, rocking all of us from one extreme to the other.

Lillith started laughing as only a reeth could laugh, her head in the air, her body shaking as she snorted out her mirth. We heard her cry, "The best of both worlds, the warrior and the soother." Other reeth reacted both inside and outside the chamber. Stomping feet shook the ground. Flapping wings agitated the air. Excited squeals and gleeful whinnies echoed through the chamber door as Lillyon pushed it open with his shoulder.

A dark grey appeared at the door. He trotted gracefully down the aisle toward us, his black wings tight against a well-toned, dappled body. Not tall, he seemed young. All eyes followed as he dropped his head to the girl baby in Jaym's arms. Breath held in anticipation, we felt Joanadon reach out mentally. "Marrair" slipped into our minds.

"Welcome, Joanadon," the young reeth said.

My heart clenched in joy. All around us, tears flowed down cheeks of homm and femm alike as we all shared in the ultimate joy between don and reeth. Cries of elation escaped Sara's lips, followed by more from the watching femm. And waves of love pouring from my daughter. Totally serene, with a face glowing with elation, Jaym raised Joana's tiny hand to stroke the grey head.

The meeting unraveled as femm surrounded Jaym, demanding to see the babies and meet their mother. At that emotional moment, femm obviously didn't care about their husbands, fathers, or brothers; they didn't care about politics; they were excited about babies. Sara, first to hug Jaym, picked up Joele. As a mere father, I couldn't get near them as I watched my son, already a charmer with his curly red hair and gleaming brown eyes, mesmerize them. Passed around the circle of femm, he happily burbled. His sister, following from arm to arm, bathed them with love and captivated their hearts with her sweet smile.

Homm milled uncertainly until they noticed Opudon vigorously shaking Stephon's hand and his fym exchanging hugs with Marn. When Ylsdon also approached the humans, a few others stepped forward to be introduced. Most returned to stand stiffly at their desks, uncertain. I stayed out of it, watching as centuries of barriers started to break down

Lillith sent me a brief vision: Pildon, his face twisted in longing, slipped out the door, past the distracted guard. "I knew he wouldn't accept this easily," she said.

Taldon finally reconvened the meeting by beating his gavel against the podium. Speakers and their families returned to their seats, and Taldon demanded that I explain.

"Before I say anything more, I ask Ylsdon and Opudon to report on their homes in Labyrinth."

Ylsdon stood at his desk and grinned, a facial expression not seen often from him. "Many of you attended my party and exclaimed at the new lighting." His grin widened. "Quodon prepared the plans and hired humans to do the work." Speakers gasped but Ylsdon gave no one time to interrupt as he explained loudly how they'd handled the project.

Opudon stood at his desk; his wrinkled face beaming. "My fym and I worked with Stephon and Marn Talmadge on the plans to rebuild my home." He strode over to stand next to Stephon. "He told the human architects the building was going to be his vacation home in the mountains and they designed exactly what we wanted. The plans are ready for council review. I plan to begin building within the month." He shouted into the growl that rumbled. "Using human contractors."

I walked before the podium and held up a hand, pulling Speakers' attention back to me. "You all saw the film at Taldon's gathering. Using a human work force, we can repair our old buildings and restore our life-style. We can provide help for our old ones and for our non-melded reeth friends. We can grow and prosper instead of wither and die."

I paused, challenging them to respond. No one did. "And now, I ask Cheradon and Puldon to share their news."

All eyes centered on the couple. Taken by surprise, they stood together, holding hands. "Puldon and I are expecting a baby," said Chera, her voice clear and strong. "We know because human researchers helped us and confirmed the pregnancy. *She* will be named Pueladon." A cheer arose from the young couples around them.

"It's time for us to rejoice, not argue," I hollered. "It's time to move forward with energy and hope."

~ Lillith

I moved in front of Joedon and waved my wings for attention in the midst of the babble. Once they'd quieted, I spoke boldly into their minds, "We reeth have one more introduction to make." Joedon glanced at me, surprise on his face, as I swept my wings forward. "Please, adjourn to the courtyard."

I walked ahead, asking Joedon and Jaym to follow and bring their human friends. Raedon and Sara dropped in behind and we filed out the chamber door. I heard Speakers milling around in confusion, but Taldon took his fym's hand and followed us. The rest trailed after.

The courtyard was filled with reeth. Don and their families gravitated to their mind-mates and before long, the courtyard was packed with reeth and don. They stood, as quietly as any large crowd could, around the outside, leaving a small center occupied by the Joe family, the Royal Couple, Taldon and me.

Lillyon and Memmyon, with their brothers and cousins, had held a corridor open toward one corner of the square, and, as the rustling died, a large group of grey reeth entered.

In their midst walked a thin human boy, tall—as tall as the shortest don—light brown hair wind-swept over his forehead. His hand rested lightly on the withers of a smallish coal-black reeth, with a broad white blaze down his face and four stockings.

The escort stopped, facing me.

"I would like to introduce Lilliod," I said. "And his mind-mate Caleb."

Gasps flew around the square. Reeth had known, don now learned.

"My friends." I thrust my voice soaring into don minds, amplified by reeth-mates standing around. "It is time to end the isolation. No more fussing. Let's get on with life." I pictured the twins. "We have the babies, proof don can reproduce with humans and pass on don powers." I pictured Ylsdon's home, lights on, warmth glowing from his windows in the dark night.

283

"We have proof humans can help fix don problems, as well as reeth problems." I waved a wing at Caleb and Lilliod. "And we have strong evidence that perhaps humans can meld, providing partners for our large population of un-melded reeth. It's time to approach humans to forge a more powerful world for us all."

In the chaos following my remarks, no one noticed Pildon, including me, standing near the back. Suddenly, he screamed and raced down the path left by the advancing Lill family. He struck Caleb, knocking him to the stone paved ground, hands clenched around the boy's throat. His continual screams, "No! A human can't!" paralyzed the crowd. The boy struggled valiantly against the strong arms holding him down.

Joedon threw himself at the pair, hands grasping for Pildon's thumbs, pulling them back from the boy's throat. With a roar, Pildon let go and spun on Joedon, plowing into him using his head as a battering ram, his arms swinging wildly, knocking Joedon backwards. As he fell, Joedon twisted and took Pildon down under him. Straddling him, Joedon locked his forearm around Pildon's neck and pulled backward. The don arched with a scream, quickly cut off. When Pildon lost consciousness, Joedon dropped him and stood shaking with fury. "Get him out of my sight before I kill him."

Two don picked Pildon up and hurried out of the courtyard. Joedon leaned over, hands on his knees and sucked in gulps of air as he struggled for calm. I enveloped him in wings, rubbing my head up and down his back.

Around us, everyone else stood quietly. For centuries, don had been non-aggressive. The quick violence stunned them.

I saw Sara run to check on Caleb, now on his feet, his head buried in Lilliod's neck. Gradually, the don standing around the pair realized the words of comfort and soothing they heard came from the small black reeth, not from me. Confused thoughts ran around the crowd via their reeth.

He speaks to us all!

He melded to a human!

He's only four!

Many a don sat down abruptly on the stone flags, struggling to order their thoughts.

Taldon asked his mind-mate to call for order. Tallyon trumpeted; his call rang over the courtyard, and the crowd became still.

"I call this meeting adjourned," Taldon announced. "Retire now, consult with your families, and come prepared to vote by roll call tomorrow at nine on the question to contact humans for help, for all of our problems."

To enjoy more of the Lillith Chronicles
Go to https://carolbuhler.com

Suggested Reading Order

Lillith

Emergence

Encounters

Revelations

Gladys

FARR

Femm Rebel

YON

MAR

Dear Father

Lilliod, Caleb and Doc

Lareina

Uninvited—the prequel, can be read at any time in the order.

Join the Lillith Chronicles Readers' Group via the website above and receive a free copy of Lillith in the digital format of your choice.

Glossary

Vocabulary

Don: humanoid native species, Planet Gareeth
Fem: female don
Femm: female don plural
Fym: don wife
Fymm: don wives
Hom: male don, or husband
Homm: male don plural, or husbands

Reeth: winged-horse-like native species, Planet Gareeth
Yon: male reeth, singular or plural, can also refer to a reeth husband
Mare: single female reeth
Mar: plural female reeth

Human: colonizers from Earth who came to Planet Gareeth 400 years in the past
Lord: head of human city-state
Lady: lord's spouse
Soer: legitimate daughter of Lord
Sor: legitimate son of Lord

Gareeth Days of the Week:

Lunday, Twoday, Wedday, Ursday, Fesday, Samday, Domday

Gareeth Months of the Year

28 days each, 13 months: Janry, Fevry, Mars, Avry, Mays, Junry, Julry, Augry, Sepry, Octry, Novry, Decry, Mers

Reeth Eye color:

Red: alarm, agitation, anger; the brighter, the stronger the anger
Purple: worry, concern; the deeper, the stronger the fear
Green: calm
Blue: pride, happiness
Blue-green: satisfaction
Orange: exasperation
Yellow: inquiry
Rose- brown: guilty, ashamed

Reeth Body colors

White: born completely white; usually do not live past teen years; often called Lethal White

Grey: born black or dark brown; their body coat greys as they age and they can turn totally white; wings are usually same color as body but can be darker

Dappled: a type of grey with circles of light grey appearing on the coat with outlines of darker grey; mane, tail, wings almost always darker

Flea-bitten: a type of grey who is mostly white with black or red flecks all over the body; mane, tail and wings usually lighter.

Brown: born brown and retain same color all their life; entire body is brown like coffee without cream; wings, mane and tail are same as body

Bay: remain the same color all their life; reddish brown to light brown body color; always has black legs up to the knees, black mane and tail; wings may be black or dark brown

Chestnut: remain same color all their life; reddish brown to light brown body color; sometimes has lighter mane and tail; wings same color or lighter than body

Red Roan: remain same color all their life, body color is mixture of white hair with red hair; mane, tail, and wings reddish; often have solid red head and face

Blue Roan: remain same color all their life; body color is mixture of white hair with black hair; mane, tail, and wings black or dark brown; often have solid black or dark brown face

Black: remain same color all their life; body, mane, tail, wings black with no white mixed in; may have white markings on lower legs and face.

Buckskin: remain same color all their life; body tan, legs, mane, tail and wings usually dark brown or black; often has darker stripe down backbone

Dun: remain same color all their life; body tan, legs, mane, tail and wings same color or maybe lighter; usually has darker stripe down backbone and may have zebra stripes on chest and forelegs

Cremello: remain same color all their life; body, mane, tail and wings all cream colored; eyes might be blue rather than brown

Palomino: remain same color all their life; body various shades of gold with lighter mane, tail, wings

Reeth Body Markings

Stripe: white narrow stripe down face
Star: white spot of any size on forehead
Snip: white spot of any size on muzzle
Blaze: broad white stripe down face inside the eyes
Bald: broad white stripe down face that goes outside of eyes
Socks: white feet up to ankle
Stockings: white feet and legs up to knee
Dapples: small, round markings of a darker color than the overall coat
Flea-bitten: small flecks of red or black on grey coat
Dorsal Stripe: dark stripe that follows the backbone
Zebra Stripes: dark stripes on chest or upper legs
Feathers: heavy, long hair around the ankles and feet, often white

Major Reeth Characters

Lilliod: Lillyon's young cousin
Lillith: Joedon's mind-mate
Lillity: Lillith's younger sister, Joeledon's mind-mate
Lillyon: Lillith's husband
Memmyon: Raedon's mind-mate
Sissith: Saradon's mind-mate
Tallyon: Taldon's mind-mate

Minor Reeth Characters

Bukkyon: Lillith's grandson, Lillene's son
Carnair: Gemdon's mind-mate
Coccyon: Samdon's mind-mate
Fennyon: Eledon's mind-mate
Lillene: Lillith's daughter
Lillolf: reeth leader, Lillyon's great-uncle
Loffert: Lillyon's cousin
Maffair: Oredon's mind-mate
Marnith: a powerful mind-reader
Marrair: becomes Joanadon's mind-mate
Memmiard: head reeth recorder, Memmyon's great-great-uncle
Quilyle: head of large Quil family
Tallalb: a guard

Major Don Characters

Eledon: physician, Ele family speaker, Fennyon's mind-mate
Joanadon (Joana): Joedon's daughter
Joedon: Supreme Don, Joe family speaker, Lillith's mind-mate
Joeledon (Joele): Joedon's son
Nandon: Nan family speaker, physician, Nellyon's mind-mate
Pildon: Pil Family speaker, non-melded
Raedon: Rae family speaker, Royal Consort, Memmyon's mind-mate, Joedon's best friend, Saradon's hom
Saradon (Sara): Royal Fem, Sissith's mind-mate, Joedon's cousin, Raedon's fym
Taldon: Chairman of Speaker's Council, Tallyon's mind-mate

Minor Don Characters

Aradon: Ara family speaker
Beedon: Unmarried young don, non-melded
Benetadon: Eledon's fym
Cheradon: Saradon's friend, desperate for a child
Dogdon: Dog family speaker

Fendon: Unmarried young don, non-melded
Gemdon: Gem family speaker
Girdon: Unmarried young don, non-melded
Goldon: Gol family speaker, metal expert
Heradon: Young fym
Holdon: Hol family speaker
Juldon: Jul family speaker, Lillith's employee
Kewdon: Kew family speaker, non-melded
Mosedon: Young fem, unmarried
Nanadon: Charge of House for Lillith, Juldon's fym
Opudon: Opu family speaker, crumbling walls
Oredon: Ore family speaker
Puldon: Pul family speaker, Cheradon's hom
Quodon: Quo family speaker, electrician
Regdon: Deceased mason
Samdon: Sam family speaker, Coccyon's mind-mate
Sardon: Saradon's father, Sar family speaker
Suridon: Saradon's mother
Twyladon: Kewdon's daughter-in-law
Weedon: Wee family speaker, Lareina producer
Wolfdon: oldest son of Wof family, non-melded
Wynnadon: Weedon's daughter, 4 years old
Ylsdon: Yls family speaker, has electrical problems

Major Human Characters

Caleb: a deaf and mute boy
Cari: Jaym's personal maid
Garard: majordomo of Lord Metz of Pith
Soer Jaym: eldest daughter of Lord Metz of Pith
Marn: Jaym's step-aunt
Stephon Talmadge: history professor, proponent of don/reeth reality
Turl: Pith Palace guardsman, Jaym's personal guard

Minor Human Characters

Captain Roml: Head, Pith Palace Guards
Claire: young girl, Wynnadon's friend
Dr, Joys Bothwell: psychiatrist
Dr. Gema Smythe: pediatrician
Dr. Lyra Grey: obstetrician
Dr. Lyle Grey: Chief Administrator, Pith Hospital
Dr. Maun Als: medical researcher
Soer Kelt: Jaym's oldest half-sister, Jill's daughter, marries Roark
Lady Jill: Jaym's step-mother
Lord Metz: Lord of Pith, Jaym's father
Lord Roark: Lord of Kavv

Seth: Pith Palace guardsman
Sissy: Young girl, Wynnadon's friend

Doc, the dog